T0304810

Praise for Andrew Miller

'His writing is a source of wonder and delight'
Hilary Mantel

'One of our most skilful chroniclers of
the human heart and mind'
Sunday Times

'A writer of very rare and outstanding gifts'
Elspeth Barker

'A highly intelligent writer, both exciting and contemplative'
The Times

'A wonderful storyteller'
Spectator

'Miller's trademark is silken prose which
gleams with acutely rendered detail'
Independent

'A delight to read'
Time Out

'A writer of astonishing gifts'
Irish Times

'One of our finest writers'
i

Andrew Miller's first novel, *Ingenious Pain*, was published by Sceptre in 1997. It won the James Tait Black Memorial Prize, the International IMPAC Dublin Literary Award and the Grinzane Cavour Prize for the best foreign novel published in Italy. It has been followed by *Casanova*, *Oxygen*, which was shortlisted for the Booker Prize and the Whitbread Novel of the Year Award in 2001, *The Optimists*, *One Morning Like a Bird*, *Pure*, which won the Costa Book of the Year Award 2011, *The Crossing*, *Now We Shall Be Entirely Free* and *The Slowworm's Song*.

Andrew Miller's novels have been published in translation in twenty countries. Born in Bristol in 1960, he currently lives in Somerset.

Also by Andrew Miller

Ingenious Pain
Casanova
Oxygen
The Optimists
One Morning Like a Bird
Pure
The Crossing
Now We Shall Be Entirely Free
The Slowworm's Song

The Land in Winter

Andrew Miller

Sceptre

First published in Great Britain in 2024 by Sceptre
An imprint of Hodder & Stoughton Limited
An Hachette UK company

The authorised representative in the EEA is Hachette Ireland, 8 Castlecourt
Centre, Dublin 15, D15 XTP3, Ireland (email: info@hbgi.ie)

6

A CIP catalogue record for this title is available from the British Library

Hardback ISBN 9781529354270
Trade Paperback ISBN 9781529354287
ebook ISBN 9781529354317

Typeset in Janson Text by Hewer Text UK Ltd, Edinburgh
Printed and bound in Great Britain by Clays Ltd, Elcograf S.p.A.

Hodder & Stoughton policy is to use papers that are natural, renewable
and recyclable products and made from wood grown in sustainable
forests. The logging and manufacturing processes are expected to
conform to the environmental regulations of the country of origin.

The authorised representative in the EEA is Hachette Ireland, 8 Castlecourt
Centre, Castleknock Road, Castleknock, Dublin 15, D15 YF6A, Ireland

Hodder & Stoughton Limited
Carmelite House
50 Victoria Embankment
London EC4Y 0DZ

www.sceptrebooks.co.uk

For the musicians

At any rate, concurrently with the development of a sane self in a sane world, I think there is always, in varying degrees, the development of a mad self in a mad world of its own creation.

On the Fear of Insanity, Roger Money-Kyrle

Nana: Shouldn't love be the only truth?
Philosopher: For that love would always have to be true.

Vivre sa vie, Jean-Luc Godard

Winter is for women –

'Wintering', Sylvia Plath

PART ONE

Risen

7 December 1962

1

He was lying on a varnished wooden board, the top of a boxed-in radiator. The board was exactly as wide as his shoulders and he knew, from painful experience, he must sit up like a man emerging from his own coffin. Roll over and he would be on the floor.

Above the radiator, a tall window was covered with thin curtains, a pattern of stripes, green, brown and red. He lifted a corner of the cloth and looked out. Deep space, the heart of night, a single small light left burning through fog above the door of the industrial therapy department.

The time? He sifted it from the air, from the many small clues it gave. Presences, absences. He had owned, when he first arrived, a watch with a brown leather strap, one of his better things. He had managed to keep hold of it for two weeks before it was stolen. He knew who had taken it: a man who choked to death in the refectory six months later, inhaling a mouthful of mashed potato. The watch must have been given to the dead man's family, along with the dozen other effects from his locker. It might have puzzled them, the nice watch they didn't know he'd had.

He let the curtain drop. He wondered what had woken him. There was no shouting, no sound of running feet, no alarm.

The place was hushed. The room he was in, a common room, a big room with a high ceiling, was deserted. But somewhere something had changed. Something had fallen or risen.

He swung himself to sit on the board, legs dangling. He patted his hair (he still had some) and looked down the length of the room. The stiff little tables with their stiff little chairs, the foil ashtrays. On one wall, screwed to the wall and out of reach, was a painting of hot-air balloons; on the opposite wall, also screwed on, also out of reach, was a photograph of the young Queen in her coronation robes.

Other than for his shoes he was fully dressed. A brown pin-striped suit with a cardigan under the jacket, the cardigan a present from his daughter, the younger one, last Christmas or the Christmas before. Red wool and warm, slightly too big, or becoming so. The older girl had stopped coming years ago. He must have worried about that once. Not any more.

Awake now, clear-headed in one of those lulls when the things they gave him had lost their force, he stood, steadied himself, and set off. In his socks he could move almost soundlessly. From the common room he entered the corridor. It was a wooden floor in the common room but in the corridor there were lino tiles, geometries in bright colours. You had to be careful not to get lost on it, not to try stepping only from green square to green square, or find yourself marooned on a red triangle. The tiles were new and part of a scheme to brighten things up. The Administrator had visited them. He had addressed them in the chapel after Sunday service, spoken from the black wood of the pulpit. 'Time for change, ladies and gentlemen! We are entering the age of opportunity!' A few weeks later the tiles arrived and a speaker was installed in the refectory, playing the same three waltzes again and again until the new man, the one with the military blazer and the scarred face, took a chair to it.

The door of the office was open. In the armchair, a figure in a white coat gently snoring. Ian, on nights this week. On the filing cabinet, the wireless, lost between stations, hissed like escaping gas then suddenly spoke, posing a question in a language he did not know. Next to the wireless was an empty Bass bottle and a packet of filterless Woodbines. He leaned in and helped himself to one of the remaining cigarettes, tucked it away in the pocket of the cardigan. The office clock said ten to five.

Pass the office and you come to one of the back wards. Each ward had a name and this was Farmer. Twenty beds on one side, twenty the other. Along the length of the room, night-lights dropped their glow like molten wax. He walked the central aisle, observing the sleeping heads and the few that watched him back. There was no babbling now, no whining. Of all the hours of day or night, this was the barest. Nobody came or went on the road outside. Inside, even the most restless had finally exhausted themselves. It would be another two hours before the shift changed.

He came to his own bed, his name, Martin Lee, written above the hook where his other jacket was hanging. Further down on the same side he stopped at the iron foot of Stephen Storey's bed. The sheets were pulled up and a pillow had been placed beneath them, the faint fake outline of a sleeper – good enough, perhaps, to fool someone glancing in from the doorway.

Was *this* what had woken him? Stephen? He was the baby of the ward, and due to go home soon, certainly before Christmas. A young man with his boyhood two steps behind him, who wrote in a small neat hand in small notebooks that his mother brought. When he arrived, carried in an unhurrying ambulance from somewhere that didn't want him or couldn't manage him, he had, for the first few weeks, opened the skin of his hands with anything that offered an edge, but they must have got something right because that had stopped. He would play chess with whoever cared to sit down with him. Recently he had been on the bench next to Martin in Mr Hitchcock's woodwork class. They made toys, all sorts, wooden boats for boating ponds, pop-guns, spinning tops. He had a flop of brown hair, a shy smile, though he looked at you clearly enough. He had once been caught singing, perfectly alone, in the shelter by the football pitch. Even the people who ran the place could see he deserved a future. So where was he?

Beyond the ward was the washroom. Martin looked for him there among the dripping taps, the smell of wet towels. There were no nightlights in the washroom but light seeped in from a lamp outside one of the frosted windows. There was a tap hissing. He found it and held his fingers under a twist of water. On the shelf above was a squat glass bottle. He lifted it, shook it. Half full? He set it back on the shelf and turned off the tap. The cubicles were behind him but he didn't bother to search them. Even when completely still, completely silent, a human being crackles like a radio mast, and he knew he was alone.

Another door, sometimes locked, sometimes not. Tonight it opened to a push. No more brightly coloured tiles; from here you walked on stone. He felt for the light switch. It lit only a single bulb under a metal shade ten yards away where the passage was crossed by another. On either side of him were heavy doors with bolts and peepholes. Most of the rooms they led to were used for storage now, though they had kept one for its old purposes. He looked in through the peepholes, saw darkness heaped like coal in a cellar. Some parts of the building (this was one) were said to be haunted, but that didn't trouble him. He thought if he could help a ghost he would, and he thought they would know it.

At the junction of the passageways he paused under the bulb. Go right and he would reach the fire door. Turn left and he would come to the laundry. He turned left. He could feel Stephen in front of him, quite close. As he walked away from the bulb the passage grew faint with shadow, but he could see his way and could have found it without the help of any light. The laundry's double doors were open and he went in. The floor was rutted from the wheels of trolleys. He moved carefully between the steel tubs and the strange machines that wrangled and pressed the sheets. Women did the work. You could watch them as they processed in their blue housecoats back to their side of the hospital in the afternoons.

Next to the laundry was the drying room. Linen hung from wooden horses suspended under the ceiling. An electric light on the side of the boiler gave the room the cool blue glow of moonlight. There was a smell of lye, and a slight bitterness, as of things that cannot really be cleaned sufficiently. In the centre of the room was a table large enough for twenty to have sat down at and feasted. It was heaped with folded sheets and towels, a heavy drift of them. Stephen Storey was lying across the top, full-length, face up, dressed and bootless. His eyes were shut, his mouth not quite. One hand rested by his belt buckle while the other had fallen to the side and lay, palm up, beside the black cloth of his trousers. There was an envelope clipped to his tie with a clothes peg. *To Whom It May Concern.* It was a hospital envelope. At some point he must have gone to the office and asked a nurse for it.

Martin touched him, his cheek, his neck. The skin was not yet cold but cooler than the air around, like a knife in a drawer. He spoke Stephen's name, softly, as though to a sleeper, and for a minute he stood there, a shade stalled among the muffled voices of his past. He thought of shaking out one of the sheets and spreading it over him, but Stephen could have done that for himself. And there was nothing indecent here. He had seen indecency, had stood in front of it seventeen years ago with his camera, a day in April, the midst of a forest somewhere between the Weser and the Elbe. Nothing here that needed hiding or hurrying into the ground. The room was friendly in its way, like the wings of a theatre, the sort of place he might have chosen himself, might still.

He stepped away from the table, paused, bowed as deeply as his stiffened back would allow, then returned to the passage. He walked beneath the single bulb and kept going until he reached the fire door. He felt for the cigarette in the cardigan pocket, rummaged in his jacket for a match, found one and struck it on the wall. When he had first come, he wasn't allowed matches, for obvious reasons, though at some point (the second shock? The third?) he had lost his faith in fire.

He leaned against the wall and smoked. Woodbines were made in a factory in the city. It was a place you could usually get a job, women and girls in particular. Some at the hospital had worked there, and some had gone the other way, from the hospital to the factory. There was a kind of trade between them. He smoked until he could feel the embers against the skin of his fingers. He ground it out on the wall. The sparks fell to the floor.

Between the metalwork room and the fire door there was an alarm in a glass-fronted box. He struck the glass with a jab of his elbow, pressed the scalloped brass of the button, then shoved the bar on the door to let himself out into what was left of the night. The fog was heavy. You could barely see the chapel. The women's wing was hidden entirely. A taste of ditches, winter fields. The sea? He walked. The fog opened and closed at his passing. So many dreams like this! At his back the first lights came on, and behind the thin curtains the place began to roar.

2

The dealer who sold him the car had called its colour *bleu nuage*, then glanced at Eric to see if he had understood. When it was obvious that he had, the dealer's smile broadened, as if he knew the deal was done – done or as good as.

The Citroën ID: fewer features than the DS but to all intents and purposes the same car, just more affordable. And this one, sitting on the forecourt, had a couple of hundred miles on the clock. That knocked something off the price.

'Didn't they like it?,' Eric had asked, and the dealer had shrugged as if to say not everyone is right for a car like this, not everyone could appreciate it.

Adjustable road clearance, air-oil suspension, rack and pinion steering, heating for front *and* rear passengers.

'The front seats go all the way back, Doctor. You can sleep in it if you need to.'

Now, driving the winter lanes, the mud, the ruts, the spray, he had to wash the car at least once a week if he wanted it to show for the lovely thing it was. Bucket, sponge, hose, the wax the dealer had thrown in as a gift. It embarrassed him a little to be washing it so often. He did not think of himself as that type of man, suburban, prissy, obsessed with possessions, but there was something voluptuous about the car he couldn't quite get over. He would in time, of course. In time he would think of it as just a car. Time would level it out, for that, he had learned (quite recently), was what time did.

The dashboard clock said twenty to nine. His first house call was scheduled for nine o'clock. It was Mrs Tallis, a schoolmistress who, he imagined, liked punctuality, but the fog was heavy still and he wasn't going to hurry. On the wireless before he left the news was of a big London smog, the worst in months, visibility down to five yards, and during the night impossible. An Air Ministry warning of more to come. Listening, he had pictured it, the shrouded buildings, Eros in a cloud, the empty parks, and for the hundredth time wondered if he had given up on London too easily, if giving up on London had meant giving up on other things. Ambition? But he'd had no good connections there, no strings to pull. A provincial with a Midlands accent he had no intention of trying to hide. And London, of course, meant weekends with Irene's parents, drinks with people he struggled to be polite to, who blathered about the impossibility of finding maids and gardeners, as if the war had never happened. And when they had first come down, the train out of Paddington, the height of summer, Gabby Miklos collecting them at the station (oh, that Mitteleuropean charm worked a treat on Irene) to take them to view the cottage, its empty rooms smelling of old fires, the garden half wild, it had felt in some way inevitable. On the train back up they hardly discussed it. They would go. Of course they would. He would be a country doctor and she would be a country wife. It seemed the solution to a problem they hardly knew they had. And if you wanted his opinion it had done her an immense amount of *good* to be out from under the shadow of her parents. More playful, more sure of herself, more like her sister, the famous Veronica. Or that, at least, had been the story of their first year. Slowly, somehow, the tide had turned. There had been an alteration. He had not worked out the cause yet; he had not had the leisure. Lack of something meaningful to do? She had complained of it once or twice. Well, that would be changing soon enough.

Up ahead, at a place where the road dipped and the fog might have passed for London smog, he saw the floating red lights of a stopped car. He slowed (disc brakes at the front, drum brakes at the rear) and came to a halt five yards behind the lights. He waited, sat there four or five seconds and was about to sound the horn when a figure in overalls stepped out of a coil of fog, peered, then waved uncertainly, a lost spaceman greeting the arrival of the aliens. Eric knew him. It was his neighbour, Bill Simmons, who had moved into Water Farm a few months after he and Irene had moved to the cottage. It had not taken long for the village to find him out – or for the woman who ran the village shop to do so, which amounted to the same thing. A rich man's son playing at farming for reasons of his own. And the father not just any rich man but one whose name showed up in the papers from time to time, stories written with one eye on the libel courts. To complete the picture there was the little blonde wife, a patient of Gabby's. She too had an interesting father, though hardly in the same way.

Slowly – and somehow with an air of resentment – the other car started to move. It was not a Land Rover but something like it, something inauthentic. It reversed, then swung off the road and bounced through the open gate into the field. Eric put the Citroën into gear. He lifted a hand, though didn't look over. He gathered speed, no longer cautious. Under the grey looming of the trees, the car flowed like water.

*

Mrs Tallis lived in a villa off the main road. He parked on the gravel. The garden had the look of somewhere preparing for a long abandonment. It was like the corner of a Victorian cemetery. There was even a small stone plinth, a sundial presumably, but looking funereal, as if it should have a stone urn on top. It would be different in the spring, of course – crocuses, daffodils – but on a day like this the spring felt almost impossible to imagine.

She opened the front door within seconds of his ringing. He imagined she'd been standing close to it, waiting for him. It was what patients often did.

'Good morning, Doctor.'

'Morning, Mrs Tallis.'

'This fog!'

'Yes.'

She asked if he would care for some tea. He thanked her. He fancied a cup; he also thought it would be useful to watch her making it, that it would give him a sense of how she was managing, her range of movement. She was fifty-six. During the war her husband, too old for the regular forces, had found a post as an auxiliary fireman and was killed in Bristol's Good Friday raid. Six weeks ago she had started getting pain in her shoulders and hips. It was worst in the morning, and it was sometimes difficult to get out of bed. He had examined her (he was good at all that, could handle people physically in a way that seemed to calm them). There were various possibilities. Rheumatoid arthritis, lupus, even Parkinson's. When he looked at the results of the blood test and thought about her symptoms, her age, he settled on polymyalgia rheumatica. He tried it out on Gabby. Though not exactly the senior partner, Gabby Miklos had a few more years' experience and a good instinct for diagnoses. It was usually worth checking the tricky ones with him. When Gabby concurred, he started her on prednisolone. The effect, which had been rapid, was proof enough of the diagnosis.

He watched her now from the kitchen table. How precise she was! Her dress, her bearing, the way she scooped tea from the caddy with the coronation teaspoon, the careful way she answered his questions. Did that come from her life as a schoolmistress? Was it about setting an example? He assumed she was lonely. She didn't smoke, but he wondered if she drank, a few schooners of sherry after dark to ward off the demons. The kitchen smelt thinly of fish, perhaps from last night's supper, a bit of grilled sole. Through the window, wintering songbirds moved in a blur around the feeder.

He enquired about headaches, pain in her jaws when chewing, any disturbance in vision. He had been reading up and knew that temporal arteritis was a possible complication. Her answers reassured him. He glanced at his watch. They went back to the hall together. On the table was a silver-framed photograph of a man in a black uniform. He had seen the picture before but only this time did he realise that the shadow at the side of the man was the plinth in the front garden.

She opened the door. 'Is it starting to lift?' she asked.

'I think so,' he said.

They stood side by side, looking out at the garden. It was the moment, a small lapse in the ritual of the visit, when something might have been said, but nothing was.

It was a five-minute drive to his next patient, just long enough to finish his smoke and smuggle the butt out of the car window. A red-brick house, two up, two down, the far end of an Edwardian terrace. There was a small garden with a pair of plaster gnomes fishing in an empty pond. At one of the upstairs windows, as usual, the curtains were half closed.

Here, he didn't even need to ring the bell: the door was opened before he reached it. The woman stood holding the edge of the door. She wore no make-up; she did not look well herself. When he had entered and wiped his shoes on the mat, she shut the door. In the dimness of the hall (a carpet of purple swirls, the dark stairs with the painted banister, the school photograph on the wall of a boy with the same dark eyes as her own), she stood close to him, as if she almost imagined he might hold her and comfort her.

'How is he today?' He spoke softly. She shrugged. A curious look came onto her face, a smile of rage. It was only there for a second.

'In and out,' she said.

He moved towards the stairs. 'I'll go up, then.' She didn't offer to accompany him and this had become their pattern. She would wait in the kitchen, a few minutes to herself when she didn't have to listen out for the ringing of the little bell.

On the upstairs corridor he felt oversized, a deep-sea diver in a Harris Tweed jacket and brogues exploring the wreck of a modest pleasure-craft, one that had foundered years ago but where everything was delicately preserved, each thing its own memorial. For form's sake, he tapped a knuckle on the door at the end of the corridor – it was always left ajar – and went in. The room's only light came from the eight inches between the curtain edges. The bed was watery greys, the man in it likewise, what could be seen of him. There was an electric heater by the end of the bed that sent up a dry, dusty heat. There was the usual paraphernalia of a long sickness, the usual smells.

'It's Dr Parry,' he said. He went to the window and shook the curtains open another few inches. He glanced down at the top of his own car, then turned back to the room. On the pillow, the man's head was a skull. His eyes were shut. Eric wondered if perhaps he was dead, and if that was the news he would take down to the man's wife in the kitchen. But the eyes opened and the gaze – the gaze of some stubborn intelligence trapped or hiding in a corpse – held Eric where he was for a moment.

'How are you today, Peter?'

A long pause. Small movements of the hands, the fingers. The gaze roamed dreamily around the light on the ceiling. Peter Gurney was thirty-eight – two years older than Eric. He had been a foreman at a quarry, one of those on the bluffs behind the surgery whose sirens they could hear even at the cottage if the wind was in the right direction, an eerie swell somewhere between raiders-approaching and the all-clear. He had still been working at the quarry six months ago.

'Are you getting much pain?'

'Not much,' said the skull, a voice like a breeze.

'That's good,' said Eric. There was a chair by the side of the bed and he sat in it. In his training he had been taught that patients, even terminal cases, should not be given regular doses of strong opioids. It was Gabby who had changed his mind about it. Gabby gave his patients diamorphine – basically heroin – as much as was needed, and as often as it was needed. Why wait for the pain to become unbearable? There were side-effects, of course, risks (respiratory arrest), but if his patients died as addicts, they were not first driven mad by pain. The old pharmacist by the surgery had found ways to make his disapproval known, and Gabby being a foreigner (and possibly *that* sort of foreigner) didn't help, but the new man, Tilly, was happy enough to order whatever was asked for. With Peter Gurney, Eric or the district nurse used to inject him; now there was a bottle and a spoon and it worked just as well, if not better.

Mrs Gurney was in charge. He had wondered if she might be tempted to try a little herself. He didn't think it very likely, though he would be careful to collect the bottle from her when it was over.

'Is there anything you'd like me to do, Peter?'

'Sometimes,' said the skull, the breeze beginning again, 'I feel people . . . close by.' He gestured, a slow fanning of his fingers to indicate the narrow spaces around the bed.

Eric waited. 'Is it a dream?' he asked. The skull rocked slowly from side to side and smiled.

The last call was to the estate. The fog was thinning fast – more mist than fog now. In the RAF he had been taught the distances you could see, could hope to see, through fog and through mist. Fog is a cloud, visibility down to a thousand yards or less. On airfields, with bombers trying to come in at night, they would soak the edges of the runway with fuel and burn it off. It worked, apparently. He'd never had to try it for himself, thank God. The war had had the decency to end before anything like that was necessary.

But even without fog it was easy enough to get lost on the estate. Hard to know what guided the planners, what shape or pattern, if any, they were trying to follow. At one end, the older houses were immediate post-war and already starting to look tatty. At the other end they were still building – brick boxes, handkerchief gardens, some gardens neatly tended, others, most, just a patch of thin grass over builders' rubble. In the *Herald* or somewhere, he had read that the population of Britain was now fifty-two million. He had no sentimental ideas about the English landscape. He had grown up in a city, had moved from its rough centre to its smarter suburbs. People going into a swoon over the Cotswolds or the

Yorkshire Dales, that wasn't for him. But fifty-two million! The whole country covered in little boxes like these! Was that the future?

He found the house. He had, he now realised, been there before. There was a swing in the garden and the remains of a rocking horse. The doorbell seemed not to work. He rapped on the wood. A teenage girl answered the door. He frowned at her. 'Julie?'

She smiled gappily. He had seen her last spring when she told her mother she'd taken an overdose of aspirin. She hadn't. She looked happy now, and he wondered vaguely at its source. Just being young, perhaps, just being alive.

They went into the front room. There was a television in there.

'She's waiting for it to start,' said Julie, nodding towards the girl curled on the sofa. 'I've already told her there's nothing till dinner time.'

'Hello,' said Eric. He put his black bag on the arm of the sofa. 'What's your name?'

'She's Paula,' said the older girl. 'She can't speak 'cause her throat's so bad.'

'Your sister?'

'Half-sister.'

She was, he thought, nine or ten. Short brown hair in little waves, enormous brown eyes. She was comically beautiful. He wondered if she'd keep it as she grew up or if this was her moment, her little flare of perfection. If she did keep it, she wouldn't be hanging around the estate for long.

'She's been crying,' said the other girl.

'Well, we can't have that,' he said. 'Shall I take a look?' He reached for the bag, opened it and took out a wooden spatula and a pencil torch. He crouched in front of the child. 'Nice and wide.' He pressed down the restless tongue, shone a light on the back of her throat, squinted.

'That does looks sore.' He took out the spatula, turned off the torch. She let him feel her neck, this little animal. She watched him with an intensity that brought him close to laughter.

'It's her tonsils, isn't it?'

'Yes,' said Eric.

'She'll have to have them out. I did when I was her age. She doesn't want to. She's frightened of it.'

'Let's try something else first,' said Eric. 'It all depends on what's causing it, the soreness. We'll try this. It may be all she needs.' He sat on the sofa, prescription pad on his knee. He wrote out a prescription for penicillin, signed it, tore it off and handed it to Julie.

'Can you pick these up at the chemist's this morning? Mr Tilly will explain how she should take them. And are there any aspirin in the house?'

The girl blushed, shook her head. Eric found a bottle in his bag. He tipped two into his hand. 'Dissolve these in a glass of water. Stir them around a bit. Give her half the glass and see how she does. Give her the rest in a couple of hours. You can get some aspirin from Mr Tilly as well. Tell him who they're for and that he can ring me if there's a problem. And she should eat.'

'She doesn't want to.'

'She has to eat. Have you got any soup?'

'We've got cubes.'

'Get a couple of tins of soup when you go out.' He turned to the child. 'What flavour do you like? Tomato?'

'Room,' whispered the child.

'She's saying mushroom.'

'You're about the same size as a mushroom,' said Eric. To the older girl he said, 'Got any money?'

She shook her head. He took out his wallet. In the little leather frame the wallet manufacturers had provided – some assumption that one *would* carry around such a thing – he had a creased photograph of Irene taken in the weeks before the wedding. The expression on her face – what could you call it other than brave? He tugged out a ten-shilling note and held it out to the girl between two fingers.

'There'll be enough change from that to get a tub of ice cream,' he said. And to the younger girl, 'Mushroom flavour, I suppose.'

At last, a smile.

At the surgery he entered by a door that meant he didn't need to walk through the waiting room. There would be half a dozen people in there by now, sitting in their coats, flicking through copies of *National Geographic* or studying the floor, fretting about whatever had brought them there, trying to get their stories straight. He had the consulting room at the end, by the main road. Gabby was at the other end with a view of the garden. The garden was not much bigger than an allotment, but Gabby had planted bulbs, tulips mostly, and there was a plum tree he harvested to make a liquor he had promised to let Eric try one day.

He sat at his desk. Mrs Bolt the receptionist (whom he had also contrived to avoid) had left his mail on the blotter. There were ten minutes before he was due to see his first patient. The larger envelope was this week's copy of the *Lancet*. He and Gabby shared a subscription. They used to have time to talk about what was in it, but they were busier now. Beneath the *Lancet* were a couple of envelopes containing publicity from pharmaceutical companies. Shiny brochures, colour photography. Sometimes there was a gift inside, though the gifts usually arrived with the reps, the salesmen – some of them ex-doctors – who sat there like friends who just happened to be passing and talked chummily about a new drug for hypertension. At the beginning of the summer he'd been offered a year's free membership of the country club, exactly the sort of place he despised, though he had, anyway, joined it.

At the bottom of the pile there was an envelope addressed in blue ink, a free-moving hand, big, confident loops for the D of Dr, the P of Parry. He picked it up, and as he did so, he glanced to the door as if he imagined Mrs Bolt bustling in, or even Gabby, with those big sad eyes that had seen God knows. But the door was shut, the settled light of morning filtering through the net curtains behind him. He was quite private.

He opened the envelope with the paper knife (Distaval in gold on the handle). Inside, one sheet of headed paper, watermarked. Had she scented it? Or was it just the press of her hand as she wrote, the nearness of her wrists with their rubbed and blood-warm smears of perfume? She had told him once the name of the perfume and he had made a point of not remembering it.

He read the letter quickly. She was, she said, writing after her bath. She was wearing only her silk kimono, the one with the lilies, and the silk touched her in a way that made her long to have him with her. She said things – wrote things – he still found it shocking that a woman might be thinking. Where did she learn such stuff? From novels? The sort, perhaps, he saw the women at the country club carrying. Fat novels to fill up their endless afternoons.

He read, he reread. She made a caress out of language. But a letter, here, to the surgery! He had told her the last time;

he'd thought she had understood. And of course, she *had* understood. This was part of a game, of how she teased him, that part of him she called Sunday-school Eric, though he'd never set foot in a Sunday school in his life.

All that she did was so extraordinarily accomplished. The maddening suspicion that she knew more about life than he did, she who hardly left the house. He considered tearing up the letter – but put the pieces where? How hard was it to imagine Mrs Bolt playing jigsaw with the fragments (*and the silk touches me in a way that makes me long . . .*)?

He slipped the sheet back into the envelope, put the envelope in the inside pocket of his jacket. He thought of his father, that steady man who rose from ganger to assistant stationmaster at Birmingham New Street, who wore a black silk trilby to the office and took it off with his ganger's hands to hang it on a coat tree. A man to be trusted with the movement of trains, the flow of crowds. His father's example – *that* had been his Sunday school, though it had had nothing to do with religion.

On the edge of his desk was the intercom box. They had installed it six months ago. It meant Mrs Bolt did not have to walk down the passage every time she had something to impart. But the buzz always startled him. There didn't seem to be any kind of volume control. He depressed the switch. 'Yes?'

'A call from your wife, Dr Parry.'

'My wife?'

'She's on the line now.'

'Right. Well, put her through.'

'Transferring her now.' Mrs Bolt had made the machinery her own. She had mastered it.

He picked up the receiver. There was a click, another click. He waited.

'Eric?'

'Is it urgent? I'm about to start. I'm probably late already.'

'The hospital called,' she said. 'They've been trying to reach you.'

'What hospital?'

'The asylum.'

'What do they want?'

'I don't really know. They wanted to speak to you. I told them I'd pass on the message.'

'Though there is no message.'

'They want you to call them.'

'All right. I'll ring them later.'

'He made it sound quite important.'

'I doubt that it is.'

'How has your morning been?'

'Same as usual. Look, I don't have time to talk now. I'll see you this evening.' In the background, the sound perfectly clear, he heard the cottage doorbell. 'Who's that?' he asked.

'I don't know,' she said. 'Probably the post.'

'I'll see you later.'

'Right-oh.'

'Bye, then.'

'Yes. Goodbye.'

He replaced the receiver and reached for the intercom. 'You can send the first one down now, Mrs Bolt.'

With his pen (a Parker 51, grey and silver, Glaxo inscribed up one side) he wrote on the blotter, in small letters, *asylum*.

3

Rita lay on her right side, blonde hair on the shadow-coloured pillow, her face in a frown as she backed out of a dream of the club, some version of itself, Chinese lanterns flickering in a breeze that came through the open door and down the empty stairs. No band on stage, the mirrored shelves behind the bar all bare. The place had been raided? She had been there once when it was. There were complicated arrangements between Eugene and the police that didn't always hold up. Sometimes they were apologetic (orders from above) and sometimes they were angry. The sight of a Negro bandleader with a diamond in his tiepin, the smell of hashish down there, and the girls, black girls and white girls, who weren't much interested in dancing with policemen. Eugene fretted about them. He said they were skittish as horses, you had to settle them down, it wasn't just about money. But in her dream the club was a place no one was coming back to, not Eugene or Gloria, not even the police. The stairs were narrower than the real ones had been, narrower and longer, at intervals (what is time in a dream?) lit like an X-ray by the neon above the street door. Something had happened in the world above. The H-bomb? Or a comet the size of London smashing the world off its axis? Go up there and she might be the last one. Endless winter in an endless night. And yet she had to see, she had to know . . .

She stirred and began to unwind herself from the sheets. The whiteness of day showed between the not quite perfectly closed curtains. There was an alarm clock on a chair on Bill's side of the bed, the alarm set for five, the time now almost nine.

The room was cold, though she'd known it colder. At the foot of the bed was a paraffin heater, but her nose told her it wasn't lit. Bill was nervous of it. He thought it would gas them with its fumes or set the bedspread on fire. He said the bedspread looked like the kind that would burn well.

She swung out her legs and sat on the edge of the bed. The dream was familiar enough, the mood if not the details. She looked down at her feet. She had on a pair of Bill's boot socks and was wearing a set of his pyjamas with the cuffs rolled up. Under the jacket she wore a long-sleeved vest. That, at least, was hers.

She listened for sounds of activity from the yard and heard, as if her sitting up was its cue, the bellowing of a cow. A train clattered past. She had learned in the last two years to tell a goods train from a passenger train, locals from the express.

She shuffled out to the corridor and down to the bathroom. There were no curtains or blinds at the window, but they weren't needed. The nearest house – the doctor's – was on the far side of the field, though today, through the fog, she couldn't see it at all. She could barely see the field.

There was a full-length mirror in the bathroom with a black japanned frame they had bought in a bric-a-brac shop on the Gloucester Road in Bristol. The woman had said it was French. It was not screwed to the wall (that was a job still waiting to be done), just propped against the faded seashells of the old wall-paper. She pulled up the pyjama jacket and the vest, held them in one hand just below her breasts. She studied the reflection of her belly, then turned side on and twisted her neck to look again. She touched her skin and flinched at the contact of her cold fingers.

Something? Nothing?

She let the cloth fall and raised her gaze to meet her own blue eyes, puffy with sleep. She reached up to pat her hair. 'You've let yourself go, dearie,' she said. She went to the wash-basin. The water shuddered in the pipes. There was a back-boiler on the Rayburn in the kitchen, but the Rayburn was as old as the house. When they moved in, she and Bill had peered inside it, like Hepburn and Bogart scratching their heads over the engine of the *African Queen*. Sometimes water came in a wild gush and your head was lost in steam; sometimes it was cold as iron and burned you the other way. This morning it was, she thought, about the same temperature as the fog. She washed her face, then cleaned her teeth. The bristles of the toothbrush turned pink, and when she spat into the basin, a little blood swirled around the plug hole.

She used the toilet and waggled her toes in the socks. When she was done she looked out of the window again. Only minutes had passed, but she could see the field now, and beyond it the blush of the doctor's roof tiles, his house like a ship anchored off the coast, riding out the weather. As she watched, a light came on in one of the upstairs windows.

'Good morning,' she said.

In the kitchen – she had pulled on one of Bill's jumpers; there were no proper women's clothes for this kind of life – she stood beside the cream steel of the Rayburn, leaned right over it (she knew which bits not to touch), then turned to warm her backside. The cat, large, brindled, was sitting on the table between the wicker egg basket and her knitting things (red wool, size 12 needles, the beginnings of a bobble hat). The cat had come with the farm. If it had a name they didn't know it. It was not affectionate. It had drawn blood from both of them, from Bill several times. It gave the impression of intending to outlast them, of being confident of doing so.

Out of the cat's reach, on top of the old meat-safe, was a saucepan of cold spaghetti and tomato sauce, the remains of last night's supper. Spaghetti was one of the things she could do. There had been a time in her life – the Pow-Wow Club, the temping – when spaghetti was a main source of nourishment, packets of it in thick blue paper from the Italian delicatessen on Park Row. You only needed one ring to make a meal. You could add anything – a tin of peas, margarine, ketchup. You could eat it bare if you had to, with just a pinch of salt. She lifted three or four strands from the saucepan and lowered them into her mouth. Like a baby bird, she thought. The thought made her tearful. She wiped her eyes with the back of a hand, then teased out more spaghetti. Tomato on her chin, on Bill's jumper.

Her morning job, the first, the only one that really mattered, was feeding the hens. Bill would have let them out after milking, but by now they would be frantic. She wetted her fingers under the tap, wiped them on a cloth, took the basket from the table and went to the back door. She leaned against the wall and pushed her feet into gumboots. You had to fight to get the door open. Like almost everything else in the house it was not well made. It swelled with the damp. It was not even a particularly old house. Above the front door a date was gouged into the plaster – 1907, the year before her father was born.

She tugged. She would have liked the strength to tear it off its hinges. She enjoyed the thought of moving through the world with unstoppable force. Attack of the fifty-foot woman! Doors, men, whatever tried to check her progress, flicked away like spent matches. She tugged again, swore at it, and the door gave. She stood on the step, breathing in the morning, the dissolving weave of the fog. The coop and the run were ahead of her. To her right she could see the end of the cowshed where a pair of rooks or jackdaws perched on the tin roof, watching her and perhaps waiting for her to start feeding the hens. On the far side of the yard the gate to the track was open. There was no sign of Bill and she couldn't see the car. He used to leave messages for her on the kitchen table saying where he was going, but not any more. He didn't have the time, and perhaps it didn't matter.

Behind the wire of the run the hens were chattering and scolding. There were twenty-five of them, brown, white, speckled. In the first year, the fox got in at dusk before the hens were shut up for the night. Some of the hens seemed to have died of sheer terror. It made her feel differently about the hunt.

They sold the eggs at the village shop, and they had a wooden box by the milk-churn stand at the end of the track. People left their money in a tin. Sometimes the money in the tin didn't add up, but sometimes they had more.

She went to the meal bin and scooped out grain, sent it, with a quick movement of her wrist, skittering across the scraped earth of the run. The hens chased it. They were lovable and idiotic. She laughed, and dug out another scoop. She began to sing: 'The mashed potato started long time ago . . . with a guy named Sloppy Jo . . .'

She filled the drinkers from the tap by the back door, then

opened the coop and looked for eggs. Some of the hens were broody. They sat in the midst of themselves, feathers puffed, and pecked at her hands when she moved them, though once the eggs were in the basket they seemed to forget them soon enough and hurried off to join the others, searching for the golden grain.

She sang again, a breathful: 'Mashed potato . . . feel it in your feet now!'

She did not, she knew, have much of a voice, but it was only hens for an audience, hens and, further off, the cows in the shed and the ones in the barn. And the bull, of course. Bill's two-hundred-guinea gamble.

She carried the basket back to the kitchen, half filled the big kettle and put it to boil on the hotplate. The droplets on the base of the kettle spat and hissed. 'A watched kettle . . .' she said, a voice that belonged to someone else. Aunt Elsa? She thought for a moment of that large cold flat in the city, of the gramophone that must have been fifty years old. She raised herself *en pointe* – or as high as she could in Bill's socks – using the steel rail of the Rayburn as a barre. Aunt Elsa's voice came through more clearly. Kick up your feet, dear, and don't forget to smile. That's it. Round you go. Now reaching up. Now looking over your shoulder. And you could pout a little here. That's it, dear. Don't overdo it . . .

The cat was watching. She stuck out her tongue at it. Aunt Elsa was dead. When she'd had a drink, she used to say that one day she was going to leap out the window and impale herself on the railings, but in the end it wasn't like that. The landlady found her when she brought up the milk. She was lying on the living-room floor in her nightie, staring at the damp stains on the ceiling.

She made tea in the pot, poured herself a mug, sweetened it, fetched her book, fetched her cigarettes and matches, dropped a cushion on the floor and sat down with her back against the Rayburn. The book was a new one. The travelling library had stopped in the village on Wednesday. It came once a fortnight and parked at the side of the shop. The librarian – also the driver – was called Keith. He wore glasses with heavy frames. He smoked a briar. She thought he fancied himself as an intellectual, and perhaps he was – who was she to say? – but mostly he was the randy-uncle type. She could sense him watching her when she was in the van with him, knew he was weighing up the pros and cons of touching. She wasn't afraid of him. She knew the randy-uncle type well enough, had received their attentions since she was twelve or so. And Keith brought things she liked, the sci-fi novels and stories he ordered for her from the big libraries in Bristol. Sometimes he placed them in a box on the floor of the van so she would have to bend over for them. Cheap thrills!

Wednesday's book was *Venus Plus X*. It had the sort of fiery cover she preferred (nothing clear, everything possible), and though she had only read twenty-five pages, she thought she liked it and had chosen well. The hero's watch was running backwards but time was flying the other way. He falls, wakes, and finds himself cared for by a man he has never seen before, and strangely dressed, maybe not a man at all. He can't work it out! Who could? And this was something else she liked, that drop into the fever of not knowing, except it's not confusion exactly, more a case of one part of you not yet ready to accept what the other part knows perfectly well.

She sipped her tea and smoked. She had forgotten to put an ashtray on the floor so tipped her ash onto the boards. It could be brushed under the Rayburn later. The butt would go into the firebox. The warmth of the Rayburn moved through the muscles of her back. All winter you hold yourself like a fist, a tension you're hardly aware of until the first warm day when you lift your face to the sun. It was far too early to start dreaming of summer – the shortest day was still two weeks off – but somehow she did begin, and it moved under her reading like a shallow stream, became part of the mood of what she read. Bill and Teddy getting the hay in, Bill showing off his farmer's tan. Lilacs plump in a jug on the kitchen table. The half-dozen nights you could sleep with the window open. And there was, last summer, that evening she'd laid the picnic rug in the orchard and they'd sat out late, moths around the jars where she had put tea-lights, the cat hunting between the trees, bats flitting, the heavy smell of grass. The dark had come slowly and hardly seemed like darkness. When the candles guttered, they had stayed on, and she had half thought they might see strange dancers under the apple trees. They had meant to do it again, had promised it to themselves, but there was always work to be getting on with. The long days needed to be used, and the summer slipped away.

After twenty minutes she shut the book. She had a length of barley straw for a bookmark. She stood, thinking how there would come a time soon when she would not be able to rise from the floor so easily. She went upstairs to the bathroom, used the toilet again, then back to the whiteness of the bedroom. She should have made a hot-water bottle, but couldn't be bothered to go back down. She felt drugged. Her own blood was drugging her. She lay down on the imprint of herself. She hauled the covers to her chin. She shivered. She could feel the beating of her heart (and somewhere inside her, a second heart ticking like a ladies' wristwatch). She thought of the doctor and of the doctor's wife, of what she was, at last, going to do today. She thought of her dream, the club like a theatre where she had been happy, or not unhappy, or not unhappy all the time. She thought, with the usual ripple of grief, of her father. And then, as if such thoughts had been small tasks to be completed, she slept.

Later, she heard Bill, became aware of his presence in the room, heard him whisper her name.

'Rita?'

She did not move, and after a while she heard him go back to the door, into the corridor, down the stairs. She slept again, and when she woke she sat up so sharply she made herself dizzy. The strong sense of having been called to by someone who could not possibly be there. The alarm clock said eleven-thirty. She walked to the top of the stairs and looked down, then went to the bathroom. The fog was gone. There was the orchard, the field, the doctor's house. She spent several minutes on her face, several more on her hair. In the bedroom she pulled a pair of jeans over Bill's pyjamas, exchanged his sweater for a thinner one of her own, a roll-neck of powder blue lamb's wool, soft as a baby blanket, a treat bought on an outing with Gloria some morning they'd come back flush with tips from the Pow-Wow.

In the kitchen, she picked out six eggs from the basket, the most handsome, washed them, patted them dry and placed them in an empty box. She went to the office to see if Bill was there. The primness of an empty room. She wrote a note on the pad on his desk. She fetched her boots, put on her duffel coat and beret and left by the front door. She walked through the orchard. In the tangled branches there were a few apples shining like decorations while others lay brown and rotting in the wet grass. At the edge of the orchard was a wooden gate with rusty hinges and flaking black paint. This, she thought, was the gate that Death would enter by. She opened it, closed it behind her, and set off across the field, where exactly nothing was happening.

4

There were still moments when it made Bill laugh out loud to think he was the lord of thirty-two acres, owned fields and cattle and a barn, that he had, in late summer, harvested a field of his own barley. Not by himself, of course. A contractor had come in a combine, a man red-eyed with fatigue and complaining about the narrowness of the lane, the narrowness of the gate, the smallness of the field. 'You want to get those hedges out,' he said. Hedges were the enemy (a waste in themselves and wasting land on either side. Expensive to maintain. Harboured vermin).

And then there were moments when he felt as if the land and the animals and everything he possessed, the machinery, the buildings – the house! – were all conspiring against him. Finding the lights in the milking parlour would not come on because mice had chewed through the wires, seeing a cow hobbling out of the parlour and knowing that probably meant another call to the vet, discovering how prone his fields were to flooding, how tall the thistles grew, how hard they were to scythe. Realising ten times a day how little he knew about what he was doing. If I was a sailor, he thought, I would have drowned by now.

This morning it was the gate. It had worked yesterday, had opened without a problem, but at some point in the night the top hinge had torn free of the post, and he would need to come back with his tools before the whole gate came away and his cows set off down the lane to Bristol.

His fields all had names. This was called Barrow. That was the name on the deeds. It might have been called Barrow for five hundred years. On old Richy's farm by Queen Camel there was a field called Purgatory.

He looked up. The sky had no depth to it. They were in a cloud, the morning light seeping downwards, like cream through muslin. Fog in the yard, the house wrapped in fog. Even in the shippon – he called the cowshed a shippon because that was what Mr Earle, the man who sold him the farm, had called it – there had been a haze above the heads of the animals, silver droplets glittering in the light from the bare bulbs slung from the beams.

He lifted the gate and began to walk it open. Somewhere in the field there were four dry cows and a pony. Usually they came to the gate when they heard him stopping. Had the fog confused them? The mental life of his animals remained a mystery to him. They certainly had a mental life; they had minds, they weren't blank. A cow had as much personality as a dog. Some of them watched him in a way that seemed thoughtful, as if they returned his curiosity with one of their own. Some liked to be handled, some not. He had two kickers – Livia and Drusilla. Drusilla had caught him in the shoulder last spring, his skin tattooed with the outline of a hoof for weeks. She was in the barn now, waiting to calve. He had looked in at her first thing and would look in again as soon as he was back.

With the gate open, he returned to the lane and saw the lights of a car. There were places in the lanes where you could pass but this wasn't one of them. He walked towards it. He had been at Water Farm long enough to recognise most of the cars that used the lanes regularly. This one was easy. Long and low, the long bonnet, the headlamps on side-wings, like frog's eyes. He waved. The whole car radiated impatience. He walked round to the door of his own car (an Austin Gipsy, and to his mind slightly superior to a Land Rover). He climbed in. For several seconds he just watched the Citroën's headlights in his rear-view mirror, then wrestled the gearbox and started to reverse through the open gate. The moment the lane was clear, the Citroën glided past.

He sat on in the cab. He had been up since five. The day was already well worn, and there was something hypnotic in the stillness, the hush, the way that beyond the further hedge, the world ended in a soft white nothing.

'I do not like thee, Doctor Fell, the reason why I cannot tell . . .'

There was a Latin version of it he had been taught at school. *Non amote, Sabidi, nec possum dicere*, something something something. The Latin master was Mr Oaks. In retrospect he seemed, like most of the other masters, a man in despair, who gave expression to it – got some relief from it – by being violent towards children. Yet the boys liked him. He was, inevitably, called Quercus. When he had had just the right amount to drink, he told them stories about the trenches. Very lights, mustard gas, wire. And because he'd been a soldier, he was put in charge of the cadets, though it was obvious he hated all things military. Mostly they just jogged around the edge of the cricket ground, sweating in khaki, while Quercus sat in the pavilion smoking and reading the newspaper.

Try explaining any of this to Rita! The life of a minor English public school. She'd had some sort of schooling, of course, had attended half a dozen places around Bristol, but they all sounded inoffensive, almost pleasant. *His* school, for which he felt a nostalgia he couldn't quite root out, his father had chosen as being at the more competitively priced end of those institutions dedicated to the production of young men who would not be out of place in a Pall Mall club (not the best ones, naturally), or an officers' mess, a shooting party. On exeat weekends his father would come up the drive in a succession of larger and more expensive cars. The headmaster waited on the front steps in his gown. They shook hands and traded remarks about the weather, his father in a voice that had more to do with unpronounceable towns sunk into the twilight behind the Iron Curtain than the chalk downs of Sussex, lying in cropped green sunshine beyond the playing fields. At some point Bill would be called over, would stand there in a rage of embarrassment at his father's attempts to dress like an English milord (the fedora, the sunglasses, the check jackets, on one occasion white shoes). Then the glide down the drive between chestnut trees, parents in smaller cars pulling over to let them pass. All of this made his father unshakeably happy, and by the time they reached the gates, wheel in one hand, cigar in the other, he might have begun to sing, one of those wavering and tear-stained songs in the language he forbade his sons to speak a single word of.

Through the side window of the Gipsy, one of the Ayrshires was watching him, her nose bubbled with droplets of dew from the grass. She tossed her head and Bill grinned at her. 'Blame the doctor,' he said. He clambered out and went to the back, opened the rear door. He had a bale of hay in there and a bale of barley straw. He dragged them out, found his clasp knife and cut the twine, kicked the bales loose. The cows began to feed. He liked the sound they made, the gentle tearing of the fodder, the huff of their breathing. The pony trotted over and took its place among the cattle. He had inherited it from Mr Earle. It cost little enough to keep and he had the impression the cows liked its company. And might a child learn to ride on it?

As they fed, he strolled deeper into the field. He had seen a heron there once, though that was when the lower field was flooded. He pictured Mr Earle walking the same rough ground: Earle who had farmed here for thirty years, who had stood in fog like this, had felt the heat of the animals, who might also have seen a heron lifting the grey width of itself into the air. To what extent was mind just circumstance? Would he begin to think like Mr Earle, to become like him? But mind must also be the history of circumstance, and his history and Mr Earle's could have very few touching points. After the sale, the farmer had retired to a bungalow at the bottom of the village. Rita saw him sometimes in the shop, buying cigarettes and tinned food. He never asked after the farm.

He drove back along the lanes. In the forty minutes since he had driven the other way, the fog had begun to break up. Stray sheets clung on, tangled in the boughs of trees, but the sky had lifted. It would not be one of those days when the fog ebbing out and the fog flooding in met at tea-time and the day was stifled, a fire that would not catch.

He drove into the farmyard and parked in front of the house. He was hungry now, but that would have to wait. He stepped down from the car and turned towards the barn that stood opposite the house on the far side of the yard. Like the shippon (that made up a third side of the yard) and the cart shed (part of the fourth), the barn was much older than the house and consisted mostly of repairs carried out over the last century and a half by farmers with neither the time nor money to do the job more thoroughly. The lower walls were stone and cob; further up there was brick, and higher still, planks nailed over uprights. The doors were wide and high enough to bring in a well-loaded hay cart. They looked, he thought, like the doors into a city, above which men in chainmail patrolled. They would be the last things to go, would survive everything until they stood on their own, like Rodin's brass doors he had seen in Paris with one of the girls (Ancient and Modern at St Hilda's) he didn't marry. Such doors were not intended for anything as trivial as comings and goings, and he went around to the far side, a much smaller door, and drew the bolt to let himself into the barn's constant evening. Light fell through gaps in the walls and roof, touching, random as memory, the stored clutter of the place. The car – a Morris Traveller – was not much used now. Rolls of fencing wire, sacks of maize cubes, the Bradley crusher (two big flywheels). There were bales of straw, a tin bath, and, stretched on its side like a shot Triffid, a streetlamp that Mr Earle had possibly meant to put up in the yard, and which would, indeed, be very useful there. And there were animals. On one side, in a makeshift loose box, two cows with mastitis, bad cases that didn't appear to be responding to the penicillin. On the other side, in a sort of sawn-down room – the remains of an old tack room? – he had Drusilla, the cow about to calve, today or tomorrow. He went to look at her. She was standing and facing him. She did not look distressed. It was not her first calf. He should, he knew, get around the back of her and see what was happening but he didn't think from her expression that she was inviting him to do so. 'I'll come and check on you after lunch,' he said. He wondered if it comforted her to see him.

When he finished in the barn, he went back to the yard. The muck heap – straw and dung – was letting go its ribbons of stink into the white air. He warmed his hands at the side of it. He didn't object to the smell. He thought he didn't notice it much any more. At the entrance to the shippon, he unhooked the chain and ducked his head under the beam. There had been stalls in here when he first arrived but they had been rotten. One of his first jobs had been cutting them out and making a big bonfire of them. It was a loose house now; the cows could move about as they chose. They bedded down on straw; they ate hay he dropped from the loft, maize and pulped sugar beet. With the dry cows out in the field and the three in the barn, he had only eight in the shippon. He checked the water troughs. He was always nervous of finding them empty and not knowing where the problem was, how to go about fixing it, but this morning there was water, blooms of casual light on its surface. He would do some barrowing later, spread fresh bedding, do a count of the bales in the loft, do sums in his head, try to work out how much winter feed he might need to buy in, think again about the advantages, the possible advantages, of making silage. He had made none this year. He had put his faith in hay. 'Good hay hath no fellow.' He had read that somewhere.

He went through an opening at the back of the shippon. Facing him was a thicket of briars, buddleia, honeysuckle, lilac. It needed bulldozing; it needed some attention from the drums of paraquat he had found in the workshop. But in the spring it was crowded with birds, and later shot out spikes and umbels of sweet-scented flowers, unruly and lovely. This was the view the bull had, gazing through the barred gate of its enclosure. Each day they had their confrontation. Bill stared at the bull; sometimes, the bull stared back; mostly it ignored him. There was no doubt it was dangerous. Dairy bulls were notorious. And was the gate high enough? There had been no incidents, or none so far, but the bull had entered his dreams, a creature whose mind was a swinging door it would be a serious mistake to find himself on the wrong side of.

He had bought it in the summer at Yeovil market. He had been leaning over the rail with old Richy, who had suddenly pointed two crooked fingers and said, 'That's him, that's the one you want.' They had been drinking in the Mermaid Hotel. He had been sitting with Richy and four or five others, Somerset aboriginals in their market suits. You knew full well that each of them, somewhere in his pockets, had a length of twine, just in case. They were not gentlemen farmers; most were tenants. When they spoke it was like listening to Chaucer. They were secretive, sly, funny. It was an obvious honour to be asked to sit with them, for in their own minds, and with some reason, they were royalty. They gave him advice, old Richy in particular, that he stored away like gold. But to drink with them! They had been swallowing strong cider since childhood. He had seen some of them top up their scrumpy with gills of gin. He was no stranger to drinking, had been raised by people who went for only very short times of the day without alcohol, but cider was something else and it had its own rules. So he had bought a bull because he was tipsy, possibly on the cusp of hallucinating, but mostly because he did not want to disappoint his mentor. Two hundred guineas! Nearly the last of his savings and certainly more than he could sensibly afford. Other farmers had looked on. No way of telling if they thought he had done well or was making a fool of himself. They knew he wasn't from a farming family; they would have recognised him if he was. A few might have known the family he *was* from, though his father's world could only have existed in their heads as a play of extravagant shadows – the London-square house, the cars, the 'business' that now and then spilled into the papers, though not yet into the *Somerset Standard* or the *Western Gazette*.

So what was wrong with the bull? And had he been sober that day, would he have seen it? Since the summer it had served only three of his cows (Drusilla's calf was sired by a neighbour's bull). Were Ayrshires not to its taste? Did it dream at night of long-lashed Jerseys? Nice big-boned Holsteins? Rita said it was the sensitive type and needed to be in the mood. He had asked her if she meant candlelight. Should he dress as an Italian waiter? Play the accordion? She had liked that, had laughed, said an emphatic yes! But he did not find the bull funny. Nor did he know what to do about it. He could have asked the vet, but the vet went from farm to farm, and it might be that when he sat down to have his mug of tea at the kitchen table, he told stories ('That lad down at Water Farm. You know the bull he bought . . .').

He tapped the gold of his wedding ring on the steel of the gate. The bull blinked. 'You're running out of time,' said Bill.

He went back through the shippon and into the yard. He crossed to the house, dragged off his boots at the scraper by the front door. In the kitchen, the cat jumped off the table where it had been licking out the inside of last night's spaghetti pan. There was no obvious alarm in its jumping; it was not fleeing, merely taking up a more fortified position under the table. Next to the saucepan was the egg basket. She had not washed the eggs, she had not washed the pan.

On the floor by the Rayburn was a mug, a cushion, a book. He picked up the book and the mug, placed the mug in the sink and examined the book. That she liked to read, he had thought of as something that made up a little for the difference in their education. But *Venus Plus X*? And the rest she came back with from the library van, flying saucers on the covers, astronauts, red planets. He had suggested other things to her. She might, for instance, like Virginia Woolf. He had known girls at the university who adored Virginia Woolf and probably wanted to be her. Did the van have any Virginia Woolf? And she had given him a look, wide-eyed, not overly friendly, then turned to the cat to ask, 'Does the van have any Virginia Woolf?'

She was right, of course. It was no business of his what she read. He should keep his nose out. And *Venus Plus X* was probably at least as interesting as something *infinitely* sensitive about a lighthouse.

He topped up the kettle and settled it on the hotplate. He opened the firebox and luxuriated a moment in the press of heat on the skin of his face. He shook in more coal from the scuttle (the scuttle, too, had been Mr Earle's), closed the steel door and went upstairs. The bedroom door was partly open. He went in, quietly. The room was curtained still. He stood at the foot of the bed. On the chair by his side of the bed, the alarm clock said ten past eleven. Lunchtime for a dairy farmer. He looked for the rise and fall of the covers, the rhythm of her breathing, but in the mushroom-coloured light there were no clear edges, just one softness blurring into another.

'Rita . . .?'

He waited. She did not stir. He bent closer, studied what little he could see of her pillowed head until he made out the fluttering of a vein in her temple. He thought for a moment of climbing in beside her, of feeling the warmth of her, like someone saying, 'You're safe now.' He watched her for a few seconds longer, then returned to the kitchen, considering if he should have a friend, someone to whom he could say 'my wife this, my wife that'. Stanhope, his closest friend at Oxford, was in South America. Six months ago he had written from Argentina to say the country was like the world's beginning and you could make on it whatever mark you chose. The people he met at market, old Richy and his ilk, were not friends. In ten years perhaps, if he stayed. His brother, Charlie, once upon a time, but not now. (In an escape film, Charlie would be the one suddenly absent on the night of the big break-out, who was windy, or was perhaps in the commandant's office drinking schnapps.) Their father, as far as he could tell, was basically friendless, and it didn't seem to have held him back. Hard to say how much encouragement one could take from that.

And Rita? Who were her friends? There were the 'girls' she had lived with before they were married, who had come to the registry office to throw confetti, though she seemed to have shed them quite easily. Others turned up in her stories, though not all the stories were entirely believable. The childhood playmate, the scamp she had roamed with in an unspecified countryside, he thought was probably an invention, something from a book.

In her room in Bristol, an early visit, he had found a photograph album under her bed with very few pictures in it, and glue marks where several had been removed. At the front, with a page to himself, was her father in army uniform, a camera round his neck, the blurred grey hulk of a tank in the background, and inked beneath it, *11th Armoured Division April 1945*.

Among the other pictures there were three or four of a grinning, fair-haired man, mostly taken in what looked like a pub. One photograph, loose in the back of the album, showed Rita on the knee of a coloured woman in what, to judge from the outfits (the outfits were sparse), was some sort of show. Later, he realised the woman must be Gloria, perhaps Rita's one real friend, until suddenly she wasn't. He had leafed through the album while Rita was in the house kitchen producing one of her inedible meals. When he had heard her coming up the stairs he'd pushed it back into the shadows under the bed and thought how nice it was, what a relief, to be free of the past.

He made tea, pouring the boiling water onto the same leaves she had used. He looked for something to eat. There were things in the fridge that should have been thrown out, things you couldn't even give to the hens. He found some cheese, a type of pungent Cheddar that stung the mouth, found the last of a sliced white loaf in its waxen wrapper. He made a sandwich, scooped a handful of chocolate bourbons from the tin behind the wireless, and took it all out to the car. He put the food on the passenger seat and went to the workshop, a lean-to at the house end of the shippon, tools suspended from nails, Earle's shotgun lying across two pegs at head height on the far wall. He was a bodger, he knew it, but a bodger can fix a gate if he tries, a temporary fix, something to get them into the New Year. He dropped tools into a canvas bag, selected a likely looking piece of timber, stowed them in the back of the Gipsy and headed out to the lanes again, one hand on the play of the wheel, the other feeding himself biscuits.

5

Irene Parry ran down the stairs in her bare feet. What if she fell? Fell and lay bloody at the bottom of the stairs? But she did not fall. She picked up the receiver and, in a voice intended to sound as if she had been awake for hours, said, 'Dr Parry's phone.'

The receiver gurgled in her ear. She was too late. She replaced it and stared at it, waiting for it to ring again. It brought her close to tears to think that her first act of the day had been this, this failure. She had heard the ringing at the edges of her sleep. It had entered her dream, a complicated and rather urgent dream involving Russians, and possibly the little cosmonaut himself. She wouldn't get it back now. Someone had been chopping mushrooms. For some reason it had frightened her.

She returned to the bedroom and put on her peignoir. She called it a peignoir, though it was more of a dressing-gown, even a housecoat, but it was quilted and quite pretty, printed with yellow and orange roses. Her feet found her slippers at the side of the bed. She opened the curtains over the small, deep-set window and looked out at the fog. The day was beginning again. For a third time? The first was when she heard the alarm on the Teasmade and the little machine going through its operations. Clicks and hissings. He had asked if she wanted a cup but she hadn't, she wanted to sleep. Did she hear him go? Or was she already with the Russians and the mushrooms? Until a month ago, she had always got up to make him his breakfast. Now she stayed in bed. It was his idea. And perhaps he was perfectly happy finding something for himself. It might be easier on his own. Toast and marmalade, the news on the Home Service. Anyway, he didn't complain.

The second waking was the phone. The third was this, the day beyond the window, the shrouded trees the far side of the lane, the stillness of the house, her own stillness, the cooler air close to the glass. She closed her eyes. Was she going to be sick? She'd had a whole week without it; she had hoped it was over. Eric said it probably was, or it might be. She went down the corridor to the loo beside the bathroom and stood there, waiting. There was a window about the size of her face, and she distracted herself with looking out. This was the other side of the house – the back garden, the ash tree, some of the field. She couldn't see the farm through the fog. She began to feel better. Things pass. She went to the bathroom, pulled the cord for the light, took off her slippers and stood on the scales. The figures swam, then settled. She stepped off and went to the mirror. It was full-length and screwed to the wall between the door and the radiator. She lifted her nightie. She gazed at herself, touched her skin, turned side on to gaze again, then let her nightie fall, buttoned her peignoir and slid her feet back into her slippers.

In the bedroom she cleaned her teeth at the washbasin. On the wall above it was a reproduction of an old painting, *The Arnolfini Marriage*. It had been given to them as a wedding present by one of Eric's friends, someone who had been with him at medical school in Manchester. The friend was ironic. Possibly the picture was a sort of joke. If so, he had not explained it, or not to her, though they had danced together at the wedding. Perhaps they were supposed to work it out for themselves.

There was a man and a young woman. The man had a face like a hairless horse. He wore a large dark hat, dark as his face was pale. With one hand he held – loosely but with, she thought, symbolic assurance – the hand of his bride. His other hand was raised in a gesture of blessing, or as if to silence her, silence everyone, while the brain behind that long white face puzzled something out. The bride was dressed in green. She was pregnant, or that was what it looked like, her free hand on the green swell of her dress. Hard to say where she was looking. Not at him, her husband. There was a bed behind them with red drapes. There was an ornate brass lamp, a mirror with something written above it, a window – open – the glimpse of a tree. Something breathless about the painting, a pause that had lasted hundreds of years, the question, the waiting, the sense that nothing can move forward until he drops his hand and says whatever it is he has decided. Then *she* can look up and say her part. Assuming she is allowed to speak at all.

She sometimes wished Eric hadn't put it up. She didn't think he even noticed it. He wasn't interested in paintings. She would have preferred a nice Renoir print, or a mirror, or just the wall. About this painting there were things she didn't know, there was some kind of mystery. It was a riddle.

She tidied the bed, picked up the cup and saucer from the carpet on his side, and went out to the stairs. She was halfway down when she heard what sounded like the front door opening. She paused on the step and held her breath. Had she mistaken the days? Was that Mrs Rudge letting herself in? But there was no bustle, no sound of a coat being stripped off, no approaching stride through the living room.

She carried the cup and saucer to the kitchen, left them in the sink and went to the hall. The noise she had heard was the post. It lay scattered on the mat. She shuffled through it, looking for the blue of an airmail, the pink stamps with the picture of the jet airliner, the dome of a building like St Paul's, which she thought was the Capitol building, or possibly the Senate. She was due a letter, but Veronica was an erratic correspondent. Nothing for weeks, then pages and pages in tiny handwriting, full of gossip and comedy. And sometimes a parcel, though none since the summer. Well, her sister was busy. She had a job! A job *and* a husband.

The post was all for Eric. Most of it looked like bills, which he had a habit of just putting into the bin, something she used to find funny. She left it all on the top of the record-player cabinet and went back to the kitchen. She was suddenly very thirsty, thirsty and hungry. She drank a mug of water standing at the sink, then plugged in the electric kettle and cut a slice of bread from the loaf, spread it thickly with butter and ate it standing up, feeding herself with both hands and looking out of the kitchen window. I'm like Hunca Munca the mouse, she thought, and for the first time that day, she smiled.

She cut another slice of bread. This time she added marmalade from one of the pots she had made following her mother's recipe. Fifteen jars in the cool of the larder, *Seville Orange 1962. S*he had not got the jelly as clear as she had hoped, but she had been proud of it and had mentioned it, casually, during the weekly phone call with her mother.

What was it she was supposed to be doing today? She hated the thought of being – what? Lazy, slack, careless, indifferent. She hated the thought of appearing like that in Eric's eyes, or even in Mrs Rudge's. She was, by nature, a hard worker; she knew that much about herself. It was Veronica, when they were growing up, who was accused, with some justice, of idleness and daydreaming. And now Veronica had a job. Irene wasn't quite clear what it was. In one of the letters, she'd said she was a glorified typist in the faculty office at the college, but it seemed more than that. Anyway, she wasn't spending her mornings in bed feeling sorry for herself.

She washed her hands, dried them carefully on a clean teatowel and went to the shelf at the end of the kitchen where she kept her library of cookbooks. She took down *Modern Practical Cookery*. She took down *The Encyclopedia of World Cookery*. She took down her favourite, *A Book of Mediterranean Food* by Elizabeth David. This had been given to her by Tessa, whom Eric referred to as her 'arty friend'. Tessa lived in London and was having an affair with a married man, a playwright who was quite well known among people who went to small theatres and cared about things like nuclear war and the north of England. She cared about those things herself, of course. She read the editorials in the *Herald*. She listened to talks on the Third Programme. She had Richard Hoggart's *The Uses of Literacy* upstairs by the bed. Eric used to talk about Hoggart. Now that she felt better she could make a proper start on it; she wanted to.

Apparently the playwright's wife knew all about the affair and accepted it. She was an actress. She accepted it, or she could do nothing about it. When Tessa came down for the party, she might ask her about it. One *was* interested. She assumed Tessa wouldn't be bringing the playwright. There was a line somewhere you shouldn't cross, though it was becoming difficult to know where it was.

She fetched her notepad and biro from the shelf beside the telephone, pushed away Eric's breakfast plate (crumbs, marmalade, the casual knife), sat at the table and uncapped the biro. There were various things to be decided. Supper tonight, that was the first. Friday supper – it should be fish, of course, but the van had not come this week for some reason. She had thought (almost her final thought before falling asleep last night) of ratatouille. She had most of what she needed – a tin of tomatoes, an onion, a red pepper, a jar of shiny black olives that Gabby had given Eric for his birthday in September. And she had garlic! A Frenchman in a comical French car (not a bit like Eric's) had appeared in the village in the autumn. He had knocked on the door in his Breton top. He had been smoking a Gauloises or a Gitanes. He had been wearing a beret. And over his shoulder strings of pink onions and ropes of garlic. He had laughed at her expression and explained in the most charming accent that he had come over on the ferry and was driving round the villages. He smelt of onions, of black tobacco, of salt, of away. She had found her purse and bought two strings of onions and one of garlic. The big onion at the bottom of the string was, he told her, the 'captain'.

'*Merci, Madame, et bonne journée!*'

'Goodbye,' she had said, then called after him, '*Bonne journée à vous, Monsieur!*' She had a school certificate in French. She'd been quite good at it.

So, ratatouille. And perhaps she would see if the village shop had something like pork chops. She might be lucky.

It was a strange thing that after three years of marriage she was still unsure of what he liked. Eric was not what her father would call 'a good trencherman'. What he did like, what he would eat without asking questions about it, was quite plain. It was what he had grown up with – they all had, to some extent, the war and so on. But a lifetime of cottage pie? Bubble and squeak? Where was the colour in any of that? He had once said she should educate him. He had meant food, of course, because there was nothing else she could educate him in.

Less pressing but more important than supper – more worrying, certainly – was the whole question of Christmas and the Boxing Day party. It would be the first Christmas they hadn't gone to her parents. Eric had put his foot down. She wasn't too sorry. Veronica wasn't coming over this year, and watching Eric and her father clutching glasses of port while trying to find something they could talk about that made sense to both of them was wearying. Her parents had made clear their disappointment. They would, she knew, go on making it clear long after Christmas had passed. It would be brought up again next year. But she was Mrs Eric Parry now. She belonged elsewhere. It was high time they got used to the idea.

As for the party, she had begun to wish it wasn't going to happen at all, but the invitations had gone out and some people had already accepted. It would not be big, about twenty if they all came. She would cater for twenty-five. Eric said people only wanted to drink at a party, that crisps and peanuts would do, but what sort of impression would that make? Please come in and have a peanut. Have two. He had also suggested that Mrs Rudge could prepare the food, but as far as she knew, Mrs Rudge could only make scones. And Mrs Rudge was the cleaning lady, not the hostess.

She opened *A Book of Mediterranean Food* and found herself looking at a recipe for grilled snipe on skewers. Now that would make an impressive alternative to peanuts. She imagined the plate being passed around. She began to laugh, startled herself, grew quiet again and turned the page. Stuffed tomatoes à la Grecque? Or dolmades: 'Little rolls of savoury rice in vine leaves'. Where could she get vine leaves? There were addresses at the back of the book where you could write off for things. Or she could set it as a challenge for Mrs Case in the village shop. She had regular deliveries from the city. There must be vine leaves somewhere in Bristol.

She yawned, looked up at the garden. The fog was threadbare now, a grey haze, like rain not quite heavy enough to fall. The garden was unkempt, slightly sad. Soaked greens and soaked browns, dead leaves turning black on the lawn. A bird feeder hung from one of the branches of the crab apple. A house sparrow was feeding. Two others waited their turn.

She got up and turned on the wireless, the Home Service. A woman's voice lost in the static. She eased the knob, a little one way, a little the other. The voice swelled.

'But what precisely did the ancient inhabitants of these isles look like?'

It was a schools programme. She listened to them sometimes. Presumably other women did the same, sitting in their houses like overgrown children.

'Woad is a common plant that can still be found growing today. It has yellow flowers and produces a blue or indigo dye . . .'

She turned it off and made a pot of tea. From the wire rack at the side of the dresser she pulled out a handful of the magazines Veronica had sent from America. She put them on the table, poured herself a cup of tea and sat down again. She knew she should be getting on with her planning but for ten minutes she would just sit and have her tea. That couldn't do any harm. And no one was watching. She thought how nice it would be to have a cigarette, and if it had been a mistake to stop, or not a mistake but not really necessary. The report might be wrong. Eric didn't think so, but it hadn't stopped him. There was probably a pack in the house somewhere, if she searched.

At the top of the pile was the *Ladies' Home Journal*, a very pretty redhead on the cover. She had looked through the magazines several times, but she nearly always found something new. And the looking made her feel closer to her sister, as if they were sitting side by side taking turns to point things out, something interesting, something absurd. In the years Veronica had been away she had come home only three times – twice on her own and once, Irene's wedding, with her husband, Morris (a whole blissful month). She was aware she did not know Veronica's daily life any more, her routine, the things she saw every day that shaped her thinking. The thought of them becoming, slowly but surely, strangers to each other frightened her. Eric had said they could go one day but she didn't like to keep asking him. On a visit to Bristol she had gone into an agency and asked about flights. They were expensive, more even than she had thought. It perplexed her that she did not have money of her own.

She opened the magazine at random – an advice column on hysterectomies. She turned the page. A picture of a crawling baby wearing Chix diapers. *Makes a change a snap!* The paper was almost sticky. Was that the colour print? She smoothed open a double-page spread of party food. Not all of it looked appetising. But devilled eggs! She had forgotten about devilled eggs. She picked up her biro and wrote it down under 'dolmades'. So, she was working after all. It was research.

Flipping over another dozen pages she came again to the quiz. It was part of an article entitled, *Ask yourself, is he a good husband?* There were fourteen questions, and if he was a good husband, at least eleven had to be answered with yes.

Does your husband –

1. *Handle money sensibly?*

2. *Share outside interests with you?*

3. *Deal understandingly with your relatives?*

4. *Choose his friends wisely?*
5. *Take an interest in your work?*
6. *Appreciate things you do for him?*
7. *Behave discreetly and conventionally?*
8. *Want the same things you do from marriage?*

She had gone through the list when the magazine first arrived, and she had gone through it again more recently. Some of her answers had changed, and it had taken her longer to answer some of the questions, to come down on one side or the other.

The magazine below the *Ladies' Home Journal* was very different. It was called *Jet*. It was 'a weekly Negro news magazine'. It cost twenty cents. It had not been surprising to find it in the parcel. Her sister was, after all, a free thinker. She was interested in the race question. Her husband, Morris, was interested too. At the college where he taught he had a coloured colleague, and sometimes the colleague came to supper.

The magazine was not glossy like the *Ladies' Home Journal*. Presumably you couldn't do glossy for twenty cents a copy. There were no novellas with their literary touches; there were no quizzes about marriage, nor any advice from doctors. Most of it was short articles about people and the things they had done, good and bad. There was, for example, a story about an ex-slave, a hundred and six years old, who had just married a thirty-nine-year-old bride in East St Louis. There was a photograph of the couple. They looked neither happy nor unhappy.

There was a story about a man shot to death for disobeying his wife. It was the wife who shot him. There was a paragraph about twenty-seven teenagers enrolling at a school in Little Rock, Arkansas, a school that had been for white children only. There were some names she recognised – Sammy Davis Jnr, Billie Holiday. Billie Holiday was photographed lying in her casket with white gardenias in her hair. But these were lives that were as remote to her as . . . she couldn't think. Chinamen with pigtails. Russian cosmonauts.

She went back to the *Ladies' Home Journal.* The world's most glamorous bachelors? The Aga Khan, Prince Orsini. She found another dish for the party list – tuna croquettes. She wrote it down with its page number in the magazine. Then she turned, carelessly, to something she had not wished to see again, something that did not belong. It was a photograph, full page, of a woman with her babies. Not a healthy woman, but one who looked exhausted, who stared out of the page with an expression that had passed beyond anger and fear. It was an advertisement for UNICEF, though probably you couldn't call it an advertisement. On the facing page a model was washing with a beauty soap: *that* was an advertisement. The woman with the babies was somewhere in Africa. The babies were twins and she did not have enough milk for them both. It was monstrous. But that, of course, was the point. That was why it was there. She could not feed them both. She must choose. The baby on the left or the baby on the right. One would live and the other would not. The first time she saw it, she had been outraged. She had made a speech in her head, had paced the kitchen. She had meant to speak to Eric, to show him. They would send money to UNICEF, a few pounds, whatever he could spare. And they would talk about it, share their disgust at a world where one woman bought beauty soap and another must choose which of her children to feed. She had meant to do it – over supper perhaps, or when he was making himself a drink, or even when they were lying in bed together under *The Arnolfini Marriage*. But Eric had to deal with people's suffering all day. What sort of wife would she be, waiting to ambush him with a picture of a woman in Africa who couldn't feed her children?

The picture didn't make her angry any more, or not this morning. Turn the page, she thought, just turn the page. There was nothing she could do, or nothing beyond accepting, finally, that this was a world in which there would always be, somewhere, a woman having to choose between her babies. As the magazine was an old one now, one of the babies would already be dead. It was a horrible and useless picture. It exhausted her to look at it, but she went on staring into the woman's eyes.

Her parents were churchgoers, C of E, the ten-thirty at St John's, where, on the wall, there was a painting, medieval, of the procession of the blessed. She and Veronica had gone there nearly every Sunday of their lives until, a week after her sixteenth birthday, Veronica had suddenly refused. Their father had shouted at her. His big hands were itching to be used. Their mother was ice. Oh, let her do what she wants, a silly little girl who thinks she knows better than everybody else.

But everybody else *doesn't* go to church, said Veronica. Bertrand Russell doesn't go to church! So they had left her, their mother buttoning her gloves, their father, his temples flushed crimson, Irene hesitating at the door, looking back, trying to send some silent support, a silent *yes*, until their father barked her name from the driveway and she had hurried after them.

Where her tears fell they darkened the glossy paper. A tear for the woman. A tear for each baby. A tear for her own mother, who was, in fact, a kind person, good and kind. A tear for her father who, when they were small, would get on all fours, pull the rug over his back and growl like a bear . . .

She sat back to weep more freely. The telephone rang. She shut the magazine, wiped below her eyes with the heels of her thumbs. On quick feet she went to the bottom of the stairs. She lifted the receiver before the bell had finished its fourth ring.

'Dr Parry's phone.'

It was someone from the hospital, the asylum. A man looking for Eric. She had brought the pad with her, and underneath 'tuna croquettes' she wrote down his name and telephone number.

'He will still be on his morning calls,' she said confidently, though she had no idea if he was, 'but I'll make sure he receives your message . . . Yes . . . Of course . . . Yes . . . Thank you . . . Goodbye.'

In the beginning, probably the first six months at the cottage, Eric used to leave a list of patients he was visiting, with their numbers, those who had telephones. She was a sort of secretary and receptionist. That was, apparently, quite normal with GPs' wives. And she had liked it. It gave her a role, albeit a small one. Then the lists became sporadic, and finally they ceased. And it was awkward, because clearly the man from the asylum assumed she had such a list. Well, she didn't.

She stepped into the kitchen to look at the wall clock, then went back to the bottom of the stairs and rang the surgery. Mrs Bolt answered. Mrs Bolt, of course, was the real receptionist, the one who was paid. She was forty-something, solid, permed hair. She wore a lot of face powder. Her private life was unguessable. She had not, she said, seen the doctor in person, but his car was outside.

Irene asked to be put through. 'Unless he's with a patient, of course.'

He was not, not yet, though there was a sense of Mrs Bolt not entirely approving of wives being 'put through'.

The phone clicked, buzzed. And suddenly she was listening to the air in the room he was sitting in.

'Eric?'

'Is it urgent? I'm about to start. I'm probably late already.'

She told him about the call. She didn't mention the earlier one, the one she had missed. 'How has your morning been?' she asked.

'Same as usual. Look, I don't have time to talk now. I'll see you this evening.'

The doorbell rang. He heard it and asked who it was, which was strange as she obviously couldn't see from where she was standing. She said it might be the post, though as soon as she said it she remembered it couldn't be because the post had already come.

'I'll see you later,' he said.

'Right-oh.'

'Bye, then.'

'Yes. Goodbye.'

She replaced the receiver and glanced to the drawing-room window. Could she answer the door like this? She patted her hair, smoothed the yellow and orange roses, and went to the hall. On her way she had the foolish idea it might be the Frenchman again but when she opened the door it was the blonde woman from the farm. She was standing there in a duffel coat and beret, bright-faced from her walk, holding out a box of eggs.

6

Next to visitors' parking and the ambulance bay there was a white-lined space with a sign that read *Medical Officer.* Eric pulled in and parked there. The space beside him was the Administrator's, and the Administrator's maroon Wolseley was there. His car was always clean. The patients washed it every week, washed it and waxed it.

He walked to the front door, finishing his cigarette. Though the day was hardly one for sitting out, the wooden benches were occupied by those in possession of grounds privileges. Most of them were also smoking. He recognised one or two.

The asylum, the main body, the part of it that looked down the drive, was mid-Victorian. It had a certain provincial grandeur that was unlikely to have been inspired by any notion that the first inhabitants, the indigent rather than the mad (though the mad were among them?) merited such surroundings. Do a good job on the hospital and you might get a crack at a railway station or even a town hall. Orange brick with ornaments of darker brick. Tall windows on the first two floors, a bell tower topped by a weather vane that must have shone once like new money but was now mostly green. Further down the tower was a clock (very like a railway clock). It said ten to three. Eric checked it against his wristwatch and was slightly surprised to find it was correct.

From the vestibule – glazed yellow tiles on the walls and a large, never-used fireplace – a flight of broad wooden steps rose between iron balustrades and disappeared into shadow. Only certain people could use these stairs, the front stairs. He, of course, was one of them. On the weakly lit corridor of the first floor, he walked past gilt-framed portraits of men with mutton-chop whiskers, high, pale foreheads – the founders, the donors, the board.

The Administrator's office was at the back of the building. There was an oak door with a brass plate on it. Eric tapped. Further down the corridor, a crouching figure was at work with a cloth and bucket.

The secretary opened the door. 'Good afternoon, Doctor,' she said. 'Please come in.'

The office was the only room in the building – or the only one Eric had ever been in – that did not smell of disinfectant and the steam of boiled food. Perhaps it did, a bit, just less than the rest of the place. It was a panelled room, high-ceilinged, with two windows giving a view of the hospital farm, the football pitch and, beyond that, on clear days, the broken edge of the city. There were two desks, one small and one large. There were four grey metal filing cabinets. There was a coal fire in the grate. On a stand in a corner, a fern shifted its fronds minutely in the room's currents of air.

The Administrator stood up behind the larger desk. He held out his hand. 'Eric. Thanks for coming. Hope we're not making a mess of your day.'

He sat. Eric took the seat opposite. The Administrator was some ten years older than Eric. A trimmed blonde moustache, watchful grey eyes, a dark grey suit, a silk tie with a golden crown embroidered on it. He was not a medical man, and from the beginning there had been a silent jostling between them as to who, in this place, had seniority.

'Sherry?'

The secretary was already settling a silver salver on a corner of the desk. A bottle of Harvey's Bristol Cream, two pretty glasses. She poured while the men watched her.

'Chin-chin,' said the Administrator.

'So what exactly happened?' asked Eric. He'd had some of it on the phone earlier, the broad outline, though that was from a charge nurse on the ward, who had sounded genuinely upset.

'One of the people on Farmer,' said the Administrator. 'You might remember him. Stephen Storey. Hadn't been here long. Quite young. Nineteen?' He looked at his secretary.

'Yes,' she said. 'He had his birthday here. September the eighth.'

The Administrator nodded. 'Dead, I think, for some hours when we found him, though you'll be a better judge of that.'

'An overdose?'

'Would appear so. Annabelle, is Ian on his way?'

'He was told,' said the secretary. 'Shall I send someone to look for him?'

'He'll be along,' said the Administrator. 'You're not in a hurry, are you, Eric?'

'I thought he was due to go home. Stephen Storey.'

'He was,' said the Administrator. 'But, of course, they don't always want to go.'

'I suppose not,' said Eric. He held his glass between the fingers of both hands. He hadn't drunk from it. He didn't particularly want to drink with the Administrator, as if they were friends. He remembered Stephen Storey better than most. He had stood out. Obviously bright. A young man who should have been at a university, not in a mental hospital. He tried to recall their conversation the last time they spoke. It was only a few weeks ago. Chess had been part of it. They had both played chess with their fathers and had both – it was hinted between them rather than directly stated – been careful not to win. The diagnosis was schizophrenia. Diagnosing people who came to the asylum was not the medical officer's business – there was a consultant psychiatrist for that – but he had the impression that the label was reached for far more often than was warranted.

'What did he take?' asked Eric. He was fairly certain of the answer but he needed to be sure.

The administrator was peering at the fern, frowning. 'The sleeping tablets,' he said. He returned his gaze to Eric and produced a smile that was also a grimace, as if now something awkward but unavoidable had entered the conversation. They both knew that Stephen Storey had requested several weeks' supply of chloral hydrate to take home with him, and that Eric had provided it.

'There was nothing,' said Eric, 'that indicated he might be thinking of anything like this. Nothing in his notes. No previous attempts. Nothing at all.'

'Suicide is notoriously difficult to predict,' said the Administrator. 'Those you think might, don't. Those who seem to be improving suddenly throw themselves under a bus. The planners, as I call them, can be very cunning. And if he had, let's say, dropped a hint, well, he wouldn't have got the tablets, would he?'

'Of course not.'

There was silence, or something close. The growl of the coal fire, the busy scratching of the secretary's nib.

'They found him in the laundry,' said the Administrator. 'Or, to be more accurate, the drying room. Somebody set off the fire alarm, so it was utter pandemonium for a while. Once heads had been counted they went in to look for him. He was lying on a table. He had a letter with him. On his chest, I believe.'

'A letter?'

'The general beastliness of the world. No hope for the future. Something of a rant.'

'Can I see it?'

'No can do, I'm afraid. The police have it.'

'The police?'

'You just missed him, in fact. Who was he, Annabelle?'

'A Sergeant Orton.'

'Orton, yes. I don't want to say officious but it might not be entirely the wrong word. And that's what complicates the picture. Stephen's mother rang them, the redoubtable Mrs Storey. She's not been a great supporter of ours. Usually the family is only too pleased to have everything managed discreetly. This time . . .' He spread his hands.

Eric nodded. He understood and he did not, not quite. What was he required to say and do? How much trouble would this cause? What sort of trouble? Had he been careless? Negligent? Would it look that way? The gesture of the Administrator's hands he understood best of all. It meant that he, the medical officer, would be the target of any censure that came, any official rebuke.

'Care for one?' The Administrator slid the silver cigarette box towards Eric. There was something engraved on the lid, a regimental crest perhaps.

'So there'll be an inquiry?'

'Hard to see how it can be avoided,' said the Administrator. 'But I know both of the coroners. I think it will all go through smoothly.'

They're masons, thought Eric. He assumed he would be asked to join at some point. Conceivably, the invitation might come from the Administrator.

There was a knock at the door.

'Come,' called the Administrator.

A man in a white lab coat came in, one of the nursing assistants. He looked tired.

'Ian,' said the Administrator, 'you know Dr Parry, I think.'

'Yes, sir, I do.'

'Then we might as well all go down. You can give the doctor the details as we walk. Whatever seems relevant.'

The Administrator stood; Eric stood. The secretary glanced at them. She was rich in secrets. The men trooped out. Corridor, stairs, a set of double doors, on the far side of which they entered the hospital proper. Asylums were much as you expected them to be. People did indeed howl; they wept, carried on conversations with the invisible, wore expressions that in normal life were only made in complete privacy or in darkness. On the colourful wipe-down chairs they sat in rows, clumsily barbered and stunned by Largactil. There was a television – an innovation of the Administrator – but it was mostly the staff who watched it. At one place on their route – they were following a corridor of bright geometric tiles – a man in a military blazer, his face furrowed with a pattern of old razor slashes, barred their way. Ian went to move him aside but it was another patient who took his arm, stepping him back to the wall.

'Thank you, Martin,' said the Administrator.

'It was Martin found him,' said Ian, once they had passed by.

'I don't think I knew that,' said the Administrator. 'And what was Martin doing in the laundry in the middle of the night?'

'He doesn't sleep much,' said Ian. 'I've often seen him having a wander when I'm on nights.'

'And was it Martin who set off the alarm? He has an interest in things fire-related, does he not?'

'I don't know about the alarm,' said Ian. 'It's possible.'

'Well, it might have been worse,' said the Administrator. 'He might have taken it into his head to light a funeral pyre.'

'I don't think he'd do that, sir. Not now.'

'Even so, I think we need to put a stop to these nocturnal peregrinations. Perhaps Dr Parry could have a look at his medication.'

'Yes,' said Eric. 'If you like.' He waited for the Administrator to mention sleeping pills but it was, of course, more effective to leave it hanging in the air.

They came at last to a door marked only with a number. From the keys he wore on his belt, Ian singled one out and unlocked the door. A room of painted stone, chill as a dairy, a small, high window, two wooden trestle tables. On the further table a form was draped with a sheet. Eric went over and drew it back. Above the table was a metal lampshade, though there was no bulb in it. The only light came from the window. It fell over the dead boy's face, evenly and softly. They had not undressed him. He was still wearing a jacket and tie. What did it say about your state of mind that you put on a tie before killing yourself? Was it evidence of madness, or just wanting to look decent, respectable even, for those who found you? Something quite normal, a normal impulse?

He uncovered one of Stephen's hands. It was cool, stiff, the skin rucked with scar tissue. He moved to the end of the table and felt his feet, pressed them through the wool of the socks. Rigor mortis starts at the head and moves downwards – moves south, as one of his teachers at Manchester liked to express it.

He shrugged. 'Twelve hours,' he said. 'Fifteen. Something like that.'

'We can't keep him here,' said the Administrator. 'He'll have to go to Bristol. It could be weeks before the body's released for burial. You'll contact the coroner?'

Eric nodded. He would need to check what the procedure was. Presumably he couldn't sign the death certificate until after the inquest.

'How many pills did he take?'

'About half the bottle,' said Ian. 'He left the rest in the washroom. I've locked them away.'

At the surgery he saw three more patients. None of them took up much time. In and out, three prescriptions, thank you, Doctor. When the last had left him and the door was shut, he checked his watch, then opened the bottom drawer in his desk. He took out an envelope of pink and cream card. On the front of it, in a swirling font evidently intended to be 'female' or at least to evoke in doctors' minds ideas of women: Enovid 5mgs. The card was too big to be hidden in any of the pockets of his jacket, so he placed it in the middle of the *Lancet* and went out into the passage. Gabby Miklos was there.

'Hello, Eric.'

'Hello, Gabby.'

'Anything in the pot?' asked Gabby. He wore a woollen suit half a size too big for him. His eyes had their usual strange brightness, as if he had just put drops of belladonna into them.

'Some nonsense at the asylum,' said Eric. 'I'll tell you about it tomorrow. Or Monday. Nothing that can't wait.'

'At the asylum,' said Gabby. He nodded thoughtfully, and studied the lino floor between them. Eric liked Gabby. In fact, he liked him a good deal – he was one of the few people he knew who did not in some way disappoint him – but it was frustrating that he seemed incapable of learning the rules of the game. As a foreigner, perhaps he couldn't be expected to.

'I'll see you later, then,' said Eric. He raised the hand holding the *Lancet* and a corner of the pink envelope appeared, showed itself like the tip of a tongue. He pushed it back in.

'Will it fog again tonight?' asked Gabby.

'Most likely,' said Eric.

Since the spring, when it had kicked off with an afternoon of pleasure that left him so altered he had not dared go home until he had sat for an hour in the coombe above the cottage, calming himself under the new green of the trees and making a kind of study of his former self and what seemed, suddenly, the banalities of the life he had, until that morning, been content to live with; since then, the outset, the very beginning, there had been various understandings between them, the most fundamental of which was that nothing of what was taking place (had taken place and would continue to) could ever be known. It was not just his marriage: it was the impossibility of carrying on in a country practice with his name mired in scandal. In a big city you might get away with it but not out here. All other understandings were derived from this one. Where they might meet and where they should never be seen together; what days and times of day he might visit, the frequency. There were to be no telephone calls unless it was urgent (Frank will be back early today). She wore, habitually, a heavy perfume, but on their appointed days it was agreed she would not use it (Irene had an acute sense of smell). He was careful of what he touched or moved. In her bedroom, afterwards, he always scanned the room, the floor, checking he had not left anything behind, something for Frank to pick up, squint at and think, But this isn't mine.

When she saw him doing it, watched him from the bed where she lay on her side, tipping the ash of her cigarette into a mother-of-pearl ashtray, she sometimes laughed. It wasn't unkind (he knew she liked him and that it might, in fact, be better if she liked him a bit less). And she, too, had much to lose, something, at intervals, he reminded her of. Reputation, marriage, house, even, potentially, her son. But she only smiled and gazed at him as if he was some bright-eyed child she had found whose ideas about the world were hopelessly naive. It was money confidence, of course. Come what may, Daddy would be waiting in his faux-Jacobean mansion, cheque book at the ready. She would not be on the streets; she would not have to take a job waitressing in a café somewhere nobody knew her; she would not be shamed. He was completely unsure what her morality was. He didn't know her in that way. He sometimes thought she was the kind of person who might choose to bring the house down simply to find out what kind of noise it made.

But if he was the one who preached caution, who insisted on it, who had once dreamed that her bedroom floor was a minefield with pressure plates under the Wilton and nasty little charges that would take his legs off, what on earth was he doing driving to her house through the dregs of the afternoon on an *unappointed* day? Was it just this business at the asylum? Had he allowed the Administrator to spook him? The Administrator! One of those types you found propping up hotel bars, some suggestion of a good war, now just out to make money and screw the secretary. As for the boy, that was another matter. He was sorry about it, of course he was. But patients died all the time. Not, it was true, nineteen-year-olds, not basically healthy ones, and not as a result of something he had given them. But if you got into a funk every time . . . The point being . . . But he could not think yet what the point was.

There was a lay-by up ahead. It would be a good place to stop and turn around, but when he came to it the car sped past, tunnelling into the teatime failing of the light.

He was not afraid of running into Frank. He knew Frank's routine. He was rarely back from Bristol before six-thirty, more usually seven. Occasionally she had visitors, other wives without much to do. That might be awkward – some of these women had sharp eyes – but he was, after all, her doctor (Frank's too, for that matter). He was making a house call. He was dropping off a sort of medicine. That should cover it.

He turned off the main road and drove at the side of a high stone wall. He came to the open gate and slowed the Citroën to walking pace. Her car was there, alone. He drove another thirty yards to the second gate, narrower, its gravel lined with woody evergreens that had got out of hand, rhododendrons and azaleas that in early summer were studded with fat blooms of pink and crimson and white. Alison called it the tradesman's entrance, and perhaps it had been when the house was new. In theory – though he did not care to test it – a car could pull up in the first drive and a car pull out of the second without the drivers ever getting sight of each other.

He parked opposite the garage. The long slope of his headlights cut across the blue of one of her lawns. Where the beams met he could see the archery target that Frank and his son, John, shot at when the boy was home from boarding school. Frank had once shown Eric his collection of bows. He had handed him an English longbow and invited him to draw it. He had managed to, but it had taken visibly more effort than he'd expected. This was at a time when they might have become friends.

He walked across the grass to the French windows at the back of the house. The curtains had not been drawn yet and a yellow light pooled around the steps. He went up to the glass and looked in. She was there, alone. He could see the back of her head as she sat on the sofa, the thickness of her hair. Smoke rose from her cigarette. There was music. He tapped on the glass, then tapped more loudly. She looked round, startled, then stood, and moved cautiously towards the glass, the beginnings of a smile on her face. Once she was sure of him, the smile widened and she turned the key.

'Well, well,' she said. He stepped inside. She closed and locked the door, drew the heavy curtains across by pulling on a cord with a handle of carved ivory like a chess piece. She reached up to kiss him, then stood back to read his face. 'Trouble?' she asked.

He shook his head. The question irritated him. He walked deeper into the room and she returned to the sofa. She was wearing black Capri trousers and a thin, honey-coloured sweater, a string of pearls the colour of snow-clouds. Her feet were bare, the nails painted crimson. The room was warm – it was always warm. Frank had installed a new system, partly at Alison's prompting (you couldn't quite be Alison in the cold), partly because of something Frank said he'd seen on television about the coming of a new ice age. All winter she only needed to wear light clothes. It was a big house, the country residence of a Victorian banker. It wasn't beautiful, was strangely proportioned, though its edges had been softened by wisteria and Virginia creeper, ivy, time. It had a conservatory with panes of ruby and green glass. In the garden there was a small swimming-pool, and a summerhouse, vaguely Alpine, for changing in. Technically there were three of them there, but the boy had been away at school for years, and Frank worked long days at the offices of the tobacco company. Most of the time, Alison was on her own, drifting from one expensively heated room to another.

'Want a drink?' she asked. 'Why don't you sit down?'

'I'm not staying,' he said.

'You could pour me one,' she said.

'You've already got one.'

'But it's nearly empty.'

He fetched her glass from the low table in front of the sofa. There was a big book about art on the table, Picasso, Miró, Juan Gris.

'Were you just missing me?' she asked. 'Or was it something else?'

He topped up the gin in her glass, shook in a couple of drops of bitters. The drops loosened themselves into filaments of pink smoke. There was an almost perfect print of her lips on one side of the glass.

'When are you expecting him?' He preferred not to say Frank's name to her.

'Not for aeons,' she said. 'It's Friday. He'll be in the boardroom with Edward Strang drinking port and working out how much filthy lucre they've made. Have you had a stinker of a day?'

'Someone killed himself at the asylum.'

'Oh!' She touched the pearls. 'How horrible.'

'He used the sleeping pills I'd prescribed. He was supposed to be going home. He asked for a month's supply, a couple of months. I couldn't see any reason not to. He didn't seem depressed. He was going to try getting a job. He seemed . . . normal.'

'Of course,' she said. 'You were trying to help. You couldn't possibly have known.'

He shrugged. He changed his mind about having a drink and poured himself a small whisky. Before he left he would wash and dry the glass in the kitchen, or tell her to.

'Darling,' she said (for she called him that sometimes and it had a rich sound to it). 'If it hadn't been the pills it would have been something else. He would have jumped off the roof or something. If a person wants out they're going to find a way, aren't they?'

'He was young,' said Eric. 'He left a note. A letter. I didn't see it. The police took it.'

'What's it got to do with the police?'

'The boy's mother called them.'

'You would have thought that was the last thing she'd want to do. Anyway, isn't it legal now? Suicide?'

'Assisting it isn't legal.'

'Oh, come on. Not even the police are stupid enough to accuse you of that. No one's going to blame you for anything.'

'I don't know what they'll do,' he said. 'The Administrator made it pretty clear that if there's trouble it won't be him in the firing line. Do we have to have that music?' He didn't know what it was. A dance band, sentimental, inane.

She uncurled herself and went to the record-player, lifted the needle. Into the sudden quiet came the hum of the heating pump, like the background sound of the world.

'Do you want something else?' she asked.

He shook his head.

'A little Mozart?

'I don't want anything,' he said. 'Why do people want music all the time?'

'It makes them happy,' she said, lowering the lid of the player. She came over to him and laced her arms loosely around his neck. She had the heavy perfume on. He had an almost irresistible urge to bite her. He stepped backwards and she let her arms drop.

'I have to go,' he said. 'I only came to give you these.' From one of the side pockets of his jacket he took out six foil sheets of small tablets. He had left the absurd pink envelope in the car.

'Oh,' she said. 'Is this what I think it is?'

'Take one a day,' he said. 'Take it at the same time each day. It'll be easier to remember. It's important to remember.'

'Thank you, Doctor. Do you think they actually work?'

'Yes.'

'And they're not going to be like the ones that made all those poor babies with arms like flippers?'

'The point of them is not to have a baby.'

She grinned at him. 'Do they work instantly?'

'No.'

'But in a week?'

He finished his whisky and handed her the glass. 'All right,' she said, 'all right. And I'm sorry you've had such a beast of a day. You're a good doctor, Eric. And a good man.'

'In fact,' he said, 'I'm not sure I'm either.'

'You'll feel differently tomorrow.'

'Better or worse?'

'Better. Much.'

They kissed, briefly. She wiped his lips with her thumb. He went out through the French windows. It was pitch black now, or seemed so after the lights. And the fog was coming back, rising and drifting like the smoke of invisible fires. As he got into the car, he remembered he had meant to rebuke her over the letter she had sent to the surgery. He had also forgotten to ask anything about how her day had been. Did that happen often? His day but not hers? For half a minute he tried to picture it, her life in the empty rooms, flicking through magazines and novels, the drink at noon, the long telephone calls to other stranded women, the insubstantial meal, the fresh packet of cigarettes, the standing at the window watching leaves swirl into the drained pool. And though he was not much given to thinking about love, did not much care for the word, thought it had been worn to a kind of uselessness, gutted by the advertising men and the crooners, and even by politicians, some of whom seemed, recently, to have discovered it, it struck him that in the end it might just mean a willingness to imagine another's life. To do that. To make the effort. And he found that he *could* do it, could view her like an attendant spirit in the room behind her, a recording angel, but that it was, indeed, an effort. He started the car (what if one day it wouldn't?) and reversed carefully between the bushes. At the junction he pulled out onto the main road just as the headlights of another car approached him down the hill. As it passed him, he thought it looked like Frank's black Zodiac, and he glanced to the rear-view mirror in time to see the car slow, then swing into the road he had just left.

7

The eggs in their box were sitting on the kitchen table. Rita had taken off her duffel coat. She had said how nice and warm it was in Irene's house and how cold the farm was. For several minutes they talked about heating systems. At the cottage there was an oil tank by the back door. The central heating ran on oil. They also had the Aga. The Aga ran on coke. There were logs for the fireplace in the drawing room, and these were delivered by an old man and his four-square daughter. Rita knew them. She said she worried the daughter was the old man's prisoner. Irene said she hadn't thought of that.

Rita explained about the Rayburn at the farm, how it sometimes exploded like a little volcano, sending a cloud of ashes across the kitchen. She and Bill were afraid to let it go out. It might be impossible to start again. It had, she thought, been burning for about a hundred years.

Each woman knew that the other was pregnant. Irene, at sixteen weeks, had begun – just – to look pregnant, and Mrs Case at the shop, who liked Rita, who thought her strange, who felt sorry for her, had confirmed it. Irene knew about Rita because Eric had let it drop one day. She was one of Gabby Miklos's patients.

'Would you like to see round the house?'

They left the kitchen and went up the stairs. Two small bedrooms above the garage at one end of the corridor, Welsh quilts on the beds, then the master bedroom (thankfully quite tidy). At the other end of the house another bedroom, the one Eric's father had died in. Irene didn't go into it more than she needed to. Mrs Rudge gave it a dust now and then.

'This is the bathroom,' she said, opening the door and standing back.

'You can see the farm!' said Rita. 'I can see you from *our* bathroom. Well, not you, of course . . .'

'How funny,' said Irene. She could not have said how it was funny. What was funny about it? That it had taken them so long to meet each other, to meet properly? Her mood before the doorbell rang – the magazines, the tears – had disappeared like the morning fog. She spent far too much time alone. It wasn't healthy.

They went downstairs. Drawing room, dining room, Eric's study (they didn't go in).

'And this is the nursery,' said Irene, opening the door to a room, whitewashed and bare, a picture window looking out onto the back garden (and the oil tank). They stood, gazing in, and it was as if, in opening the door, they had surprised the future, and in the depths of the room, cheeks flushed just the right shade of pink, a child returned their gaze. Or two children, of almost exactly the same age.

They circled back to the kitchen (you could do that in the cottage, leave the kitchen by one door and re-enter by a second at the other end). By the time they settled again at the kitchen table, the two or three minutes it took, each had said what the other already knew, had exchanged due dates and begun on the list of symptoms and complaints, laughing about things that in private made them almost despair. Rita was a month behind Irene. She said she had nothing to show yet.

'At night I look a bit pregnant but that's just my tea.' She said her teeth hurt and her gums bled. She said she needed to go to the toilet all the time.

'Oh, yes,' said Irene, deciding she would also use the word 'toilet'. 'There's a toilet downstairs when you want it.' She smiled, and felt, somewhere in mid-Sussex, her mother's back stiffen a little.

'I'm still wearing my pyjamas,' said Rita. 'Actually, they're Bill's. I have to roll up the bottoms.' She stretched out a leg and pulled up the denim to show the pastel cotton stripes of a man's pyjamas.

So they moved on to husbands. In the garden the songbirds had settled into the shelter of the hedges and bushes to wait out the short winter afternoon. Larger birds cruised a sky the colour of old porcelain.

'It must be nice being married to a doctor,' said Rita.

'I suppose it is,' said Irene, wondering what Rita meant by 'nice'. A doctor's income? A doctor's standing? 'It must be jolly hard work being a farmer's wife. All the animals to care for.'

'Like Mrs Noah,' said Rita. 'But Bill does most of it, and we don't have lots of animals. Fifteen cows, a bull, a pony, some hens. A cat.'

'But that does sound a lot!'

'One of the cows is about to calve. She's called Drusilla. They've all got names, though none of them is Daisy or Bramble. We've got one called Nefertiti.'

'Goodness,' said Irene. 'She must be terribly grand.'

'Bill was at Oxford,' said Rita, as if that explained the naming of cows after queens of the Nile. 'He was studying law but dropped out. It was his father who wanted him to do it. Wanted a lawyer for the family business, one he could trust.'

Irene nodded. She had heard things about the father. What had Eric called him? Anyway, he had rubbed finger and thumb together to make the money sign.

'Your husband's father, was he a doctor too?'

'Oh, no,' said Irene. 'He worked on the railways. He started out doing something quite simple. A labourer, really. He ended up as the assistant stationmaster at Birmingham New Street. He passed away a couple of years ago. Just after we moved here. Eric was always rather in awe of him.'

'Bill can't mention his without making a face like he's sucking a lemon.'

'They don't get along?'

'Nothing would make Bill happier than to find out he's adopted.'

'Families are awfully complicated, aren't they?' said Irene.

'And now,' said Rita, 'we're making our own.'

The truth of this. They were quiet for a moment, sombre. They looked out of the window. A train passed without stopping at the station. 'Goods train,' said Rita, almost to herself.

'Would you like some Guinness?' asked Irene. 'I usually have a glass about now. Eric bought a whole crate of it. It's full of iron.'

From the larder she fetched two slim dark bottles. She took two glasses from the dresser. She bent the tops off the bottles with an opener that had a handle of some kind of horn. Each woman carefully poured the black beer into her glass.

'Here's how!' said Rita, holding out her glass across the table.

They tapped glasses and sipped the beer, then each carefully wiped away the foam moustache from her upper lip.

'Did you grow up on a farm?' asked Irene.

'For a year or so, during the war. They were relatives of Dad's, second cousins or something. They couldn't decide if I was part of the family or a sort of servant. They weren't very different from their animals.'

'You must have been glad to escape,' said Irene.

'I must have. But you hang on to home, don't you, even if it's not very nice? Anyway, one morning they drove me to Bristol with my little suitcase and introduced me to Aunt Elsa. I'd never even heard of her before. A big cold flat at the top of a house on Cotham Brow. She'd been a dancer when she was young, and when she was too old for that she became a teacher. She had about three pupils, young girls like me. I don't know how she managed to pay the rent. She taught me all these funny old dances. There was one called the Moth, and I was in this costume she'd made out of net curtains. I had to flit about like a little moth around a candle flame. You can guess how that ended. But it suited me well enough when I got older. I had my own key. I came and went as I liked. I left school at fourteen and got a job in a hotel. By the time I was sixteen, I was making four pounds a week.'

'Gosh,' said Irene. A farm of horrors, an eccentric relative, four pounds a week in a hotel. She wanted to offer something similar but, of course, she had nothing similar. 'When we were young,' she said, 'my sister Veronica and I tried to learn how to dance from a book. There were black feet and white feet. It was impossible to follow, and when we started going to actual dances at people's houses we had to dance with each other because we were doing something quite different from everybody else.'

Rita laughed. 'I've got a sister,' she said. 'She's five years older than me. I don't know her really. She stayed with Mum when Mum went. In Bristol somewhere, I think. Is your sister round here?'

'She's in America,' said Irene. 'She married an American.'

'Lucky thing! Wouldn't you like to live there too?'

'Oh, I don't know. Eric says we could go one day. Just for a visit.'

'They must need doctors in America.'

'Eric says you still have to pay for doctors there. They don't have a health service like ours.'

'Gabby Miklos is my doctor,' said Rita. 'He comes from the same place as Bill's father.'

'Does he? But isn't your husband's name Simmons? That sounds quite an English name.'

'That's just the name his father chose when he came here. Bill told me his real name once, but I've forgotten it. It ended with an *i*.'

'Well, I suppose that's not very English.'

'Don't you think he looks like Peter Lorre?'

'Who?'

'Gabby Miklos.'

'Gabby? I think he's more like Omar Sharif.'

This pleased them both. Gabby Miklos as Omar Sharif.

'Do you ever go the pictures?' asked Rita. 'You and your husband?'

'He's awfully busy,' said Irene.

'When I lived in Bristol,' said Rita, 'I used to go all the time. The ABC in Whiteladies, the Eastville Hippodrome, the King's in Old Market. Bristol was full of cinemas. They're starting to close now.'

'People watch television,' said Irene.

'You've got a nice one,' said Rita. They had passed it on the tour of the house. 'Bill says we can rent one soon. Lord knows if it will work on the farm.'

'You might have to play around with an aerial,' said Irene, and for a few seconds they sat with serious faces, imagining the waves from the transmitter seeking out lonely farmhouses, though Water Farm was not particularly lonely. There was the village, the station. If you walked up to the top of the coombe at dusk, you could see the lights of the city.

'I used to go with Dad,' said Rita, 'to the cinema. We even went during the war, you know, when he was on leave.'

'He was in the forces?'

'The AFPU. That's the army film and photography unit. He was a photographer before the war, so they just got him to carry on with it, but it wasn't weddings any more. The last part was the worst, I think. Once they got inside Germany. The things they found. Do you remember the smell of khaki? That sour smell it had?'

'I can a bit,' said Irene. Her father, too, had worn it. And, of course, after a while it was everywhere.

'The first film we saw together was *The Invisible Man's Revenge*.'

'Weren't you frightened?'

'I don't think so. Dad was with me, and the cinema was the most wonderful place I'd ever been. We saw all the Flash Gordons, Buck Rogers, *Mars Attacks the World* . . .'

'Our father never took us. I think he thought it was . . .' She almost said 'common'. She floundered for a second but Rita seemed not to notice.

'The ones I like best,' said Rita, 'are when the aliens arrive and everyone just wants to shoot at them but there's one man, usually the scientist nobody listens to, you know, the boffin, who's quite handsome when he takes his specs off, and he begins to understand what they're *really* saying. They haven't come to do us any harm but to teach us. They know much more than we do. They could solve all our problems if we just listened to them instead of blowing them up.'

'Do you believe in aliens?'

'Of course,' said Rita. 'Don't you?'

'I'm not sure,' said Irene, though what she was most unsure about was whether Rita was serious or not.

'They might not arrive in flying saucers. They might just walk out of the fields one day.'

'And what will they look like?'

Rita shrugged. 'Can I use your toilet, Irene? I'm bursting.'

When she came back she found Irene standing by the Aga. She asked if Rita would care to stay for lunch and she said she would, she would love to, thank you. They laughed at how hungry they were, and it was odd, thought Rita, it was very peculiar, how she could laugh like that when two minutes earlier, sitting on her own in the small green-painted room, staring at the washbasin with its smear of light from the frosted window, she had been going out of her mind. The narrow voices had been waiting for her, the ones she'd heard first as a teenager after the war, and again when she lost the child – though 'lost', as they liked to remind her, was not really the right word. With the new pregnancy they'd come back, men's voices, older men mostly. She used to know how to distract them, but they didn't run after the thrown ball any more. They had become subtler, more distinct, less in her head and more in the air around her. Today they were pretending to find things funny. Little Rita Lee talking to the doctor's wife. What a hoot! Little slutty Rita Lee. Filthy, child-murdering Rita Lee. The poor woman will have to scrub her kitchen top to bottom, she'll have to fumigate it, she'll have to take a bath with Dettol in it. And when her husband comes home, the *doctor*, he'll give her pills to calm her down and then he'll march over to the farm and tell Bill that if his disgusting wife tries to visit again he'll have them both arrested . . .

They were old-style comedians: their own jokes were the best. But then, as if they had failed to plan beyond the first assault, they became confused, repeated themselves more shrilly, lost words, lost sense, became a single voice, a mouth snapping at the dark, a man, a dog-man, a dog, until, swiftly as it had begun and with as little warning, it was over, and she watched the marks of her fingers fading from the white of her thighs. She breathed into her hands. Sometimes she could smell the rot but today there was just the tart smell of beer. She had cried, in a very disciplined way, for no more than a minute, then stood shakily, pulling up the pyjamas and the denim. In the water-cool air of the room, her voice hidden by the flush, she said, 'Gloria, Gloria.' And checked her face in the mirror, practised an easy smile, and came out.

They had scrambled eggs on toast.

'I do this,' said Irene, scattering a pinch of Madras curry powder onto her curds. 'My mother does it. I think her mother did too.'

Rita tried it and said it was delicious. When the food was finished they drank tea and Rita fetched her cigarettes from the pocket of her duffel coat. She offered them to Irene, but Irene said she had stopped. She had read the report from the Royal College. She hadn't smoked in months. Eric still did. She didn't mind other people smoking. She fetched an ashtray, the nice one of red Murano glass.

'Where did you meet him?' asked Rita. 'Your husband?'

'Eric? At a tennis party. You know the sort of thing. A few

sets and then lots of drinks and milling about on the lawn . . .' They smiled at each other. The fiction of Rita knowing about tennis parties would be allowed to stand.

'It was August. I was there with my sister, Veronica, and there was some boy I was quite keen on, though when I think about it now I can't understand why. He'd just finished at Sandhurst. He was awfully correct and old-fashioned. Hoping to have a crack at the Mau-Mau or whoever it was.'

'Perhaps he had nice eyes,' said Rita.

'Yes. I don't remember his eyes,' said Irene. 'Anyway, it was hot and I had probably drunk too much punch, just out of thirst. I thought I'd take a walk around the garden. There were big trees at the far end and it looked wonderfully cool. So I wandered off on my own and it was such a relief just to be walking and not having to listen to someone going on about politics or get roped into playing an endless game of croquet. Those parties were rather strange when I think about them. Get young people to run round in the heat, fill them with alcohol, and see who gets engaged the next week.'

'Was he at the bottom of the garden?'

'He was. I didn't see him at first because he was sitting in the shade. I'd noticed there were some chairs down there, but I couldn't see anybody sitting in one. He was in his tennis whites and a blazer, just looking at the trees and smoking. He wasn't part of our set – I didn't recognise him. I'm still not sure who he came with. Rather oddly, neither is he. He didn't stand up, which most of the other boys at the party would have done, so we had a slightly awkward conversation with me standing and him sitting. And he had an accent – he's from Birmingham – not strong, but that was different too. I honestly couldn't say now what we talked about. He was a few years older than most of the others. There was something . . . complete about him.

We talked for ten or fifteen minutes, then I just had to leave. I don't know if I lost my nerve or what it was. I said I had to get back, that they would be looking for me. He grinned as if he thought I was the most ridiculous person he'd ever set eyes on.'

She paused; she was slightly breathless. She hadn't told the story in a long while – who would she tell it to? Mrs Rudge? – those minutes at the end of a garden, the smell of the mown grass, the heavy summer flowers, and this man who looked at her and spoke to her in exactly the way she had been waiting for. The memory disturbed her. It excited her. She had not wanted to make love for weeks, it was the last thing she had wanted, what with feeling so sick and tired, so strange to herself. Now, without warning, ten past two on a Friday afternoon, she did. But the eyes looking into hers were not Eric's. She got up and fetched the kettle, topped up the teapot.

'You'll have to tell me your story now,' she said.

On the table between them were the magazines, the cups and saucers, the glass ashtray. Time lay slack.

'It's not half as romantic as yours,' said Rita. She was turning a box of England's Glory between her fingers. The ship appeared and slowly disappeared.

'I was temping in a place called City and County on Corn Street, an estate agent, all sorts of property. I can touch-type and I've got shorthand. I taught myself shorthand out of a book. One morning, in through the door comes this young man wanting to talk to the manager, Mr Partridge, who we called Birdy, though not to his face, naturally. It was his voice made me look up. Nicely spoken. Quite gentle. Well, you've probably heard him speak.'

'Yes,' said Irene. 'We've said hello and things. It *is* a nice voice.'

'Well, like I say, I looked up and caught his eye and he

smiled. I was a bit smarter then. Hair done and a proper face on. You can't go to work in a place like C and C looking like this. And I could hear what he was saying to Birdy. He wanted a farm, nothing big, just somewhere he could set himself up. I don't think Birdy knew what to make of him. Tall young man, obviously educated, but something about him that made him hard to place. I didn't know what to make of him either. I'd seen my share of Somerset farmers, and they weren't like him, I can tell you. So, I thought, he wants *land.* He'll grow white roses and keep peacocks and walk around with a pair of thin dogs, a book of French poems in his pocket. It's boring in an office so you have to daydream a bit or you'd go barmy. Have you ever worked in an office, Irene?'

'No,' said Irene. 'Though when I finished school, I was sent somewhere to learn to type. I used to type things for Eric but there's someone at the surgery who does that now.'

'Mrs Bolt,' said Rita.

'Yes, Mrs Bolt.'

'I wouldn't want to get on the wrong side of her,' said Rita. 'She looks like a storm trooper.'

Irene grinned. She knew now she would always think of Mrs Bolt as a storm trooper, a parachutist perhaps, and that all the powder she wore was to cover the blue of her shaved chin. 'Did you speak to him?' she asked.

'No chance of that with Birdy there. We weren't supposed to speak at all unless it was "May I go for lunch now, Mr Partridge?", "Is it all right if I go for my bus now, Mr Partridge?" But a couple of days later he came back. Birdy was out with a client and it was just me and this girl called Mary, an Irish girl and about the shyest person you ever met. He wanted to see one of the farms Birdy had told him about. He was in a bit of a hurry, had to get back to London that afternoon – he looked a bit browned off. So I said, "If you've got a car, I'll go with you now." "You?" he said, and I said, "That's right," and he looked at me like he didn't know what to say. I thought, This'll either get me the boot or they'll give me a rise. Excellent display of initiative, Miss Lee. That was my maiden name, Rita Lee. It was fine with me either way. There were other offices. And if I was really stuck, I could always go back to the Pow-Wow.'

Irene nodded. The Pow-Wow. She would remember to ask Eric what the Pow-Wow was. Rita lit another cigarette. She drifted the smoke through her nose. A lock of hair, more caramel than blonde, swung down over her brow. She was, thought Irene, like an out-of-work actress. Her lazy beauty.

'He did have a car,' she said, 'and I found the keys to the farm. I knew where things were kept. I said to Mary, "Please inform Mr Partridge I am out with a client." She almost curtsied. And off we went. It was a lovely sunny morning. We chatted in the car and I told him things about the area. I'd heard Birdy do the spiel often enough so I knew how you were meant to make it sound. I told him things about the farm he still believes. We got lost in the lanes but he didn't mind, and then we found the turning and bumped down the track and there it was. It had been empty for months. It looked a bit of a mess – it probably still does. I'm just used to it now. I started showing him around. I was wearing heels and walking across the farmyard, telling him the land was in good heart and just hoping I didn't turn an ankle.'

Irene pressed her hands together, laughing. 'You sold him the farm!'

'More or less.'

'And were you given the boot?'

'If I'd walked in on my own, I reckon that would have been

it, but Bill came in and said how helpful I'd been and how interested he was in the farm. Laid it on pretty thick. Birdy didn't like it, though. I'd forgotten my place. I certainly wasn't going to get any thanks. As for the agent's fee, when Bill bought the farm Birdy pocketed all of that.'

'What an unpleasant man,' said Irene.

'I wonder sometimes if Mary's still there. She was very young and pretty. I'm not sure she'd know how to fight him off.'

'But you and Bill?'

'He'd already asked for my phone number. Said he might have more questions about the farm. We still joke about that. Got any more questions about the farm, sir? I could tell he liked me but it was still a bit of a surprise when he called. He was very formal. Wondered if we might meet – only if it was convenient, of course. He'd got a list from somewhere of pubs and hotels, but I said we should meet on the roof terrace of the new department store in Broadmead. You know where I mean? You can have a cappuccino or a milkshake and they do nice meals if you fancy something more. So that was where we went. I meant to arrive late, but somehow I was bang on time. I never do that so I must have felt it was different. The sun was out after days and days of rain, and the terrace was chock-a-block, but he'd got us a table near the balcony and it was like being on the deck of a liner. Believe it or not, we did talk a bit about farming. I tried to impress him with my knowledge of cows. Then he was telling me about his family and how he didn't really belong with them and the new life he wanted that was going to be completely different and real and honest, and it was like he'd been saving it all up, waiting to find someone he *could* talk to. We were up there for hours. I was dizzy from all the cigarettes and coffee. I'd been quite unhappy for a while. I hadn't been very well. And all that just seemed to lift away.'

The story ended. The women smiled at each other. The tea had travelled through them. Irene went to the loo upstairs. Rita returned to the downstairs toilet. It was Rita who was back first. There had been no voices this time. When they weren't there, it was hard to believe in them. She had wondered a few times if it was quite common for people to hear voices; perhaps if she mentioned it to Irene, made a sort of joke of it, it would seem quite normal. She'd tried that once with Dr Miklos but he hadn't laughed. Asked a couple of questions. Seemed to know more than she had told him.

'We're having a party,' said Irene, when she came back. 'On Boxing Day. Nothing grand. Twenty people or so. Would you like to come? You and your husband? But you're probably going away for Christmas.'

'Us? We're not going anywhere. The only place we could go is Bill's lot in London, and we never go there.'

'It's still in the planning stage,' said Irene. 'I don't know if anybody will come at all. I suppose they will.'

'We'll come,' said Rita. 'We'd *love* to come.'

'I've been trying to think of finger food. I want it to be more than just peanuts and crisps, things like that.'

'A proper spread,' said Rita. She had once, in Bristol, been to a house party with Gloria and Byron, somewhere along City Road, and in the little garden someone was roasting what looked like an entire goat.

'Have you ever made tuna croquettes?' asked Irene.

'They sound nice,' said Rita. She wasn't sure what a croquette was. She imagined something like a crumpet.

'And devilled eggs. And quiche.'

'And cocktail sausages!'

'Yes,' said Irene. 'Everyone likes those.'

'What about music?'

'I hadn't thought about that. We've got a record-player, we just don't have many records. We could put the wireless on. We'll probably do that.'

'I promise not to come in Bill's pyjamas,' said Rita.

'I promise not to wear a housecoat!'

They laughed, sat at the table again and started to talk about clothes, remembering the nice things they had, the touch of rayon, of taffeta and silk.

8

The gate was mended. Or it was not truly mended but it would do, it would last until the better weather, it would serve. Bill washed his hands at the kitchen sink. You had to be careful with the hot tap. Sometimes the water was boiling; it leaped from the tap and scalded you. The Rayburn was the heart of the house but it was uncontrollable. Certainly he did not know how to control it.

He went upstairs to see if Rita was still there but the bed was empty. His pyjama jacket, the one she wore, was on the floor. He picked it up and, after looking at it for a moment, lifted it to his face. When he first knew her she used to wear a perfume, something vaguely lilac. Had she stopped using it or had he just stopped noticing it? The scent of her in the cloth was not perfume. It was musty, not unclean; the skin's winter bloom. And something milky? She could not, surely, be making any milk yet. The smell was probably on his hands, on his overalls. At least she had got out of bed, that was something. During the last month she had taken to lying half of the day in bed, smoking and reading and sleeping. It was her condition, of course, but it was also just Rita. Not much of a farmer's wife, but then he was not much of a farmer. He breathed her in again, felt the flickering of a confused longing, then tossed the jacket onto the sheets and went downstairs.

In the office he found her note on his desk. *Taking eggs to the neighbours! Back later.* He frowned. He could not see why the doctor should have his eggs for free. He did not approve. He folded the note then dropped it into the wastepaper basket by his feet. It was Mr Earle's basket. Presumably he hadn't thought he would need it in his new life in the bungalow.

The office was at the front of the house. It looked across the yard to the barn. He would need to go out there soon to check on Drusilla. He had learned from watching the vet, from listening to him, how to reach inside a cow, what to feel for, how in the darkness of her body to work out which way a calf was lying. Front hoofs or back? But Drusilla didn't much care to be examined. He did not know which way the calf was lying. He stared at the barn, imagining himself busy over there, purposeful, then shut his eyes for a moment, for several moments, until some dispute of distant rooks called him back and he opened them again. The fireplace, unlit; the sagging but comfortable old sofa; the bookshelves he had put up and that held a strange mix of books – things on farming by men who made it sound rather more straightforward than it was – and some of his required reading from Oxford (*The Book of Fallacies*, *On Liberty*, *The Invisible Hand*). There was half a shelf of novels, paperbacks mostly – Lawrence Durrell, Joyce Cary, Nevil Shute, George Orwell. *Animal Farm* felt quite a different book now he lived on a farm. He should reread it and decide if Orwell knew anything about farming. At the near end of the lowest shelf was a couple of years' worth of *Farmers Weekly*. The magazines were helpful, he had learned things from them, but he thought they were aimed generally at farmers with more than thirty-two acres to play with.

He ordered himself to work. He sat at the desk, opened the milk ledger and unscrewed the cap of his pen. Each day, twice a day, he weighed the milk and wrote the results on a scrap of paper with the stub of a pencil he kept beside the can of Cetavlon udder cream in the milking parlour. Later, he copied the figures neatly into the ledger. His aim was forty pounds of milk per cow per day, but since September he had achieved it only twice, and in the last month not at all. There were many factors, and most of them he did not fully understand. Feed was a big part of it. He lay awake at night thinking about silage. As against haylage. As against hay. Good hay hath no fellow. Should he grow some kale? How could he get more clover into his grass? What should he plough up next year and re-sow? Re-sow with what?

Underneath the paperweight – a red-rimmed boost gauge he had found, pristine and still in its box up at the airfield – were letters from the bank, mostly from Mr Harrison, the manager. Harrison had visited the farm once. His wellingtons, which he took from the boot of his car, were spotless, and one imagined them to have their own faint pattern of pinstripe. As they toured the yard, Rita had come out. She had shaken hands with him, treated him to her showgirl smile, had stood slightly too close to him. It hadn't changed anything. The loan was what it was, useful but not enough, the sort of money his father kept in cash in a drawer in his office.

He filled in the ledger, capped the pen, blew the ink dry, then pushed back the chair and took the two strides to the sofa. He lay down, head towards the window. There was a moss-coloured picnic rug on the back of the sofa and he dragged it over himself. A soft white light, objective, fell across his face. The last of his summer tan had faded. He looked pale, though not unhealthy, a hint of shadowing around his eyes, fatigue mostly, but also a feature inherited from his father and from wherever that line led. He had not met any of his father's relatives; he had never even seen a picture of one. He imagined them in different ways – as silent servants in a castle in a forest (climbing stone steps with guttering candelabra). As dark-eyed bourgeois in a gabled house overlooking the cobbled square of a town (globed oil lamps, a draped piano, plum trees in the garden). Or he imagined them as sacks of hair, boxes of spectacles, gold rings, their clothes billowing with fire . . .

He slept for an hour. Something woke him, though he could not have said which side of sleep it came from. He disentangled himself from the rug and stood up. He stared at the open milk ledger as if all possible meaning was there, in the pink grids, the inked columns. Then he strode to the front door, dug his feet into his boots and hurried across the yard to the barn. He had the impression he was following just behind the dragged hem of a dream. In the barn, Drusilla was much as he'd left her, except now, in the straw at her feet, there was a calf. The cow stared at Bill, then lowered her head to lick the dark, slick flank of her offspring. The calf did not move. It lay there, casually, uselessly. Bill swore. He cursed himself. It might, of course, have been dead inside her for days. Or it might have been fine and needing only a tickle of straw up its nose to make it breathe and live. He left the barn and headed to the milking parlour where he kept the storm lantern. He would need to see what was hanging out of the back of her, what might still be inside her. He would need to see the sex of the calf to know what his loss was. Later, he would try the knackerman, though he didn't always want to come out for a calf, which meant burying it on the farm and for weeks seeing the turned earth and remembering that was when he was sleeping, tucked up like a child under a moss-green rug.

Other failures attended. He recited them as he looked for the lantern, found it, found it was out of paraffin, found the paraffin and slopped it clumsily into the reservoir. Down from Oxford without a degree. The whimsical purchase of a farm you couldn't possibly make money from however hard you worked. The whimsical purchase of a bull that didn't like cows. A marriage – also whimsical? – to a woman more suited to being a mistress than a wife, whose past he thought he would be better off not knowing too much about. Endless questions of character, his rather than hers. Of what he was and what he should be. He couldn't place himself! At twenty-nine years old! Unformed still.

Through all this, the dull litany of self-reproach, his father moved with his heavy head, his blue-green gaze, the bulk of him so impressive to a young boy watching him in the bath, the water's green surface flecked with cigar ash. Was failure how he fought back against his father, his father's plans for him, the ugliness of his father's mysterious life? He disliked his mother, too, of course. He assumed his father had chosen her because she was damaged and incurious, and possibly for her bookkeeping skills, but he had no struggle with his mother. He talked to Rita about his father, sometimes speaking with a tone of unnecessary insistence as though she had contradicted him, had taken his father's side, doubted him. Less frequently they spoke about *her* father, whether they should visit him together, whether he was getting better, whether or not 'getting better' was the right question, whether the past was something, eventually, you just recovered from (green grass over rubble). It was a good subject for them, fathers. Easier, somehow, than talking about children.

When he had done what he could in the barn, he made lunch for himself in the kitchen. It was a late lunch and he was light-headed with hunger. He found a tin of oxtail soup, heated it to just the far side of tepid and swallowed it with slices of bread. Everything tasted of paraffin.

After eating he went to the office and from the long drawer took an untitled manila folder and went out to the Gipsy with it. There were jobs to be done in the yard but they could wait. He reversed to the parlour, loaded three churns, and drove slowly along the track to the lane. He left the churns on the wooden loading platform (it was built from old sleepers that wept their tar in summer). He checked his watch. Ten to three. The lorry would be along in an hour.

He turned the car and followed the lane in the opposite direction to the one that led to his fields, his broken gate. The lanes were a labyrinth, though one he was learning to navigate. Here and there he passed the mouths of tracks, holloways, broad green paths he had never been down and that led who knew where. An old farm perhaps, a worked-out quarry, a sacred hill.

He had made this trip for the first time last summer, an afternoon of strange un-English heat that shimmered the distance. He had heard a story and he wanted to find out if it was true. Since then he had made the journey at least once a week. Rita knew nothing about it. No one knew. He needed the pressure of a secret. Speak too soon and he would hear himself, and it would sound hopeless, impossible.

Another mile and the hedges were replaced by the rusting poles of a metal fence, the wire mostly gone. Beyond the fence was a grazed and empty space, cleared ground dotted with buildings and the remains of buildings, stark shapes radiating abandonment. Teddy, the old boy who helped with the hay and did a bit of milking, had mentioned it first. Twenty years ago he had watched the planes lifting over the heads of cattle, seen their shadows on the corn. In the bar of the Jubilee he had drunk with the airmen, noisy, good-natured boys, some from half a world away – Canada, New Zealand. One of them, said Teddy, touched still by the wonder of it, was black as night . . .

At the blank windows of the guardhouse he turned onto the perimeter track and followed it towards the stump of the control tower. After the tower there was a row of huts with asphalt roofs. He had explored them; they were rotten and sad, stencilled numbers, a few stencilled names by empty lockers. A row of jakes like men at prayer. His little Massey tractor could flatten the lot in an hour. He thought the huts might welcome it.

A hundred yards further on was the only large structure left more or less as it must have been in 1945, a bomber hangar, like a Nissen hut on the heroic scale, big enough to shelter a football pitch and a decent crowd. The roof, the great curve of it that was almost everything, almost the entire structure, was weathered but basically intact. The concrete frontage with its shut steel doors of rusted blue had been built with strange robustness for a place that must always have thought of itself as temporary, there only for the duration. Tacked onto one side was a small brick annexe with a square brick chimney, from the top of which a little thorn tree grew, like petrified smoke.

He entered through the annexe, its brief dark, the sourness of damp mortar. Inside the hangar, light fell through a scatter of rips and high windows, complicating in the stilled air and settling on patches of concrete stained with blooms of spilled oil. It always took him a minute or two to get used to the acoustics. On a windy day the building had an extraordinary range of groans and claps and rattlings but today there was barely a breeze and the hangar gave off only a low and almost inaudible humming, as if from buried cables.

He walked to what he judged to be the more-or-less centre of the floor. He turned, slowly, a full circle. Here and there were pieces of junk, things left behind when the last lorry pulled out. Lengths of chain, scaffolding poles, a cannibalised lathe. In a far corner were the remains of an office – wooden desk, metal-frame chair, a wall telephone. On one of his visits he had lifted the receiver and said something daft ('My wife is not herself today'). On that occasion he had felt suddenly observed and had peered out through the glassless hatch, almost frightened.

He arched his back to gaze up. Sometimes you saw a bird, something small, angling its flight to the curve of the roof. Getting in might be easier than getting out. He shifted a couple of feet to where the light fell more strongly. He opened the folder. It was figures mostly, figures and sketches and question marks. The plan had not occurred to him on that first visit, nor on the second, but it was there, he thought, the bones of it, when he walked in for the third time. He had asked around. It turned out the site belonged to an estate with parcels of land all over the county. He wrote to them and had received a reply that did not discourage. They were, he understood, interested in money. The airfield made them nothing. They were open to proposals.

In his scheme, the hangar would become a barn, one he would fill with beef cattle. He had an estimate of five hundred head, Herefords probably, bought from all over, fattened through the winter and sold at local markets in the spring. As far as possible he would grow all the feed himself – potatoes, grain, maize. He would construct a raised central aisle, a concrete ramp, wide enough for a tractor and trailer. Bedding would be straw; the cattle would spread it about themselves once the twine was cut. He would need a weighbridge, a crush, troughs, piped water. He would need a stockman and at least one other man. But everything would be kept as simple as possible. Whatever could be automated would be. Factor in all the overheads he could think of – labour, vet's bills, light, power and water, transportation, deaths – and he should, in theory, make a clear profit of better than ten pounds a head.

It was not an original idea; he didn't claim that. He had read about similar schemes – *Farmers Weekly* seemed to think it was the future, things done at scale, the rise of the specialist. He had kept his ears open at market. He had corresponded with a man in Ireland who was doing something along the same lines (Poor Tree Farm, Fermanagh, Ireland, had been enough of an address). The farmer turned out to be an enthusiast and had replied at length. Above all, he had trusted to figures, to the close arithmetic of small margins. He had his mother's quickness with numbers, numbers in columns, numbers to be set against each other in a constant shuffling down the ruled page.

He needed fifteen thousand pounds to set it up. He didn't have it. He didn't have a thousand. The entire farm was worth less than three thousand. He had not dared to speak such a sum aloud. To Rita he assumed that fifteen thousand would sound like fifty thousand or five hundred thousand, fabulous and irrelevant. And imagine old Richy's face! The joy with which he would tell the others! Can't manage fifteen cows but wants five hundred now. He thought they might egg him on. The whole county would take an interest.

He shut the folder and stood perfectly still. He tried to fill the hangar with the heave of phantom beasts but found himself picturing only the dark span of bombers, and the sound of them, those engines that must have made the great arc of the roof tremble. At school he had seen them often enough passing southwards in the last of the dusk. Once they had crossed the coast, they turned off their navigation lights and there was only the fading throb of the engines, a sound you heard in your head long after they'd gone.

In London, home for the holidays, he had roamed about with a gang of boys, coming and going as they pleased, unnoticed, undisciplined, on licence of some kind. In Regent's Park one summer morning, not far from the boating pond, they came across the wreckage of a downed German plane, a Dornier, part of the previous night's raid. There was no sign of the crew. The bodies had been removed or they'd bailed out. Before it was cordoned off they looted it. Among the shattered glass of the cockpit he found a scrap of charred paper, a few lines of printed text, a small, neat swastika at the bottom of the page like an elaborate full stop. He had shown it to his father, who had studied it for half a minute, then balled it up and burned it in an ashtray. His father had found the war inconvenient, though not necessarily unprofitable. He hung Union Jacks from the windows on VE Day but might have been content to hang out other flags had things gone differently. As a foreigner, a man who spoke with an accent, he must have had trouble with people who thought he should be interned, that on the roof of his house at night he was not fire-watching but signalling to the enemy with a torch. He always had his certificate of naturalisation with him, carefully folded in his wallet. Bill had seen it once (he was a little spy in the house), and read there for the first time that the name his father arrived with was not Simmons but Somogyi. For a while he had been very anxious that people – people at school – would somehow find it out, that he was not really Bill Simmons, vice captain of the under-15s cricket, but Bill Somogyi, the foreigner's son, an alien. He didn't even tell his brother, Charlie. He was still not quite sure why. Perhaps it was in case his brother had liked the name and started using it.

In the garden they'd had an Anderson shelter (it was still there) though sometimes they had preferred the greater safety of the Underground, he and his brother in pyjamas and dressing-gowns and school shoes, reading comics and weighing themselves on the machines. You couldn't hear the raid but when something fell close, a fine grey dust lifted, then settled. In the morning, people shuffled up the stairs to look around and see what was still standing, gather rumours about who had copped it during the night. After one raid they passed, on their route home, a house that had taken a direct hit and been opened like an exhibition. Most of the front wall had disappeared and you could see the rooms and the furniture, the wallpaper that would now soak up the rain and slowly fade in sunlight. From the sliced upstairs bathroom, a bath had tumbled down to lie across the pavement, right way up. During the war he saw stranger and more disturbing things (a man mad with grief tearing at his clothes on Camberwell Road) but the bath had stayed with him, though over time he remembered it differently. With taps, without taps; small and dented, or pristine and white as a throat. And more than once, in those years immediately after the war when it was like the war was still on but without the interest or the freedom, he had dreamed of it. In one of the dreams there was a woman in the bath, naked and beautiful and perfectly dead.

At the far end of the hangar the air was sifting into shadow. If he allowed himself, he could imagine this was a place that didn't much care to be disturbed, that to be there at night would be to hear birds with the voices of young men reporting the failure of their engines, the loss of height, the impossibility of knowing, in such weather, on such a night, where they were.

He made his way out through the annexe. It was lighter outside but there was already the slight veiling of the air that meant the fog was coming back. He started the Gipsy and began to drive on the grey ribbon of the track. As he crossed the end of one of the runways – there were two in a narrow X – he stopped to look down the length of it. He was not, he decided, much interested in the past. The war, the finest hour, his childhood. Those years were white ash to be dusted from his hands. If he wanted things he would have to take them – 1963, for example. Why should it not be his? He thought it could be. But he hung on a moment, held by whatever it was that had not quite found stillness here. The planes were fuelled and bombed up. The crews had been bussed out an hour ago to run their checks. They would know tonight's target. They would be sitting now in the glow of gauges, already cold, a bit of banter but mostly silent. And then, when all was ready, somewhere along there at the edge of the runway, in the thickening gloom, the light of an Aldis lamp would flick from red to green.

9

Eric liked to wash when he came home. He would go up to the bedroom, take off his jacket and tie, roll up his sleeves, turn on the taps beneath *The Arnolfini Marriage*, wash his hands and face, pressing the water into his face, moving his hands back to wash his neck, the back of his neck where all day his collar had chafed him. Then he dried himself and in the colder months put on a cardigan or jumper and came back down, sometimes whistling. He was not whistling tonight. He stood at the edge of the drawing room watching Irene lay a fire. She had meant to do it earlier, but she had gone up to change and fallen asleep on the bed. When she woke she needed to dress and busy herself in the kitchen.

She placed the kindling over a sheet of last week's *Herald*, the crumpled face of Kennedy smiling at her from the ashes (*they* had Kennedy, *we* had Macmillan; it seemed to say everything). Once the fire was lit and starting to draw, she stood and said she would make some drinks. She was wearing a dark blue dress with a cream collar. She had put on a new pair of stockings, had pearl studs in her ears, lipstick ('Snow Pink'), a spot of Chanel on wrist and throat. He had come into the house like thunder or the promise of it. When he noticed her

– properly – the dress, the earrings, the brushed and pinned hair, he asked if they were expecting company.

'It's Friday night,' she said. 'I just . . .'

'I'm on call all weekend,' he said.

'I thought it was Gabby.'

'Well, you thought wrong.'

These moods were not unusual. They did not, as a rule, last very long. And she understood, understood perfectly, that it was part of her role to absorb them. Goodness only knew what he had had to deal with during the day. He was entitled to let off a little steam in his own house.

'A beer, or something stronger?' she asked.

'A beer,' he said.

She was gone for two or three minutes. When she came back he was doing things to the fire, jabbing it with the poker.

'Did I make a mess of it?' she asked.

He hung up the poker then took his glass of beer, thanked her without looking at her. Her own drink was sweet vermouth. Being pregnant had changed her sense of taste. She would not have liked it before, would have found it cloying, but now it pleased her. She sipped it and felt its warmth in her throat. She longed to be touched.

'Supper won't be long,' she said. They were both standing. He was staring at the fire. She had never quite got used to the way they could suddenly find themselves like strangers in a waiting room. She thought it probably happened in every marriage. She assumed it did. It was not something you could really ask people about.

'Was it a difficult day?'

'Why?'

'You look tired.'

'Do I?'

'A little.'

He nodded.

'Why don't you sit down?' she asked.

'Because I'm happy standing. Why don't you sit down?'

She sat on the sofa, her glass between her hands. Very lightly, she rubbed the skin of the glass with her rings. 'I had a visitor today,' she said.

He picked up the scuttle and shook a few lumps of coal into the fire. The flames were buried. He swore and began to work again with the poker.

'When you order coal,' he said, 'order the right sort. This stuff's like house bricks.'

'What is the right sort?' she asked.

'Am I the coal merchant? Tell him what we want. Describe it.' He jabbed again, letting through a tongue of blue flame. 'Nutty slack,' he said.

'Nutty slack?' she repeated, and for a second they teetered at the edge of laughter. If they had caught each other's eye. But he wasn't ready yet. She would have to be more patient.

'It was Mrs Simmons from the farm,' she said. 'She brought some eggs.'

He looked round at her. 'What are you talking about?'

'My visitor. From Water Farm. Rita Simmons.'

'What about her?

'She came over with some eggs.'

'What did she want?'

'She didn't want anything.'

'She must have wanted something. What did she charge for the eggs?'

She knew this move. It meant, I grew up where the prices of things mattered. If the nearest shop was dear, you walked to the next. Clothes were bought in the rag market. Socks and stockings were darned. Collars turned. Sheets turned. There were no luxuries. She also believed this was true only of his earliest childhood and that later on he and his father had lived quite comfortably in a nice house in the suburbs. In her own family, between the ticking of the grandfather clock, the smell of beeswax, there was a constant unvoiced anxiety about money.

'The eggs were a present,' she said.

'Which you accepted.'

'They were just eggs.'

'And now we must offer something in return. Isn't that how it works? I hope to God you didn't invite them to the bloody party.'

'They're our neighbours,' she said.

'And?'

'That's what one does, isn't it?'

'You mean it's what your mother would do. In fact,' he corrected himself, took a new course, 'I can't imagine your mother ever inviting a *farmer*'s wife to any of her little gatherings. If she did they'd have to use the tradesman's entrance.'

'She's pregnant,' said Irene.

'I know,' he said. 'I told you that.'

'It was nice to talk to another woman.'

He nodded.

'Did you go up to the hospital?' she asked.

He nodded again.

'Was it anything urgent?'

'It was nothing.' He put his glass on the mantelpiece and felt for his cigarettes. 'You know who's up there, don't you?'

'At the hospital?'

'The asylum. The bin.'

She shook her head. She waited. She was oddly nervous.

'Your new friend's father.'

'Rita's?'

'The same.'

'He works there?'

'He's *in* there.'

'Her father?'

He lit a cigarette and spun the match into the fire. 'Yes. Her father.'

'A patient?'

'Patient, inmate.'

'Why?'

He pretended to find this funny. 'Why do you think?'

'But you know him? You've seen him?'

'Of course.'

'Is he . . . very disturbed?'

'Your classic lunatic, you mean? The sort they have on television in a play written by someone who's completely bloody ignorant? No. He's not.'

'Does she visit him?'

'I have no idea.'

'How awful.'

'You don't know that. He might be happy as Larry. Three meals a day, a roof over his head. Cushy.'

'Will he come out?'

'They're all coming out. That's the new plan. Empty the asylums and have them living in society. It'll be delightful. I assume she failed to mention any of this.'

Irene shook her head.

'So what did you talk about?'

His news had confused her; she found it difficult to remember. They had talked about husbands, of course, but she wasn't going to tell him that. 'Films,' she said.

'Films! And what the hell does she know about films?'

'Actually, she seemed to know quite a lot.'

The table was laid in the kitchen. They had napkins with silver rings. She had put a candle in the terracotta candlestick they had bought on their honeymoon in Mallorca. She lit the candle then fetched the casserole from the slow oven in the Aga. She had made coq au vin. At the shop there had been no chops; there had been a quartered chicken. He had liked it the last time she made it but the last time he had been in a very different mood. When she served him he asked what wine she'd used, and when she told him he allowed a flicker of annoyance to cross his face.

'Shouldn't I have?' she asked.

'Isn't there some sort of cooking wine you can use?'

They started to eat. They were people dressed in wooden clothes they could barely move in, who possessed only a dozen words each, the poorest. She was slightly afraid of him – afraid *for* him. He had the expression of one tempted by recklessness. She wanted to cry 'Oh look!' and point to something, a shooting star, the marks of the stigmata blossoming suddenly in her palms. But with heads down they ate the good food hungrily. Their bodies were blind and grateful to have sustenance.

After supper they sat in the drawing room – Irene on the sofa, Eric in the leather wingback chair – and watched television. They watched *Dr Kildare*. Eric had scoffed at it when he first saw it, had kept up a commentary so that the programme seemed a string of inanities, but more recently he had watched it in silence and obviously enjoyed it. Irene liked it too. She found she was content to watch all sorts of things, had quickly got over her discomfort at just sitting, doing nothing useful. For the first month after the van delivered the set, she always had her sewing box open, but she had given that up. It was difficult to remember what they had done before the television arrived. Had they talked more? Read more? Gone to bed earlier?

After *Dr Kildare* it was *Benny Hill. Benny Hill* was one programme they had agreed not to watch, yet tonight they did. The leering face, the goggle eyes. Once or twice she was tempted to laugh; she almost thought it clever. At nine-fifteen they watched the news. The headline was the previous night's smog in London. Film showed people and cars moving very slowly. When interviewed, more than one person said it was worse than the blackout.

There was a report about the British nuclear bomb test in Nevada. The government said it was for essential military purposes. They were perfecting the trigger mechanism. The test had been underground so there was no mushroom cloud to show. At Ford, the industrial dispute had not been resolved. Feelings were running high on both sides. The weather for tomorrow, mild and cloudy, some rain in the north and west. Colder by Sunday.

They started watching *Television Playhouse*, but after twenty minutes and one more cigarette, Eric said he was going up. At the bottom of the stairs he paused and turned to her, and in a voice quite different from the several he had used throughout the evening (the voice of an actor in the wings, tired, no longer anybody), he said, 'Your cooking's a bit wasted on me, isn't it?'

'Not if you enjoy it,' she said.

He nodded and went up. She carried on with the play. It was a type of comedy. She could hear him when he went down the corridor to the bathroom. She should go up too, of course. That was what she had wanted. It was what, hours ago, she had longed for. She left the television on and went to the kitchen. She would clear up. She would leave the kitchen spotless. She would pay particular attention to the wiping down of surfaces. Nothing would be left on the draining board. She would sweep the floor. She would set the table for breakfast. She would erase all evidence of the evening. Her mother sometimes talked about sluts. A slut was the other thing you could be. The good wife wrings out the cloth in hot clean water, she puts the cutlery in jars of Silvo, she wears rubber gloves to protect her hands because it's important they remain as soft as if she did no work at all beyond snipping the occasional rose in the garden.

She fetched the dustpan. She wondered if her mother would think Rita was a slut. A slut with a mad father. She didn't know much about madness. Sometimes you saw people in the street, old people usually, strangely dressed and talking to themselves. Did you catch it, like a virus? Did you inherit it from a parent? Or did something happen to you, something so awful you could never get over it? She must be very, very careful never to mention it. It would be horribly embarrassing, unforgivable. Imagine her own father like that! And briefly, staring furiously at the dustpan in her hand, she did, saw him in a ragged uniform, gazing up at her from sunken eyes, his head a skull . . .

She replaced the dustpan in the cupboard, checked the Aga had enough fuel to see it through the night. She glanced at the clock and went back to the drawing room. It was smoky in there, a haze of smoke curdling under the beams. Tomorrow she would air the house properly, have the windows wide for an hour, let the day roll in like surf. And she would take a walk, up to the coombe perhaps. It was unhealthy to spend so much time indoors. She slipped off her shoes and went on stockinged feet to the television. The play was over. It was a courtroom drama now, big faces full of passion. She pressed the chrome 'off' button, then stood a moment – when had *this* become a habit? – watching the dot at the centre of the screen pulse like a small heart or a failing star until, with a suddenness she could never quite anticipate, it blinked into absence.

10

Rita was leaning over the wireless. One hand held a lit cigarette while the other tried to settle the dial on Radio Luxembourg. The signal came and went. Was it the fog? From the Rayburn, the smell of sausages turning to carbon. Beside the frying pan a saucepan of water was boiling. The potatoes were in the sink.

Suddenly the music came through perfectly. She lifted her fingers very gently from the dial and stood back. Bill came in and took the pan off the hotplate. He looked for somewhere to put it. On the table two candles of different lengths were burning in the mouths of wine bottles. He laid a doubled cloth on the table and put the pan on top of it. Rita watched him. 'Are they ready?' she asked.

'They're inedible,' he said.

'Almost nothing is inedible,' she said. 'And anyway, we have luncheon meat.'

He wasn't angry; he wasn't even irritated. He had just taken a bath. The water had been hot and there was plenty of it. The god of the Rayburn was in a good mood. He had wallowed in the water watching an interior film of the first day when he, the stockman and Teddy – because it would take at least three of them – herded the cattle from the backs of lorries into the transformed hangar, their winter quarters. Then he would come back to the house, dusty and dungy, and everything would be at risk, everything, and it would all be much better like that. He would be awake. He would have something to fight for. It would bring out the cunning in him.

She put a glass on the table for him and filled it with cloudy cider. He was still practising with cider – you needed to practise. The kitchen was hazy from the burned food and Rita's cigarettes. There was candlelight, and on the dresser a table lamp with a shade of orange raffia that Rita had brought with her from her room in Bristol. The wireless signal drifted; she played with the dial. For a few seconds a voice spoke rapidly, passionately, in Russian or Arabic or who knew. It seemed to be pleading with them, to be passing on urgent news; then the music was back, Marcie Blane singing 'Bobby's Girl'. Rita turned to face Bill across the table. She started to mouth the words, the song's half spoken, half sung introduction. She swayed her hips. She kept her eyes on his. It was a show. It was put on just for him. He looked back, grinning, though not fully at ease.

'I know just what to say . . . I answer right away . . .'

The club, of course, the Pow-Wow. He knew about it, knew where it was in Bristol, had once walked past its door in daylight, the name and the neon wigwam unlit. It was nothing much to look at. A late drinking place, a cellar with a bar, somewhere bands played. It had what the newspapers would call 'a mixed clientele'. Exactly what Rita had done there he was less sure of, but he didn't think it was the accounts.

'I wanna be . . .' – she was singing now rather than miming

– '*Billy's* girl, I wanna be Billy's gi-ir-ir-ir-irl. That's the kind of girl I want to beee!'

The show ended. He tapped his applause on the tabletop. She was drinking gin. She was a little high but not very. He took one of the sausages from the pan. It was gritty but he'd had worse during national service. He'd certainly had worse at school.

Rita fetched the luncheon meat. She opened it with the little key, peeling a thin strip of tin, then shaking the meat onto a plate, where it sat, glistening and blatant. She cut two thick slices of bread. She found the cheese. She put it all on the table. Now she was pretending to be a teahouse nippy. 'Everyfing to your liking, sir?' He'd seen her move through a half-dozen different personas in as many minutes.

He asked if she had been sick today. She said she hadn't. She thought her teeth might fall out but other than that. She sat opposite him. Her cigarette smouldered in the ashtray. It was a small brass ashtray with an engraving of Winston Churchill on it. It had come from a pub in Bristol. It was odd because you had to put out your cigarette on his face.

For a while they were too hungry to talk. They attacked the luncheon meat from different sides and ended with a thin slice in the middle, which Bill cut neatly into two. The cat approached and he threw it a piece of the meat. They laughed, watching the cat investigate, then abandon it.

'I went to the doctor's house today,' she said.

'Oh yes.' He had forgotten about it, the note on his desk. 'I saw him on his way out this morning. I was in the lane and I could tell he didn't much like being held up. A man with a very well-developed sense of his own importance.'

'He *is* important,' she said.

'Is he?'

'You are too.'

'Thank you.'

'She's pregnant.'

'So you told me.'

'We couldn't stop talking.'

'About babies.'

'She's a month ahead of me. Got a lovely little bump. It was a relief to have someone to talk to about it.'

'Her lovely little bump?'

'Being up the duff.'

'Men can't understand,' he said.

'I'm not sure they try very hard,' she said. 'You're probably better than most.'

'Thank you again.' He cut more bread. 'Do we have any pickle?'

'We've got mustard.'

'Can you eat cheese with mustard?

'We've been invited to their Christmas party,' she said.

'I don't like parties,' he said. It was half true.

'It'll do you good,' she said.

'Will it?'

'I can hardly go on my own. They already think you beat me.'

'We don't know them.'

'I'm going to help her with the food. We're going to roast a goat.'

He yawned. He was madly tired now. 'What are their names again?'

'You know their names,' she said. 'Irene and Eric.'

'I knew someone at school called Eric. He was light-fingered.'

'She's got a sister in America.'

'She's posh,' said Bill. 'We've said good morning to each other. She's definitely posh.'

'So are you,' said Rita, 'but I don't hold it against you.'

'I come from ill-gotten gains, my dear. There's nothing remotely posh about us. Posh people think my father's a jumped-up little immigrant, which he is. They'd send him back if they could work out where he came from.'

'Their house is ever so warm. You could sit around in your underwear.'

'Did you?'

'I like her.'

'I can see that.'

'She *is* quite posh.'

'But you're not going to hold it against her.'

'Do you think she's lonely?'

'Isn't that what what's-his-name's for? When is this party?'

'Boxing Day.'

'Cows still need to be milked on Boxing Day.'

'Has Drusilla had her calf?'

He turned over the black end of the blackest sausage. 'Not yet. I'll look in at her later.' He leaned back on the chair and shut his eyes. He did not want the day to end with news of a dead calf. He would tell her tomorrow, or he would tell her if she remembered to ask. He had left the carcass in the barn by the door, covered with a tarpaulin. He hoped nothing would get at it in the night. The knackerman, who travelled in a Commer van with ropes and a bolt gun, had said he would call tomorrow. It was a bull calf so he wouldn't have kept it anyway. He sighed. Pieces of the day moved through him in a juddery procession. The doctor's car in the fog, the bull in its endless sulk, Rita's hair on the pillow. The hangar with its ceaseless soft rain of light . . .

*

She watched him fall asleep, his length folded awkwardly over the chair, legs stretched out, feet in thick grey socks, one sock with a hole under the big toe. She knew how to darn but she didn't much care for it.

'What's a croquette?' she whispered. His lips twitched but he didn't reply. She turned off the wireless, shook out another cigarette. If she went to buy a fresh packet in the shop tomorrow, she might run into Irene. Possible, though not likely. Could she call in again? So soon? What would that look like?

She would see her at the party, of course, but that wasn't for weeks, and then her friends would be there, her old friends, people more like her. Her background, her class.

She rolled smoke through her nostrils; she ran a finger over her eyebrows, smoothing them. She needed a plan and it didn't take her long to think of one. It would involve a train ride, a few shillings of spending money. There was nothing complicated about it so long as Irene was game, and why wouldn't she be? Despite the things the voices told her, Irene had liked her too. It hadn't just been politeness.

On the mat beside the back door the cat was staring at her, waiting to be let out. She didn't want to struggle with the door and wake Bill. She went out to the hall and the cat followed. She opened the front door and it slipped past her, trotting towards the cart shed, melting into the fog. What could it do on such a night? What did it want?

She stood in the doorway, her arms folded under her breasts. The animals were quiet. She imagined the bull in his pen, the night moving like a river through the big sack of his head. The world, the fog-world in its brittle glass sheath of now, was aching for an arrival. Stare long enough, hard enough, and it might be happening already, the figures gathering in the yard, then one stepping forwards, thin as a prisoner, and passing on the astonishing news. A rescue mission, a harvesting. And she could lead them over the field to collect Irene (no need to pack, they have everything). Two women stealing out of the house in gumboots, coats over their nighties. For years it would be spoken of, the young wives who had disappeared without a trace one December midnight, who were now, perhaps, residents of Ledom or living on Mars. There would be men from the newspapers, government scientists taking photographs of the scorched grass where the craft had set down and risen. At the shop, Mrs Case – 'I know what I know' – would become famous . . .

She stepped back into the hall and closed the door. There was a big key and there were bolts but she left them as they were. Who would think of breaking into a place like this?

In the kitchen he was still asleep. She would wake him in a while and they would go up to the cold bed together. She filled the kettle for the hot-water bottle, settled it on the hotplate. Her book was propped against the egg basket. She dropped a cushion on the floor and sat with her back to the Rayburn. She found her page and, frowning slightly, started to read, one hand holding the book, the other beneath her clothes touching the heat of her belly, that place, still very strange to her, where life was doubled.

14 December 1962

1

'Some,' he said, 'prefer to do this in two goes. Two blocks, if you like. I do it all together, which I think works perfectly well. Why do twice what you can do once? As the bishop probably didn't say to the actress.'

He glanced up. He said it to his students, perhaps, and got the desired response. Eric nodded. He was watching the other man's hands, his quick work with the knife. Then the knife was set aside and he reached in, lifting what he had freed – heart, lungs, stomach, liver, kidneys, almost the whole butcher's shop from gullet to bladder, gathered it and, in a single movement marked only by a thin trail of pink spots, carried it to the marble surface of a table, a kind of bed-table on trolley wheels that lay across and above Stephen Storey's bare feet. The bowels were already in a bucket. The ribcage, removed with the help of gardening shears, had a little table of its own. The body was almost empty now. They would do the brain later.

The pathologist was a man called Seven ('The number rather than the river'). Eric wondered if he should make some admiring remark. It *was* well done. Of course he must have done it a hundred times, five hundred, emptying them out, men and women, the occasional unlucky child. Most of what he removed would go back later. Stephen would be closed, the great wound sewn tight with a single thread. He would be made decent. His mother might want to see him again. That was likely.

'How does the liver look to you?'

Eric stepped closer. 'Normal?'

'The layman,' said Seven, 'is always astonished at the size of the liver.'

For several minutes he busied himself. He moved between his tools. He had the lipped scissors now. He worked them into the oesophagus. There was a clock on the wall. It was already after midday. On Eric's drive into the city, rain had slapped the windscreen of the car. In here, in the basement, the outer world might be doing anything. It might be on fire, the four horsemen cantering around College Green, slicing the heads off policemen.

'Did you treat him much?'

'Very little,' said Eric. 'He wasn't there long.'

'At the asylum?'

'Yes.'

'What's it like there?

'I think they do their best.'

Seven bared his teeth as if he had heard something amusing. He was ready for the stomach now. He fetched a metal jug from the counter next to the sink.

'Remind me, Parry, where did you train?'

'Manchester,' said Eric.

'How did you like the dissections? Were you a fainter?'

'I suppose the first time was . . . I don't know . . . uncomfortable. I don't remember anybody fainting.'

Seven held up the stomach and made a cut. The contents drained into the jug. They watched carefully. 'Something for our friends in Toxicology,' said Seven. 'I'll get them some blood from the femoral. From the look of this, there's not much doubt about the pills. Are you a married man?'

'Yes,' said Eric.

'I think Gabby Miklos said you live in one of the villages.'

'Yes,' said Eric. He gave the name.

'Not too dull for you? A young man?'

'It suits us,' said Eric. 'And there's a station in the village. If you want to go away.'

'A nice place to bring up a kiddy,' said Seven. He had lit upon the heart. He prodded it, examining the vessels on its surface. Eric thought Seven was about fifteen years older than him. Clearly he did not think of himself as young any more. Where, in those fifteen years, did the change occur? How close was he to it?

'And Gabby,' said Seven. 'What's his story? Somehow one never really wants to ask.' He lifted the heart, held it in both gloved hands. 'Take a guess,' he said. 'Win a prize.'

'What am I guessing?' asked Eric.

'The weight.'

Eric leaned. Lean closer and he could bite it. Then Seven would bite it. Between them they would devour it. Dab their lips. 'Four hundred?'

'That would be a heavy one. I'll go for three.' He rested the heart on the scales. The needle settled at three-ten.

'Bingo,' said Seven, softly. He returned the heart to the marble surface. The room's electric light slid over the lenses of his glasses. He fetched a hacksaw. Pretty much all of a patholo-gist's equipment could be found in a kitchen or a garden shed.

'Descartes,' said Seven, 'believed the soul might be found in the pineal gland. He must have seen dissections, at Leiden, perhaps. Does it seem strange that an intelligent man should think such a thing?' He touched Stephen's head, his hair of two shades of brown. He was peering down at him as if looking for the grain in the skin, somewhere to start. Eric cleared his throat. He said he was sorry but he had to go.

'An appointment with the living,' said Seven. 'Yes, you run along. I don't think there will be any surprises here. We'll let you have a copy of the report, of course. No one's to blame, Parry. A poor boy out of his wits. Not the first I've had in here. He won't be the last.'

For three seconds they regarded each other across the corpse, fell free of their roles, were bare as travellers.

'Just leave the lab coat on the back of the door, will you?' said Seven.

He drove and smoked, sometimes scattering ash across his thighs. The rain was over for now. Sunlight fell from a broken sky and lit up the glass in the roofs of the railway sheds, touched the water of the Cut, gave the grassed rubble of a bombsite a winter's grace. He fretted at the slowness of the traffic, recited certain lines he had in mind to say later, practised and refined them, swapped a tender word for a blunt one, then swapped it back.

He left the city by the Bath road. He passed the gates of the hillside cemetery where his father slept, where his father would wake at the last trump, where he rotted, where he was nothing, where he was a stone in the winter grass in a row of other stones. At the funeral, a dozen old comrades had come down from Birmingham and he'd had the notion one might take a whistle from his pocket and sound a blast on it, as if for a departing express.

Up the hill through Brislington, the traffic thinning, the city thinning, until he came free of the last of it and was passing fields where a tractor with an escort of gulls was churning the earth. Could you plough in December? What would you sow? Living in a village, living next door to a farm, should have taught him something but it didn't seem to have done. The round of the seasons was largely a mystery to him. He thought it probably was for most people.

At Keynsham, a small town without prospects, a dormitory for the city, he turned onto a quieter road, heading north now, almost north. He saw the red-brick hull of the chocolate factory. Among other things they made the chocolate-covered 'delight' he sometimes kept in the glove compartment, a rose-flavoured jelly. He had liked it as a boy too. Now and then his father had remembered to buy it from one of the kiosks at the station and bring it home in his briefcase.

He drove through a village. On the far side of it the road was just a lane. He didn't know where it ended. Perhaps it just petered out. He turned off between a pair of pillars and followed a potholed driveway to a clearing by the edge of the woods. He switched off the engine, brushed the ash from his lap. He could see for miles from here. When he wound down his window there was the sound of rooks. 'I'm sorry,' he said, 'but it's for the best. Don't you think?'

He opened the door, climbed from the seat and stretched. For the first time since the pathology lab, he inhaled deeply. He felt the cold air washing him, smelt the earth, the litter of rotting leaves under the trees.

Five minutes later he heard her car. She parked close behind his own. When she got out, he thought of the care she had taken with her appearance and what it was to be a woman, always having to think about that. She walked over and kissed him.

'Hello.'

'Hello.'

It was Alison who had told him about this place. He didn't know who she had been here with before. With Frank? When they had come up in the summer it was a sort of Eden. They had taken a long ramble and lain together in a hollow of unmown grass, listening to larks.

'Been here long?'

'About ten minutes,' he said.

She took his arm. 'Let's walk.' There was softness to her voice, a touch of melancholy he took comfort from. She understood already. She was, after all, an intelligent woman. None of this would surprise her.

'When I was leaving last week . . .' he began.

'You saw Frank.'

'Did he mention it?'

'He said, "I thought I saw Parry's car," and I said, "Did you?" And that was it. I made him a big drink. He was already quite refreshed. He fell asleep on the sofa with his mouth open.'

'Still . . .' said Eric.

'Still,' she said, smiling, imitating his voice.

They walked towards the old house. It came into view, Bath stone, shuttered. Whoever once owned it had a passion for hydrangeas. The uncut flower heads, dry as money, rattled and whispered when the wind caught them.

They came to a favourite place, a turn on the path. From here you could look back at Bristol and see more or less the entire city. On a clear day you could look far beyond it, into Wales.

'A policeman came to see me,' he said.

'Your past catching up with you?'

'It was the thing I told you about. At the asylum.'

'Surely not!'

'He was all right. Reminded me a little of the policeman in the Priestley play.'

'I thought the point of the policeman in the play was that he *wasn't* a policeman.'

'This one seems to be.'

'You could probably speak to someone who, you know, would speak to someone.'

'Pull a string?'

'Yes.'

'Is Frank a mason?'

'If he is, he hasn't told me.'

'Would he?'

'I don't know. Sometimes I think he tells me everything. Sometimes I think he doesn't.'

'He brought the letter with him. The one they found with the body. The suicide note.'

'You read it?'

'Yes.'

'And?'

'It was rather good. Certainly not a rant. A list of reasons for not being here, or not staying. Some of them personal. He didn't believe he would ever be fully well. Most of it was to do with the state of the world, the H-bomb and so on. He thought we would probably use it soon. He said he had lost faith in us. Human beings. He thought we were addicted to violence. That we were incapable of learning or changing.'

'We're not,' she said quietly.

'Not what?'

'Addicted to violence.'

'Us or people generally?'

'I see a lot of kindness,' she said.

'The one doesn't preclude the other. Himmler adored his daughter. He called her Puppi.'

'Puppi?'

'Doll.'

'Well,' she said, 'they lost.'

'Yes, they did.'

They stood, looking out. The distance was constantly shifting.

'I was at the post-mortem this morning,' he said. 'For the dead boy. I haven't been to one of those for a while.'

'I was at the hairdresser's' she said. She squeezed his arm. 'Come on.' She turned them back towards the cars. They went in silence. They had sometimes seen deer up there, plenty of rabbits. Once, in the distance, an old man wheeling a barrow, like a figure from a Book of Hours. When they reached his car she left him, went to hers and came back with a small box wrapped in dark green crêpe and bound with a ribbon of gold satin. They sat in his car together. They lit cigarettes.

'I can't really give you something like this at the party, so it's Merry Christmas now, darling. And I realise you probably have a thousand objections to being given presents, by me at any rate, and you probably made me swear once not to, but I wanted to and I've done it and, yes, you do have to accept it.'

While she spoke he was peeling away the green crêpe. Inside, in a case of stippled leather, was a watch. Lift it on two fingers, it had a good weight. He turned it over and saw his initials engraved on the steel.

'The body is Rolex, though the mechanism is something else. The man assured me it was good quality. Swiss gnomes. I thought a brown strap better than a black. Match your eyes. You can say something if you like.'

He thanked her. Presumably she imagined he would wear it when they were together. Or that he would lie to Irene, tell her it was a bribe from a pharmaceutical salesman. They leaned towards each other and kissed. The heavy perfume was somewhere in the depths of her skin, but it was yesterday's rather than today's. She was good at kissing. He didn't know what that was about, if it was just physiognomy. Seven might be able to explain it, tease out the secret with his knife. He wondered if he smelt of the lab, a whiff of formalin.

'And this is the other bit of your present,' she said.

She unhooked the catch of his trousers. He helped her. When his trousers and underpants were down by his knees, she made him hard and began to work the damp, smoky heat of her mouth around him. He gazed at the crown of her hair. Such thick hair! Whorled and stiff from one of those strange metal hoods women sit beneath at the salons. He had only ever done this once with Irene. It had not been a success. Nothing worse than a woman who was *trying*. It had been kind of her, he recognised that; she had wanted to make him happy. She had thought, perhaps, it was among her wifely duties. It had slightly surprised him that she knew about it at all. Had she got it out of *Lady Chatterley*? Or had her sister told her, Veronica of the slightly shorter tennis skirt? She, at least, seemed to have escaped the anti-sex atmosphere of the house they had grown up in. Her college-professor husband probably got his fair share of this. Fleetingly, he wondered if his father had ever had his cock sucked. It was, thankfully, unimaginable. He stroked her neck. He stroked one of her ears, the jewel in the lobe. Ahead of him, in the far distance, somewhere over Gloucestershire, there was a brightness in the air, like a shard of glass. It was a plane presumably – much too high for a helicopter – though it didn't seem to be moving in the way a plane moves. Had he not been otherwise engaged it might have puzzled him.

When he came his body jacked forwards and he grunted like a boxer. She sat up and smiled. He dragged up his clothes, fastened his trousers. She was studying her face in the mirror on the underside of the sun visor. She patted her lips with a tissue.

'Merry Christmas, Doctor.'

'I detest Christmas,' he said.

'I know.' She stretched over and kissed his cheek.

She left first. He sat for a few minutes, trying to decide what had happened. Clearly, it was not going to be as simple as he had thought. Each secret meeting tied another thread and tautened the ones already there. It still had to be done, of course. Not because he was tired of her. He wasn't. She represented some sort of fundamental ambition he was very reluctant to give up on, was almost afraid to give up, but if he didn't do it, didn't tidy things up, it would end in a way he wasn't in control of, and that frightened him more. The dream of sitting in the stationmaster's chair, the red phone ringing, the big trains hurtling towards some catastrophe in the fog, was one he had so far avoided but fully expected. There would be tears but it would be civilised. He would say something about Irene's pregnancy. She would, surely, as a woman, understand how that changed things. He thought vaguely of the New Year, everybody sober again and looking down the barrel of winter. That might be the right time. He dared not leave it later.

He got out of the car to arrange his clothes more carefully and to let the wind carry away the scent of her. He looked for the glint again, that strangely manoeuvring brightness he had seen, but for now at least, the sky was empty of novelties.

2

Bill crossed the yard in the rain, following the beam of his torch. He had slept in an extra half-hour but the night was still intact. He hummed the tune of a hymn they used to sing at school in the fabulous tedium of Sunday services. In the parlour he switched on the lights. There were two bulbs but today only one came on. The farm – one of the few pieces of information Mr Earle had offered up unbidden – had had no electricity at all until 1955.

He turned on the vacuum pump then fetched the bucket and filled it with water and disinfectant. He went to the shippon and greeted the cows. They followed him out. Two lengths of chain from the shippon to the parlour made a small collecting yard. The first two cows presented themselves at the door of the parlour, the same two as usual. They looked at him like neighbours come to borrow a cup of sugar. They wore the rain like suits of light. They knew their places in the parlour, were perfectly used to it now. One lifted her tail and voided herself. The other licked the parlour wall, experimentally. He washed their teats then squirted a little gush of fore milk into a jug, checking for lumps or shreds. He fitted the suction cups and stood to check the dial of the vacuum gauge. He tapped the glass and the needle settled. Each cow took about five minutes, give or take. Drusilla was in the last pair. For two or three days after losing her calf she had bellowed and seemed to search for it, but she was back to her old sullen self and he was careful around her. He had seen cows with their back legs in fetters to keep them from kicking. They shuffled like convicts. He didn't care to see it, though he knew that more experienced men would tell him the animals did not object, did not suffer, barely noticed. They were not pets. Rita made a fuss of them but that was Rita. Last summer she wove a garland of wild flowers and crowned her favourite. The cow wore the garland long enough for her to take its photograph with one of her father's cameras (the same camera he had carried in the war, probably the one he had photographed the camp with). The picture was pinned to the office door.

By the time milking was over and he had hosed and scrubbed down the parlour, he didn't need the torch any more. The buildings were like features on a beach the receding tide exposes. He fetched the leash and the cricket bat from their place by the shippon door and went through to the bull pen. The bull was easier to handle at this hour. The half-light veiled their gazes and made them, perhaps, less threatening to each other. He studied it a full minute, then let himself into the pen and clipped the lead to the brass nose ring. The bull's breath on the back of his hand, the heat of its idling heart. He touched its haunch with the tip of the bat. It moved, stiff-legged. He led it towards the dispersal yard. When they fell out of step he felt the sudden tug, as though he were holding a planet on a kite string. In the dispersal yard the cows were tearing gently at the hay. He led the bull into the midst of them, unclipped the leash and backed off. He closed the gate. The bull stood with its blackness bleeding into the air, unmoving, as if swallowed by its own mythology, as if turned to basalt, bewitched. The cows showed no obvious interest. They did not look up or stop their feeding, but the bull's presence reordered their world entirely. It was all fact. Two hundred guineas' worth.

'Just fuck one,' whispered Bill. He checked the latch on the gate and walked away towards the house, practising cover drives and flashier hooks to the sound of scattered applause, the phantom heat of a distant summer. He was young still, but already so much was irrecoverable.

In the house he cracked six eggs into a china bowl. He added salt and would have added pepper if he could have found any. He beat the eggs with a fork, found the frying pan in the sink, washed it and set it on the Rayburn. Onto the scarred steel of the pan he dropped a knob of butter not much less than the size of his fist. Butter, he thought, was the secret. He poured in the eggs and pushed the pan to the edge of the hotplate. He looked for bread in all the likely places but there wasn't any. There was a packet of water biscuits. He had seen them before but he couldn't remember when. They smelt OK and had kept some of their snap. He stirred the eggs, lifting the curds from the bottom of the pan. When it looked about half a minute from perfect, he carried the pan to the table and sat down with it. Fork in one hand, cracker in the other, he began to eat. With his mouth full, he reached for the wireless, turned it on and moved the dial from Luxembourg to the Home Service. It was a review of the day's stories, Polaris versus Skybolt, thirteen Africans and a white policeman killed in South Africa, Gaitskell to visit Moscow, Red spies in Germany. The spacecraft *Mariner 2* was about to make its closest approach to Venus after a flight of a hundred and ten days. In a basement flat in Pimlico, a poodle called Mitzi had been burned to death. The cause of the fire was a mystery.

Rita appeared and he turned off the wireless. She was in her pyjamas, his pyjamas. She sat down beside him. Her face was puffy.

'Hungry?' he asked.

He put some of the egg onto a cracker and passed it to her. She ate it and licked her fingers. He gave her another. When it was finished, she pushed back her chair and went up the stairs. He put on the kettle. Before it boiled he heard her in the bathroom, retching. He went to the bottom of the stairs and called up, 'Need any help?'

After a few seconds she sent back her no.

By the middle of the day she seemed perfectly well. They changed their clothes in the bedroom on different sides of the bed. It had rained steadily for most of the morning but it was easing now, the sky growing lighter, higher. Bill put on a suit of carded grey flannel, a clean though unironed shirt, his college tie, grey socks. Rita put on a woollen dress of grey and beige checks. It was one of her dresses from before, one of the quieter ones. She asked him to zip her up. He came around the end of the bed. She lowered her chin to lift her hair from her nape.

'I can't decide,' he said, 'if I should look more like a businessman or more like a farmer.'

He had told her where he was going but not the sums involved, not what he was going to ask for.

'I could wear the green tweed,' he said, 'the Donegal.'

She was sitting on the bed rolling up one of her stockings. 'The Donegal,' she said, putting on the accent. He changed jackets, showed himself to her. She nodded, then went down to the bathroom to do her make-up.

When they said goodbye, she offered her hand and they wished each other luck. It was part of a game he wondered if they would ever come to the end of. He didn't even know what the game was. She looked older in her make-up. As usual, he could not quite decide if her eyes were blue or grey or even slightly green. She had done her lips with particular care. He leaned and kissed her forehead.

'Thank you, Reverend,' she said.

The branch of the bank he dealt with specialised in farms and farmers; it was in a county town, westwards, towards the coast. On his journey he passed the surgery and looked to see if Parry's Citroën was outside but it wasn't. The hills behind the surgery were raw pink cliffs of quarried stone. Further on, the land was flat and green, riddled with small rivers, a region prone to flooding, a refuge for bats and dragonflies and flocks of shy migrating birds. It was secretive, drenched. The rivers were full of eels, or had been once. In the county museum you could see eel traps woven from split willow, each distinct as a man's signature.

He parked in the town centre, one end of the market street. He had the buff file with him. He opened it against the steering wheel and glanced at the top page. He had done it all as neatly as he could, but it was probably time to invest in a typewriter. Rita had office skills. That, after all, was where he had met her. She could type things up while the child slept.

He was early – ten minutes or so. He went into a newsagent and bought an Aero bar. The shop next door was a gentlemen's outfitters and he stood at the window eating chocolate and looking at the clothes. There was a lot of corduroy, checked shirts of heavy cotton, sensible rainwear, scarves. Three trilbys hung from lengths of fine cord, like a squadron of flying saucers. Most of the mannequins were dressed for the shoot, for point-to-point, a county fair, but one stood slightly apart. From its moulded hair and slender orange face it seemed intended to represent a younger man. It wore, among other things, a jacket described as 'slim cut' and 'Italian', a garment with frivolous though attractive buttons, a narrow lapel, a hint of yellow satin lining. It was not thorn-proof. You did not walk a dog down a muddy lane in a jacket like that. It was an experiment perhaps, something the proprietors had discussed anxiously, after looking at the newspapers, after being troubled by dreams of dancing. How many young men were there in the town who might be interested in such a jacket? Where would they wear it? But young men had cars now. They weren't condemned to spend their lives on the same narrow ground as their fathers and grandfathers.

And so into the bank, where the tellers sat behind the polished brass grilles of their positions, local boys and girls with an aptitude for counting. Say to them 'slim cut', 'Italian', they might blush. There was a small coal fire, a clock like a station clock. The minute hand juddered to half past. Bill gave his name to the secretary outside the manager's office. She found it in the diary, stood and knocked at the door. She leaned in, then held the door wide.

'A very good afternoon,' said Harrison, standing behind his desk. 'Please . . .' He gestured to the chair on the other side. They shook hands and sat down. They smiled at each other. There was only one reason for farmers to come to see Harrison in his office, to come at their own request, but for half a minute they allowed themselves the pretence of something else, like seeing the doctor and wanting to exchange a few pleasantries before telling him about the blood that had started appearing in the toilet bowl.

'And your good lady wife?'

'Very well, thank you,' said Bill. 'In fact, she's expecting.' He had not intended to say this. He had told very few people about the pregnancy. He had, for example, told nobody in his own family.

Harrison smiled. 'The blessed state.'

'Yes,' said Bill.

'My sincere congratulations to you both.'

'Thank you.'

Harrison offered cigarettes from a box of polished black Bakelite. 'Virginia this side, Turkish the other.'

Bill didn't smoke, not unless he was drunk, but he thought he could hold it and wave it around a bit. There was a desk lighter, an ashtray that looked to have been made from the brass base of an artillery shell. They were ready now.

'So,' said Harrison, 'you would like to discuss a business proposal.'

Bill opened the file. He passed the top two sheets to Harrison, who put on a pair of glasses and began to read. The top sheet was the broad outline; the second was the figures. Harrison glanced at the first sheet and turned to the second. An almost imperceptible raising of the eyebrows. When he looked up again, Bill began to talk. He spoke, more or less fluently, for fifteen minutes. He had rehearsed it around the yard. The cows had heard it, the bull (not Rita). He listened to himself. He had been afraid he would at some point begin to sound unhinged, that he would embarrass himself. Now he took courage. He liked the way he sounded. If the plan was eccentric, perhaps it was the right sort of eccentric. He leaned forwards slightly. He wondered if he was enjoying himself. Harrison did not interrupt. Occasionally he nodded or made some soft noise in the front of his mouth.

'I confess myself intrigued,' he said, when Bill had fallen silent. 'And if you will permit me to say so, I think you show the ambition of the new generation. A more conservative man might have come looking to expand his herd a little. Another five cows, another ten. You want five hundred.'

'Is it something the bank could be interested in?'

'It's a great deal of money.'

'I've costed it very carefully,' said Bill. 'I hope you can see that. It has to be done on this scale. If I tried to do it in a small way, if I halved the numbers, it wouldn't work.'

'A game not worth the candle.'

'Exactly.'

'And,' said Harrison, running a blunt finger down the page, 'you estimate the profit as ten pounds a head . . .'

'On a sale price of nine or ten pounds the hundredweight, which I think is realistic.'

'And you would sell in local markets?'

'Between March and June.'

'Costs?'

'Around sixteen hundred a year.'

'That includes labour?'

'Yes. But labour will be minimal. This is all about automation. One man with a tractor, trailer and side-chute will be able to feed the whole herd in half an hour.'

'Feed them on . . .?

'Pea silage, potatoes, barley meal. I'll grow as much of it as possible on the farm. There's plenty of usable land around the hangar. I'd apply for a ploughing grant.'

'Breeds?'

'Anything that makes good beef. Herefords, South Devons.'

'And how will you transport them?'

'Lorries. Lorries are probably the future. But the railway is close by and I'd certainly use that.'

Harrison nodded. 'My predecessor,' he said, raising a hand to gesture towards a portrait on the wall behind him of a man who strongly resembled Clement Attlee, 'liked to remind us that a bank was not a casino. I'm sure he had never been inside a casino. Nor, for that matter, have I. I doubt that you have. But we understood his meaning. We are not here to gamble. If we take risks – and Mr Naughton always spoke the word with distaste – they must be finely calculated. If your beef enterprise did not go as planned, it would be a considerable loss for both of us.'

'But I think it will go,' said Bill. 'As planned, I mean.'

'You will forgive me if I point out you have limited experience of farming. And with beef cattle, none at all.'

'I would employ a good stockman,' said Bill. 'That's essential.'

'You would be the financial brains.'

'I would be the manager,' said Bill.

Harrison rested his hands on the blotter. He pressed his fingertips together. A tip of tongue touched his upper lip and withdrew.

'I will be very frank with you,' he said. 'I deal with a lot of farmers, small and not so small. If almost any one of them had brought me a scheme such as this I would, as politely as possible, have turned it down. But then, who among them would bring me such a scheme?'

He picked up the sheet of figures again. He read in silence. Around them the life of the town went on, the slow wrapping-up of a winter's afternoon. The portrait of the former manager was clogged with shadow. Was he dead now, Mr Naughton? Or old somewhere, very old, an untouched cup of tea on the table, his hands mottled and, to his own gaze, strange.

'If you could find a guarantor,' said Harrison, 'or, better still, someone who might put up a portion of the capital. Half, say. That would change the complexion of things. Is there anyone who might be able to help in that way? Someone in the family, perhaps.'

For a few seconds Bill focused his gaze on the ashtray where their cigarette butts lay, like pieces removed from a game, an exchange of pawns. 'I suppose you're talking about my father.'

Harrison widened his eyes a little. He waited.

'My father and I,' said Bill, 'are not . . . close.'

'No?'

'We have very different ideas.'

'I see.'

'About everything.'

Harrison nodded. His eyes behind the lenses of his glasses were colourless but not cold. For the first time it occurred to Bill that Harrison might actually like him.

'We haven't spoken for a long time,' he said. 'I was supposed to go into the business.'

'The family business.'

'Yes.'

'Property.'

'More or less.'

'Your father was disappointed?'

'I imagine.'

'He doesn't approve of farming.'

'He doesn't know anything about farming. I doubt he's ever set foot on a farm in his life. Unless it was before he came here.'

'To Great Britain.'

'Yes.'

'And you think that if you spoke to him about this' – tapping the paper of figures – 'he would not be interested?'

'I'm certain of it.'

'Wouldn't bite.'

'Sorry?'

'If it was put to him as you have put it to me. As a business proposition. Something to appeal to him in that way. Not really to do with farming at all, but with pounds, shillings and pence. You would be speaking the same language.'

'We will never speak the same language,' said Bill. 'My father, Mr Harrison, is a very peculiar man. It's difficult to explain unless you've met him. He doesn't . . . change.'

'I think I felt something like that about my own father,' said Harrison.

'Did you?'

'For a time.'

'And later?'

'Oh, later . . .' said Harrison. He looked towards the door as if hunting for some expression, a line from the poets. In the end he just said, 'No.'

The clerk who showed him out shut the bank doors behind him. There was the jangling of keys. Business was concluded for the day. Bill looked down the street, unsure for a moment where he had left the Gipsy. The little shops had their Christmas windows in; they glowed appealingly. He wondered if he might find a tearoom, somewhere he could sit and think about what had just happened. The meeting had been a failure, of course. He had come away with nothing, not a farthing. And yet it didn't quite feel like that. What did it feel like? Like one more click of the tumbler when you open a safe? (In his father's house there were three safes, or three he knew about. Almost certainly one he didn't.)

And what had Harrison meant about speaking the same language? Sly dog! In those big cabinets in his office he kept files on everyone, must do. Or he kept files on those with well-to-do fathers. It might have been interesting to see how much he *did* know, or thought he knew. What were his sources? Newspaper clippings? Or was there someone higher up the chain, someone in Threadneedle Street, a department that dipped its ladle into dirty water and sipped it?

He crossed the road. He was walking without paying much attention to where he was going. One could not, in a town like this, become importantly lost. He saw a place called the Lite Bite but it was closed. Try one of the pubs? There were several, most looking like hulks on a mud flat, but he was too late and too early for the pub. He walked on, then paused in the yellow light spilling from the window of a shop for women, a sort of haberdashery. A girl in stockinged feet was reaching up to hang a Christmas star above a display of artfully tumbled bolts of coloured cloth. Drifts of lace stood in for fallen snow. The girl, he thought, was no more than fifteen. Left school in the summer? Her upturned face was settled, concentrated. Then she suddenly knew herself watched and turned quickly to look out, saw Bill and grinned. Something forward in that expression, though it might only have been because of the glass between them.

3

The rain was over and the day was not especially cold, not for December. They bought tickets and went out to the platform. There were three others waiting for the Bristol train, two women and a man. Because this was the country and not the city, there were discreet nods of acknowledgement. Irene and Rita sat on a bench together. Rita had on her duffel coat; Irene was wearing her sheepskin. In just a week, thought Rita, Irene had changed from looking pregnant when you knew to look for it to being obviously so – or, at least, if you saw her without her coat on. For herself, nothing much seemed to have altered. The dress was a little tight across her middle but not uncomfortable. Irene had a big safety pin fastening the pleated skirt she wore. They had laughed at it and agreed that soon they would just walk around in sacks.

The station was red brick and slate. Two chimneys, larger really than the building warranted, took smoke from the coal fire in the waiting room and the smaller fire in the ticket office. The women sat side by side, looking at the deserted platform opposite. It was as if in the house and then the walk up the lane they had exhausted everything they had to say to each other. They were beyond mere politeness, but had they arrived at what came next?

'Bill's gone to see the bank manager,' said Rita, after a long minute of silence. 'He has plans for the farm, but he's very mysterious about it.'

'Banks rather frighten me,' said Irene. It wasn't true. She didn't know why she had said it.

'I've met him,' said Rita. 'The manager. He came out to the farm once. The driest of dry old sticks. I suppose your husband has to do all that sort of thing too. It is a sort of business, isn't it? The surgery?'

'I think they have someone in Bristol who does most of that, an accountant. Anyway, it's probably quite straightforward. It's not as if they have to sell anything. Not really.'

They were silent again. Clouds moved on a westerly breeze.

'You must know a lot more about it than I do,' said Irene. 'Business.' She said it brightly but felt a curious pang of shame.

'Only what I saw them doing, Birdy and co. Bill's mother is a bookkeeper. He says that's the only kind of cooking she ever did. You know, cooking the books.'

'For the family business?'

'That's right.'

'What exactly is it they do?'

'Buy old houses and rent them out. Bill says his father owns whole streets in London. I've never met him.'

'Not even at your wedding?'

'We got married at the registry office in Bristol. I had the girls from the house and Bill had his friend from Oxford. A registry-office wedding only takes about fifteen minutes. Afterwards you wonder if it really happened. I met his brother once.'

'Is he like your husband? Like Bill?'

'Oh, no. Charlie's a playboy. Or he wants to be. He calls up now and then when he's pie-eyed. He's just bought an E-Type Jaguar. A purple one.'

'Goodness! Purple.'

'Here we are,' said Rita.

They stood up. About half the trains that came through now were diesels, but this was a small green steam engine that drew up noisily, mashing the air, and draping the whole length of the platform in a mist sharp with the reek of cinders. They walked down until they found an empty compartment. They sat opposite each other by the window. When the train shuddered into motion they grinned, like children on an outing. Slowly, then more swiftly, the familiar countryside slipped past. There was the meadow with the two horses in it, there the abandoned house, now the long view to the south. They talked about trains and train journeys. There are always things you can say about trains. Irene began on a story her father had told her about a man on the commuter train to London who always stood to shut the window in the moments before the train entered a tunnel. All the regulars knew he would do it. If anyone else tried they'd be stared at. 'And the strange thing was, he was completely blind!'

Rita listened, made listening noises. She lit a cigarette. She wondered if she would make it to Bristol before throwing up, if it would be wiser to be sick in the train toilet rather than risk it happening on the walk to the cinema. This was the worst week so far for nausea, for headaches, for tiredness. It was also the last week of what she had experienced before, nearly four years ago, though she could not honestly remember how it had felt then, if it had been better or worse or about the same. How could you forget things like that? The rest she had not forgotten, though with Nembutal and gin she had sometimes tried, that half-reel of film starting with the scene of a careless girl on a bus, an overnight bag on her lap. You didn't need to take much with you. A nightie, a dressing-gown, a wash bag, a change of underwear.

Eugene – after accusing her of trying to trap him, then apologising (you could watch him, hunting around for his better self) – had offered to drive her, but they both knew he couldn't risk being seen with her going *there*. In the city you could be hidden; in the countryside you were always seen by someone. And Eugene had a club to run. Also, as it happened, a marriage, and while Annie could never have had many illusions about him, everybody had their limits. She could have asked Gloria, but no visitors were allowed at Nanny Simpson's so she couldn't have come further than the gate. And had Gloria given up on her by then? What if she'd said no? So she had walked the mile from the bus stop on her own, past empty fields, bungalows, the frantic barking of tethered dogs. It didn't have a sign or anything. There were no ambulances outside. High hedges, neatly clipped. Gravel drive. Not a soul until you rang the bell.

Later, she saw some of the others, girls like moths in the panelled corridors. There was a rule about names; you weren't really supposed to talk at all. It was a big house with a beautiful staircase. Some of the windows had stained glass in them, knights and dragons. The procedure took place the following morning. She knew next to nothing of what it entailed, the mechanics of it, and she was careful to keep it that way. She didn't even know who did it. There was talk of doctors but she didn't meet any. When it was time to leave, you had a few minutes alone with Nanny Simpson in the office. She gave you things – pads, aspirins, warnings. The bill had been settled on the way in. Eugene had given her cash from the till. Cash was preferred. Then the much slower walk back up the lane with her bag to the main road. When the bus came, the driver gave her a look. That stop must have been notorious. At the depot they probably had a special name for it, something blunt.

*

As the train pulled into Temple Meads station, she was crying, and Irene had moved to sit beside her. She had a hand on her shoulder. Rita dabbed at her eyes with a tissue. She asked if her mascara had run and Irene said it hadn't.

'Just a funny turn, dear,' said Rita, in a funny voice.

They got down onto the broad platform and crossed to the barrier. Slamming doors, the movement of the crowd like the flickering of grey fire. They gave their tickets at the barrier and left the station through the hall. Rita was in charge now. She felt the draw of the streets, the deep relief of being back among them. There were buses they could have taken but they decided to walk (they weren't old, they were young; they weren't ill, they were pregnant). One route would take them past the Pow-Wow and she was tempted. She could point it out, quite casually, tell Irene, I used to work in there. Did you? That's right. Arrive around seven, have a drink, listen to the band on their last run-through. A dance with Gloria, sometimes with Eugene, if Annie wasn't about. Then a quick brush-up in the Ladies', swallow something to get you through and it was showtime . . .

Other than in dreams she hadn't seen the place in a long while, not even the outside of it. Was the neon wigwam still there? It wouldn't be open at this time of day, of course; she'd be unlucky to run into anyone. She was tempted, but she was wary, and where the routes divided she took the other way and they went through Broadmead, looking in the windows of the new shops. If you'd known this part of the city before the war you probably didn't know it now. Here and there something remained, some building mysteriously spared, standing at the edge of memory, human and dark. The rest was glass and concrete. Angular dummies in winter modes. Doors opening into scented air. Some excitement of money.

*

At the cinema, the manager was lounging by the open doors. He wore a yellow waistcoat and a crimson bow tie.

'Afternoon, Rita.'

'Hello, Tony.'

It was not a cinema that got first-run films, not any more. That evening they would be showing John Wayne in *The Searchers*. For the matinees they cultivated small but specialised audiences of pensioners, housewives, loafers. They showed European films, German or Swedish mostly, that always had some nudity. They showed horror films. These, too, often had some nudity, the servants of Satan in billowing see-through robes. And they showed science-fiction, in which there was romance but little nudity. They screened the films in double-bills. Today it was *Journey to the Seventh Planet* followed by *First Spaceship on Venus*. On the glass of the ticket booth, Tony or someone had stuck up a clipping from the newspaper about *Mariner 2*.

They bought their tickets and went to the sweets counter. Rita bought a pack of Rolos. There were only about ten other people waiting. Irene tried to place them. She was imagining what she might say to Eric, the story (funny) she would prepare for him, but the people did not seem to belong to any category she could easily identify. In the midst of them a black man appeared, carrying a sort of metal suitcase. It looked heavy.

'Cutting it fine,' said Rita.

'Show can't start without me, Reet.' He looked at Irene. 'Come with a friend today,' he said.

'Irene, Byron. Byron, Irene.'

'Nice to make your acquaintance, Irene.' He hurried on, went through a door at the back of the room.

'Byron's the projectionist,' said Rita. 'I've been up there with him before. The projection box. There's more to it than you might think.'

'Are people allowed to go up?'

'Tony doesn't mind. And Byron can do what he wants, more or less. A good projectionist is hard to find. The cinemas try to steal them from each other.'

Irene looked at the door the man had gone through. She wanted to ask a question but couldn't think how to frame it. The words.

'I used to work with his sister,' said Rita.

'You're lucky,' said Irene.

'Am I?'

'You've met lots of . . . different sorts.'

'You'd better believe it,' said Rita.

They went up the stairs. An usherette in a maroon uniform showed them to their seats. They were in the front row of the balcony. The house lights were on. The auditorium was sour with last night's smoke. Along the row from them an old man unwrapped his sandwiches. He used a folded newspaper as a tablecloth.

'He's always here,' whispered Rita, her breath tickling Irene's ear. 'You'll get a whiff of fish paste in a moment.'

They had a Rolo each. Irene peered over the edge of the balcony. A scatter of hats down there, but most of the seats were empty. Once your eyes got used to the dimness of the house lights, you could see how shabby the place was, though once it must have been almost grand. Red plush, gilding. Above the screen was a plaster lyre, still with some of its gold paint.

'A year from now it'll be bingo,' said Rita.

'How sad,' said Irene.

'You've got to give the people what they want,' said Rita, another of her voices, northern.

Irene leaned back in her seat. She touched her belly. The safety pin was uncomfortable. She needed maternity clothes.

She couldn't go on with pins and letting things out, she might be enormous by the end – some women were. With Veronica she used to play a game, stuffing pillows up their school sweaters and walking round the bedroom complaining about their backs. Even then, perhaps, they were afraid. They had to make a cartoon of it, the future when their bodies wouldn't be for running any more. And in the meantime the men went on, hardly changing at all. Serge, worsted, flannel, tweed. The 8.04 to Victoria. Cheerio, Daddy, cheerio, dear.

The lights went down. There was an advertisement for a car showroom. Irene thought it might even be the one where Eric had bought the Citroën. It was filmed in summer, the trees opening and closing in a summer wind. Then an advertisement for an electrical business, 'five minutes' walk from this cinema'. Would people really rush out to buy fuses and wire flex? The last was a cigarette advertisement. That one worked. Rita lit up and blew her smoke high towards the shifting light of the projector.

For a few seconds the screen was blank, a restless grey broken only by zags and flickerings. Irene sat stiffly, waiting. Sometime between Victory in Europe and Victory in Japan, she had gone one afternoon to the Orion in Hassocks with Veronica and their friend Carole. Before the feature there was a newsreel called *An End to Murder*. It was about the trial of the guards of the Belsen concentration camp. It showed scenes from the camp as it was when the British Army first found it, a place in a German forest where the dead were piled like firewood. It showed boxes of wedding rings, large boxes. At the end of the film, British soldiers used flame-throwers to burn the camp down. She was fourteen. She had, that summer, started her periods, but after the film she missed a month. There may have been other reasons – food was not plentiful, in some ways it was worse than during the war – but she thought the film was the cause of it, and she still did. The fire burned the camp down but it could not take away what had happened there. The guards, women among them, were brutal idiots, but she knew, even at fourteen, that they would be replaced, that it wasn't an end to murder at all, that it would go on somewhere else, always keeping a little ahead of the cleansing fire.

There were still newsreels sometimes. Most of them now were about science or the Royal Family, but when the lights dimmed, those first moments in the dark, she was always coiled, waiting to be shown something one could not make sense of, that stunned the mind.

She felt Rita take her hand. She let her. She felt one of the toffees being smuggled into her palm.

The film came on. She sucked her sweet. She relaxed. The film was set in 2001. Men's fantasies had become reality. At first, they were pleased. Then the fantasies began to threaten them. The beautiful women they had created ensnared them. There was a monster they shot at uselessly with their machine guns. The colours were bright but blurred, seeping beyond their outlines. The best bits were of the rocket moving through empty space.

At the interval the girl in the maroon uniform reappeared from a room below the screen. Around her neck was a tray of drinks and ice creams. When she came up to the balcony, the old man went through every item on her tray before buying a tub of vanilla ice cream. Rita bought a carton of Kia-Ora fruit squash. She said it was full of vitamins. During the second film she got up and left. Ten minutes passed, fifteen. Irene went to look for her. She had to squeeze past the old man. She wondered if he would touch her but he didn't.

The Ladies' had a varnished wooden door on a heavy brass hinge. You had to lean your shoulder against it. Inside, the light bounced off the tiles, dazzling after the auditorium.

'Rita?'

She was in the end cubicle, kneeling on the floor. Irene squatted behind her.

'I shouldn't have had the juice,' said Rita. She stretched forwards, racked again. Irene held her head, those waves of hair, blonde and honey, she had been curious about.

There was no more. They leaned against the wall of the cubicle, one behind the other, like riders on a scooter.

'I'll make you feel sick,' said Rita.

'I seem to be through that part,' said Irene.

'Do you ever talk to it?' asked Rita.

'The baby? Not really. Do you?'

'There isn't much there yet, is there? It might not even have ears. When do the ears grow?'

'I'm not sure,' said Irene. 'I could ask Eric.'

'Our cow lost its calf,' said Rita.

'I'm sorry,' said Irene.

'Bill had to deal with it all.'

'Poor Bill.'

'Yes. Poor Bill. Poor cow.'

They were silent awhile. They could hear, though faintly, the swelling music from the film.

'Your friend,' said Irene, 'the projectionist.'

'Byron?'

'Yes.'

'He's all right. It was his sister Gloria who was my friend, really, but I haven't seen her in a long time.'

'She went away?'

'I think she just changed her mind about me.'

'The only coloured people I've ever spoken to are bus conductors.'

'You won't find any in Bristol,' said Rita. 'The company won't hire them.'

'That shouldn't be allowed,' said Irene.

'No,' said Rita, 'but it is.'

'Sometimes my sister sends me magazines from America. In one of them there's a photograph of a man who was born a slave. He was getting married.'

'This city,' said Rita, 'made a lot of money from slaves.'

'Billie Holiday is dead,' said Irene.

'I know,' said Rita. 'Poor Billie Holiday.'

They helped each other to stand. Rita washed her face at one of the basins. They stood side by side, looking at their reflections in the mirror. On one tiled wall there was a poster of Marlene Dietrich. She was dressed in a black suit with a black hat. She was on a balcony, and behind her a city, exotic, lit, rejected.

'Sure you're all right now?'

'Right as rain.'

They went back to the auditorium. Rather than push past the old man again they sat in two empty seats beside the aisle. The film, which had not been easy to follow even in the beginning, was now incomprehensible. The thing they ran from, these men with dubbed voices, was always somehow in front of them. Irene shut her eyes, saw against the lids an afterglow of the screen, puffed white and luminous, like gardenias. She slept, and woke with the house lights going up, the sound of seats flipping back.

In the foyer, in a recess under the stairs, there was a bar. The manager was there. He invited Rita and Irene to have a drink. Rita wanted a Babycham (that had been another of the advertisements, the wide-eyed fawn in the enchanted forest). The barmaid, who was also the manager's wife, took two small bottles from the mirrored shelves behind her and emptied them into two broad-bottomed glasses. Rita passed one to Irene, raised the other. 'Here's how!' she said.

After a few minutes, Byron joined them. The manager's wife poured him a glass of mild. He sipped it, wiped the froth from his lips, seemed satisfied. Irene peeped at him over the rim of her glass. She wanted to speak to him but had no idea what she could say. Return to Liverpool Street, please. The manager handed out cigarettes. Byron said the reels of *The Searchers* had still not been delivered. The man who drove the van (his name was mentioned) was lazy. He could not be depended upon. He was later every week.

'Country's going to the dogs,' said Rita, laughing.

'You're not wrong there, girl,' said Byron. His voice had authority.

The manager's wife wore false lashes. Her hair was the colour of ochre. She was nineteen or she was forty. She looked at Irene and made a movement with a drawn eyebrow and a corner of her lips that meant something Irene didn't fully understand. None of the people at the bar were the kind her mother would be pleased to see her in the company of. And they were having a sort of party, in the middle of a Friday afternoon, like they had nothing else to do or they didn't care about doing it. Just standing there by the bar, smiling in the soft pink light that bled almost secretly from angular art-deco lamps on the wall.

Boxing Day

The kitchen table was covered with plates and serving dishes. Some of the plates were covered with foil. At the centre of the table the dolmades were arranged on the prettiest plate. She had written to an address in London, a shop in Soho, and the vine leaves had come by return of post.

Rita had helped. She had chopped carrots for the dips, shelled the hard-boiled eggs (from her own hens), fished olives from the jar, cubed the Gouda cheese. Later, she took Irene upstairs to look at her clothes. Her skills in the kitchen were like a child's but she knew about clothes. She made Irene try on four different outfits. In the beginning, Irene had been shy, stupidly shy, standing in front of her in just a slip, but Rita hardly seemed to notice. She was a shop girl in a high-end store, a boutique. She played with zips and hooks and hemlines; she smoothed the fabrics over Irene's belly. The fourth dress – a pattern of thin red lines on a cream background, a large, soft, pretty collar – Irene had not worn since before the wedding. It had a cloth belt that Rita unpicked with a pair of nail scissors. Then, after tugging the dress this way and that, she walked behind Irene, slipped her hands through the unzipped back of the dress and made two quick cuts in the lining either side of the waist.

'Mend and make do,' she said, going to the dressing-table and starting to search through the jewellery box. She picked out a pair of jasper earrings. She said she had a string of red beads at the farmhouse, that she would fetch them, and she did, immediately, walked over and walked back. The beads were nothing precious, they might even have been a type of plastic, but wound in loose throws round Irene's neck, they made a show of themselves. They looked entirely correct. They picked out a lipstick, chose a bangle of marbled glass (a present from Veronica on her first trip back from America). Shoes were a problem. Were her feet swollen? Rita crawled most of the way into the wardrobe, came out with a pair of court shoes that she dusted on her sleeve.

Then she was gone, and suddenly it was time to change back into ordinary things and hurry down to the station to meet Tessa and the playwright off the London train. And Tessa would *not* stop talking, had looked almost desperate as she stepped from the carriage with more luggage than could possibly be needed for a two-night stay. The playwright, David, gave the impression of looking for something to dislike but there was only the curious sadness of the lane at dusk. It was poor material.

She had shown them up to the spare room at the end of the house. There were two single beds, a view of the front garden. The bathroom and the loo were just across the corridor.

She had, for a time, been troubled by the question of whether putting them in the same room, even with separate beds, made her an accomplice to adultery. She had spoken to Eric about it and he had said something about her 'voicing' her mother's thoughts then, more gently, 'They're adults, aren't they? It's for them to worry about.'

It was hard to argue with that. And she had been impressed

by the way he seemed to know his own mind. But how were you supposed to decide? What did you base it on? If no one was hurt, what did it matter? But perhaps somebody was hurt? Somebody who would find her actions contemptible?

As soon as Tessa had her on her own in the kitchen she said how perfectly, perfectly ghastly Christmas had been. David had been *devoured* by guilt. There had been telephone calls with his wife, calls that sounded like scenes from his plays. He was drunk by lunchtime, had refused to eat the lasagne she had made, then fell asleep in an armchair, woke and ate it cold, almost the entire thing. Of course, *she* was a bit blotto by then and had said, 'Why don't you just go back if it's all so bloody unbearable?' He had looked at her like she was an idiot. In the evening – his way of trying to make up for it all – he read her excerpts from his travel diaries, though that always made her nervous because he wanted her to say things, observations and so on, and it felt like a sort of test. She hugged Irene and wept. She asked if it was wonderful to be pregnant, if being pregnant made sense of everything. She herself *ached* to be a mother. She took a bath, a long one. David asked to use the telephone. For ten minutes, while he and Irene stood at the bottom of the stairs, he was very charming and intelligent.

Eric, who had said he would be back at four, was back at six-thirty. He went up to the bedroom and changed, came down, played with the cuffs of his shirt, his jacket, went back up and changed again. This was unlike him. She made him a drink. He started eating the cocktail sausages and she offered to heat up a tin of soup, make him a sandwich. He said he wasn't hungry. He took another sausage, laid the stick on the side of the plate. If she had been asked to write down a single one of his thoughts she could not, with any certainty, have done it. He was in the drawing room now, talking to David. She had heard some of it, a wary probing that seemed to cost them both an immense amount of effort.

Was everything ready? The food, the drink, the decorations? What she liked best was the large vase in the dining room, in which she had placed three red and three white amaryllis. The flowers had arrived in a van two days before Christmas, boxed, the heads closed, the thick stems cool to the touch. She had kept them in the chill of the unheated nursery, then moved them last night into the dining room, lifting the heavy vase with difficulty. She had timed it perfectly. The dining room was not as warm as the drawing room, but overnight the big fleshy beaks had opened. Each time she passed through the room they were louder. They had become the centre of the house, an annunciation.

The doorbell rang and she flinched. In the glass of the kitchen window she saw herself, the cream dress mostly, like a photographic slide that hadn't been properly developed.

Gabby came into the kitchen. He was like a bird whose arrival heralded better weather. He was wearing a brown corduroy suit and a maroon bow tie. He kissed her hand and performed a little mime of amazement at the sight of the food. He had come on his own. There was no Mrs Miklos. Eric had said he wasn't interested but didn't say in what. Marriage? Sex? He asked if it was permitted to try one of the dolmades. He bit the parcel in half, did not spill a single grain of rice.

'You have Greek blood,' he said. 'Nothing else can explain it.'

He helped her to carry through some of the plates to the dining room. He touched the white petals of one of the flowers. She looked at him, meaning to say something, ask something perhaps, but nothing came out.

The bell rang again. Eric came through.

'Your wife is a genius,' said Gabby.

'I know,' said Eric, not looking over, going to the door, his face set.

It was the neighbours from up the lane, the Duckworths, Phillip and Christine. Phillip Duckworth was in antiques. They came in, rubbing their hands. The wife's nose was pink from the cold.

'The snow is in the Midlands,' she said, 'and travelling south at the pace of a family saloon.'

'The latest from the Air Ministry,' said her husband, stamping his feet on the mat.

Coats, hats and scarves were being stored in the empty nursery. Irene led the Duckworths into the drawing room. They had met at the village fete in August and again at a fundraising evening for the Congo (an unwell-looking young man singing songs by Dowland). They had not been in the house before. Mr Duckworth paused to examine a decanter of blue Bristol glass in a niche above the sofa. 'A very nice example,' he said.

They were introduced to the playwright. He was wearing a leather jacket and a blue shirt he had described to Irene as a working-man's shirt. He was poking the fire, a glass of beer in his other hand. The Duckworths admired the Christmas tree. Eric fetched their drinks (two fingers of Scotch, no water). Irene brought in the cheese sticks. Gabby put on a record, Acker Bilk, 'Stranger on the Shore'.

'Oh, lovely!' said Mrs Duckworth. 'I will *never* get tired of it.'

'Someone,' said the playwright, 'should beat him to death with his own clarinet.'

Tessa came downstairs. 'Hello, everyone,' she said, 'I fell asleep. I was dreaming of trains. I couldn't get off . . .'

She had brought a bottle of vodka with her and had explained to Irene that it was different from other drinks, less fattening, and was practically the only one she allowed herself now. She had the bottle in her hand. Eric fetched her a glass. She half filled it and raised it above her head. 'Lechaim!' she said. Gabby looked at the carpet. The playwright said that when Chekhov was dying, when he knew he was dying, no false alarm this time, the real thing, he sent out for champagne. Mrs Duckworth asked if Chekhov had been a Jew.

'He was a doctor,' said the playwright.

'You can be both,' said Eric.

'I'm not a Jew,' said Tessa, 'but sometimes I *feel* like one.'

The bell. 'I'll get it,' said Eric. He returned a half-minute later, passed Irene and said, 'Your chums from the farm.'

She went out and found them taking off their boots and coats, unwrapping themselves. Rita had on a shimmering green dress, forest green, beetle green, quite short. If you looked with care, if you were paying attention (if you were a woman or a doctor), you would see she was pregnant; you would guess it and look again and be sure. She had done her eyes Egyptian-style. Her lips were bright as cherries. She held up a string bag. 'I've brought records!'

Bill carried their coats and gumboots into the nursery. Irene had only seen him in his overalls before and usually wearing some sort of hat. In a suit and tie he looked almost dashing. He smiled at her shyly. He reminded her of someone but she couldn't immediately think who.

In the drawing room she introduced them as her neighbours from Water Farm. Rita curtsied and people laughed.

'Thank God,' said the playwright. 'People with some honest dirt under their nails.'

'David worships the land,' said Tessa, refreshing her glass.

'David does *not* worship the land,' said the playwright. 'David just happens to think we took a terribly wrong turn somewhere around 1500.'

'What was that?' asked Mrs Duckworth. 'The wrong turn?'

'We started getting interested in money.'

'I think you'll find we were interested in money long before 1500,' said Mr Duckworth.

'Oh, *interested*, yes. But it wasn't everything. There was religion. And not the sort of Sunday nonsense that goes on now. God was alive and knew every field in England.'

He shouted the last few words. There was a short silence, then Acker Bilk's clarinet began again its dreamy upwards swooping. Rita went over to Gabby and shook hands. The playwright drew closer to Bill. He asked if he felt a blood connection to the animals.

'I'm aware of them,' said Bill. He mentioned the bull.

'A bull!' said the playwright. 'You should have brought it with you. That's what this party needs.'

The Duckworths were talking to each other. Irene considered joining them (where had Eric gone?) but went instead to the kitchen and shut the door. Her party skills had deserted her. She used to be good at it. Not as good as Veronica, but Veronica was an exception. Veronica had talent. Even so, she had known perfectly well how to circulate, drop in and out of conversations, how to make people feel she was interested in them (she generally was).

She opened the kitchen window and put her nose out. Her sense of smell, always good, had sharpened with the pregnancy. She could smell woodsmoke. She could smell the oil tank (which they had been promised would be odourless). She could smell water and earth, and something else, something ebbing from the darkness, not unwelcome. What had Mrs Duckworth said? The speed of a saloon car? She lifted her face to it, and as she did so, she felt the child move, not a fluttering any more, not butterfly wings. This was a shove from inside. It made her gasp.

'Don't jump!' cried Tessa, coming into the kitchen with her glass and bottle. 'The buggers aren't worth it.' She laughed. 'Any ice? Don't worry if not. It's just that it tastes less like petrol when it's cold.'

There was plenty of ice. Irene ran a tray under the tap and they took turns hitting the back of it with a steak mallet.

'I don't think,' said Tessa, 'David can make up his mind which of them to seduce.'

'Who?'

'Your farmers. I mean *she*'s very pretty in a sort of chorus-line way, but I think he wants to play Birkin to whoever it was. Tom? Gerald? You know. In the D. H. Lawrence. Wants to get into his birthday suit and wrestle madly beside the fire.'

Irene nodded.

'I think he does bat for the other side sometimes. Or he *thinks* about it. That probably disgusts you.'

'Not really,' said Irene. 'Have you seen Eric?'

'Someone said he'd gone out.'

'Out? Why?'

'Who knows, darling? It's a party, isn't it?'

The lights of the black Zodiac nosed about, looking for a space. Nobody wants to be boxed in. Eric waved but thought they probably couldn't see him. Then the headlights caught him. The beams seemed almost to lift him. He narrowed his eyes and pointed. The car turned and parked at the edge of the lane, two wheels on the verge. As the headlights went off the interior light came on, a dim yellow light that showed them, all three, all doing slightly different things – Frank talking, Alison looking past him towards the house, the boy in the back nodding at whatever his father was telling him. The driver's door swung open.

'You sure it's not going to get flattened by a gritting lorry?' asked Frank.

'I shouldn't think so,' called Eric. 'I meant to bring out a torch. Sorry.'

'Don't worry,' said Frank. 'We can see in the dark. We practise it. Don't we, John?'

And, in truth, they came without difficulty. The men shook hands. Eric led the way into the house.

'Acker Bilk,' said Frank. 'Very smooth.'

'I think it's on repeat,' said Eric.

The boy, John, was wearing what looked like his school uniform. He was fifteen, with a big frame he was starting to grow into. He had Alison's eyes, her eyes in Frank's face. Frank was wearing a business suit. His tie had a fat knot. It wasn't a college tie – he hadn't been to university. Nor was it anything regimental: like most of them there, he was a couple of years too young to have played a part in the war, and one didn't have ties to recall the tedium of national service. Rotary Club perhaps, junior Chamber of Commerce. Or just something Alison had picked out for him on one of her afternoons drifting around the shops on Park Street.

She handed Eric her coat. In the privacy of a single second she rested the full weight of her gaze on him. He had seen her at perhaps ten parties before, most of them at her house. But had he seen her like this? Her beauty was solemn. The generosity of her mouth, her skin that seemed to have been kneaded with butter. At the same time, she looked as if she had not been sleeping well, as if she had been listening to the teachings of three a.m. and taking them as gospel. Then she flashed a smile at someone behind him (Mr Duckworth looking for the little boys' room) and the weight was gone. The dress she had on he would later hear her telling the farmer's wife was French tweed. It was the colour of oatmeal. She wore pearls, three rows (he knew them, the Bulgaris), and three or four bracelets of silver, one a kind of pale lemon gold. As he carried their coats through to the nursery, as he came back to ask them what they would drink, as he ushered them into the drawing room, he took soundings, groped in the darkness of himself, that city in a blackout. Was this thing he had with her a vulgar bourgeois nonsense, or was it the one thing in his life that felt like life, that he was in fact proud of? Conscience is there to make us smaller. He understood that much. Reeve across the line into the bigger life and the world would find some way to throw you back, or not the world, but society, of which he, as the local doctor, was supposed to be some sort of pillar. Yet there, creaking in his leather jacket, was the playwright, his mistress the other side of the room, neither of them looking like outcasts. They weren't shunned. Nobody cared. And not for the first time he wondered if Frank had someone in Bristol, whether if he caught him out of earshot tonight when they both had a lot more alcohol inside them, he might tease a confession out of him . . .

He went to the kitchen to pour drinks. Beer for Frank, gin for Alison, ginger beer for the boy. He put the glasses on a tray, another bottle of beer for the playwright (he had started to like him), then added the bottle of Black and White to top up the Duckworths. When he gave Frank his beer he thought he heard him say something about making a good waiter. Maybe that wasn't what he said.

'Need anything, Gabby?'

Gabby held up his glass, still mostly full. 'I injected myself with heroin before coming out,' he said, and smiled as if it was an old joke between them.

'Right. Well, there's plenty of beer in the kitchen. You know your way. Probably some heroin in the house too.'

The playwright took his bottle. The Duckworths accepted more whisky. They both looked like they could soak up a lot of it.

'And me, please,' said the farmer's wife.

He rested the bottle neck against the rim of her glass. 'Say when.'

'When,' she said, looking at him rather than the glass. He turned away, lost his bearings a moment, then found them.

'This is lovely,' said Alison, lifting the last two glasses from the tray and passing one to her son.

'Is it?'

'You know it is.'

He asked the boy what he'd got for Christmas.

'A new bat,' said the boy.

'He broke the old one hitting a six over the pavilion,' said Alison.

'Impressive.'

'I suspect you were a bowler rather than a batsman.'

'I wasn't much of either.'

'But now it's rugby,' she said. 'I shall have to stand on some windswept touchline cheering him on.'

'That won't be necessary,' said the boy, not sounding like a boy any more but a man already weary of dealing with the antics of women.

'There's nothing I'd like better,' she said. She gave him a fierce smile. He absorbed it. How awful, thought Eric, to have children.

Hallam was the next to arrive. He was an eye man and worked at the hospital on Lower Maudlin Street. They had overlapped at medical school and been friendly for a time. Now and then Eric referred patients to him. He seemed to know his work. He had brought a friend with him, perhaps ten years younger, whom he introduced as Terrence.

'You don't mind, do you, Parry?'

'The more the merrier,' said Eric. Terrence grinned. He was missing one of his front teeth. He wore suede shoes, though the suede was balding. He looked luckless, as if he'd spent his childhood in care and was now enjoying some brief respite before new disasters overwhelmed him.

Coats, drinks. Eric took the new arrivals over to Gabby because that seemed the easiest thing to do. Gabby knew Hallam and he would, somehow, know how to talk to Terrence. He left them and propped open the door between the drawing room and the dining room with a fishing float of bubbled glass. A few people drifted through and began to pick things from the plates on the dining table. The record-player was in the dining room. It was housed in an antique cabinet, an old press or coffer of dark wood, a date on the front (1712) between a pair of rudely carved dog roses. Rita lifted the lid, then the needle from the record. The vinyl spun silently.

'Goodnight, Mr Bilk,' she said. She found the sleeve and put the record back with the half-dozen others in the rack at the side of the turntable. She looked to see what else they had. Frank Sinatra (she didn't like Frank Sinatra), *The Music of Spain* (various artists). Then a sleeve with a big picture of Christ's face – a drawing like chalk on a blackboard, Christ's eyes turned skywards, the thorns radiating from his brow straight as nails. She had theories about Jesus Christ; she was curious. She put it on, just to have a taste of it, but then the sounds, like something prowling, something crossing a dark space unstoppably towards them, made it impossible to move. When the voices came – and they came unfairly, leaping from the dusty speaker, stunning her – so did Dr Parry. He reached past her and lifted the needle.

'No thanks,' he said.

'Sorry,' she said. 'What is it?'

'*St John Passion*. Not really party music.'

He put it away and pulled out the album beside it. 'What about this?'

'God bless the child who has his own . . .' sang Terrence. He was peering over their shoulders, a glass in one hand, a lolling wedge of quiche in the other.

Eric put the record on, settled the needle. Terrence pirouetted and returned to the table for more food. Unlike the others he seemed genuinely hungry.

'Irene told me your dad was a train driver,' said Rita.

'I doubt that she did. He worked on the railways but he was never a driver. He started out as a plate layer, if you know what that is. He ended up as the assistant stationmaster at Birmingham New Street.'

'I've been to Birmingham,' she said.

'I won't ask if you liked it. People generally don't.'

'All depends on what you're doing,' she said.

After the braying of a trumpet the music had slowed to something like confession, shuffle. A voice that seemed to come from a numbed mouth, stung.

'Did you go to see your father yesterday?'

'Oh, yes,' she said. 'I went.'

'How was it?'

'Christmas morning at the asylum?'

'Yes.'

'Someone had found the box of paper crowns. They all had them on. Staff too. Do you know why the staff wear white coats?'

'Tell me.'

'You wouldn't be able to tell them apart if they didn't.'

He nodded.

'There was a man with a slashed face,' she said. 'Had a red crown on. He looked quite dangerous.'

'I know the one,' said Eric. 'The captain. Or perhaps the major.'

'Dad said he was all right once you got to know him.' She laughed.

'You get a different perspective.'

'Shop floor,' she said.

'How did it start?'

'What?'

'With your father. His being . . . unwell.'

'Dad?' She tilted her head. 'The war, I suppose.'

'He had a rough time?'

'He saw things.'

'He was disappointed.'

'Disappointed?'

'In us.'

'That's a funny way of putting it,' she said. 'What are you disappointed in?'

'Me? I don't know. Getting older?'

'I thought we were still young.'

'I thought so too.'

'Irene's lovely,' she said.

'Does she talk about it?'

'Getting older?'

'Disappointment.'

'Not to me.'

'You know, your father doesn't really need to be there any more. The old hospitals will be closed in a few years. Emptied. Might he like it on the farm?'

'He'd burn it down,' she said.

They pooled their gaze on the spinning record, the way it carried a rippling blade of light.

'I'm going to make a jug of something strong,' said Eric. 'People are still half sober. Got any ideas?'

'Gin and anything,' she said. 'Lots of ice.'

He left her. For half a minute she thought about her father, saw him as she had the day before, the other side of a Formica-topped table with its pattern of cigarette burns like spilled grain, some women in the corner singing the first line of 'Good King Wenceslas' again and again and again. She had told him she was pregnant and he had told her about the dead boy in the drying room. Like two swift moves in a game.

She lowered the lid of the cabinet. When she turned, Terrence was dancing on his own. She grinned at him: she liked people who knew how to be unhappy.

The doorbell rang and Irene came through. There was the touch of colder air, of voices raised in greeting, then a man's voice riding effortlessly over the shrilling of the women. He appeared, swathed in a camel-hair overcoat and a paisley muffler. He was carrying a cardboard box. He looked at Rita.

'Can I take your fings for you, sir?' she asked. It was her maid-of-all-work voice.

He bared his yellow teeth. From somewhere beneath the camel hair came a shout of laughter.

'Come on,' he said. 'You're going to be the first. Lucky dip.' He held out the box. She went over. It was full of packets of cigarettes and cigars, cheerful in their cellophane.

'Don't mind if I do, sir.' She took a packet of Embassy.

'Merry Christmas,' he said.

He was twenty years older than the other men, perhaps twenty times richer. Now and then Eugene had organised parties for men like this, exclusive gatherings, not at the Pow-Wow but in houses across the city, mostly in Clifton. Estate agents would let a flat for the afternoon. Champagne and lingerie. No great harm.

'This is Edward Strang,' said Irene. 'Rita and her husband have the farm next to us. Water Farm.'

'A farmer's wife. Well, well. I wouldn't have guessed it.'

Mrs Strang came in. She looked shrewd, slightly worn out, like the keeper of unpleasant secrets. She wore a coat of pale mink. Behind her was a girl introduced as Cassy. She was too young to be their daughter, too old for a granddaughter. A ward of some kind. She looked at Rita with the same expression of rage she must have worn in the dark of the big car on the drive over to a party she didn't want to be at.

When the new arrival had shed his coat and scarf, his leather driving gloves, his black hat (Irene and Rita working together), he marched into the drawing room shaking the box. Alison knew him: Frank worked for him. She took a packet of Passing Clouds. Eric took a green pack of Three Castles. The eye man helped himself to cigars, the mid-range Castellas. Mr Duckworth also took cigars. Terrence asked for Rothmans and Edward Strang said, 'Oh dear.' Someone explained. Eric moved in his wake, a lighter in one hand, in the other a glass jug tinkling with ice.

'What is it?' people asked.

'Drink it and see,' he said.

'What do you think, Gabby?' called a voice. 'Is it safe?'

'He's a doctor,' said Gabby. 'He has taken oaths.' For almost the entire evening Gabby had been standing in the same place beside the television set. People came up to him, spoke a while and moved off. Neither he nor Eric was on call. They had hired a young Welshman who was sleeping at the surgery on a camp bed.

The jug was a great success. Eric went back to the kitchen to make another. John and the teenage girl were put together in the centre of the drawing room. She was high-coloured, restless. When prompted they gave each other the names of their schools, then fell silent. Alison sent them to fetch plates of food and hand them around. Tessa was talking to the Duckworths. She had made the mistake of trying to match them drink for drink. She was leaning against the wall by the fire. She was starting to look hunched. Frank was talking to Edward Strang's wife. Edward Strang was trying to persuade Irene to have something from his box. ('Oh, that's all nonsense,' he said. '*Nonsense.*') The playwright, sweating in his leather jacket, was telling a small man in a brown suit – it was Tilly, who ran the chemist's next to the surgery – about the state of London theatre.

'But it gets worse,' he said. 'Olivier is in some unspeakable tosh at the Saville where everyone has to put on a northern accent and pretend they've been raised by fat violent women in the slums. But they're all from *enormous* houses in the Home Counties! They were raised by nannies. It's excruciating. I'd rather go to the sodding *Mikado*. At least you know on the way in it's going to be complete balls.'

A cry went up: 'The jug's back! Three cheers for Eric!'

Acker Bilk was on again. In the dining room, Terrence had taken one of the red amaryllis and was playing it like a clarinet. The eye man stroked Rita's thigh as he passed her. She looked round, but he was already making some remark to Edward Strang's wife, who allowed herself the smallest of smiles.

'Is that your husband?' asked Alison. She pointed with her chin to where Bill was standing, indecisively, at the bottom of the stairs.

'Yes,' said Rita. 'He's always a bit lost at a party.'

'You've got the handsomest man in the room.'

'Where's yours?' asked Rita.

'Oh, somewhere.'

'I like your dress.'

'French tweed,' said Alison, 'but I bought it for the lining.' She reached down and turned the hem.

Rita fingered it. 'Raw silk,' she said. 'And nice silk stockings too.'

'Are you two going to swap dresses?' asked Eric.

'That's right,' said Alison. 'Why don't you come upstairs and help us?'

He filled their glasses and left them. They lit cigarettes.

'How far along are you?' asked Alison.

'Fifteen weeks, I think. We could ask Gabby.'

'He's your doctor, I assume, rather than the child's father.'

'I'm assuming that too,' said Rita.

'Here comes *my* baby,' said Alison.

John and the girl approached. The girl carried a bowl of pink dip; John had a plate of carrot batons and crackers.

'*The Midwich Cuckoos*,' said Alison. 'Do you know it?'

'I saw the film,' said Rita. '*Village of the Damned*.'

'Oh, yes,' said Alison. 'Horrible, wasn't it?'

'Mind your backs!' said someone (Mr Duckworth?). Tessa was trying to reach the stairs. She had her eyes shut.

'Here we go,' said the playwright. 'Bang on cue.'

Bill caught her as she began to fall. 'It's awfully stuffy, isn't it?' he said.

'She's not going to make the stairs on her own,' said the eye man.

'Pick her up, Bill,' called Rita.

He did. Farming had made him strong. He carried her up the stairs, thinking of Drusilla's calf. Irene followed. Some of the guests clapped.

'She's in the room at the end,' said Irene. 'Door on the right.'

He laid her on the bed nearest the door. Irene switched on the bedside lamp. The room was calm, the air warmed to something pleasant by the radiator under the curtained window. You could hardly hear the party. It was like the roar of distant surf.

When Eric's father was dying, the first spring they were in the house, he had spent his final weeks in this room. He had had liver cancer that soon spread everywhere. He turned yellow, shrank, was swept with panic, then, some gift of exhaustion, resigned himself. There was a moment at the end when they were sitting, she and Eric, either side of the bed, each holding one of his father's hands. They had been there a while, perhaps as long as an hour, late afternoon, the birds cutting dark lines of flight across the garden. And Eric had suddenly stood and lifted the sheet over his father's face. It had startled her. She had not been aware of any change. In the thinness of his wrist she thought she could feel a pulse still. 'No, no,' said Eric, 'he's gone.' And how could she argue? The son, the doctor. So she let go of his hand and settled it on the covers as she might, from a boat, have let go the hand of someone in the water. She had liked him very much. A decent, unimaginative man. The possibility that the sheet had been pulled over his face while he was still alive troubled her for a long time. It still did.

'I'm going to be sick,' said Tessa. Irene fetched the plastic bowl from under the sink in the bathroom. When she brought it back, Tessa sat up, gripped the sides of the bowl and vomited.

It went on for two or three minutes. When it stopped, Irene put the bowl on the floor. Tessa cried noisily. Bill stood with his arms crossed, lips pursed.

'I can manage now,' said Irene. 'Thank you so much.'

'Oh, that's all right,' said Bill. 'Rita's been queasy for weeks. I'm quite used to it.'

He left them. Irene held Tessa's hands. Tessa apologised and started to cry again. 'I'm a horrible, useless, pathetic woman,' she said.

'You're not at all,' said Irene.

'I *am*. You know I am.' She groaned. 'Nothing more vile in the whole bloody world than a woman who . . . steals another woman's husband.'

'I expect it's more complicated than that, isn't it?' said Irene.

'I've met her, you know. His wife. Did I tell you she's an actress? Hedda Gabler at the Garrick. He reads me all her reviews. He calls her a classic bitch but he's in awe of her. And the children. Adorable . . .' She began to choke on her tears. She waved frantically for the bowl. Irene held it. There wasn't much more.

'There's always a bloody price tag,' she said. 'Nobody gets away with anything. Or perhaps it's just the women who don't.' She looked up at Irene, like a child who's stayed up far too late. 'If I sleep a bit . . .'

'Yes,' said Irene. 'Sleep a bit. You'll feel much better.'

She eased off Tessa's shoes, stripped a blanket from the other bed and laid it over her. She stood watching her drift to the edge of sleep. She pitied her, though did not think her assessment of herself entirely wrong. She left the lamp on and carried the bowl across the corridor. As she started to open the loo door, a man's voice barked, 'Steady the Buffs!' She shut the door and called an apology. She was turning to go back into the spare room (she had to move carefully, the bowl was almost half full) when the loo door swung open and Edward Strang came out. He peered into the bowl. 'Not yours, I hope.'

'No,' she said. 'Someone else.'

'Lovely party.'

'Thank you. I'm so pleased you were able to come.'

'The question,' he said, 'is whether we'll be able to leave.'

'You mean the weather?'

'I mean those jugs of gin your husband's plying us with.'

'Yes,' she said. 'I don't know where he's finding it all.'

'In the name of the Father, the Son, and London dry gin,' said Edward. He zipped his trousers. 'I suppose you want to get rid of that.'

'Yes,' she said.

'You carry on.'

He strode away along the corridor. There was a shifting column of smoke at the top of the stairs. He entered it and descended like a man wading into the sea. She stepped into the loo. It was a small space and it stank. She emptied the bowl, flushed, opened the little window and backed out. She was in the bathroom before she took a deep breath. She rinsed the bowl then washed her hands. She took the bowl back to the spare room and left it by the bed. Tessa was deeply asleep, her face tilted to the side, the skin between her brows pinched into a frown that Irene was tempted to smooth out with her thumb. (Once, during the war, on retreat before her confirmation, a priest, very high church, had rubbed a cross of ashes onto her forehead and she had liked it.)

She walked towards the top of the stairs but paused outside her bedroom. Before going down, she would have a minute to herself, check her make-up, perhaps a spray of perfume. Imagine going down with some lingering whiff of what Edward Strang had done still clinging to her! She stepped into the bedroom but stopped by the door. There was a woman in there, standing by the washbasin, looking up at *The Arnolfini Marriage*.

'Hello,' said Irene.

The woman turned. 'Sorry,' she said. 'I got lost.'

'That's all right,' said Irene.

'It's a lovely party.'

'Thank you.'

'How's that poor girl?'

'Tessa? She's much better, thanks. She's sleeping now.'

'Best thing.'

'Yes.'

They looked at each other across the bed, the buttery light of a bedside lamp. They had talked at parties before, a few words, nothing memorable. The last time was probably the pool party in the summer, but there had been a lot of people there, people Eric didn't really approve of, business types, the management of the tobacco company, the board. At one point, somebody (it was that very fat man, Geoffrey something or other) found an arrow and pretended he'd been shot with it and staggered over the lawn and fell with an enormous splash into the swimming-pool. It was, actually, very funny.

'Do you like it? The picture?'

'I'm never very sure,' said Irene. 'He's such strange-looking man.'

'That big hat.'

'Yes.'

'The bride doesn't seem too sure about him either.'

'She's miles away.'

'One theory is that the painting is a memorial to her. That it was painted after her death. When you think of it like that, it makes more sense, doesn't it?'

'I didn't know that,' said Irene. 'I hope it's not true.'

'Oh, it's probably not. I've no idea really. How far along are you now?'

'About nineteen weeks.'

'You look lovely. Blooming.'

'Thank you.'

'Some women just look completely exhausted.'

'Yes, I suppose so.'

'I wonder what makes the difference.'

'The dark,' said Irene. She meant it as a joke but it didn't quite come over as one.

'That sweet creature in the green dress. She's preggers, too, isn't she?'

'Rita? Yes.'

'Bliss to have someone to talk to about it. Who understands.'

'Oh, yes. Very.'

'It's funny how you forget. My boy will be sixteen in February. Valentine's Day. I can remember giving birth, of course. You don't forget that. But being pregnant . . .' She moved her hands. Some suggestion of spilling. 'I wasn't a very good mother. I'm not brilliant now, but when he was born I didn't have a clue. I was twenty-one. I don't think I liked my baby very much. I know that's an unforgivable thing to say. The district nurse terrified me. She had no time for mothers who weren't managing. I got over it in the end, but it probably took a year. One thing I was sure of was that I didn't want any more.'

'He looks a lovely boy,' said Irene.

'Oh, he looks a bit of a thug. He's very bright. He impresses me. But they *are* rather frightening, aren't they? Children? All that rage for life. Yours will be an angel, of course. You'll be a wonderful mother.'

'I don't know,' said Irene. 'I suppose you can't know until you've done it.'

'What kind of father do you think Eric will be?'

'He was very close to his own father. His father raised him really.'

'The railway man.'

'Yes, that's right. Did he tell you about him?'

'He must have done.' She shrugged. 'Anyway, you didn't come in here for a chat. I've been horribly rude. I'm going to leave you in peace.'

'Oh, don't worry about that,' said Irene. 'I enjoyed it.'

'I did too,' said Alison. She smiled and walked around the end of the bed. As she came close to Irene, she stopped and looked back into the room.

'Which side does he sleep on?' she asked.

People had at last started to migrate into the dining room. There was too much smoke in the other room, a blue cloud, an atmosphere only certain people, like the Duckworths, seemed able to bear. Most of the food on the dining-room table had been eaten. Eric had gone to look for more, and when Irene came down he was cutting up pieces of cheese on a plate next to the Aga. He said he was going to make sandwiches. He stared at her, his eyes bright with gin. He asked if she had changed her dress.

'No,' she said. 'It's the same one.'

She went into the larder, where she had half a dozen more plates of food prepared. Sweet things and savoury. She took off their foil hats.

'What's happening upstairs?' he asked.

'Tessa was unwell but I think she's all right now. She's sleeping. Then I bumped into Edward Strang. Then I had a conversation with Frank Riley's wife.'

'With Frank's wife?'

'Yes. She was in the bedroom.'

'Our bedroom?'

'She said she'd got lost.'

He was silent a moment. He started cutting one of the slices of Cheddar into thin strips. 'What did you talk about?'

'Oh, I don't know. Babies.'

'Babies? What does she know about babies?'

'And she asked what side of the bed you sleep on.'

'Did you tell her?'

'I couldn't think of a reason not to.'

'It's none of her bloody business. How's that for a reason?'

'None of it mattered,' said Irene. 'Could you open the windows in the drawing room? Someone's going to faint.'

She carried the tray through to the dining room. On one side of the tray there were porcelain ramekins of fruit fool, each with a sponge finger to use as a spoon. The playwright, smoking one of Edward Strang's cigars (he had gone for the Wills Whiffs rather than the larger Castellas), helped himself, and immediately got a dollop of cream on his jacket. He didn't notice it. In the morning, Irene would find the end of his cigar in the ramekin. She would find one of the amaryllis in the downstairs loo, one of the dolmades under the sofa, two glasses almost buried on the lawn. One glass, which had found its way into the back garden, set down like an offering next to the crab-apple tree, she found in mid-March, a week after Eric had left, and shortly before she did too.

A voice asked where the young people were. Someone said they'd gone outside. Frank said he'd look for them. 'Why?' asked Alison. He shrugged and stayed where he was. He patted his suit pockets and took out a packet of Passing Clouds.

Despite the colour it was marketed equally towards men and women.

At the end of the dining table nearest the uncurtained window, Bill found himself beginning a conversation with Gabby Miklos. For the last half-minute he had been trying to catch Rita's eye, make the signal that it was time to leave. They had talked about it on the walk over, or he had. He was to do a little mime of milking, a small up-and-down movement of his fists. But Rita was busy touring the room, making people laugh, doing her voices. She was with the big man now, the one who'd arrived with the box of tobacco. He was gazing down at her, delighted. In Bill's right ear, Gabby was saying something. It sounded like a question but it wasn't in English.

'No,' said Bill. 'I never learned it. My father, I suppose he was leaving all that behind him. Sometimes in songs, you know, when he was in a good mood.'

Gabby nodded. Yes. Leaving it all behind. Even so, at some level? Deep down?

Several times during the party, Bill had got the impression Gabby wished to speak to him. For some reason he had been reluctant to do so and had been careful not to meet his gaze. It was the wrong setting. Too much noise, too much smoke, the strange heat. But the wrong setting for what? They were, he thought, standing closer than was really necessary. The room was noisy but not crowded. They must look as if they were exchanging secrets. He tried again to get Rita's attention. He sent her a silent message – shouldn't that work between husband and wife? – but if she received it, she ignored it. She was telling a joke. He couldn't hear it but he knew which one it was. Anyway, it was too late. Gabby was talking about *his* father, an amateur scientist, who revered Charles Darwin and had a beautiful cabinet of slender mahogany drawers in which he kept his collection of moths and butterflies and beetles, all of them pinned to ivory card with their Latin names beside them in such small writing it was as if the insect had dipped one of its feet into black ink and written its own name. 'These were my delight to look at as a child, though I confess they also frightened me a little . . .'

They had a wireless at the house ('a Zenith Stratosphere, quite impressive, with little wooden doors you could close to cover the dial'). At some point it became unwise to have such an item. They moved it to the cellar and listened to the BBC in the dark. Uncles wrote from America. From five thousand miles away, they could see more clearly. His father complained that he was too old to move, and, anyway, really, why should he? So they waited. They listened to *him* on the radio. It was obvious madness. It would blow over. Wasn't the world full of civilised people? This wasn't the Middle Ages. He put his faith in reason and good manners, kept it even when he was refused service in shops he had gone to for thirty years, even when his sons could no longer attend school, even when the clubs he belonged to, where they drank coffee and discussed *Acherontia styx*, suggested it might be better, for his own sake really, if he no longer attended. Then the name calling (hardly new). A broken window. Rat poison for the dog. They had money. The piano lessons continued until two days before the order to pack a suitcase and wait outside the house. The piano teacher was among those who received the order. The local police collected them. They wore hats with green . . . feathers?

'Plumes,' suggested Bill.

'Ah, yes,' said Gabby, looking pleased. 'Plumes.'

They were marched up the hill to the cemetery. For a week, they lived in the open. On one occasion – he was a slender boy with quick eyes – he got back to the house to fetch an item his mother had hidden and now wished for. Inside, he found several of the neighbours. Among the things they were looking at was the cabinet of narrow drawers containing the insects. They were very surprised to see him, somewhat annoyed, not at all embarrassed.

He lapsed again into the old language. Bill shook his head. 'No, no. Remember?' He saw Rita coming out of the coat room with the string bag of records in her hand. The eye man stopped her. He wanted to see what she had and she showed him.

There were those who thought they would never leave the cemetery. Was it not, after all, a most suitable place? But that would have been the old way. Now things were done differently. When they left the cemetery, they were forbidden to take their suitcases with them ('and, please, you will imagine you are the one who goes there after us to find a thousand suitcases among the grave stones'.) At the marshalling yard the order came to drop all valuables on the ground – money, rings, whatever they still had. There was a high price for trying to keep something back, and quite close to where he was standing a woman paid it. He knew her – not well, but he knew her. After that, two days on the train. Or it was one day, or it was five.

'I am sorry,' he said.

'It's all right,' said Bill.

In the wall of the wagon there was a small window about the size of a human face and at each station they stopped at he looked out and saw how everything was normal, how for others the world had not altered. The stations neatly swept. The summer trees in leaf (it was July). At one station, a woman and child waited drowsily on a bench for a different train. Finally, after moving at the pace of a slow running through forests of the darkest green, past houses with thatched roofs and fields where the farmer watched the wagons with knowledgeable eyes, they arrived at a place no one had been before, because it was somewhere that had not existed before.

'People ask now how this could happen, but how is very well explained. There are many documents. There are the reports of meetings where everything is discussed even to the smallest detail. How it happens is perfectly understood. There is no mystery. So please, tell me, what is the question we must ask instead?'

'I don't know,' said Bill, quickly. He felt, but did not want to look down to confirm it, that Gabby had taken hold of the sleeve of his jacket. The air between them had become a kind of skin, a membrane. It vibrated. Outside the dining-room window the teenagers stood at the edge of the light, looking in. They watched the room blankly. It was either exactly what they had expected or it was incomprehensible, a piece of experimental theatre, something they would have to write about, laboriously, for an exam.

When Gabby began again – *Häftling, Sonderkommando, Judenlager* – Bill, staring at an abandoned cheese stick on the tablecloth, began to withdraw his heart. He did it as subtly as he could, an inching back that might, with luck, seem no movement at all, a disappearing act, a party trick (the corpse wrapped in a rug carried out under the very noses of the police), but all was glass to Gabby Miklos and he sensed it at once. He looked up and smiled at Bill. It was, after all, not his first failure.

'Your wife is dancing,' he said.

It was true. In the centre of a broken circle of guests, some of whom attempted to keep time with clapping. A dance danced on the spot, one that involved clever, repetitive movements of the feet and ankles. A dance somehow faster than the song.

'It's called the mashed potato,' said Bill.

Her thickened waist seemed no encumbrance. Her hands steadied the air. Her expression was abstracted. She looked somehow less familiar to him, to not be among his possessions, barely his memories. In the doorway to the drawing room, Mrs Duckworth observed it with polite interest, then swayed, just once, as if they were on a liner, and somewhere in the dark above them, the unlit bridge, there had been a shift in course.

She danced the full three minutes. There was applause. Edward Strang said they would all do it now. 'Put it on again!' he ordered. He took off his plum-coloured jacket, folded it and dropped it onto the floor. 'Come on, everybody. Follow . . .' He couldn't remember her name. He pointed at her.

Coats were found; coats were brought out of the still-bare nursery. Coats, gloves, scarves. Is this one yours? Eric went outside to help with the manoeuvring of the cars. The hollow sound of slamming doors, the cut of yellow lights. The teenagers were discovered glitter-eyed with cold. Rita helped with the clearing of the dining table. Had anybody looked in on Tessa?

'Who?' asked the playwright. He laughed. He was following Bill around, explaining his ideas for a revival of working-class culture. A full-frontal assault on bingo and telly. There was going to be a festival in Middlesbrough. Brass bands, folk music in the pubs. He himself was updating sketches from the *Commedia dell'Arte*. Harlequin would be a union man, Pantelone someone from the coal board.

'Your wife should come with me,' he said. 'She's authentic.'

Gabby had slipped away. No one saw him leave. In a day or two a little note would arrive in the post, a half-dozen lines on good paper. The chemist found Irene in the kitchen and thanked her. He looked like a man who had seen marvels. Eric came in, rubbing his hands. Whatever he had been before, he was sober now. Bill tapped Rita's back. 'Come on,' he said. 'I'll be milking in a couple of hours.'

They took off their shoes and put on their boots. Bill had a torch. They stood at the back door.

'Will you be warm enough?' asked Irene.

'Perfectly,' said Rita. She leaned and kissed Irene's cheek.

'Thanks for putting up with us,' said Bill.

At the other end of the kitchen Eric had one of Irene's magazines open on the kitchen table. 'Cheerio,' he said, without looking up.

They walked away into the darkness of the garden. They found the little gate behind the ash tree and began to cross the field. It was like leaving the harbour for open water, and like open water the field was colder than the garden.

'Gabby was telling me things,' said Bill.

'Was he?'

'Trying to. I think he wanted some sort of fellow feeling but I'm the wrong fellow.'

'By tomorrow afternoon,' said Rita, 'nobody will remember anything they said to anyone.'

'They'll remember you,' he said.

'What? A fat girl dancing to a pop song?'

'I nearly socked what's-his-name in the jaw. The one with the leather jacket.'

'David.'

'He thinks you're authentic.'

'I am,' she said.

'He wants you to go to Middlesbrough with him.'

'Do you want me to?'

'It's about saving the working classes from bingo.'

'I have to save the middle classes first. They're in a terrible state.'

'Hello . . .' said Bill.

They saw it first in the beam of the torch. A second later it touched their faces – an ear, a cheek, the crease of an eye. Bill shone the beam skywards. In the cone of light the flakes skittered, twisted, seemed briefly to rise rather than fall, then fell decisively, filling the darkness with a whispering that had no clear source, no centre. They shut their eyes. They tasted it. Stone-flavoured, the tips of the sky. It filled them with a great excitement of change. They laughed, standing there in the centre of the field. Then she gripped his arm, leaned into him, and with heads bowed they pushed on, no longer quite certain of their direction, the torch playing over shifting veils that seemed sometimes to rush at them, then parted to let them through.

PART TWO

The Land in Winter

Thursday, 3 January

When Bill opened the front door he felt the house inflate, lift slightly. He fought to get the door shut, then shouldered his way across the yard, head down, weaving like a drunk. At milking time (and somehow, despite the cold, the machines still worked), the snow had been gusts and flurries. Now it was the air tearing itself to shreds. Snow from the sky, snow from the ground where it had been lying for days. He stepped inside the shippon, half expecting to see the cows blowing like wastepaper, but they stood, blotchy and solid, regarding him, this bundled figure erupting out of the storm, with their usual mild curiosity. He caught his breath. 'How do you like this?' he asked.

He climbed the ladder to the loft. The steel roof shook, groaned, somehow held. He fancied it was warmer here, above the animals, than it was inside the house. If the house became unliveable, if the wind ripped the chimneys off, they could do worse than shelter here. They would have mice for company but there were mice in the house too.

He dropped three bales through the trapdoor, then climbed down and cut the twine. On Dartmoor and on Exmoor helicopters had been carrying bales of fodder for the animals

– cattle, ponies, sheep – though no helicopter could fly in this. They were also, of course, carrying provisions for people. Farms were cut off, villages, entire towns. Okehampton, for example. You couldn't get close to it.

He checked the water. The tap (it sat there like a small god) was stiff but turned and the water flowed. He went out again. The storm gathered him, shoved him forwards. He shouted to hear the nothingness of his voice. He reached the barn. The dry cows and the pony from the field were in there. He had brought them in just in time, a couple of days before New Year. Even a tractor was of little use in the lanes now. He petted the pony. It was trembling slightly. He wished he had brought something for it. There were apples from the autumn stored in the back bedroom of the house. They had used half a dozen in a pie, and there were about two hundred left. The room smelt powerfully of apples. The rest of the crop, most of it, was under the snow in the orchard.

From the barn he tacked his way to the cart shed. This was where he had moved the bull. He had hauled out the buck rake and the Ferguson plough. He had made a pen from a pair of gates and some of the scaffolding from the hangar. Had he left the bull in its old home behind the shippon, it would be up to its muzzle in snow by now. He checked to see if its water was frozen, if there was food in the trough. It liked the maize cubes and ate a lot of them. Now and then, the snow curled in and blew over the bull's back, melting into the heat of it. Bill turned towards the house. He had done what he could. The farm would stand or it would be scattered over the county. Nothing he could do out here would make any difference. One end of his scarf worked free and whipped his face. He felt for the door handle. When he got the door open, it drew him inside as if he had hold of a sail. He shut it, leaning his back against it. He was dizzy, half deaf, infested with cold, yet felt the urge immediately to go out again. What was that? A sort of hunger? In the kitchen, Rita was sitting at the table with an eiderdown round her shoulders. Cigarettes, ashtray, book. She stood and helped him peel off his gloves. She put them on the Rayburn to dry. She touched the numbness of his face.

'What's it like out there?' she asked.

At the kitchen window, Eric smoked and watched the garden come and go. Irene was cooking but now and then, in her apron, she joined him and they stood together, their eyes following the darting of the snow.

They had plenty of food left over from the holidays. The heating was working – the oil-fired central heating, the Aga, the open fire in the drawing room. There were cold spots, but you expected cold spots in a cottage. The end of the house taking the brunt of the wind was noticeably cooler, but the kitchen was at the other end and they were perfectly comfortable.

They sat to eat. It was a beef stew, and Irene had made dumplings. Eric adored dumplings. He decided to have a bottle of beer with his food and she fetched it for him. They sat facing the window. The wireless was on but turned down low. You could hear a voice but not what it was saying, not exactly. A list of lost roads perhaps, an update from the Air Ministry.

In theory, he was on call, though other than give advice over the phone, there was very little he could do. He had not left the house in days. The Citroën was safely in the garage. The garage was an ice house, its one window like a sheet of crystal so that the car sat in light the colour of cobwebs. He had given the car a thorough clean, had sat inside it, getting interestingly cold and wiping everything down with a damp cloth and a chamois. He had emptied the ashtray. He had removed from under the passenger seat a tissue with a print of lipstick on it, of lips.

He had expected to feel restless in the house, trapped. Instead he felt a certain pleasure in surrendering to what he could not change. It was a long while since they had spent so much time together, just the two of them, no distractions. The last occasion was probably their honeymoon. When he asked her she agreed, yes, probably the honeymoon. And something in the way she said it (she said it simply enough) made him understand this was a truth much nearer the front of her mind than it had been of his. It cut him a little, and he began to act in ways he knew would please and reassure her. They talked about Veronica, the possibility of a trip out there in the spring (were there rules about pregnancy and flying? How late could you leave it?). They talked about the baby, a good-humoured tussling over names. There was a resolve to get the nursery finished, and on New Year's Day he had spent a couple of hours sanding down the window frame and priming it. They talked about his work in the way they used to. A mood of confession crept over him and he warned himself to be careful, while at the same time wondering how it would be if he held her hand and told her, in his gentlest voice, what had been going on. Not all of it, obviously. He would assure her it was over. He had been lost but he was back now, had found his way home. It might be an occasion for celebration rather than anger and tears. It might be the jolt they needed.

They had discussed family and friends. They had laughed – really laughed – at the memory of Tessa and her absurd playwright 'boyfriend'. They sat close to the fire in the evenings, sipping whisky and pretending to be colder than they were. They got out the baize-topped card table and played whist and rummy. He taught her a version of poker he had learned in the air force. She tried to explain the rules of bridge. She used to play with Veronica and her parents. The Duckworths were probably bridge players, and that, too, was somehow very funny, the thought of bridge evenings with the Duckworths, who were, fairly obviously, alcoholics.

They watched television, though the weather or the work-to-rule by the power unions made the reception erratic.

They listened to music. He put on the *Passion*. He didn't really like playing it. He had bought the record because the music was stored on it in the way he imagined memories were stored in the brain. He had seen it only once, a church in Manchester, sitting in a cushionless pew by candlelight after an afternoon in the anatomy theatre (where the technician had shown him a trick for peeling back the skin). He could barely remember now why he had gone, and why on his own, only that he had reeled out at the end, avoiding everyone's eyes and walking for hours in a sort of trance, ending up in the depths of Salford. The *Passion* was evidence of something, and to that extent it was awkward for a man like himself (BSc MD FRCGP). The music called to what, when Bach had written it, was easily named, but now seemed quaint, a gown with lace cuffs blowing around between the night buses . . .

They had listened together on the sofa and at the end of it Irene smiled, said nothing, left him alone for a few minutes. Imagine Alison Riley having such tact! Though when he did imagine it, it didn't seem particularly unlikely.

*

A patient rang. She had a child with a temperature. Any rash? No? Good. Fluids, aspirin, bed rest. See how he is tomorrow. Another call, this from a woman complaining of dizzy spells. He knew her and knew there would be fewer dizzy spells if she drank less. He suggested she make a meal for herself, something hot. Did she have food in the house? She did. She went through it, tin by tin. He thought she just needed to speak to someone, that she was probably frightened by the weather. He thought how much he liked being a doctor. He remembered his father's pride in it. It is a powerful thing to please your father. It is a powerful thing to disappoint him, even his ghost.

He telephoned Gabby, who lived in a flat quite close to the surgery. He could, with a little effort, get in. 'Any customers?'

'Quiet as soup,' said Gabby.

'They'll get the line cleared soon,' said Eric. There was a station at a walkable distance from the surgery.

'This morning,' said Gabby, 'a policeman delivered my milk. In the storm.'

'Yes,' said Eric. 'The country is strangely obsessed with milk.'

In the afternoon, the blizzard blew away towards the north. For an hour the air was perfectly still. The ash tree was a frozen fountain. Several times they said to each other how beautiful it was. The dusk came swiftly. In the garden, the snow lay in subtle undulations, each with its deepening blue shadow. The cold descended and the land tightened. Eric went out to read the gauge on the oil tank. It was lower than he had expected. He didn't mention it to Irene. They'd be all right for a while and weather like this couldn't last.

In bed that night (in place, perhaps, of making love, to fend it off), he told her about Stephen Storey, chloral hydrate, his role in it all. Irene was wonderful. She defended him to himself, was rational, changed the nature of her touching. In the silence that followed they shared the calling of an owl. The house was strangely quiet, perhaps because without oil the radiators had ceased working.

'There'll be no burials,' he said, 'until it thaws. The ground will be like iron.'

She leaned her head against his shoulder. Soon they were both asleep.

Saturday, 5 January

The sun came out. Rita phoned. She asked if Irene wanted to build a snowman with her in the field between the farm and the cottage.

'All right,' said Irene, laughing. 'I'll meet you there in half an hour.'

On the wireless, still no news of the coaster *Ardgarry*, missing in the Channel since before New Year. The leader of the opposition, Hugh Gaitskell, had been taken ill. No one seemed to know exactly what the trouble was. Twenty-seven cup ties had been cancelled. More bloodshed in the Congo.

Eric was taking care of the fire in the drawing room. There were embers from the night before. He laid kindling on them, and when they caught, he placed a handful of small coals on top. Irene brought him fresh coffee. She told him what she was going to do. She supposed it was a bit silly, but still.

'It's not silly at all,' he said. 'Get some air and exercise. I'm going to clear the drive if I can find a shovel.'

In the bedroom she looked for warm clothes. She chose the land-girl dungarees she had bought in the army surplus store in Bristol. They were not flattering (this land girl had possessed an ample backside) but the bagginess left plenty of room for her bump and, anyway, she would have her coat over the top of it.

The bedroom was untidy. With two of them in the house, two of them constantly and no Mrs Rudge coming in, the room was littered with draped clothes (most of them Eric's), with shoes and slippers left where they had been taken off. The washbasin wasn't particularly clean, the bed was unmade, there was an unemptied ashtray on the windowsill next to an open copy of the *Lancet*. But somehow it pleased her. It would need a good tidy, of course it would, and she would get round to it after the weekend, but the sight of his cufflinks on the dressing-table next to her earrings, his pyjama jacket dropped over her long-sleeved vest, the hot-water bottle on the floor, where, at some point in the night, he had kicked it out – all of it said, here is a comfortable space where life is shared, a nest with its twigs and moss.

She went down for her coat and scarf. She heard the scrape of the shovel. The sound pleased her more than she could have explained.

Outside, the cold caught in her throat. It made her eyes water. She stood by the back door, pulling her woollen hat over the tips of her ears. The child shifted in her. She shivered, partly from the cold, and set off across the garden. There was a fine surface of ice on top of the snow; each step was a breaking of the surface, then a sinking into the softer snow beneath. The sun threw her shadow to the left. It warmed one cheek. It made the snow hard to look at.

As she passed through the gate beside the tree, she saw Rita coming from the other side. They waved to each other. The field was less sheltered than the garden, and the snow had been blown into shallow dunes. She saw Rita stumble. 'All right?'

she called, her voice sharp as a bark in the brittle air. Rita waved again. They met more or less in the middle, touched each other's gloved hands, their faces flushed.

'Surviving?' asked Rita.

'Yes, thanks.'

'We're burning the furniture.'

'Are you?'

'Not yet, but soon.'

'How are the animals?'

'Oh, they don't mind it much. Bill brought them all inside. Do you want some milk? We can't get rid of it. The lorry can't get through.'

She offered the bag she was carrying. There were three bottles inside, one of them a wine bottle. They had improvised tops of tin foil and rubber bands. There was also a carrot in the bag and two pieces of coal.

'I've never actually made a snowman before,' said Irene. 'I don't know why not. We had snowball fights and things like that. What do we do?'

Rita was already doing it. 'It's just big snowballs,' she said. 'We roll them up like this.'

Irene bent to help. They worked either side of the ball with their heads almost touching, their breath in clouds, their shadows blue and restless over the broken snow.

'Any new horrible symptoms?'

'Nothing horrible,' said Irene. 'A bit up and down. Mostly up at the moment.' She turned her head to smile at Rita. 'And you?'

'Less tired, but I had a headache yesterday that made me want to bury my head in the snow. Bill said there was a god who gave birth to a daughter when his head exploded.'

'Athena,' said Irene. 'Or that was the daughter's name.'

'I thought you'd know,' said Rita.

The body was done. They started to roll a second ball. Irene began to find the bending awkward. She stood and stretched her back. Rita joined her. 'We mustn't give up,' she said.

'Definitely not,' said Irene.

'I suppose your husband can't see any of his patients. Are they dropping like flies?'

'He speaks to them on the phone. I think Gabby's seen some. Eric says he goes on skis.'

'Nothing stops Gabby,' said Rita. 'The man they couldn't kill. Has your husband ever delivered a baby?'

'He's done a few. Not first-time mothers.'

'Bill's delivered some four-legged ones. There's quite a lot of heaving involved. Bits of twine.'

They were quiet for a moment. Fear like a touch, a caress. And how *strange*, thought Irene, that she, who was going to have the child, should know so much less about it, the reality of it, than Eric, who was not. Her knowledge came from magazines, from obscure hints her mother dropped, from glimpses in films and novels. None of that would help her.

'If you're late and I'm early,' said Rita, 'we might be on the ward together.'

'I'd like that,' said Irene. And she thought she would, almost more than anything. To enter the machine together.

They set the new ball on top of the first and began to scrape up snow for the head.

'There was a woman giving birth in Devon,' said Rita. 'They sent the helicopter for her.'

'It's pretty bad in Devon, isn't it?'

'It's pretty bad here.'

'Was she all right?'

'The woman? I don't know. I think so.'

They lifted the head. The finished snowman was not much shorter than Rita. They discussed which way he should face and settled on east – towards the village and not looking at either of their houses. Rita screwed in the carrot for a nose; Irene gave him eyes of coal. They stood back to admire their work. They named the snowman David after the playwright.

'He wanted me to go to Middlesbrough with him,' said Rita.

'Did he? Why?'

'To wake up the working classes, I think.'

Irene smiled at her. She felt proud to have a working-class friend. 'Tessa should probably give him back to his wife,' she said.

'The wife might not want him,' said Rita.

At the edge of the field, by the shadow-line of the hedge, a dog, or something like a dog, raised its head into the light, studied them a moment, the two women upright in the bareness of the field, then dropped out of sight again, soundlessly.

Tuesday, 8 January

They had heard the whistle of a train the previous afternoon. Eric had managed to get down to the station to find out what was happening. (Every outing had a tinge of heroism to it.) The stationmaster was there. He wore a military greatcoat and was sowing the platforms with ashes and cinders. He said the plough had been through. You could get to Bristol and from there the line up to London was open. The other way was good as far as Weston, possibly Bridgwater. Of course, another storm like the last, or just a night of the wind blowing in the wrong direction . . .

'But you'll be able to get to the surgery, Doctor, if that's what you want.'

'That's it,' said Eric, and for several seconds they stood together at the platform's edge, like Russians in an old story, something with a title like 'Confusion'.

She made him breakfast. She made porridge with the last of the creamy milk Rita had given her. She made coffee and toast. The larder wasn't bare, but it would be in another a couple of days. She would try the village shop later, though she didn't know if it would be open, or if it was, if it would have anything in it.

She sat with him while he ate. He said the porridge tasted of wine. He grinned at her. She had shown him the bottles the milk had come in.

'You'll be glad to get back into the world, won't you?' she said.

'I can't leave poor old Gabby to do it all on his own. I'll be gladder still to get back here tonight. Looks fairly grim out there.'

They said their goodbyes at the front door. She fussed with his scarf. They kissed, lightly. He had shaved with the electric razor she had given him for Christmas. His skin was very smooth. He put on a dark green Loden cap. He didn't usually wear hats – he had the idea they made him look shifty – but today, partly for Irene, he would.

'I'm just going outside,' he said. 'I may be some time.'

She went to the dining-room window to watch him walk down the path he had cleared on the drive. Once he was on the lane – here, the going was harder – he turned and waved, and she waved back and went on watching until he was out of sight.

At the station there was a distinct feeling of wartime. It came back to him very easily, the uncertainty and boredom, the nagging hunger that was only partly to do with food. His time in the air force – he had got his wings though never completed his operational training – was a collection of small stories he had told once or twice then given up on. He rather despised people who seemed unable to move on from the war, though at the same time he understood very well what it was they missed.

There was no waiting room on this side of the station, the down line. People coughed; a woman hugged herself. Most, including Eric, smoked as they waited. It warmed you up a bit. A bell rang. The stationmaster crossed the line. The train was only fifteen minutes late. Five carriages, their floors slick with melted snow. He sat in a compartment near the rear of the train. The windows were fogged. He thought if he wiped them he might see his father out there. He wondered if it was high time he stopped imagining his father was following him about, watching him and judging.

He found Gabby at the surgery; Mrs Bolt had made it in too. There were three patients in the waiting room, none of them his. He went to his consulting room. He touched the radiator. It was on, just, but seemed to make no difference to the temperature of the room. He sat at the desk in his coat and looked at the messages Mrs Bolt had left for him. None looked especially urgent. If people couldn't see the doctor, perhaps they found they could take care of themselves. The last message was from Mrs Gurney, with regard to her husband, Peter. If Dr Parry was able to make a house call . . .

There was some mail too, New Year greetings from some of the pharmaceutical companies. One envelope contained a copy of the pathologist's report on Stephen Storey. There were no surprises. There had been enough chloral hydrate in his system to kill him twice over. It was no cry for help. It was definitive, and in part he admired it.

He put the report back into the envelope and the envelope into one of the drawers in his desk. He went back to the radiator and played around with the valve. Gabby knocked and came in.

'Morning, Gabby. Your room any warmer than this one?'

'Ice inside the window when I arrived this morning,' said Gabby. He was wearing a knitted grey polo neck under his jacket, on his feet what looked like climbing boots.

'The Romans understood central heating,' said Eric. 'Apparently they took the secret with them. Listen, is your car up to the weather? I'd like to see Peter Gurney if I can. I'd borrow your skis but I've never done it.'

Gabby dug the car keys from a trouser pocket. He tossed them over and Eric caught them.

'Irene likes the snow?' asked Gabby.

'Seems to. She built a snowman at the weekend with the farmer's wife.'

'With Rita Simmons,' said Gabby, and a look of quite unnecessary sadness came over his face.

Alone again, Eric went to the filing cabinet, took out the brown medical files of the patients he had to ring, sat at his desk, turned on the lamp and picked up the phone. One fall, though nothing broken, by the sound of it. The others were seasonal ailments, chest infections, two cases of what he assumed was flu. No lumps found in breasts, no appendixes about to burst. He was done inside forty minutes.

Mrs Bolt brought through a cup of tea. There was no biscuit, though he suspected she had some somewhere. Gabby got biscuits? He revolved his chair to look through the net curtains of his window. He knew and had always thought it strange that the word *chair* in French meant 'flesh'. A car passed slowly, headlights on. A minute later a bus went past, like a ferry in heavy weather. He thought of ringing Alison; he had, he knew, been thinking of it ever since he woke up. He had dreamed of her? He tried to weigh up the likelihood of Frank being at the house. He considered the different ways Frank might get to the office in Bristol. The main road was evidently all right with a bit of care, and probably better the closer you got to the city. And if he didn't want to drive, there were at least two small stations he could stop at to take a train. Either way, the odds were she was on her own, and if Frank did answer, he could say something about having a patient out his way, and what were the roads like? He swung back to the desk, picked up the receiver and dialled. He did not have to look up the number. He pictured her, slightly startled at the sound of the ringing, then resting her cigarette on the lip of the big ashtray, crossing the room. On bare feet? Surely not even Frank's house was warm enough for that now. He waited. She would say, through a smile, 'I thought it was you.' She would say something mock-dramatic about the snow. He would tell her about Gabby's skis. Or he would, to begin with, be slightly sullen, so she would understand the difficulties he was facing. He listened; the phone rang on. The pause between one ring and the next seemed unusually long, as if the ice on the line, on the wires that crossed the white landscape, the weight of the ice dragging the line down, stretching the copper, had somehow made the whole apparatus run more sluggishly. And suddenly he was unnerved, as a child might be halfway up or down an unlit staircase. He replaced the receiver and stared at the blotter on his desk. In one corner something was written in his own cramped handwriting. He couldn't read it at first. He tilted the head of the lamp, drew it closer, and saw that the word was *asylum*.

Irene went to the shop. She wore her boots. She had thick socks on and her warmest stockings. The snow, even where a sort of path had been made, sometimes came to the tops of her boots.

The shop was open – Mrs Case had, after all, only to come downstairs and put on the lights – and Irene was not the only customer. The old farmer, Mr Earle, was there, buying cigarettes, biscuits, tea. He picked out a tin of steak and kidney. Mrs Case asked if he was making a pie for himself.

'I'll just heat it up,' he said. He had large, red arthritic hands.

'It'll be very nice whatever you do,' said Mrs Case.

There were gaps on the shelves but the shelves were not empty. Irene put two tins of tomato soup into her basket, a box of Oxo cubes, what looked like the last bag of flour. There wasn't much in the vegetable rack, a few carrots and swedes (there was already talk of a vegetable shortage). She took a bag of sugar; she took a lemon for no reason but the shine of its waxed skin, its history of sunlight. Was there any meat?

'There's some rabbit,' said Mrs Case. She showed it, the thin, bloody haunches. 'The doctor got away on the train, then,' she said. It wasn't a question. She knew everything, sucked knowledge from the air, heard all footsteps.

'Yes,' said Irene. 'Thank goodness for trains.'

'Might not have 'em much longer,' said Mr Earle. He had lit one of his newly purchased cigarettes. Mrs Case put an ashtray on the counter for him.

For a few minutes, in the frigid air of the shop, they discussed Dr Beeching and the closure of the branch lines. This winter might give them a reprieve, show the government their worth. A bus was a poor replacement for a train. As for cars, Mr Earle did not have one and neither did Mrs Case.

Irene carried her shopping home. She thought about Mr Earle, his life in the bungalow. Was he in his sixties? Farming had probably been a struggle he was glad to give up, though sometimes, even now, he must wake in the early morning imagining the animals were waiting for him and his life still had some purpose. What did he do now? Drink tea, smoke, look at the paper? Her own parents were not old – upper-middle-class people aged more slowly, of course – but how long before she looked at one or other and saw, gazing back with rheumy eyes, an old man, an old woman? Yes, they would grow old and die.

She would visit their graves once a year and throw away the dead flowers. And she in her turn would die, and her child would put flowers on her grave. And then the child would grow old and die, and the child's child, and so on until it all stopped, countless little lives, her own perfectly invisible among so many. Mrs Case, Mr Earle, Eric, the Duckworths. Even Gabby. So much dying and nobody really knowing what it was for. She turned onto the drive and walked past her own footprints. Her thoughts had not depressed her, they had not brought a sense of futility. If anything, they had made her feel lighter.

In the kitchen she unpacked the basket onto the table. She boiled the kettle and prepared some tea. While it brewed she rested her hands on top of the Aga. She was lucky, she knew it. The universe might be a vast purposeless toy slowly winding down but she had a warm house. Think of the creatures out there in their burrows, shivering, barely alive, their terror of the cold. She poured her tea and sipped it. Was the house, though, slightly less warm than yesterday? She touched the nearest radiator, then put on her boots again and went out of the back door to look at the gauge on the oil tank. She rubbed the frost from it. The needle lay at the bottom of the dial. She knocked on the tank's steel side and it gave back a drunken, hollow sound. She returned to the kitchen and shook more coke into the Aga. They could manage for a few days. The lanes would be cleared soon and the tanker would come. It was no great hardship. Had she not grown up through a war? She finished her tea, went into the drawing room, got onto her knees and laid a fire. There was coal in the scuttle, there was wood stacked up. She had no reason to suppose there wasn't plenty of coal in the bunker at the back of the house.

The fire caught and brightened. An odd urge to sing to it. She stood (here is the animal standing, a female, gravid) then went up the stairs to the bedroom. She started with the bed, stripped off the sheets. After washing and mangling she would put the rack by the fire and finish them off on top of the Aga. She spread new sheets on the bed. She could do hospital corners.

When the bed was made she fetched the Ajax and a scourer from the cupboard in the bathroom. She cleaned the sink under the Arnolfinis. They watched, or *he* watched. She tidied the bits and pieces on the dressing-table. She emptied the ashtray into the wastebin and put the bin by the door. She picked clothes off the chair. She sniffed one of his shirts and decided it could go into the tub with the sheets. Mondays were washdays but Tuesday would do: there wasn't a law.

She folded his pyjamas. She folded the cream Guernsey he'd been wearing at the weekend and placed it in the woollens drawer, smoothing it. She held up his tweed jacket. She tried to remember how you cleaned tweed. She thought you probably just steamed it. If she hung it in the bathroom, suspended it over the bath while she had a soak? First, however, with a little washing powder and warm water, she would sponge it. She fetched a towel, fetched a bowl (it was the same she had used with Tessa but it was perfectly clean now). She spread the towel on the bedroom floor, laid the jacket on top. She was on her knees again but she didn't mind. She was working; she was adding to the list of things she would be able to say to herself at the end of the day she had done. He had, of course, things in his pockets. She took out a prescription pad. She took out two pens, a matchbox, a sweet wrapper, an envelope. The car keys! She pressed the jacket with her palms to be sure she had got everything. She dipped her sponge into the soapy water. She started dabbing around the collar, then placed the sponge back in the bowl and picked up the envelope. Blue ink, a free-moving hand. Big D for Doctor, big P for Parry. She turned it, then lifted it to her face and sniffed it. She could smell Eric, a tangle of scents that included the surgery, the car, his body and the tweed itself. And beneath it another scent, not strong but quite distinct (aniseed, iris, vanilla). The envelope had been opened with a blade rather than a finger. She parted the lips, reached in, and drew out the single sheet of paper. She read it (*the silk touches me in a way that makes me long . . .*), then read it a second time, looking for several seconds at the name and address on the embossed heading. After a third and final reading she returned the paper to the envelope and replaced the envelope back among the other things she had taken from his pockets. She dipped the sponge and squeezed out the water, then sat back on her heels, peering around the room as if she had never seen it before.

Gabby had a Morris Minor. Its colour was the green of bathroom fittings. It wasn't the latest model. A split windscreen, the dash bare as a Jeep's. On the passenger seat there was an alarm clock. It had a loud, insistent tick. When Eric sat in the car and closed the door, it was all he could hear. It would be like travelling with a time bomb. He pulled out onto the main road. The bulldozed snow was thrust up at the sides of the road, in places as high as a man. He drove at twenty miles an hour. He passed houses with lights on, with smoke drifting from the chimneys. He saw trees holding what must be half a ton of snow and ice. There was almost no one out of doors. A woman pulling her shopping behind her on a sledge waved at him, at the car. One of Gabby's patients, presumably. He waved back.

When he reached the road that Peter Gurney's house was on, he could go no further. The side roads, the residential streets, had not been cleared. He left the car in the yard of a small industrial site, a candle factory. With the threat of black-outs, it was probably a good time to be making candles. He crossed the main road and waded through the snow to the Gurneys' house. He almost walked past it. Everything was altered, disguised. He rang the bell and waited, shuffling in his boots. He rang again. A boy's face showed at a downstairs window. Eric waved and pointed to the front door. Another short wait and the door was opened by Mrs Gurney. He entered the house, took off his boots and stood in his socks on the purple carpet. The boy was there too. Eric smiled at him. 'Why isn't there a snowman out there?' He gestured to the garden. The boy looked at his mother. She was wearing a thick jumper that probably belonged to her husband. Her hair was shorter and it looked like she might have cut it herself, in a mirror, by candlelight.

'I'll pop up, then,' said Eric. He started on the stairs, climbing from the dimness of the hall to the subtler dark above, the grey snow-light that filtered through the window at the end of the corridor. The door of the sickroom was shut. He raised his fist to knock then let it drop, turned the handle and went in. The room was icy. When he drew back the curtains, he saw the window was open and that there was snow on the carpet. Peter Gurney was in the bed, eyes shut, mouth slack. Eric leaned over him; he touched his throat. He drew back the covers. Blue pyjamas, a pair of thick black socks on his feet. He pulled the covers up again. How long had he been lying like this? Two days? A week? He went back down the stairs. The boy was gone but the woman was still there. She looked proud in a fragile way, defiant, as if daring him to punish her, strike her, even. Then she stepped forwards and rested her forehead against his chest.

Later, he used the telephone to speak to the undertakers. They would come in the morning. It was Phillips and Sons. They had collected his father from the cottage. They were perfectly reliable. The snow would not stop them.

*

At the end of the day he came home on the train. He had, foolishly, not brought a torch, and more than once he stumbled as he went up the lane. He let himself into the house. It was about seven o'clock. He took off his boots and coat, hung up the Loden cap. In the dark of the drawing room the fire was almost out. He put on a light then worked with the poker, put fresh coal on the fire. He used the bellows. When he was satisfied, he went through to the kitchen and poured himself a drink. Had she gone to bed already? It was possible. She had done that a few times since she had become pregnant, spent half the day in bed, but not recently. He looked into the slow oven of the Aga. There was a pot in there, a steel casserole. He took it out and lifted the lid. A smell of herbs, and something sweet, slightly musty. He fetched a spoon and tasted it, then went upstairs. The bedroom had been tidied (though for some reason the unemptied waste bin was still by the door). The bed was made. On the bedspread there was a sheet of writing paper from his study, a note that said she was feeling very tired and would sleep in the spare room.

There were three spare rooms – or three until the baby came. He knew which of them she wouldn't be in. He went down to the other end of the house, the two small rooms above the garage. He opened the door of the first and leaned in. Was she there? Yes, she was there. He sensed her as much as saw her.

'All right?' he whispered. 'Need anything?'

There was no answer. He closed the door and went back to the kitchen. He finished his drink and poured himself another. In his black bag he had the mixture from Peter Gurney's house. If he wanted a proper drink, he could try a teaspoon of that. He grinned at the black window. He ate his supper out of the casserole, standing up at the Aga. He had no idea what the meat was;

he didn't like it much. When he had finished, he sat in the drawing room to watch television. If he had it on low it wouldn't disturb her. He recognised the programme, an American courtroom drama, part of a series about a father-and-son legal team who defended tough cases. It wasn't unintelligent, or it wasn't unintelligent for television. He lit a cigarette. The day haunted him but the day was over. A woman was apparently arranging her own murder. She paid a man to shoot her. The man was nervous. He was a killer but he'd never done anything like this before. The woman checked her hair in the mirror, then calmly turned to face him. 'Are you ready, Mr Jones?'

The picture failed before the programme finished but he could see how it was going to turn out. He sat on, watching the static or whatever it was, the scattering of photons, the storm behind the thick curved glass of the screen. The screen was about the same size as a window in an airliner, but this wasn't a plane, it was a spacecraft. By morning they would be in a new galaxy. A sun would rise but a different sun. He would wake Irene and show her. Her face would be bathed in the glow of it, both their faces. The thought made his eyes fill, though he could not quite see what it was he had touched in himself. He switched off the television, banked the fire and went upstairs. The bedroom was cold. He changed into pyjamas but kept on his socks. He cleaned his teeth at the basin. He looked at the picture of Arnolfini and his wife. There was a dent in it he hadn't noticed before, a half-moon, almost a tear, in the man's black hat. He probed it with a finger, then sat at the end of the bed, wondering if he could be bothered to go down and fetch tea for the Teasmade.

Wednesday, 9 January

The milk yield was down – the lowest since he'd started – but as there was no one to collect it, it hardly mattered. The lanes had been partly cleared by tractors and shovels (he had played a small, though not, he thought, inglorious part in this). It was possible the lorry would get down before the week was out. Until then, whatever they couldn't use on the farm or sell through the village shop, he poured down the milking-parlour drain. The hens were all right. Rita made them a kind of porridge in the morning with corn and scraps. There were fewer eggs and they were smaller, but the hens, who didn't much care for rain, seemed to find the snow quite interesting.

The bull worried him, but the bull always did. When he came back, he might try it in the barn with a couple of the cows he was pretty confident weren't pregnant, see if the cold was no impediment. Alternatively, he might have it towed away and turned into corned beef.

He had a breakfast of fried eggs and Camp coffee. He lit the fire in the office. There was a small front room but they rarely used it, and it was now impossibly cold. He heard the bath running. At some point the pipes would freeze. He hoped it wasn't while he was away. In an emergency she could always go to the doctor's house. No doubt things were snug enough over there.

In the bedroom he changed out of his overalls and peeled off most of the layers beneath, things he had reached for in the dark of five-thirty. He kept on his long johns and vest, put on a clean shirt, a pair of woollen trousers. He chose a tie, a V-neck sweater (maroon), then shrugged himself into the Donegal jacket. He looked for clean socks, couldn't find any and kept on the ones he was wearing. He went down to the bathroom. The door was shut. He knocked. 'Decent?'

'Is that the milkman?'

He went in. She was in the bath. The heater was in there and the room smelt strongly of paraffin. He crouched by the side of the bath. She looked at him. He wiped a drop of water from her cheek.

'Teddy's coming at four to do the cows.'

'They'll probably like that,' she said. She was sitting in the water with her knees to her chest.

'One day,' he said, 'we'll have a bathroom you can grow lemons in.'

She grinned. In the water, no make-up, she looked very young, or somehow young and old at the same time. (Stanhope had once said he did not believe in childhood. It was an odd thing to say, though they were at the bottom of a bottle of port. Easier, really, not to believe in adulthood.)

'You'll be all right?'

She nodded.

'You're sure?'

She nodded again. 'Good luck,' she said.

He kissed her shoulder. 'If the trains are buggered, I'll be back in an hour.'

He had packed a holdall. He carried it down and placed it by the front door. He checked the fire in the office. He shook more coal into the Rayburn. The cat watched him. 'Try to be nice,' he said.

He drove out of the yard, caught between the exhilaration of setting off and a nagging disquiet at leaving Rita and the animals. Already people were saying it was worse than forty-seven. Colder, more unrelenting. It wasn't just rivers that were frozen. For a mile from the Kent coast, the sea had turned to pack ice. A mile! Nobody could remember anything like that. But it was just for a couple of days, and Teddy knew infinitely more about farming than he did, certainly about cows. And later, years from now, he might look back at this – the Gipsy edging across the snow, like Lieutenant Kijé's sleigh – as one of the great moments of his life, the act of daring that changed everything.

At the station he enquired about the line. The stationmaster was cautiously optimistic. Trains were getting through on the main lines. He couldn't answer for the branch lines, of course. The picture was complicated.

'*Caveat emptor*,' said Bill.

The stationmaster nodded. He shifted a column of tarnished pennies half an inch to the side. Bill went out to the platform. Among the clutch of people on the opposite platform he saw the doctor. They were wearing almost identical dark green caps. They nodded to each other across the vagaries of air, then looked away, in different directions, like dogs picking up a scent.

On waking, lying in the morning dimness of the spare room, she had cried again. When she heard Eric leave she cried more openly, more passionately, then got up and used the bathroom, went down to make tea, looked, once, at his plate and cup on the table, then stood with her back to the Aga, staring out of the window at the snow.

In her memory of the day before a woman was changed – but changed to what? She had wanted to fall and been surprised that she hadn't. Fall and hit her head on the edge of the washbasin so that when he came back he'd find her teeth all over the bedroom floor like a broken necklace. She had howled (in an English cottage) and pictured the unborn, the tiny red stoma of its mouth, stretched into a howl of its own. You go mad among familiar things. What you learn, you learn too quickly. And not some comical vileness about a woman in silk, a woman who *writes it down*, but about herself, her self-deceiving, her part in a farce. And thank God she had not seen herself like that, in the grip of it, had not carelessly glimpsed herself in a mirror. She would never be free of it. She would have turned herself to stone.

Then it was like acting. She couldn't keep it up. She had slumped. The first shock was over. She had legs still, arms. She could see. She could pass for human. She had gone on with the day (it seemed incredible to her now). She had cut up rabbit meat to make a stew. She had smoked half a cigarette and thrown up in the downstairs loo. At tea-time or whenever it was she wrote three notes on paper from his study, burned two in the fire, left one on the bed.

He had leaned in at some point. Had she been the kind of woman who puts a boning knife through a man's chest, that would have been her moment. He would, for a second, have thought it just the blackness of the room flinging itself at him.

She drank her tea, put her mug in the sink and stood under the kitchen clock. Subtract five hours. She found, somewhat frighteningly, that she couldn't, or not without difficulty. She understood she was exhausted; she understood she would remain so. Among the things that had been taken from her was rest.

In her fist she had a piece of paper. She went to the bottom of the stairs, lifted the receiver and dialled the operator. When the operator answered, Irene gave her the address and the number, replaced the receiver and waited. Sometimes it took half an hour or more, but today the operator called back after a few minutes and put her through. It was Morris who answered. He was groggy and had, quite obviously, been asleep. Irene apologised.

'Don't worry about it,' he said. 'I'd have to get up in a little while anyway.'

He asked her about the snow. She told him. He said they'd had some too, just a little. More later, probably. He had such a kind voice. You wanted to ask him questions, quite difficult ones, just to hear him explain.

She heard Veronica: 'Who the *hell* is it?' The phone was passed over. Each detail of this, the sounds of movement in the American morning, was fragile and precious.

'Irene?'

'Hello.'

'It's not Mummy or Daddy, is it?'

'What? No, no.'

'And the baby?'

'The baby's all right. It's fine.'

'It's just that, darling, it's not quite six o'clock. A faculty party last night. A reception for the new vice-provost. There's a drink called a Manhattan. Very unwise. Are you sure you're all right?'

'Yes.'

'Well, that's good. You know, I think I might have been dreaming of you. I think we were wearing those pleated checked skirts. Do you remember them?'

'What were we doing?'

'In the dream? Lord knows. Waiting, I think.'

'I dream about you too,' said Irene.

'Of course you do, darling.' There was the click of a lighter. Morris was asked to bring an ashtray. 'But one interesting thing that *did* happen last night was a conversation with a man called Stone. He's head of department. He's basically your boss, isn't he, Morris? And he's been trying to persuade me to study again, study properly, and said it was high time the college had some female professors. There's only two in the entire place and one is so ancient she claims to have met Emily Dickinson. Is that possible, Morris?'

'Numerically possible. If she'd been a young child.'

'Anyway, darling, I think it's all rather exciting. Can you imagine your sis as a professor? I thought the stern but sexy sort.'

'Stone,' said Irene.

'He's the sub-dean of liberal arts. Moustache like a walrus.'

'Associate dean,' called Morris. He was further off now, dressing or speaking through the open door of the bathroom. Irene had a clear mental picture of their house though she had never set foot in it.

'Associate dean,' said Veronica, a voice full of smoke. 'It's worse than the army. They're obsessed with titles. You're not frightened about the baby, are you, darling?'

'No.'

'And Eric's fighting fit?'

'He takes the train now because you can't drive in the lanes. Or not in his car. It's very low to the ground.'

Veronica started laughing, something about the idea of a car low to the ground. A *low* car. She told Morris.

'It's a Citroën,' said Morris (closer now). 'They have pneumatic suspension. Hydro-pneumatic. The car rises when it's started.'

'Does it?' asked Veronica.

'Yes,' said Irene. 'I think it does.'

When she finished the call she sat on the stairs for a minute then stood up and called her mother. At the sound of her mother's voice she shook. She was almost sick again. Somehow, she spoke. Her mother was magnificent. She didn't even seem surprised. She was equal to it. She gave instructions very calmly.

Bill changed trains in Bristol. So far so good. The London train was waiting on platform three. He had time to buy a newspaper. He would read about the cricket. He would think about sport and nothing else. The idea pleased him immensely. A group of nuns was boarding the train. He didn't know what sort they were. They had enormous white starched linen hats that only just fitted through the carriage doors. They weren't called hats, he knew that. Wimples? But that wasn't right either.

He found a seat in a compartment with a soldier, two men who looked like commercial travellers, and a woman he decided was a librarian. He sat next to the soldier and opposite the woman. The soldier lit a cigarette, cupping the match in his hands to shield it from a wind that wasn't there. On the platform there were nuns saying goodbye to the nuns on the train.

'Daughters of Charity,' said the woman. Her voice was aimed at Bill but loud enough for the others.

'Extraordinary headgear,' said one of the men.

The echoing blasts of a whistle. They pulled slowly from the shed into the morning snow-light of the unbeautiful city. A sky the colour of sheep's wool. Idle cranes above an unfinished tower block. Bill settled back and opened his paper. There wasn't much cricket news; the third Test was still two days away (Smith was out and Murray was in; some speculation as to whether the Sydney ground would take spin).

He read a story about big, bustling Christine Truman, the will-she-won't-she girl of British tennis, who had solved the mystery of why she quit Australia in just three words: loneliness, depression and weight. There was a picture of her at a foggy London airport with her mother. She didn't look fat, she looked strong. The sort of woman who, when she was through with tennis, might make an excellent farmer's wife. On the same page was a small article about a statue of a madonna in Sicily that had started weeping tears of gold. How could you make sense of people who believed in weeping statues and at the same time had practically invented organised crime? At some point these things must touch. He closed his eyes. He thought that the woman, the librarian, might be watching him, but he didn't mind. The movement of the train gentled him towards sleep. The soldier lit another of his small, bitter cigarettes. Very slowly, the paper slid from Bill's lap.

Irene packed her case. It turned out it could all be done. Opening and shutting drawers, choosing a dress, picking between two tops. A hairband, a nightie. In her purse she had only a pound note, two half-crowns, a threepenny bit. She went downstairs, through the dining room and into Eric's study. The smell of him, his cigarettes, the smell of the books, of old journals. She knew he kept money in the desk, in a spare wallet. Reserve cash. She found the wallet. It had three five-pound notes in it. She took one. She would find a way of returning the money. She would ask her father. In the drawer with the wallet was a box, and inside the box a watch she had never seen before. She held it to her ear. It was ticking. The time looked right. She would have to hurry.

When she was ready, the case packed and nothing to do but this, she took the letter from the pocket of his tweed jacket. The jacket was in the wardrobe; she had hung it there with everything returned exactly as she had found it, the prescription pad, the keys. (Was that cunning? Was she cunning?) She took the letter down to the kitchen and propped it on the table against the wooden fruit bowl, facing the door he was most likely to come in by.

She put on her sheepskin coat, tied on a headscarf. She put on gloves and boots. Briefly, her nerve failed in her. She wanted, almost desperately, to lie in bed with a hot-water bottle, lie there for days, catatonic. Outside, the cold examined her immediately. She started to walk up the drive, the blue case in her right hand, her breath in rags over her shoulder. At the station there were three cars outside. Two looked like they'd been there a long time, their roofs heaped with snow; the other she recognised as Bill's car, the thing like a Land Rover but not. She braced herself to meet him. She practised a line in her head. She imagined her smile. The ticket hall was empty. She swapped her boots for a pair of shoes from the case. She left her boots with the others. No idea when she might pick them up. They might end up in Lost Property. They might be sold in the spring.

She went to the ticket window and the stationmaster greeted her. 'Change at Bristol, then Reading, then Guildford. After that you'll have to see what's best. Can't tell you from here. You'll go by Crawley, perhaps.'

She thanked him and watched him pick tickets out of a drawer. She paid him and he counted out her change.

'Bristol train in fifteen minutes, if he's on time.'

She went onto the platform. One man but not Bill, not anyone, she thought, from the village (smart overcoat, green trilby, face like a bird). She went into the waiting room and sat, from habit, beside the fireplace, though there was no fire in it. She dabbed her nose with a tissue, a sheet of pink loo paper, then balled it up and hid it in her sleeve.

At Waterloo, Bill moved down the platform in the wake of the nuns. The woman in his compartment had informed them that the headgear was called a *cornette*. Now, the white of the starched cloth against the gloom of the station, he thought they were like a flock of gulls.

The station was busy, dizzying. The rest of the country might be grinding to a halt but the capital was, apparently, undaunted. (London can take it! St Paul's above the smoke of last night's raid, a whistling milkman picking his way over rubble. Some of that was true, some of it just part of a story the country had not yet grown tired of telling itself . . .)

A woman's voice recited the arrivals and departures. Crane your neck and you could see her up in her glass booth. Half the trains, certainly the long-distance ones – Padstow, Exeter, Portsmouth – were delayed or cancelled. He had, perhaps, been lucky to get through.

He bought a cup of tea and a bun at a kiosk. The attendant took his money with mittened hands. It was two years since he was last in London; he had not expected to be so excited by it, his return. He watched, with deep pleasure and an odd sense of involvement, a man buying flowers at a stall. Flowers in the depth of winter! He watched porters flinging sacks of mail into the back of a van; he caught the dreaming smile of a woman, who passed, briskly, dressed he thought for the West End, a smart day out at the shops, tea at Fortnum & Mason.

When he left the station he found it was snowing again, not heavily but steadily. The streets were slush and shovelled grey snow. He caught a bus going south, got down at the Elephant and Castle. He could walk from here, preferred to. The snow was the type you could enjoy – big flakes in no hurry to arrive, goose-down, not the grit of ice that raked your face in the big storms. He set off down Walworth Road. Unlike the Elephant and Castle, where the wrecking ball and the bulldozers were making an almighty mess of the mess already made by the Luftwaffe (no phoenix rising there), Walworth Road was more or less as he remembered it. Buildings in their blackness seemed like ruins, and some of them were. A woman passed him pushing a pram. There was no baby in the pram; it was full of coal. He glanced through the window of a café where men and women, still wearing their coats, bent over plates of fried food. The market, Clubland, Baldwin's the herbalists, the slender turret of the church (it took a direct hit in 1940), he recognised it all, but he had always been an outsider here. No one was going to step out of a pub or a bookie's to clap his shoulder. He was six when they sent him to his first prep school, an hour on the train out of Waterloo, his tin trunk in the guard's wagon, the compartment's bristly seat irritating the backs of his bare legs. That first school was the sort of place Dickens might have recognised, Orwell certainly, though he had no recollection of ever being homesick. He had not run away or attempted to harm himself. He had been beaten, though not buggered, for which he knew he must be grateful. His first summer he won a small brass medal for the long jump. Home, it turned out, had been the perfect preparation for not being at home.

As he walked, he tried to remember what it was in his father he should appeal to. His father was not an obviously greedy man. His interest in money was layered and hard to locate. In the holdall, Bill had the Manila file he had shown to Harrison at the bank. He had finessed it, checked the figures a third and a fourth time (he had them by heart now, like poetry). He would pitch it somewhere between swagger and deference, make it sound as if the scheme was not an abandoned aerodrome and five hundred head of cattle that did not, to all intents and purposes, exist, but something actual and solid that his father was being brought into at the last moment as an act of filial generosity, a settling of debts.

He entered the square. The garden at its centre, the plane trees as tall as the houses, was solemn with fresh snow. The railings, which had been removed during the war – was anything ever made with them? Could you make Spitfires out of old railings? – had been replaced. There was no traffic. He walked in the middle of the road between the parked cars under their fur of snow. The short afternoon was already giving up, the dusk descending from the bare canopies of the trees. Turn back? Something seemed to say it. If he could have been confident of catching a train he might have done it, but the woman up in the glass booth shook her head and, anyway, it was too late to lose his nerve now, to reinvent the day. As he turned the first corner of the square, the unlit windows of the house greeted him, the prodigal. He saw that the neighbouring houses had been smartened up in the last couple of years. Their cream paint was fresh; they had no long rust-coloured stains running down their faces. His father's house stood between them shamefully, though also with a shrug of indifference.

He pressed the bell. It was answered by a man he had not seen before, short, with oiled black hair, his eyes and cheekbones suggesting some connection to an old colony – Singapore, Aden, Sarawak. He was, evidently, a servant. There was always a servant in the house; they came and went. Most were people who owed his father rent. They put on the white jacket with the steel buttons rather than face eviction. The same jacket was used again and again.

'Hello,' said Bill. 'I'm Bill.'

The man stood aside. Bill edged past him into the L-shaped hall. He put down his holdall, hung his hat next to his father's (was Togoland still in the Empire? Samoa?) and started into the house. If anything had changed here, it had changed very little. The same excess of furniture, of pieces stranded rather than placed, as though carried in on the tide. The Heal's sideboard, the antique French chairs with legs like whippets, the big sun-faded salmon-pink sofa with the strange stains on it, so that you would not be surprised to see it roped off as a crime scene. The next room had a billiard table. That at least was new, some inspiration of his brother's presumably; their father played no games of any kind, seemed not to understand what they were.

He found his mother in her room at the back of the house, a small withdrawing room, a closet, a sort of boudoir, windowless. She was sitting on the daybed. She looked up at him as he stood by the open door. She was smoking. There was an empty glass on the floor by her feet.

'You're letting the heat out,' she said. It wasn't said unpleasantly.

He kissed her. There were magazines, cushions. The dark green wallpaper might have dated from the house's beginnings. A two-bar electric fire threw a watery opal light against her shins. He paused to let her ask about his journey. When she didn't, he said, 'Where's Dad?'

'He's in the shelter. He's waiting for you.'

'The air-raid shelter?'

'He's made a steam room in there,' she said. She looked at him helplessly. 'He's been ever so excited about seeing you. Ask Colin for a towel.'

'Who's Colin?'

'He answered the door, didn't he?'

Bill nodded. 'And Dad's waiting for me?'

'He's not been very well, Billy.'

'You look well,' he said, though she didn't. Her life was coming out in her face in ways that couldn't be disguised. He would say to Rita, Mum's a complete ruin, and as for Dad . . .

She held up her glass. 'And tell Colin to put the other half in here. Today, if he pleases.'

He took the glass. The first lesson any new servant was taught, perhaps the only important lesson, was how each member of the household liked their alcohol served. He found Colin in the large, cream-tiled 1930s kitchen. Something meaty was boiling on the stove. He handed Colin the glass; Colin gave him a towel. The kitchen had a window overlooking the small garden. Smoke gusted from a stack at one end of the Anderson shelter's earthed-over roof. There was no snow on the roof, and for a yard all around the shelter, the grass was a vivid, improbable green.

'What do I do?' asked Bill. 'Get changed and run out there?'

'That's about the size of it,' said Colin. His voice was pure south London. He had been born, perhaps, not far from there.

As they pulled into Reading the guard walked through singing, 'All change!'

The journey had been uneventful. There was no one on the train Irene knew. No one had questioned her right to be there. No one had asked her where she was going or why. It was snowing again. She couldn't remember where it had started. Swindon? Didcot?

She changed platforms, going up and down deserted concrete stairways. She was cold. Her feet were very cold. She thought with real longing of her boots at the station in the village. She asked a man if this was the right platform for the Guildford train. He wore a bowler hat, the rim collecting snow. He assured her that this was indeed the right platform, or if it wasn't they were both lost. He laughed. 'We could end up in Peking.'

Irene smiled and walked away, hoping to find somewhere to get a cup of tea and perhaps a sandwich. There was nowhere. A train pulled in. There were no announcements. She went back to the man in the bowler hat. 'Do you think this is the Guildford train?'

'I will if you will,' he said. He opened a carriage door for her and she climbed up. There were three others in the compartment, all men. She had her ticket tucked into the wrist of her glove. One of the men lit a pipe (so much fussing to light a pipe, they must like that too). One of the others drew a folded copy of *The Times* from the pocket of his Gannex. He was opposite her and she read the headlines. Threat of power cuts for the whole of the South. Gaitskell in hospital still but rather better. A tattooed man had been arrested in connection with the Co-op murder.

They began their journey.

'Guildford station,' said the man who she had asked about the trains, who had sat beside her and who now had his bowler hat on his lap, 'is thirty miles and twenty-seven chains from London Waterloo.'

'Is it?'

'I wonder if you can tell me how long a chain is?'

'I don't think I know,' she said.

'Oh, have a guess.'

'Half a mile?'

'Now that would put Waterloo somewhere in Suffolk, wouldn't it?'

She shook her head. His eyes, blue, small, were like a child's, though she thought he was probably only a few years younger than her father. His chin where he had shaved it looked painfully raw.

'Have another guess,' he said. 'Three guesses and you're out.'

The man reading the paper said, 'Twenty-two yards.' He spoke without putting the paper down, a bored voice, as if many times he had answered the same question in much the same circumstances.

'Yes. That's right,' said the man beside Irene. He sat back, his smile tightening. 'Twenty-two yards. You'll remember that now.'

She looked out of the window. There was nothing much to see, just the spinning of the snow against a white sky and a white land. The man with the paper turned the page. The engine whistled. She wondered if there was a restaurant car on the train. She should go and look, but she felt ridiculously tired. She had slept only an hour or two last night and it was catching up with her. When the guard came, she would ask him; she would lean forwards and say, Excuse me, is there a restaurant car? And the guard would say, Two carriages back, Madam. Then, after a decent pause, and careful not to catch the eye of any of the men, she would get up and go back two carriages, and there would be a woman working in the car, a cheerful sort a bit like Rita, and while she was pouring the tea from a big metal pot, they might have a completely harmless sort of chat . . .

The man beside her was sitting very close. She felt his heat. She leaned slightly towards the window, feigned an interest in the nothing happening outside, shifted her weight an inch away from him. It was hard to tell how fast they were going. Not very, she thought. The engine whistled again. The sound was almost visible – a tattered pennant streaming in the wind. The dotted line of a fence climbed a hill towards a spinney of black trees. She saw the flicker of horses in a field beside the track. Were they racing the train? Three, four horses, stretched in the gallop, the snow kicked up behind them. Something in her went out to meet them – how wonderfully alive they were! How unconcerned! – then she clipped her forehead against the window glass and came almost to her feet with the force of the train's braking. A parcel shot from the overhead rack. Luckily it didn't hit anyone. The train screamed and juddered to a halt. The carriage rocked, once, and was still.

'Tigers on the line,' said the man beside her. 'No cause for alarm.'

They sat. She rubbed her head discreetly. After a few minutes the man with the newspaper started to read it again. No one left and no one came. The snow fell. A chain, she thought, is twenty-two yards. He was right: she wouldn't forget it. With her gloved hands she squeezed her knees. She was cold and hungry and alarmingly close to tears. She was, in truth, starting to feel unwell. She couldn't imagine why nobody did anything, why they were all just sitting there getting colder and colder. Then, at last, the guard. He came by along the corridor. He didn't stop or even glance in at them. He was hurrying, the keys on his belt jangling. She waited for him to come back. He would, surely, have to come back. He had gone one way and would, eventually, return. She waited. He didn't return. Fifteen minutes passed, twenty.

'I'm expecting,' she heard herself say.

The man with the pipe frowned. The man opposite lowered his paper just enough to look at her over the top of it. After a few seconds, the man beside her (one half-turn of the bowler hat) said, 'Consider us informed.'

The voices arrived about two hours after Bill had left. She was in the kitchen making tea and it was like an insect had flown past her ear. She had been waiting for them. She didn't think they would waste such an opportunity, their girl (their 'gal' as the American-sounding one called her) all alone, no one to run to, blub blub, boo-hoo. They were not loud, not yet. They were exploring the house, making themselves at home. It was better sometimes just to let them be, not to rile them. She was in the office now, looking at the milking figures in the ledger. Through her hands she turned the red-rimmed gauge Bill had found at the aerodrome. She liked it. It was made for a measurable world. If the voices began to be angry with her – and they would, for they, too, could not help themselves, they, too, were driven forwards – she might hold up the gauge like a charm. It might impress them, buy her a few minutes. It was the sort of thing people did in the stories she liked to read.

The phone still worked. That was something. She tried Irene. When it was obvious there would be no answer, she went up to the bathroom and looked out across the field. The doctor's house was a house in a fairytale. White roof, white garden. There were no lights on and she could see no smoke from the chimneys, though she couldn't be sure, not with a gusting wind and a white sky.

In the bedroom she slid out her lingerie drawer and checked on her supply of pills. She knew what was there, more or less – Nembutal, Seconal, three or four Dexamyl; some chloral hydrate (to be mixed with the Nembutal for several hours of something like non-existence). Did pills go off? Most of these dated from Pow-Wow days. Or did the cold preserve them, like the apples in the next room? She made a pattern of them, a spiral on top of the chest of drawers, then swept them into her hand and returned them to their home in the cup of a black bullet bra. They were perfectly well hidden there. Bill was not the type of man who explored a woman's lingerie drawer.

In the office she tended the fire. She smoked. She leafed through copies of *Farmers Weekly*. Heaven knows when the library van would be back. Would the librarian find her attractive once he realised she was pregnant? Would he still leave the box on the van floor? And was it very sad she hoped to be found attractive by a man who meant nothing to her, who, if he touched her, she would bite?

The voices found the office. They hung fatly in the air, trying to draw her into conversation. At fifteen, when it started, she'd thought she was Joan of Arc. God was speaking to her, but God with his mouth full, God with a stocking mask on, like a bank robber. It took weeks to know them for what they were, pub bores, dreary assassins, men who, when asked why they had strangled the girl and left her body in the woods, would genuinely have no idea. One had become very clever at impersonating her father. It was going on about something long ago; it knew things her father didn't. The others were waiting to see how she took it. She picked up the phone to try

Irene again, but put it down without dialling. She stood and went out to the front door, started pulling on boots, coat, scarf, hat. She went out to the yard. It was better there. She felt steadier. The snow had tidied the yard, everything but the midden, which melted whatever fell on it. She pulled her hat down over her ears and entered the orchard. The trees – each bough with its load, each twig rimed. Here and there, in the net of bare branches, an apple hung like red glass.

Out of the gate she began to cross the field. There was something curious about the acoustics of walking in snow that created the impression of an unseen companion close behind her. It was hard going. She had liked the snow at first but now she wanted it to disappear. She came to the snowman. He had lost his nose and she wondered who or what had taken it. The eyes were still there, the blank staring towards the village.

By the time she reached the cottage garden, her breath was hot in her mouth and her legs ached. She tapped at the back door. It'll be cosy in there, she thought. I'll tell her everything. She waited, tapped again, peering through the glass panel in the door, peering from one world into another, then followed the path around the side of the house to the front door. She rang the bell. She should have brought eggs again and she hadn't. There was a muddle of footsteps in the snow around the door. They led towards the drive, the gate, the lane. She returned to the back of the house. She looked through the kitchen window, put her nose right up against it. What if a stranger's face looked back at her now, loomed suddenly from the shadows? But the kitchen was empty, the whole house empty. You could feel it. On the table, the signs of someone's breakfast, and propped against the turned wood of the fruit bowl, a piece of paper or, looking more carefully, not a piece of paper but a letter, already opened.

Inside the shelter, Bill sat opposite his father. There was a large stove. There was a pot of simmering water on top of it. The light came from a single hurricane lamp. His father was naked.

Bill, who had started out with his towel around his waist, was now also naked. His father had said, 'What are you doing? You think you'll catch something? We sit like Turks.'

It wasn't said unpleasantly.

His father was smoking a cigar. He had, when Bill came in, been reading a newspaper (the *Wimbledon Evening News*), the paper sodden from the steam, the grey corners hanging like rags.

Though his father had no interest in games, he understood it was an important part of speaking the language, so for half a minute they spoke about the cricket. ('Will they win?' 'Who?' 'The English.' 'Probably not.') It hurt to breathe. Bill heard the echo of old bombs, the *poum*, *poum*, *poum* of the anti-aircraft battery in Hyde Park. His father's face came and went out of shadow as the flame in the lamp swayed in the glass. The floor was stamped earth, black.

His father's cock! The hair that came up his belly and spread all over his chest and shoulders. His neck was thinner than Bill remembered it; you could see its rigging. And the fat was going out of his face. It had been a very round face, moonish, round, fat, but hard. Now it seemed to be melting, like a wax mask. One day soon they might see the features of a perfect stranger. The stowaway, the spy, the survivor.

'Mum said you've not been well.'

His father shrugged. He touched his chest, somewhere around the heart. Then he leaned forward, touched Bill, his right arm, and smiled. 'You are stronger,' he said.

'That's farming,' said Bill. They grinned at each other. In a fight in the dark, inside the shelter, who would come out and walk all bloody over the snow? I might win, thought Bill, my hands around his throat, his eyes starting to pop. I might win.

'The farmers I knew were peasants,' said his father. 'They were people who washed once a year by swimming in the pond. They married their sisters. They were lazy but their lives were endless work.'

'Well, I don't have a sister,' said Bill.

'I could only make boys,' said his father.

'How's Charlie?' asked Bill.

'Your brother?' A sway of the hand. It meant Charlie was, essentially, a failure, but that no one was surprised by this and there was nothing to be done. It might even be funny.

'Has he got the Jag still? The E-Type?'

'It's purple,' said his father. 'I asked him, what is wrong with red or green? Green is a good colour. He told me the future will be purple. Maybe he's right. He sometimes is. I don't go out enough, not any more.'

'He's working for the business?'

'Who else will give him a job?'

'How is the business?'

His father nodded. 'How is your wife?'

'She's quite purple,' said Bill.

'Then you'll be ready.'

'For what?'

'The future.'

His father drew on the unfolding cigar. A glow, a cloud. Then he tossed it into the pot of water on the stove. He reached down into the darkness around his feet and came up holding what looked like a small broom of twigs.

'I made this myself,' he said. 'I think it's a good one. You lie on the bench. Lie down on your front.'

They started to shuffle around, two souls in hell. There was a mood of confusion, hilarity. Bill lay down and his father started to beat him with the twigs. He beat the backs of his legs, he beat his backside, he beat his back. It wasn't particularly painful, or no more than it was supposed to be. His skin sang. Soon they were laughing, coughing and laughing. How awful, thought Bill, to be loved by such a man.

At last the guard did come back. He had snow on the shoulders of his coat. He was going from compartment to compartment, sliding open the heavy doors.

'Line's blocked,' he said.

'We're going back to Guildford?' asked the man with the pipe.

The guard shook his head. He wasn't young. He looked like a man operating at the very edge of himself. 'There's a goods train behind us and he's stuck too. One of his wagons jumped the rails when he braked. The nearest plough's at Portsmouth. He'll come out but he won't be here any time soon.'

'So we sit here?' asked the man with the paper.

'There's a school,' said the guard, 'about a half-mile from here. We're going to get down on this side and walk to it. It'll be a bit nasty but it's not far. You'll be much warmer there.'

'This lady,' said the man with the bowler hat, 'is in a delicate condition.'

'She's pregnant,' said the man with the pipe. 'She told us so.'

'Right,' said the guard. 'You think you can make it, Miss? You can almost see it and we can't leave anyone.'

'Oh, yes,' said Irene. 'That's completely fine.' She smiled. She put on her brightest face. Anything was better than sitting here, waiting with these men. She tried to visualise it, half a mile. From the cottage to the Duckworths' house? Or was that more like a quarter of a mile?

They were told to leave their luggage. Once the line was clear they would come back and finish the journey.

'That might be tomorrow,' said the man with the paper.

'It could be,' said the guard. He moved on. There were other compartments, other passengers to be readied.

The signal to disembark was a last hoarse whistle from the engine. They climbed down into the snow at the side of the line. It was not a blizzard but it was heavy, and there was a bladed wind that lifted the snow like spume from where it lay at the top of the cutting. The engineer was at the head of the party. The guard took up the rear. They moved off in a column, fifty or so people, some calling, some laughing, most in silence. A man's hat blew past Irene's face. There was, at most, another hour of daylight left. They walked beside the train. At the head, beyond the cooling engine, they saw where there had been a sort of avalanche. Could they have just dug through? Perhaps, with enough shovels. They laboured up the bank. Irene lost a shoe and had to feel for it in the snow. People behind her grumbled. At the top of the bank they moved into a field. There was no shelter. She followed the black legs of the man ahead of her. She gripped the collar of her coat. She remembered as a child marching with Veronica behind their father around the dining-room table while the gramophone played 'The British Grenadiers'. She tried to remember the tune; she couldn't, not quite. Or she could remember something, but was it the 'Grenadiers' or 'Lilliburlero'? The gramophone was an old wind-up Decca. The dining table was one of the good things they had. There weren't many. It was rubbed every week with beeswax and could hold an entire afternoon on its surface. Dining tables are what separate us from the savage. Or record-players. Or marching. What was beneath the snow? Autumn stubble? She staggered, steadied herself, glanced through the purpling air to the edges of the field where it ended in a blur, a sigh. The wind worked at her. A good woollen hat would have been infinitely better than a headscarf. Nothing had been thought through properly. She had acted on impulse and she was ashamed. She should have stayed at the cottage and confronted him. She should have shattered his precious record of the *Passion*, gouged the vinyl with her thumbnail, dared him to strike her. She angled her head in an attempt to keep the wind from blowing into her ear. Her feet had been hurting but now she couldn't feel them at all – she wasn't even sure she still had her shoes on. The sense of her body as a shelter, poorly made, a thing of gaps through which the wind tore hungrily. They came to a gate, a line of elms. A road? The whole column paused, standing there as if lost, then moved on, slowly, shuffling past the dragged gate like prisoners, like the remnants of a defeated army. On one side of the road the snow was higher than their heads, much higher. The shapes of snow are the shapes of water. She fell, got up. How quickly she was coming to the end of herself! Soon now they would realise they had made a terrible mistake to leave the train. She felt a flash of rage, a moment later just the grief of walking. Again she fell, sprawling forwards onto all fours, doggish, the snow up to her shoulders. Someone helped her. She was being held. A man's arm was round her waist, his hand on her belly. 'No!' she cried, and broke free, stumbling forwards, blindly, as if against a great surf.

Home to a dark house, darker. He turned the key, entered, and stood in the little hallway, listening. If this house had anyone in it they were lying still as death.

Into the dining room. No warmth, no light. His fingers smoothed the wall, feeling for the switch. You put your intelligence into your hands, you hope. When the light was on he looked at the furniture. The dining table's balance seemed precarious. He went through to the drawing room, dropped his coat over the end of the sofa. He looked at the fireplace where there was no fire. He went upstairs, leaned into the unlit bedroom, whispered her name. He looked into the spare room where she'd slept the previous night.

'Irene?'

He went to the kitchen and turned on the lights. That first instant when you see but don't comprehend; the instant that follows when you understand everything with an exactness you will never be able to repeat, because you will never quite have the courage or the honesty. He picked the envelope up (took hold of it as you are supposed to grasp a nettle), studied it with a strange, dead curiosity, then rested it back against the fruit bowl. At the bottom of the stairs he shouted her name.

The sound of him – he didn't hold back – lifted petals of white ash in the grate. In its niche, the blue glass sang.

He made a drink, though making it was just pouring gin into a tumbler. He searched for his cigarettes and found them in a trouser pocket. He started laying a fire but gave up before lighting it. He looked at the phone and thought of Gabby. Hello, Gabby. Listen.

Upstairs, he stood by the bedroom door, examining the room, trying to work out what could be saved. He got onto his knees and peered beneath the bed. He laughed at himself.

He went down to the kitchen and looked for something to eat. The remains of last night's stew? No thank you. He got out the bread and a tin of salmon. He made a sandwich and ate it standing at the Aga. He went to the table and picked up the envelope again. He took out the letter. His fingers weren't quite clean and he left marks on the paper, a print of brine, a pink fleck of fish.

My Darling Man . . .

Well, wasn't this what he wanted?

'You're free,' he said. 'You old sod. The house is yours. Happy 1963.'

He poured another drink. Second or third? The taste of it, something between flowers and formaldehyde. Was Gabby just a little in love with Irene? He must be in love with something. Gabby and Irene, Eric and Alison. Frank could fuck right off and take that unpleasant boy with him. If I was the new king, he thought, I'd have to kill the boy, too, so he didn't wake me up some night with an axe.

He needed to warn Alison, of course. Then again, Irene would hardly be running off to tell tales to Frank. That wasn't her style. She'd keep very quiet about it all. She didn't like fuss. But leaving the letter like that in the kitchen – was *that* her style? And what did he know about her style in a situation like this? He didn't know his own.

He was cold. 'You've had a bit of a shock,' he said, his physician's voice.

He went up to the bathroom and stood in the dark there, smoking and gazing out of the window. Through the branches of the ash tree, he could see a light. And he remembered – suddenly and with huge clarity – seeing Bill Simmons at the station, Bristol side. Had a bag with him. Off on a trip. So the wife, the little blonde, was probably on her own tonight. He could go over with the last of the gin, sit by the fire with her, make her laugh. Then do it with her, slowly, in front of the fire. You can't knock up a pregnant girl. He thought she'd probably like it, the great screw beside the flickering fire with the doctor.

He ran a bath. There was no oil in the tank, but the water was heated by the Aga and the Aga was still burning. What if Irene was over there, at the farm? But he knew where she was. He undressed and got into the bath. The shock of the water as your balls go in. He sat there in the steam observing his white legs under the curves of the settling water. Emotions were stacked up like work. To be this tired, he thought. To be *this* tired.

After two minutes he got out. He dried himself. He rubbed his head vigorously. In the bedroom he took his pyjamas from under the pillow and put them on. He put on socks. He found his Guernsey in the drawer and put that on. He cleaned his teeth at the sink and thought that one day he would just have them all out, have porcelain teeth, like a doll. He spat, and arrived, abruptly, blissfully, at the edge of tears, but he wouldn't let them come. It was unsafe. It would be like being sick and unable to stop until you threw up your own heart. He looked at Arnolfini and his wife, then went down the corridor to the spare room beside the bathroom. He got into the bed his father had used, if used was the right word. He lay on his back. The curtains were undrawn. There was a blue glow that he thought must be the moon, a winter's moon. He fumbled with the sheet, got it free, and drew it up to cover his face.

Thursday, 10 January

You break the surface but all night the river has carried you and you recognise nothing. She had, she understood, lost the child. There was only a stone inside her now, a white stone.

She pushed down the covers. She was wearing a nightdress patterned with small, faded flowers. It wasn't hers; it didn't fit her. She dragged it up and stared at herself, expecting blood, perhaps a lot of it, but the sheets were dry and clean, her legs and thighs likewise. Then the child moved in her and she made a sound, birdlike, a strange sound that fell out of the heat of her mouth. She caressed herself, her belly. She spoke in a whisper, addressing what lay unfinished there the other side of the taut skin, said every sweet thing her heart could supply. When it was done, she lay back on the pillow, breathless, and gazing up at the ceiling, its pattern of white plasterwork. The hollowness was there still but it must belong to some other part of her. Her head, she thought. Her head like an abandoned hive.

'You're awake,' said a voice.

On a chair, by one of the big windows, almost lost in its light, there was a girl. She had been knitting, and stood slowly, holding her needles and a ball of red wool. She smiled at Irene, or slightly to one side of her, then came down the aisle between the beds and stopped at the end of Irene's. She looked at the wall and smiled again. She was twelve? Thirteen?

'I'll fetch the housemother,' she said.

'Is this a hospital?' asked Irene.

'Oh, no,' said the girl. She had a voice like a flute. 'It's not a *hospital*.'

She went on up the long room, passing by the ends of another eight or ten beds, all empty. She had on brown leather shoes almost the same colour as the parquet floor. She turned, brushing the end of the last bed with the dark stuff of her skirt, felt for the door, opened it and was gone.

Irene waited. She listened. She got out of bed and sat on the side of it, letting her blood settle. There was a big fireplace but no fire in it; a mantelpiece, bare. At the end of the room the two windows were mullioned. She tottered towards them, steadying herself with the metal bed frames.

The view – downwards – was of a slated eave and a small courtyard. In the centre of the yard was a pole – iron? – from which chains hung down. Further off, beyond the brick wall, the black line of a telephone wire travelled in swoops above the soft white tonnage of the snow. A child emerged from a door she couldn't see, a little boy in a bobble hat and belted coat. In his gloved hands he held a cup or little dish. He stepped, cautiously, in the direction of the metal pole, then threw the contents over the snow, cast them like seed. He was, she realised, feeding the birds, but for the moment no birds came.

The car was the purple of an aubergine; it was purple soaked in itself, a purple surface with purple depths, though someone had plumbed them, perhaps with the edge of a coin, a sequence of gouged lines on the driver's side of the bonnet. You had to see it from the rear of the car looking forwards to understand that what was drawn there was, in fact, a gibbet.

'Yeah,' said Charlie. 'Some mamzer.'

'A mamzer?'

'A pisher.'

'Oy-vey!' said Bill. His brother's imaginary Yiddish life: this, too, he had forgotten – or just pushed away. It started when they were teenagers and he must have got it out of books or films because there was no Yiddish in the house, not unless it was in the back of one of those big cupboards that stood like sarsen stones at the edges of several rooms, a family in hiding. But Bill knew what the cupboards contained: the hoarded newspapers, the folded blackout curtains, broken gadgets (a 1920s vacuum cleaner in one, like the remains of a small vegetarian dinosaur), the jigsaws his mother's parents had sent every Christmas, a thousand pieces of the sea, the boxes never opened. The Yiddish was an affectation. Charlie was made up of such things. He had told them once that he wanted to be an actor. Nobody had paid the slightest attention, but it might have suited him better than being a rent collector.

They got into the car. The day was white, windless, still as a painting. They were looking back at the house and Bill thought he saw the shade of their mother at one of the windows. Charlie talked him through the switches and dials. The seats were comfortable (purple leather with red piping). The speedometer went up to a hundred and sixty.

'Think it can?' asked Bill.

'Not between here and Paddington,' said Charlie.

There wasn't much traffic, that or Charlie was good at avoiding it. The car prowled down ploughed streets of flat-faced houses. Suddenly, the river. It wasn't frozen here (it was further up), but the water was sluggish and moved around the piers of the bridges in sticky black ripples thick as hawsers. As they crossed to the far bank – long views in both directions – the city briefly made sense. Then they were back in the slotted world of blind streets, half of them building sites. Buses moved like lava. The car edged westwards, just ahead of its growl.

They didn't speak much. Charlie smoked (Kensitas). He looked pleased. The nice thing was happening that he had imagined, carefully, more than once. Bill stared out of the passenger-side window. He was almost dreaming. He had woken at five and was half out of bed before he realised he had no cows to milk.

'Do you remember,' he said, 'coming out of the Underground one morning after a raid and there was a house that had been hit, and the whole front wall was gone and there was a bath on the pavement, like it had just landed there? Do you remember that?'

'A bath?' said Charlie. 'I think so.'

Bill nodded. He thought he probably didn't.

She was back in bed again, lying like a good girl (and wasn't that how it always was, one good kitten and one bad, one good mouse and one bad?), the sheets pulled up to her chin. The day was at slack-tide or already on the turn. She listened to the housemother's arrival, the drag along the corridor, the complaint of boards, the mouth noises, words or their damp beginnings. There was something brisker at the side of her that turned out to be a dog, a spaniel, with liver-coloured patches. It sat by the door, alert as a courtier, while the house-mother came down the room to Irene's bed. There was a chair and she lowered herself onto it, spilling a little over the edges. Both thick legs were bandaged but it looked habitual rather than anything urgent. She smelt, strongly and bitterly, of tobacco. Small yellow teeth, eyes of porcelain blue. Her hair was the colour of dust. She smiled. 'There,' she said, 'that's better, isn't it?'

She adjusted herself in the chair. If the chair gives way, thought Irene, there was nothing in the world that would raise her again.

'So, my dear, you may call me Miss Watkins, or just Mother, as the children do.'

She produced a packet of cigarettes from a pocket in her apron, shook one out and lit it with a kind of swift brilliance. She had a nice lighter, a Ronson.

'So, what's it to be?'

'I beg your pardon?' said Irene.

'Miss Watkins or Mother?'

'Oh. Miss Watkins?'

The housemother nodded. She drew on the cigarette; the ember crackled. She seemed to be looking out of one of the windows.

'We were very worried about you, dear. You were in a right old state when you arrived. We had to put you to bed straight away. You've been asleep almost twenty-four hours.'

'Have I?'

'Yes, dear, you have. In that bed. We're not using this dormitory at the moment. This is Willow. All the remaining children are in Birch. Lots of them went home at Christmas and, of course, they haven't come back. And my assistant Miss Bernard is also absent. She is trapped in Rottingdean. I have only Cook and Mr Grant to help me.'

'Is this a school?' asked Irene.

'Yes, dear. What did you imagine?'

'The girl who was here when I woke . . .'

'Dorothy.'

'She's blind?'

'They're all blind. Blind or as good as.'

'A school for the blind.'

'That's it, dear.'

'Are the others here? From the train?'

'He marched them up to the top of the hill and he marched them down again.'

'They've gone?'

'They could hardly have stayed, could they? Fifty of them, wanting loaves and fishes. Did you want to say goodbye?'

'No. Not really.'

'And it's like I said, dear, you were in a right old state when they brought you in. Hysterical. Coming out with all sorts.'

'I'm sorry if I was a trouble.'

'I say to the children, dear, what does sorry *mean*?'

'I was awfully cold.'

'You were. And not the only one.'

'Of course,' said Irene. 'Everyone must have been the same.'

'We're not talking about everyone, are we?'

'No?'

'When you're cold and hungry, so is the little traveller.'

It took Irene a moment. She nodded. She was being chastised.

'There was a very pleasant gentleman who explained your situation. Not that I needed anything explained. In the war I was with the Women's Voluntary Service. I saw terrible things all the time. Do you remember much?'

'The war?'

'Yes.'

'Quite a bit.'

'But you were too young to play a part.'

'Yes.'

'We had beetroot red jumpers and felt hats.' The cigarette was finished. She stood and carried it to the empty fireplace then returned to her seat. She took out and lit another cigarette. 'You were running away.'

'Not really,' said Irene.

'And where you go the little traveller has to go. He hasn't got a choice, has he, dear? Come rain, come shine. Have you felt him moving?'

'Yes.'

'And what do you think he would say to you?'

'About what?'

'You know about what.'

'I was going to my parents' house,' said Irene. 'I ought to ring them.'

The housemother nodded. For a while she was silent. Very faintly, through the floor, the voices of children.

'There'll be time for all that. I'll have one of the girls bring you up a nice cup of tea. And when you're feeling stronger you might read to them. They're tired of my voice.'

'If you like,' said Irene.

The housemother stood up again. Everything a wrestle with elemental forces. The dog, understanding the time had come, also stood.

'We can't be forever just pleasing ourselves. There's an old-fashioned word, dear. Duty. I'll know you'll forgive me being so frank.'

'Yes,' said Irene. 'Of course. Thank you.'

'Winnie came by one time. To the rest centre in Stepney. Waved his hat to us. It's not disrespectful to call him Winnie. We felt we knew him.'

'Mr Churchill?'

'That's right, dear. Well, we've had our chat. I'll look in later.'

She shuffled to the door. The dog fell into step beside her. When they were gone, Irene lay back on the pillow, frowning up at the pattern on the ceiling, the plaster net. She played the entire scene back in her head, carefully. She was trying to decide if the woman, too, had been blind.

The office was two rooms on the fourth floor of a house in Paddington. From the window Bill could see the ribbed sheds of the station. There was a young woman typing. There was a man in a leather jacket leaning against the wall reading a paperback. The overhead light was on. There was a calendar on the wall, a small picture of George VI, a clock.

'Big brother,' said Charlie. He flourished an arm at Bill. 'He's the one they spent the money on.'

The young woman glanced up, briefly. The man in the leather jacket was called Derek. His part was not explained. Charlie opened some mail. He made a telephone call. 'That's the coppers,' he said, when he finished the call. 'We're all old friends.'

He took a set of keys from a board of brass hooks by the door. 'Forty-six?'

Derek nodded and pushed himself away from the wall.

Charlie said, 'Can you hold the fort, Julie?'

'I've got a dentist's appointment,' she said. Her voice was querulous, thin as a child's. She wanted pleasure; instead she had this.

The men began on the narrow stairs, Derek at the front, the

brothers a few steps behind him. On the landing two floors below, a door that had been shut on the way up was open now. There was the chatter of sewing machines. Charlie walked in and Bill followed. Three men in waistcoats and white shirts sat on a workbench under bare bulbs. Further into the room a half-dozen women fed cloth into machines they sped with their feet.

'Got big brother with me today, Mr Nencel,' said Charlie. 'Going to show him how the other half live.'

One of the men on the table nodded but kept his attention on his needle.

'Mr Nencel worked for Knize in Vienna. Made a suit for Marlene Dietrich.'

'That I have never said,' replied Mr Nencel.

'You might make my brother a suit. He could use one. What do you say?'

'Possible,' said Mr Nencel. He looked up at Bill, a gaze supple as tape.

'Dove grey,' said Charlie, 'double-breasted.'

'Blue,' said Mr Nencel, 'and single-breasted. Two buttons. A bit of mohair in the cloth.'

'Mr Nencel,' said Charlie, 'tells stories with clothes. Isn't that right, Mr Nencel?'

'That's right.'

Each of the men on the table had his shirt sleeves rolled, the material held out of the way with sprung metal bands. Each had a row of numbers on his forearm.

'Göring's telephone number,' said Mr Nencel, noticing the noticing. 'Come back and we'll dress you. You'll look like Raf Vallone.'

'Or Rock Hudson,' said Charlie.

'Delon,' said Mr Nencel. 'You know Belmondo?'

'Dirk Bogarde,' said Charlie, 'Tab Hunter . . .'

They settled on Mastroianni, Brioni's 'Roman style', though something about it made the tailor laugh. Then he bit the thread and was enclosed again, hidden in his work.

Derek was outside, waiting for them. He wedged himself into the back of the car. He was bigger than either of the brothers – taller than Charlie, broader than Bill – and sat slightly above them, a black Achilles, the brothers his charioteers.

It was not a long drive to number forty-six but West London was a chess board and there were no simple journeys. They descended a street of cheap hotels – the Alexandria, the Shangri La, the Tudor Court. They were slowed to walking pace by a man leading a horse and cart; every ten strides he blew on the bugle he carried. They crossed squares where the houses waited on their knees for the demolition men. On a wall, in yard-high letters, a misspelt shout for the White Defence League.

At the house, Charlie rattled the keys in the lock and shoved the door with his shoulder. There was a man in mid-descent on the stairs. He froze. Derek spoke to him. Some patois? The man came down and passed them in the hallway. He was dressed for finer places than he seemed likely to find in the neighbourhood of number forty-six. His eyes met Bill's. There was, on each side, something resembling a bow, though its terms were historical and uneasy.

They climbed the stairs. It was not, of course, the first time Bill had been in a house like this, but it was the first time in two years. He paused on one of the landings, wondering if he should leave. Charlie leaned over the banisters of the flight above. 'You out of puff? Thought you'd be fit.'

They were there to prepare a room for a new tenant. In one corner of the room stipplings of black mould reached from skirting board to ceiling. On the wall by the window, water from the roof had frozen into slender tributaries of ice. The bed, a place where sleep or love might have been attempted, where someone had dreamed, was stripped to the sagging mattress. There was a gas fire. Derek crouched to turn the tap. No gas. The meter was at the bottom of the house. If you wanted to kill yourself, you would have to go down with a handful of shillings and walk back up, five flights down and five back. Time to think it through.

Against the back wall a piece of furniture resembling a sofa. Above it was a square of darker wallpaper.

'There was a picture there,' said Charlie. 'What was it?'

'*Summer*,' said Derek.

'If it's not nailed down . . .' said Charlie.

Bill stood by the window. The light was the only clean thing in the room. In the road below, a group of boys circled the purple car.

'Someone up here once,' said Charlie, 'used to trap pigeons with a coat hanger. Roasted them like chickens. He had to go. All pigeons are the property of Her Majesty the Queen.' He laughed. 'Where is he now?'

'He's around,' said Derek.

They made small alterations. There was a lock-up near the station where they stored furniture.

'At least change the mattress,' said Bill. 'And burn that one, for Christ's sake.'

'Nothing wrong with it,' said Charlie. 'You'd sleep on that, wouldn't you, Derek?'

'Slept on worse,' said Derek.

'You've forgotten things,' said Charlie, 'or you never bothered to learn them. Walk down through the house and knock on doors. People will tell you they're glad to be here. Roof over their heads, an address to give to an employer. You can't work without an address. We rent to the people others won't touch. And if you think this is bad, you should see the places Cyril Kaye rents out. Better or worse, Derek?'

'They're pretty bad.'

'The people here *like* us,' said Charlie.

'That must be why you've got a gibbet carved into your car,' said Bill.

Charlie shrugged. Derek was looking again at the patch on the wall where *Summer* had been. The room was five pounds ten shillings a week. Key money was three months in advance. All transactions were in cash. The room would be gone by the weekend. There would be no need to advertise.

They went out again to air that smelt of coal smoke and iron, of history stacked like skins in a tanner's yard. They dropped Derek off at the lock-up. Then Bill and Charlie drove into Soho. Charlie claimed to know Jack Spot, to know where to buy speedballs from the son of an earl, how to park for free on Beak Street. They sat, shoulder to shoulder, each aware of some brotherly urge to hurt the other. Soho was charming in the snow. A window full of oranges, another of cigars. The strip clubs were just opening, the jazz clubs not yet. At the doors of small cafés, men like El Greco saints stood smoking in their heavy coats, imperturbable, between miracles. Sometimes, just looking is enough.

The housemother brought in a tray of food. She had two of the children with her. From its place in a corner of the room, a bed-table was rolled down the aisle to Irene's bed. Irene asked if the lights could be put on, if that would be all right. They looked at her, the ribbon of her voice.

'Of course, dear,' said the housemother.

One of the children swam to the far wall where the brown switches were. At the third attempt he found them. Under metal shades like coolie's hats, a half-dozen bulbs came to life.

They stayed while she ate. She forked mashed potato into her mouth. She had not understood how hungry she was.

'That's it, dear,' said the housemother. 'Clear your plate. Every last scrap.'

The tea had a chalky scum. She drank it. There was a tinned pear in sugar juice; that was what she liked best. The tray was taken away. When they were all gone she looked for her clothes and found them (not her shoes) in the wardrobe between the windows. She put on her sheepskin coat and went out to the corridor. She passed by the top of the stairs. She approached doors and opened them, cautiously. Like a dowser she followed the subtleties of water, heard the hissing of a cistern, and found a bathroom with three baths and six basins. Behind brass-handled doors, three toilets (in an institution, all WCs are toilets). She chose the one at the end with the narrow window. She sat in silence, in the cold, her hands like flowers at dusk, bearing their own light.

When she came out she wanted a mirror. There wasn't one. She opened the taps at the sink. Ice water one side but on the other a warmth that turned to heat and steam, the water coming in glassy gulps that broke on the veined china. She washed her face, dried it on one of the rough little towels. On a painted shelf above the basins there were melamine cups, each with a small toothbrush in it. She wondered how the children would know their own cup from the one beside it. She chose one of the brushes and cleaned her teeth, returned the brush to the cup, leaving it exactly as she'd found it.

She went back to the dormitory. The last of the daylight lay against the windows. She climbed into bed still wearing her coat. She was thick-headed, recklessly tired. Whatever they had put in her tea was folding her like linen. (Chloral hydrate? She knew that name from somewhere.) She was, she supposed, in need of rescuing, but could not decide what that would mean. At the very least she needed to make a telephone call, though perhaps there was no urgency. The snow had changed things. They were in the world differently now, people understood that.

She lay on her back, then writhed onto her side, trying to make herself more comfortable. It was a child's bed – she was too big for it, an imposter, an alien. She tried to gather herself but the self she sought was a shoal of fish swimming far below her. Pull closer and it dissolved into a thousand darting fragments . . .

Yesterday, the day before, the week before, the year, all of it needed *thinking* about. Where to begin? She had been deceived, but the source of the deception was not as clear as it should have been. She couldn't understand why she did not hate Alison Riley, and if there was some truth in the saying that people get what they deserve, though surely it was a terrible thing to believe and something in her refused it, utterly. Should she take off her rings? (But how she had once longed for those rings!) She saw herself flinging them at the snow, saw them glint in the air, then bury themselves beneath small shadows. Her hands would be lighter. Her life? She sighed like a grand-mother. Her teeth were cold, the sheets smelt of lye. She was being sifted, cleared out by cold and silence. Freedom, she thought, would be comfortless. It would be like this room. It would not feel like home, or not like any home she knew.

The woman who ran the club stood at the end of the bar nearest the door, greeting people on their way in, saying cheery-bye, ducks, as they stumbled out (one flight of stairs and then the city).

It wasn't a big place and it was painted in dark colours. There was an unimportant window at one end, a sticky downwards fade of electric light. Once you picked out the faces of individual drinkers it was obvious that almost everyone was ill. There were a few younger ones, men and women, who looked as if they would be OK for a while, a year or two. You had to admire it, the wastage.

They took a small round table at the edge of the room. It had just been abandoned and someone had left a face on it made from a half-slice of lemon and two bottle tops. Charlie got the drinks in. He came back with four glasses of what he called 'big gins'. Four meant he wouldn't have to go back to the bar for a while. The barman was often abusive. He had his favourites. Apparently Charlie wasn't one of them.

The brothers raised their glasses. Charlie's first big gin disappeared in a single swallow. He wiped his lips. 'We have to help Dad,' he said.

'There's nothing wrong with Dad,' said Bill.
'How would you know?'
'He looks all right.'
'No, he doesn't.'
'What's wrong with him, then?'
Charlie shrugged.
'He's getting old,' said Bill.
'We don't know how old he is,' said Charlie.
'No,' said Bill. 'We don't.'
'I can't help him,' said Charlie.
'Why not?'
'I'm not the right one.'
'And I am?'
'Of course you are.'
Bill moved one of the bottle tops from the face, then put it back. It was curious how two bottle tops and a half-slice of lemon worked perfectly well as a human face.
'You're the one who stayed,' said Bill. 'You work with him.'
'He talks to himself,' said Charlie. 'Not in English.'
'So?'
'He didn't do that before.'
'Maybe we just didn't hear him.'
'I don't stay because I like it,' said Charlie.
'Move out,' said Bill. 'That nice room we were in today.'
'You've come back to skin him, I suppose,' said Charlie.
'The old man,' said Bill. 'The pater.' He frowned at the oily surface of his gin.
'Whatever he was running away from,' said Charlie, 'has found him. It's tracked him down. It's moved into the house. It's following him around.'
'What does it look like?' asked Bill.
'I don't know,' said Charlie. 'Perhaps it looks like you.'

They laughed.

'Am I to blame for everything?' asked Bill. It sounded like a genuine question.

'I'll tell you what,' said Charlie.

'What?'

'I had a revelation. I actually had it in the khasi here. In the club.' He searched for his cigarettes. 'Did I leave them in the car?'

'No idea.'

'Do you have any?'

Bill shook his head.

'For some reason they only sell Gitanes at the bar.'

'The revelation?' asked Bill. 'The khasi?'

'It's that Dad came here, to this country, to make you. And the point of making you was that you would hate him. Good, eh?'

'I don't hate him.'

'An English gentleman, educated. Someone with taste. Someone who would be ashamed of him.'

'I don't like what he does, if that's what you're on about. I don't like what you do.'

'A snob. A liberal snob. A bit of a lefty. But mostly a snob.'

'And you? What are you, Charlie? A businessman? You're not a businessman. You're not even a proper criminal.'

'I've seen the future,' said Charlie.

'I know,' said Bill. 'It's purple.'

'It's full of people like me,' said Charlie.

'I doubt that,' said Bill.

'What I'd forgotten,' said Charlie, gazing at Bill, a crooked little smile on his face, 'is how much you *look* like him.'

'Balls,' said Bill, though his brother had impressed him. He went to the bar for another round.

'Which one are you?' asked the barman. 'Rosencrantz or Guildenstern?' The drinks were expensive. Bill waited for change but there wasn't any. Carrying the drinks back to the table, he stood above his brother and saw how his hair was thinning at the crown. It pinched his heart to see it, as if he had seen death there. At seventeen Charlie had been pretty; at forty he would look like a bald edition of their mother. He sat down. They raised their glasses.

'Have you got a picture of your wife?' asked Charlie.

'No,' said Bill.

'What do you think about that?' asked Charlie. He pointed with his chin to where two men were dancing together to music from the jukebox. Bill watched them, a middle-aged man and a younger man, a slow waltz. And it was like an ENSA show, or theatricals in a prisoner-of-war camp, Stalag Luft something, to distract from the digging of a tunnel. It also looked uncomplicated, as if they might just be in love.

'Dr Parry,' said Eric. He had not been back long. The ringing of the phone had frightened him, like a klaxon going off in a dream. He stood at the bottom of the stairs in his coat, slightly breathless.

It was Irene's father.

'Hello, Eric. We were expecting Irene last night but we haven't seen her.'

'No?'

'No.'

'Or heard from her?'

'No.'

There was a pause. Irene's mother would be in the room. She would be staring at her husband. He would be hating every second of it. He would also, presumably, be worried, angry.

'The trains are pretty awful,' said Eric.

'Yes.'

'I thought she would be with you.'

'No. We haven't seen her.'

'And she hasn't called?'

'No.'

'I see,' said Eric. He felt a heat of confusion. 'I'm quite sure she will. Call you or call here.'

'Yes. One of us, I expect.'

'We can let the other know,' said Eric. 'I mean, if she calls here, I'll call *you.*'

'Right.'

'Some of the lines might be down. The ice.'

'Yes. They might be.'

'Or she might have stopped en route. To wait out the weather.'

'Do you think so?'

'I'll call either way,' said Eric. 'I mean, if I hear from her or if I don't.'

'Thank you.'

'And if she calls, I'll ask her to call you.'

'If you would.'

'Of course.'

'Goodbye, then.'

'Yes. Goodbye.'

Eric replaced the receiver. His pregnant wife was lying in the snow. The snow fell into her open eyes; the snow was burying her. Or she had thought better of it? Had decided against the lottery of trains, been told at the station such a journey was impossible, and settled on a more convenient hideaway, just out of sight? He went up the stairs to the bathroom and looked out. A light faint as a star, a light that trembled like a star. He went down again. He needed a drink. He thought of the expression 'to collect oneself', of what it meant and how it might be done. He was slightly surprised to find he was still wearing his coat. There are times when your body just follows you around, like a dog or a younger brother. He took his cigarettes, the remaining fifth of that silly bitch's vodka, and went out to the garage. He sat in the car. He imagined himself out driving, the windscreen running with stars. Aloud he said, 'A week ago I was happy.' A half-minute later he added, 'No, I wasn't.' He nodded, and took a drink from the neck of the bottle.

The children were in bed. The housemother had tucked them up. She had read to them in the voice they were tired of. All this Irene had heard – the sound of their boots, the calling, the hushing, the opening and shutting of doors. When the housemother came in she feigned sleep, lay on her side facing the windows, listening to her approach, the drag of her walking, the smell of her (something like Vicks balsam she may have been rubbing into a child's chest). Then she heard her go away again, the fading slap of her feet on the stairs. She waited for what she guessed was another half-hour, then slid from the bed. She felt her way to the door. There were no lights on in the corridor, but again she was guided by the tricks of water, old plumbing. Bathroom door, bathroom, then a half-minute of stroking the wall to find the switch. There was no lock on the door. So be it. She chose the middle bath. Would the water still be hot? Had the children used it all? But it *was* hot, some old furnace in the cellar fed by mountains of coal, of split logs. Or just the remains of the passengers from the train, the three men from her compartment, pipe, bowler hats, newspaper, the works, lifting in the pink heart of the fire, fluttering, then settling back as ashes . . .

She ran the cold water, stirred it in, the water swinging in the grey enamel. She stripped swiftly, hanging the nightie from one of the hooks, the sheepskin a couple of hooks further down. She lowered herself through the steam. She would have had it hotter if it had just been her. Could hot baths really lead to miscarriages? A hot bath and gin to bring it off? She thought it was probably untrue, the sort of thing Eric would scoff at. But out there somewhere, a girl trying it?

She washed with a bar of white, sharp-smelling soap. She was warm at last. The warmth or the water woke the baby. It turned in her – a heel the size of a rosebud – low down in her abdomen. 'Little traveller,' she said, and started to cry. One day, out walking with the child, just the two of them, she would explain it. It would be their joke.

She lay back, her head pillowed on her hair, hair darkened by winter. She let her eyes close. She was . . . on a plane, BOAC, a stewardess with white gloves (she looked like Princess Grace of Monaco) bending down to ask if there was anything she needed. (My gloves? Put them on while they're still warm. Your hands are small too.)

Behind her, the door opened. She stayed completely still, moved nothing but her eyelids. She braced for the housemother's voice, for the scolding to start, but a boy came into view, nine or ten, his pyjamas printed with stars and rockets. He paused. He had been deeply sleeping, dreaming perhaps. What did he sense? He raised an arm, swept it in a graceful arc, clearing the air ahead of him. Then he reached for the brass handle of the nearest toilet, went in, leaving the door wide, pushed his pyjamas down to his knees, emptied his bladder, dragged up his pyjamas and came out, murmuring to himself some incantation to a bathroom unexpectedly haunted, his words (unintelligible) a kind of purple dotting, like violets through snow.

In the dining room, where four heaters of different types were at work, sending out shimmers, fumes, battling the yard-deep cold that sat on the uncarpeted floor, Bill and his family were gathered for the evening meal. And somehow the chandelier was working, coaxed into life by Colin the servant (half an afternoon up a stepladder, plaiting wires). They sat beneath its rain of light. Bill's father was sporting a silk tie and tinted glasses; he was grinning at something and playing with a butter knife. Bill's mother had painted her eyelids with a heavy green shadow. If she closed her eyes (rather than staring at her husband and sons) it might seem two scarabs had been laid there in a funerary custom peculiar to Barnet or Waltham Forest, or wherever it was they would row her back to at the end.

Charlie was explaining modern art. He had begun it humorously, something about sex and unbelief, about words written over the top of other words, but now his voice was thick with emotion.

'We should have a dog in this house,' said his mother. 'I don't mean an Alsatian. A small dog.'

Colin came in with the trolley. It was loaded with bottles. Had they eaten already? Bill looked at the table, the tarnished silver. He didn't think he was drunk but he certainly wasn't sober. He was, for example, smoking a Gitanes from a packet he had bought in the club. 'You *should* have a dog,' he said. 'One you could put in your handbag.'

'Thank you, Billy,' said his mother.

'It'll do its business in there,' said Charlie. 'Imagine it. You reach in, a strange warmth . . .'

She made a face, yet looked as if she might enjoy more stories of the terrible things the dog would do. 'Colin will take it out to the square,' she said. 'Won't you, Colin?'

'I will,' said Colin. He was moving round the table, pouring drinks. Another thing: the glasses in this house were bigger than the glasses in other houses. You could barely hold them.

'Binkie,' she said. 'That's what I'll call him.'

'Why not a chicken?' asked Bill's father. 'They're small. They make eggs. A dog doesn't make eggs. Not a small dog. Bill will find you a chicken.'

'We had trouble enough with them in the war,' she said, confidently, though nobody else could remember them. Chickens? Where? In the garden? It was getting harder perhaps to remember the war, or remember it accurately.

The glasses were full again and there was a lull in the conversation while they renewed their thirst. My mind, thought Bill, is like a fly in a matchbox. At Oxford, during the short period when he was interested in being a sort of intellectual, he had gone to the Union to hear a debate on the Argument from Design. At the conclusion he had followed Stanhope through the 'Noes' door, but it was entirely unclear to him now who had won. It bothered him. It might be important.

'You're going to be grandparents,' said Charlie. He was holding a silk tulip from a vase of them on the table. He pointed it at Bill and fired it like a ray-gun.

'Yes,' said Bill. He had told his brother at the club. 'You are.'

In the silence that followed, Colin wheeled out the trolley. They heard it rattling down the passage.

'It's just a baby,' said Bill, quietly.

'What do we do, Dad?' asked Charlie. 'Smash all the glasses?'

Their father tilted his head. He knew, he didn't know. On the table in front of him was a pill pot. It was elaborate and silver, like a small medieval pyx. As with many of his possessions it had the character of loot. He opened it.

'You're supposed to take it with your food,' said his wife, angrily.

The dining room overlooked the square. Bill noticed that the streetlamps were starting to flash. 'Raiders approaching,' he said. Then the light from the chandelier began to flicker. It started slowly and speeded up. They watched it, their upturned faces swept with shadow, like a film of themselves, something from the dawn of cinema, the faithful receiving manna, the unfaithful about to be expunged.

Eric had a torch but kept the beam low by his feet. He was, or wished to be, a kind of shadow flitting across the field, a will-o'-the-wisp. He came to the snowman. It startled him, though, of course, he had known it was out here somewhere. He played the light over it. It looked solid, frozen to the core, an iceman more than a snowman. If I was a child, he thought, I might imagine it following me.

He pushed on, wading the snow, at one point stumbling onto his knees like a supplicant, three seconds of stillness, of why not stay like this? He arrived at the little gate. It was wedged open and would not be shut again until the snow had gone. He entered the orchard. He had not been in here before. There was no obvious path. The trunks of the apple trees were about the same height as he was, and two or three times his head was touched. Under his boots the fallen apples were a sort of rubble. When he came free of the trees he switched off the torch. The house was to his left; to the right, the blackwork of unlit buildings, presumably the yard.

They had a dog? He didn't think so. A real farmer would have had a dog. But if not a dog there was something here. It had listened to his coming through the orchard, had scented him. He could hear the damp weight of its breathing. He veered away from it, towards the house. Light flowed from an uncurtained window on the ground floor, a lozenge of yellow light on the snow. He touched the stone of the house, and slowly, a type of lizard, brought his face close to the glass.

She was sitting on the floor in front of the fire. She had on a coat. She was smoking and talking. He could – just – hear her voice, though not the words, not what she was saying. On the floor around her, objects in a circle (a camera, a ball of wool, something that might be an alarm clock; also a half-dozen sweets he decided, looking more carefully, were probably pills of some sort).

The overhead light was on, the desk lamp, another lamp on the floor beside the sofa. There were no shadows where his wife might be hidden. Had he seriously expected to find her here? He was not so drunk or so lost that he did not know to treat his recent thoughts with some suspicion. And if he had – the two of them plotting and laughing – what then? Burst in on them with his cape swirling? Thrash them with his silver-headed cane?

She darted the end of her cigarette into the coals. She hugged her knees. It was, he knew, outrageous to watch her, but how rare the chance to see someone sitting in the maze of herself, all unsuspecting, bare as a branch. Doctors should be trained like this, at windows, at night. Or they could put it on the telly, secret filming of people alone (when he suggested it, they would tell him it was disgusting, shameful; then they would do it). One night, of course, you might see yourself. It would change you.

He shivered. He had forgotten to wear a hat; he had forgotten gloves and a scarf. He was starting to be very cold but it was difficult to stop it, this watching. She held herself more tightly. She rocked a little. She was less like this? She didn't seem it, perhaps the opposite. He remembered their talking at the party and how he had gone away to make the jug of gin with a different opinion of her. He considered knocking gently at the front door, and when she answered, he would say (laughing) that he would be glad if she would sell him some eggs. He would do his best to look reassuring, and might say something about her knowing where he was if she needed help. It wouldn't have anything to do with seduction. Sometimes he hated sex and sex thoughts. He would be kind; it wasn't beyond him. And he was picturing all this, their short exchange at the door, the tone of his voice, of hers, the establishing of some sort of trust, of how comforting that might be for both of them, when the light disappeared and she cried out, an awful sound, a wail of despair and terror. He waited. He dared not move – couldn't. Then a match flared and her face showed at the window, no more than an arm's reach from his own, just her face, wide-eyed and rippling with the movement of the flame. Last on Earth, first on Mars. Either way, abandoned.

She was drying herself with a child's towel, rubbing down the shine of her skin, the towel rough, boiled in the copper a hundred times. The bath had been a great success. She needed to learn how to win, and the bath had felt like that. It had not been offered: she had taken it. She had done what a man would have done, a man who takes unauthorised baths, unauthorised time, unauthorised people. And where did they learn that? At school? From their fathers? In clubs? Did it have something to do with money?

She was dry, more or less, naked other than for her rings. She was wiping the soles of her feet, steadying herself with one hand on the curled rim of the bath. The pads of her feet were scuffed and bruised from her walk across the field. Then a sound, too slight and subtle to be named, and the lights went out. She straightened herself and waited. The darkness settled, and somehow she knew it was a darkness that went on for miles and miles, that if she stood on the roof with the frost creeping over her skin, she could turn a full circle and see not a single pinprick of light anywhere.

In her head, a scheme of the bathroom, something captured by her clever brain, though it would, of course, fade, perhaps quite quickly. She navigated around the end of the bath, reached out and touched the nightie. She pulled it on. Two hooks further down was her sheepskin. Thank God for the coat! She about-faced, moved past the basins (touching them with a trailing hand), turned to where the door must be, found that it was, sought the handle, opened the door, and did something like looking out, though there was nothing to look at. The landing had a darkness of its own, more perfect than the bathroom's. The dormitory and her bed were at the end on the right. The stairs would be on the left about halfway. She must stay away from the stairs.

She found the right-hand wall, and partly facing it, began to move forwards over the boards. Her eyes were wide, searching for light, anything, a dot, the moon through a keyhole, but the dark was faultless, and she began to live in her fingers and the sketches of memory. Slowly, slowly, bare feet on the bare wood, the company of her breath. Then the wall gave way and her hands pressed empty air. She gasped, teetered, and stood in a kind of fluttering stillness, as if at the edge of a crevasse. She was – she could sense by the play of air – facing an opening she could not account for, that should not have been there. The picture in her head dissolved. She turned to study the nothing one way and the nothing the other. And she felt it go into her, an utter bewilderment. What had she forgotten? What mistake had she made? She had exited the bathroom by a different door? Entered a different corridor? One where the stairs were on the right, not on the left? Her room, then, was not ahead of her but behind . . .

All the warmth and comfort of the bath was gone. As on the walk from the train, there was a moment of fury. This had been *done* to her. As on the walk, it changed nothing.

Cry out for help? The children would rescue her. What was this to them? They would trail drowsily from their room, they would take her hands and guide her, this grown woman lost in a corridor. A woman who would be a mother by the time the hawthorn blossomed.

So she recovered herself in some obscurity of shame. She conjured up her sister (Don't get in a state, darling, it's really not so difficult). Somewhat to her surprise she thought, too, of Gabby Miklos, the weight of his shadowed gaze, how, in one of the pockets of his corduroy suit, he carried the disasters of the century.

She moved to the side, one step, another. She was, she guessed, in the middle of the passage; she was wherever she imagined herself to be. She shut her eyes, raised her arms, hands open, fingers splayed, and tempted by some fancy that her baby could see, was slung from her ribs like a lodestone, or some small bird, swift, swallow, that crosses half the world to a familiar garden, she began to inch forwards, somnambulist, votary, divinely blind, approaching the shrine.

Friday, 11 January

'Don't!' she shouted, when the telephone rang. Then she lunged at it as if it would sink out of reach if she didn't catch hold of it immediately.

The voices were out for a stroll. They had started addressing each other with elaborate titles. Wing Commander, Herr Professor. They knew they were in charge now. The night had been a great success. They were looking forward to the next.

'Water Farm,' she said.

'Hello, Water Farm.'

'Bill!'

'Did I wake you?'

'It's the afternoon,' she said. 'Isn't it?'

'It is here,' he said. 'Are you all right?'

'Yes,' she said. 'Where are you?'

'Regent's Park. Just been to the zoo. Think I was eight last time I was there.'

'Did they remember you?'

'I don't think so, but I was in the reptile house and they don't give much away.'

'What was your favourite?'

‘A toss-up between the flap-necked chameleon and the crested water dragon.’

‘Lovely,’ she said. ‘I wish I’d been there.’

‘Me too.’

‘There was a blackout last night.’

‘And in London,’ he said. ‘We sat around the table wondering who had the carving knife.’

‘I couldn’t find the torches or the lamp or anything.’

He told her where they were.

‘I know,’ she said. ‘It’s light now. I’ve found them. Are you coming back?’

‘Not today,’ he said. ‘I haven’t had the chat still. He’s hard to pin down.’

‘Like the crested water dragon.’

‘Actually, more like the flap-necked chameleon.’

‘Are you hiding from them?’

‘I thought I might try to miss the first three or four rounds of drinks. How’s Teddy been?’

‘I wave to him through the window and he waves back. He has sacks tied around his trousers.’

‘Any milk collections?’

‘I saw him taking churns up on the tractor yesterday.’

‘That’s good. And the bull?

‘Missing you.’

‘What’s the weather like?’

‘A sky of hot nude pearl,’ she said.

‘What?’

‘It’s in one of your books,’ she said. ‘One of the novels in the office.’

The phone beeped. She heard the drop of a new coin.

‘Next beeps, I have to go,’ he said. ‘Out of shrapnel.’

‘So you won’t be back tonight?’

'If I go without the chat the whole visit's been pointless. I'll try to get back tomorrow afternoon. Sunday at the latest. Can you hold the fort until then?'

'I'll have to, won't I? How's the brother?'

'Charlie? Unbearable. Talks codswallop.'

'Though in fact you're quite glad to see him.'

He laughed. 'Yes. Oddly I am.'

They fell silent. In the background, like the whisper in a shell, a city of millions.

'Sure you're all right?' he asked.

'The cat disappeared.'

'There are stories,' he said, 'of cats drinking from cow's udders. They stand on their hind legs. I think old Richy told me that.'

'So it's probably not true,' she said.

'Probably not.'

The beeps again. They hurried their farewells, spoke over each other. She thought she heard a bus. Then the line went dead and she put the receiver back in its cradle. She stood at the desk, her hands on her belly. Should it worry her that she was not getting bigger, or should she be pleased? She had slept on the sofa. The blankets were at one end in a tangle. On the floor was an ashtray, an almost empty packet of Embassy, the lamp she had brought in from the kitchen, the novel (*Justine*) she had started reading at half past one in the morning when, like a shout, all the lights came on again. In front of the fire was the protective circle she had made – the boost gauge, her father's Zeiss Ikon camera, a selection of the pills from the lingerie drawer, her knitting things, the photograph of the garlanded cow, two copies of *Farmers Weekly*, August 1961. It had not protected her very much.

She went up to the bedroom. She opened the wardrobe and

began to sort through the clothes, shifting them along the metal rail. She picked out a dress of mohair and red wool, a pink crêpe slip to wear beneath it. She laid out clean underwear, a pair of winter stockings, then stripped off, dropped everything she was wearing onto the floor and wrapped herself in the chill of the new clothes. She did her make-up in the bathroom. Cold enough in there to condense her breath. She put on earrings (diamanté petals around tiny purple amethysts). From a box on top of the wardrobe – she had to stand on a chair to reach it – she took down her rabbit-fur hat. She drew on the coat and buttoned it to her throat. The day already had the character of a memory. She looked at the alarm clock beside the bed, calculated, and decided that if she cut through the Parrys' garden she would be at the station in time to catch the half past.

In the office, where the fire was dying, she picked from the floor the blue triangle of a Dexamyl and swallowed it with a mouthful of cold tea. She wrapped a couple of the Nembutal in a tissue and put them into her purse. She put the photograph of the cow into her purse next to her library card. She hunted through the desk for some money and found three pound notes at the back of the milk ledger. In the kitchen she opened the Rayburn's firebox and shook in what was left in the scuttle. She put on boots and gloves. She carried the kitten heels in a string bag. As she opened the front door, the bitter air caught in her throat and she had a fit of coughing. When it was over she crossed the orchard and went out through the wedged-open gate into the afternoon glare of the field. There were tracks here – her own from yesterday, and a second set that moved over the snow in what seemed a series of hesitations, looping, erratic, some blind creature chasing a scent. But if these were an animal's tracks it was one that went upright in boots. Irene? Who else would cross the field? Irene had come! Irene had stood knocking at the farmhouse door, stood there for God knew how long, and got no answer (the farmer's wife was out cold on the sofa).

She started over the field, long strides, the tops of her boots rubbing at her stockinged calves. She imagined finding the snow suddenly spotted with blood, spots that turned into splashes. When she reached the garden, the cottage looked exactly as it had the previous day – lifeless, all windows dark. She rapped on the back door, she tried the handle. She went to the kitchen window and put her brow to the glass. The envelope was still on the table, though now there was an empty bottle beside it. Had that been there before? She didn't think so, though yesterday felt immensely distant, and her self of yesterday a younger sister who had yet to learn what the night can teach.

She looked at what she could see of the tiled floor. No one was lying there. She squinted through the doorway between the kitchen and the drawing room. She tapped a gloved knuckle on the glass and waited. The Dexamyl was starting to work, the first threads. For a few hours the voices would lie on their backs, frozen, beaks wide but silent. They didn't like it (they had ideas about their dignity) and there would be a price to pay, but she would pay it later. When she stepped back from the window it became a mirror. It held her, not unkindly – unless to be held at all is unkind – a figure in a garden, posed against the whiteness of a winter's afternoon. Irene was fine. Irene did not need her. Irene was somewhere in the south, white drapes lifting on a warm breeze, the sound of people playing tennis . . .

She went around the house to the lane. The road had been

scraped, the snow shoved into muddy sloughs at the verges. The cold was making her eyes water and she was afraid her mascara would run. She also didn't care.

She rang her parents using the telephone in the school office. The office window looked out at the courtyard. The iron pole, the trampled snow. It was her father who answered. She explained about the trains. She told him where she was, as far as she understood where she was.

'They had no business setting out from Guildford,' he said. He passed the phone to her mother and Irene explained it all a second time.

'I'll probably just go back to the cottage,' she said, when her mother asked when they should expect her. 'I think it would best. We can talk it over, Eric and I.'

'Daddy's been furious.'

'Has he? I didn't mean to upset you both.'

'Well, naturally we are upset.'

'I'm sorry,' said Irene. She had thought it would be comforting to hear their voices. In fact it just made her wish she had kept it from them, told them nothing. The memory of herself on the phone to her mother that morning made her blush. 'I may have overreacted,' she said. 'It was just a letter.'

'It might not have been what you thought?'

'I don't know.'

'Marriages have their ups and downs, Irene. Not all men are like your father.'

'No. Dear Daddy.'

'And one has made certain promises, of course. Important ones.'

'Yes.'

They spoke for another few minutes. They discussed the suitcase she had left on the train. It had her name and address on a label so it would find its way back. There was some hint that if she had come for Christmas none of this would have happened. Veronica's name was mentioned. For years her parents had discussed Veronica as a problem. Now it seemed they were preparing to speak of her as a great success.

When it was over she stood in the office on her own, wondering if this was how it would feel when they were gone, when she had buried them both in the churchyard with the clipped yews, the tower where a faceless clock struck only the quarter-hours. This mix of loneliness and gratitude, the faintest ache of indifference.

On the walls of the office there were group photographs of the pupils posed outside the front of the school, a succession of summers, the earliest looking as if it was from the very beginning of the century. Why do we imagine the past as more innocent? Because it came before Belsen? But it didn't come before hunger or slavery. We confuse it with our own childhoods, perhaps, though even they, growing restless under glass, are not what they once were.

In the courtyard a half-dozen flakes of snow fell but no more. The office door opened. When she turned, the housemother was there, smoke pouring through her nose.

'Come along, dear,' she said. 'We're all waiting.'

Mrs Bolt spoke from the depths of the box: 'Mrs Riley on the line for you, Doctor.'

'OK. Thanks. Put her through.'

He picked up the phone. He had tried her yesterday and again this morning, twice. He had begun to persuade himself she had left, had quit the country to wait out the remainder of the winter in South Africa or Jamaica. Now she was calling *him* and he felt unprepared, absurdly nervous.

'Hello?'

'Hello,' she said.

'How are you?'

'I'm all right. How are you?'

'Yes,' he said. 'I'm all right. Keeping warm?'

'Yes, thanks. Are you?'

'We've run out of heating oil.'

'What a bore.'

'Yes.'

There was, somewhere at the back of her voice, a tightness he didn't think he'd heard before. Perhaps she imagined Mrs Bolt could listen in on them, though as far as he knew that wasn't possible.

'Irene's away,' he said.

'Is she?'

'Gone to her parents.'

'You're on your own, then.'

'Yes.'

'Are you on call this weekend?'

'Tomorrow. Gabby's on on Sunday. What's it like where you are?'

'You mean the snow?'

'Yes.'

'Not too bad now. We can get in and out.'

'Right.'

'Can you?'

'What?'

'Get in and out.'

'Well, I've been using the train, but they've ploughed the lanes, most of it. Icy, of course, but if I was . . .'

'Because I was just wondering if you could come here.'

'Yes? When?'

'Tomorrow.'

'Tomorrow's Saturday.'

'I know.'

'What time?'

'Around four?'

'Four?'

There was a pause. 'Yes,' she said.

'You're sure?'

'Yes.'

'All right,' he said. 'Good. We need a proper talk, in fact.'

'Around four, then.'

'Yes,' he said. 'Around four.'

She put her receiver down first. He replaced his. He had

patients in the waiting room. He needed to buzz Mrs Bolt, have her send the first one down. He looked through the lamplight. He had never told Alison Riley he loved her, mostly because he had never been perfectly sure that he did. Would he tell her tomorrow, at four? Tell her his marriage was over, that the whole thing was going to come out, that they needed to brace themselves, to make a plan? And again, he suffered the brief fantasy of control, followed almost at once by the certainty that he was about to lose everything of any value in his life. 'Better kill yourself,' he said. It felt important to keep the option open, though he thought almost everybody he knew was more likely to do it than he was. Mrs Gurney, for example. Or Gabby.

He reached for the intercom and flicked the switch. 'Thank you, Mrs Bolt. I'm ready now.'

He glanced down at the pile of patient records on his desk. The top one was a young mother whose baby was never quite well. The mother was not overly bright. She didn't really know how to look after a child. She would sit across the desk, pale, frightened. The child would be crying. At some point he would crouch in front of them. The mother would lift the child's clothes and he would put his stethoscope to the small, hot chest. The child would cry more passionately and he would close his eyes, listening to the roar of its heart.

She followed the housemother through the panelled hall of a refectory, then down windowless corridors to a door whose brass plate was dotted with small fingerprints. The spaniel sat waiting for them. Beyond the door was a classroom. Rows of sloping desks, a raised desk at the front for the teacher, and two windows looking out at what, beneath the snow, must be an expanse of lawn, the dark wings of a cedar tree at its centre.

The children sat huddled at the desks. The youngest at the front looked no more than five or six. At the back they were teenagers. Irene saw the girl who had been sitting with her when she woke. She smiled at her and was briefly perturbed that the girl did not smile back.

'Good afternoon, children,' said the housemother.

The children chorused their response. The room was cold but not impossible.

'Today is a very exciting day because we have a visitor with us, Mrs Parry, who was on the train that got caught in the snow. Mrs Parry has been staying with us as our guest and she has kindly agreed to speak to us. So, children, let us clap our hands nice and loudly to tell Mrs Parry how grateful we are for her time.'

The children clapped, the younger ones with wild enthusiasm.

'Thank you, children,' said the housemother. 'That will do. And now Mrs Parry will address us.'

Irene inclined her head and spoke into one of the housemother's surprisingly small pink ears. 'What would you like me to say?' she asked. She had imagined she would read from one of their story books but there were no books.

'That's up to you, dear,' said the housemother, shaking a cigarette from her packet. 'Just tell them who you are. You're a messenger from the wider world. The bearer of news.'

She lit the cigarette. How familiar the children must be with the snap of her lighter! Irene surveyed the class. She felt slightly giddy, as if she'd had a couple of vermouths, though there had been no tell-tale scum on the tea this morning. If she fainted, the children would hear it but they wouldn't know what had happened, not at first. They sat in their bulky knitwear, their faces tilted like the palms of hands. Only the dog returned her gaze.

'Well,' she said, 'it's awfully nice to meet you all.' It was her Joyce Grenfell voice. At the back of the room one of the older girls shifted the heavy plait of her hair from one shoulder to the other.

'I live on a farm,' said Irene, 'and we have lots of different sorts of animals. We have cows, mostly, and we like to give them all very special names . . .'

For an hour she had sat in a new café in Broadmead (tangerine walls, curved fibreglass benches, teenagers on dates) not eating her plate of macaroni *au gratin*. Later, she had a port and lemon in a pub. A man spoke to her but went away when she told him port was the best cure for morning sickness. Now she was in the warm and that was almost the best of it. Two big Kalee projectors, the smell of carbon dust, the racketing of the film through the gates. She was looking through the scratched glass of the observation window. On the screen Natalie Wood was kissing Warren Beatty. The audience – not a full house, barely half – was smoke and shadows. The ninety-second alarm sounded; the second reel was ready to go. She heard Byron move across to the far projector. She was watching out for the cue dots at the top of the screen. First dot, switch on the motor; second dot, roll.

'There,' she said, but he had seen for himself. The second reel began to turn. It seemed like something so easy to get wrong. He came back to the other projector and unloaded it. She watched him work. She had seen the film before; it wasn't new. He started to load the third reel. He checked the carbon rods. Though you weren't supposed to smoke up there, she begged a cigarette and turned back to the window.

When the intermission came he unscrewed the cap from the rum and topped up their glasses.

'Here's how,' she said. She drank, greedily. Byron drank too, but modestly. He studied her over the rim of his glass.

'You don't know how cold that farm is,' she said.

'Cold everywhere,' he said.

'Bet you wish you were back home, don't you?'

'Home? Every day.'

'Think you'll ever go?'

He shrugged. He had been in England for seven years. The last two he knew he would never leave. 'So where's your old man tonight?'

'Bill?' For a moment she thought he might have meant her father. He nodded; she explained.

'You should have gone with him.'

'Somebody needs to keep an eye on the farm.'

'You keeping an eye on the farm, Reet?'

She stuck out her tongue. For half a minute they were quiet together. Music was playing in the auditorium. Choosing the music for the intermission was another of Byron's jobs. Tonight it was Charlie Parker, 'A Night in Tunisia'. It was one he played quite often.

'So, how's Gloria then?' she asked, breezily, not looking at him. Sometimes he would tell her things and sometimes not. It seemed to depend on how, at any given moment, he viewed it all, her and Gloria, the history of those days.

'Gloria's OK.'

She waited.

'You know what she's up to now?' he said.

'I don't know anything.'

'Going to night school.'

'Gloria?'

'Twice a week on the bus. Satchel full of books.'

'She doesn't like buses.'

'Some place at the edge of the city. Never misses.'

'Blimey,' said Rita, frowning, 'night school.' Then, softly, 'Good for her,' and meant it, though there were pictures here very hard to reconcile. The pair of them walking home some hour of the night when even the lady-killers were in bed, the hiss-hiss of Gloria's satin dress, the little hussar's jacket with the fox-fur collar one of her regulars had given her. And Gloria on a corporation bus in harsh yellow light, a satchel on her lap, off to night school at the edge of the city. Was that what it meant to change yourself? You become what the others could not imagine, or had failed to? In their sleep, that chamber of drugged velvets at the centre of her head, the voices stirred.

'Going to do some A levels,' he said.

'Yeah?'

'Try for the university.'

'She'll make it.'

'You reckon?'

'Of course she will.'

'Because the university is so full of girls like my sister?'

'It's 1963, Byron. World's changing.'

'Changing all right. Wouldn't care to say what it's changing into.'

She held out her glass. 'To Gloria.'

He reached out with his own. 'To Glo,' he said.

The bell rang for the end of the intermission. He stood, suddenly in a hurry. Rita turned again to the window. She watched the ice-cream girl saunter back to her little room beneath the screen, draw the curtain. For a few seconds you could see her silhouette through the thin fabric, then the lights softened and she was gone.

When it was over, when the heavy doors had been swung shut, the night's takings counted, some of the litter between the seats collected (once, famously, they found a prosthetic leg in the dress circle), they gathered – Tony and Mrs Tony, the usherette, Byron and Rita – in the pink light of the foyer bar. Rita told jokes; she ground her teeth and drank gin. When she tottered off to the Ladies', Tony and his wife exchanged meaningful glances. Tony turned to Byron. 'Someone needs to walk her back to the station,' he said.

'And that should be me?' asked Byron.

No one said anything.

They cut through St Paul's on pavements imperfectly swept of snow, that here and there were glassy with ice. There was nothing in this part of the city he didn't know – the shadows in a doorway, how the light of a streetlamp rested on a third-floor window, who came and went, at what hour. He longed to find himself somewhere new, to be wandering, in a loose light suit, a city like Alexandria, somewhere that blazed with strangeness, where even the sky was strange. She held his arm. She was skittish. He didn't know what she was on, but she was on something.

At the top of Portland Square, rather than turn down towards Pritchard Street, she drew him onwards across the top of the square. Ahead of them a neon wigwam flicked from blue to green and back again.

'You joking?' he said.

'Why not?' she said.

'You know why not.'

'One quick drink,' she said.

'No way,' he said.

'Ten minutes. A last drink.'

'You don't understand what no means?'

She smiled at him, walked the last yards on her own and rang the bell. Music seeped from a vent beneath her feet. A young man in a suede jacket answered the door. He asked if she was a member.

'I used to work here,' she said, 'but I don't remember you.' She brushed past him and started down the stairs.

The club was busy, though not yet packed. On really busy nights you had to slide between the hot bodies; the men's hands were everywhere. As she came through the dark place at the bottom of the stairs, she saw Eugene mixing drinks and carrying on at least two conversations with men leaning at the bar. She sat at one end of a red bench from which she could see both the bar and the band.

'Five minutes,' said Byron, catching up with her. He went to the bar and brought her back a half-pint of Guinness. She took one of the Nembutal from the tissue in her purse and swallowed it with the beer. On stage a teenage girl was singing 'Strange Things Happening Every Day', but singing it more as blues than gospel. She had a white silk flower in her hair, a voice that was too big for her. The song shook her. She had been taught to give everything or she couldn't help herself.

When Rita turned away she caught Eugene studying her from behind the bar. He nodded, half smiled, renewed his attention to the glass he was filling. Very cool! He had, she thought, put on weight. His sandy hair was longer but there seemed less of it. He told her once he had begun in a rabbit hutch in County Cork. He was the funniest man she'd ever known. Was he a rich man now? The club would always do well: it was, somehow, tethered to the future. And she assumed he still arranged afternoons in the rented flats for those older men, local princes of commerce, highly respectable sorts, who, having won the war and survived the fifties, wanted some fun while they still had it in them. That little show she did with Gloria, that always went down well. Big tips! But when Gloria stopped coming (what did that man say to her? What did he call her?), she'd had to do the show with Iris or Peggy and it wasn't fun any more. You sober up and see what's in front of you. The men were fools and she was too, a bigger one. And Eugene? 'We're just making ourselves a dishonest living, girls. Button your coats and I'll buy you hot whiskies at the Rummer.'

Tonight she felt sorry for him (did he not, under the blue lights of the bar, look tired, exhausted even?) but tonight she felt sorry for everyone. She had never loved him; he had laughed her into bed and she had let it happen. Or more than that, she had wanted it to, had said something to him about two lonely people (ah, that's right, he'd said, undoing the little hooks). As for the rest of it – the doctor who charged five guineas to test her urine, the sad arguments about who was to blame, the walk up the lane to Nanny Simpson's, what did any of that matter now? She hadn't come to frighten him. She would go over there soon and say, It's all water under the bridge, Eugene. I just wanted to see if the place had changed much. I dream about it sometimes . . .

'Drink up,' said Byron. He'd seen Eugene's wife, Annie. Rita didn't see her until she was standing at the table.

'You've got a ruddy nerve,' said Annie.

'Hello, Annie,' said Rita. 'You've cut your hair short.'

Annie picked up the Guinness glass and emptied it into Rita's lap. 'Don't come back,' she said. 'Stupid cow.'

When they were outside again, Byron said, 'What did you expect?'

'I don't know,' said Rita. 'I'd forgotten she was like that.'

'Well, you remember now. When's the last train to this place you live?'

She said she didn't want to go back.

'I thought that was coming,' said Byron.

'Gloria won't mind, will she?'

'Gloria has to work tomorrow.'

'I'll sleep on the sofa. Under my coat.'

'You got some trouble at home?' said Byron.

'I'm pregnant,' she said. 'In case you hadn't noticed.'

He nodded. He hadn't. They stood there a moment, washed by the neon. He had no reason to suppose his sister would be pleased to see Rita Lee, but there were rules here, and he did not care to leave a pregnant woman at the station on her own at night. They set off. It was only a ten-minute walk. She chattered; he half attended. He had his hands thrust into the pockets of his overcoat. She took his arm again. She was reminiscing. Oh, the fun they'd had! Now and then he felt her shiver.

The house was just off City Road. They climbed the stairs. He waited for her at the top with the key in his hand.

Inside the flat he called to Gloria. Her room was at the back of the house. She came out in a silver-grey corduroy dress, a black cardigan. Her hair was tied in a strip of green velvet.

'She missed the last train,' said Byron.

'Hello,' said Rita. She started to sob, little waves, pulses of grief that seemed to rise in her almost mechanically. 'I'm just cold,' she said.

'Cold and pregnant,' said Byron. He went off to his room at the other end of the passage. There was only so much you could be expected to do.

Gloria came down to fetch Rita. She took her hand and led

her into her room where the gas fire was burning. On the table by the window a bottle lamp seeped its light onto the rugs. She took Rita's coat.

'Annie threw beer over me,' said Rita.

'You went to the club? You crazy?'

Rita shrugged.

'Take off the dress,' said Gloria. 'I'll get you something to put on.'

In the wardrobe she found a candlewick dressing-gown. Rita put it on over her slip. When Gloria took the dress to the kitchen, Rita sat on the sofa in front of the fire. There was a round, wood-frame mirror above the mantelpiece – had it been there before? – and wedged into the frame was a postcard of a bay with blue water and blue hills. A nurse's uniform hung from a brass hook on the back of the door. There was a type-writer on the desk, a portable. Above it, a film poster for *The Day the Earth Caught Fire*.

She curled up on the sofa. When Gloria came back she was nearly asleep.

'I made you tea and toast,' said Gloria. 'How long you been pregnant?'

'Ages,' said Rita.

'It doesn't show much.'

'It's a very polite baby,' said Rita. She sat up, took the tea and the plate of toast. She was extraordinarily hungry. Between mouthfuls she explained about Bill, where he was, what he was doing.

'You two get along?' asked Gloria. She had met Bill once, right at the beginning. He had seemed an odd choice but at least he wasn't married.

'We do all right,' said Rita, 'though sometimes he looks quite surprised to see me there.'

'At the farm.'

'That's right.'

Gloria sat on the sofa beside her. They looked at the feathers of the gas fire. Soon, from towers across the city, bells would strike the hour.

'You, a farmer's wife,' said Gloria.

'It's just a game,' said Rita.

'Won't be when the child comes.'

'Won't it?'

'You know it won't.'

'I don't know anything,' said Rita. 'Not any more. It isn't supposed to go like that, is it? By the time the baby's born I won't know my own name.'

'You can give the child what you didn't have.'

'Or what I did? How long should I leave it before I take the kid to meet Grandpa in the bin?'

'You're just frightened. You'll be all right when the time comes. You'll see.'

'Byron said you're going to night school.'

'Best thing I ever did.'

'You going to be a teacher?'

'I'm going to be someone who thinks.'

'And you're nursing now.'

'Up at the infirmary.'

'Got a nice smart uniform.'

'They soon let me know if it's not. Strict up there. And I'm on earlies this week. Got to be up at five tomorrow.'

'I'm sorry.'

'Doesn't matter.'

'I shouldn't have come.'

'It doesn't matter.'

'You're not angry?'

'Why would I be angry?'
'I don't know. I'm the bad penny.'
'I'm not angry, Reet.'
'I could always do what I did last time.'
'Last time?'
'At Nanny Simpson's.'
'You *joking*? No way that's going to happen. You hear? It's not like before. You're married now. You got a husband, a home. Forget about that place. Forget about the Pow-Wow and Eugene, all that craziness.'

She turned to study her, this friend she had not seen in how long. The robe was too big for her. She was there like a sickly child, one who has to be watched through the night. How much trouble was she in? How lost? Was it serious? There had been no big bust-up between them. She could hardly remember now what it was. A coolness, a misunderstanding, some home truths (Gloria to Rita). She'd had her own unhappiness then, her own troubles, and did not think Rita had the right to say she understood what she didn't and couldn't.

She lifted the plate and cup off the sofa and drew Rita's head onto her chest. She had put a shilling in the meter so the gas was good for another half-hour. She stroked Rita's hair. She remembered the smell of her. She said things to calm her, slipped back into something like her island voice. She remembered how Rita liked that, a language at the edge of singing, the voice her mother and grandmother had soothed her with in the time before. It slowed your heart. It slowed both their hearts. Slowed the baby's too? She drew out, like a poison, some of the coldness in Rita's body. She felt her softening. She was close to sleep herself now. The gas made you drowsy and she'd walked miles on the ward today. She settled her head against the cushion. Along the passage, from Byron's room, came the singing of Fats Domino – 'I want to walk you home, please let me walk you home . . .'

To be held. Wasn't that what anybody wanted? To be held, if only for a night?

She slid further towards sleep, the peace of it. Rita had an arm loosely around her waist. At evening class last term they had looked at slides of paintings and there had been one, Toulouse Lautrec, of two women sleeping in a bed, and you could just see their heads above the piled covers and though they were both redheads she had thought at once of herself and Rita. The teacher said the women were probably prostitutes but the teacher doesn't always know.

His father stood in the doorway. Bill got out of bed. He put on a jacket over his pyjamas, looked for his socks and found he was still wearing them. His father watched all this. Finally, he fetched the folder from the holdall and followed his father along the corridors of the night-time house.

His father had two offices, one in the basement and one in the attic. They went to the one in the attic. If the Gestapo arrived or the Flying Squad or the Kray twins, the office in the attic would be the last of the fall-backs, the place you made your last stand, where you decided they would never take you alive.

There was a metal-frame desk, grey steel cabinets, an electric cooker, a safe like an unliftable shut mouth. There was a bar stool, a chair upholstered with beautiful toffee-coloured Italian suede, another chair of plain yellow wood, like a schoolroom chair. A small window looked from the back of the house towards Bermondsey. If there were stars, if there were not.

His father was in a paisley dressing-gown. He wore a yellow silk scarf. He had on black leather shoes and seemed, under the dressing-gown, to be wearing what he had been wearing during the day. To warm the place, he turned on the electric rings of the cooker. They gave off the smell of some impending electrical disaster. He poured them both little glassfuls of colourless liquor. There was half a cigar in the ashtray on the desk and, after giving it a gentle massage, he lit it with a piece of paper he set alight from one of the rings. He asked what the child's name was.

'It doesn't have a name yet.'

'Elizabeth,' said his father. 'After the Queen.'

'Yes,' said Bill. 'That's a possibility.'

'Or Winston?'

'There are probably quite a lot of little Winstons already.'

'Or Bill?'

'Bill?'

'Bill Junior.'

'Would you like me to name it after you?' asked Bill.

'Well,' said his father, 'you would have to know my name first.'

'I think I do,' said Bill. 'I looked at your naturalisation certificate. It was in your wallet.'

'You looked in my wallet?'

'It was a long time ago.'

His father nodded. 'So you want to call the kid József Somogyi?'

There was certain thrill in hearing his father say it. Hard to tell what that was. Some brush with truth, with history. The very speaking of the name opened the door to a courtyard, just wide enough to see who was gathered there. Then (to Bill's relief) the door swung shut again.

They drank the liquor. Bill opened the folder. He began to explain to his father the scheme for the old hangar. It came out like a fairy tale, as perhaps everything must at two a.m. He laid the sheet with the figures on the desk in front of his father.

'You should show this to your mother. She's a human computer. She's like IBM.'

'All right,' said Bill.

'She's not well.'

'No?'

'How could she be well?' Without looking at the sheet of figures, his father touched the corner with one blunt finger. 'They add up?'

'Yes,' said Bill. 'I've gone over it many times.'

'Automation.'

'As much as possible.'

'You like people?'

'Some of them,' said Bill.

'You like your wife?'

'Yes.'

'When you were little . . .' said his father. He gestured with the cigar. Nothing followed.

'You would be a sleeping partner,' said Bill.

'What if I wake up?'

'You wouldn't need to.'

'Every year you can send me a big steak.'

'Every month, if you like.'

'I'm not a rich man,' said his father. He was grinning.

'Of course,' said Bill.

'The bank will give you something?'

'If I can raise half.'

'The banks,' said his father, 'are the greatest thieves of all. Remember that.'

He filled the little glasses again, stood and walked around the desk to where a half-dozen leather briefcases lay discarded on the floor behind the door. He picked one out, dusted the leather with the sleeve of his dressing-gown, placed it on the desk and undid the catch. Then he went to the safe and squatted in front of it. Bill could hear but not see the turning of the tumbler. When his father rose again he was holding wedges of cash in either hand. He put them on the desk and went back for more. He made four trips before shutting the safe.

'Have a look,' said his father.

The bundles were held together with rubber bands. Bill picked up the nearest and flicked through. This wasn't money crisp from the teller's drawer: it was cash from a purse, a trouser pocket, a teapot on the mantelpiece, the underside of a mattress. Money saved, money hidden, money handed over between the covers of a rent book to a man standing on the landing with an Alsatian. On the newer notes, the young Queen, offended, jowly, would not meet his eye.

'How much is there?' asked his father.

'I'm not sure,' said Bill. 'Ten?'

His father nodded. He looked pleased to have a son who could recognise ten thousand pounds when it was piled on a table in front of him. 'Put it in the briefcase,' he said.

Bill stood up to do it. He put in the money carefully while his father watched him. The case was big enough but only just.

'Should I give you something?' asked Bill. 'A receipt or something?'

'It's a gift,' said his father. 'Do you give a receipt for a gift?'

In the bedroom, by the light of a bedside lamp – one of those curious old wartime 'Emergency' lamps, a cycle bulb in green glass – Bill sat on the bed with the briefcase beside him. Now and then he opened it to look inside. The money showed like flowers at dusk, like the crumpled blooms of the evening primrose that grew in scattered spikes behind the shippon in August. He got off the bed, raised the case, lowered it. Guess the weight and win a prize! He laughed, softly as he could. For the length of a corridor on his walk back from the attic he had feared he might be at the beginning of some attack of self-loathing, of moral nausea. But it wasn't the beginning of anything; perhaps it was the end. He felt full of vitality. If Rita had been there he would have made love to her. It had been a while since they'd done that. He thought of her expression when he showed her the money. He imagined (with another burst of stifled laughter) showing the money to the bull. He slid the case under the bed. He would have felt happier locking the bedroom door but there was no key. He put off the lamp and slid under the covers, anxious now for sleep, for no untidy thoughts to eat away at the moment's triumph. And he did what he had done before in this house, reciting in a whisper to his pillow the names of London's hidden rivers. Once upon a time he knew them all, but now he stalled at Walbrook, heard the hollow roaring of its flood, was briefly frightened, then let it carry him (black petals, small hands) to where the waters widened and rose towards the morning.

Saturday, 12 January

His first patient was in the village, the bungalows at the bottom of the lane. He would walk down – it would only take ten minutes. There was a wind, on the sharp side, but it wasn't snowing. He put on a heavy coat, leather gloves, a scarf. He decided he didn't need boots: his beetle-crushers would do. He took his bag and set off (I am the doctor walking through the village). As he passed the shop the shadow of Mrs Case waved to him and he waved back. It was Mrs Case who had rung him about Mr Earle. A neighbour of Mr Earle's had been worried and had spoken of it in the shop. It was understood that one of Mrs Case's roles was to pass on information to the appropriate person. Generally this meant himself or Constable Hill. Occasionally, a message might be carried to the parson.

The bungalows were quite new, certainly post-war. They were built in a semi-circle around the looped end of the lane (if you want to keep going, there's a path through wasteland that brings you out onto the Bristol road). Each house was pebble-dashed and had a patch of lawn at the front, another at the back, just big enough to sit on and watch the washing dry. There was no sound of playing children. They were council properties and almost all were lived in by retired people, some of them quite elderly.

Mr Earle's house was number three. Eric pressed the bell. When there was no answer he squinted through the living-room window. The curtains were partly closed and the room unlit, but he could see Mr Earle in one of the armchairs. He tapped on the glass. Slowly, Mr Earle looked up. He nodded, gravely, but made no attempt to stand. Eric went round to the back. The garden, with its single tea rose, its blackcurrant bush and lean-to shed, must be strange to a man who had once run a farm. The back door was unlocked. It led directly into the kitchen. He called, 'It's Dr Parry, Mr Earle.'

The kitchen was a mess. He went through to the living room. The room was very cold. He opened the curtains.

'Hello,' he said.

'What you doing here?' asked Mr Earle. He looked alarmed, as if he had already forgotten the face at the window.

'One of your neighbours thought you might be poorly.'

'I'm all right.'

'Yes?'

He was wearing pyjamas, with a ribbed jumper (padded elbows) over the pyjama jacket. His left foot had a slipper on but the right was bare. Eric took off his coat and draped it over the other armchair. He got down onto one knee. 'Mind if I have a look?' he asked.

He could have cut the material with his scissors but the cloth was loose and he was able to raise it without touching the leg. Along the shin and the outside of the calf, the skin was shiny, sausage pink and badly blistered.

'Fell asleep in front of the fire,' said Mr Earle. 'Like a daft sod.'

'That one?' asked Eric, nodding to the two-bar heater, unplugged, the other side of the little hearth.

'That's him,' said Mr Earle.

'When did it happen?'

The farmer shrugged.

In the kitchen Eric set the kettle to boil. He took the plates and saucepan out of the sink. He took off his jacket and rolled up his shirt sleeves. He washed his hands, drying them on a clean handkerchief. (Irene kept that top drawer well supplied; it was the sort of thing one had hoped would happen in married life.) He went back to the living room.

'How do you feel about going to hospital?'

'Not going to any hospital,' said Mr Earle. 'Go in, you don't come out.'

'I thought you might say that,' said Eric. 'Are you in much pain?'

Mr Earle made a face. His pain was his business.

Eric opened his bag. He took out tweezers and scissors, carried them to the kitchen to sterilise them with the boiled water, came back and started to debride the wound, cutting away the dead skin and some of the blisters. He worked quickly. Two or three times the old farmer flinched and Eric apologised. He was trying to decide what kind of condition Mr Earle was in. Clearly, he was extremely tough. Many of his age, a burn like this, sitting in the cold, would have had hypothermia. The worry, of course, was infection, but there seemed very little sign of it. Had the cold helped with that? He cleaned the wound with tap water and a solution of iodine. He dressed the leg with mesh and a net bandage. He took the farmer's blood pressure. It was low but not alarming. In his bag he had the bottle of mixture from Peter Gurney's bedside. It was that or aspirins. He didn't think aspirins would make much difference. With a little persuasion ('You don't want me to call that ambulance, do you?'), Mr Earle took a sip from a teaspoon. It was no more than a few millilitres.

In the kitchen Eric made a pot of tea, then went through the cupboards searching for food. There was a tin of baked beans, a tin of marrowfat peas, a tin of steak and kidney. He heated up half of the steak and kidney and tipped it into a bowl. He sat with Mr Earle while he ate it.

'How are you feeling now?'

'I've had worse than this.'

'Do you need the toilet?'

He did. Eric fetched an empty milk bottle and Mr Earle half filled it. The poor shrunken phallus.

'Right, let's get you into bed.'

It took ten minutes to get him down the short corridor to the bedroom. The room was plain, nothing on the walls, no photograph on the chest of drawers. No children, no wife. Was it very bitter to be so alone? Would he find out? There was a high old-fashioned bed, one that had more to do with farmhouses than modern bungalows. Eric opened drawers in the chest until he found some clean pyjamas. He wasn't bothered about the jacket but the trousers needed changing. He was told to bugger off but the job got done. He manoeuvred the farmer into bed, both of them working hard. He drew the curtains, leaving just a few inches of the white day to fall across Mr Earle's large red hands.

'I'll get the district nurse to come in at teatime,' he said. 'You'll like her. Mrs Drysdale. She'll change the dressing and make you something else to eat. You don't need to be shy with her. I'll be back in the morning.'

He packed up his bag, put on his jacket and coat and left

the house. He wondered if he should have insisted on the hospital. What sort of state was his heart in? But a man in his sixties was surely entitled to refuse treatment. If he died in his bed, what of it? He had done what he could to make him comfortable. Across the world, perhaps a hundred thousand people would die today, so the farmer would leave in company.

As he walked up the lane it started to snow, big flakes tugged about by the wind. A heavy fall now and the lanes might become undriveable again quite quickly, but by the time he reached the shop it had stopped. He went in and spoke to Mrs Case. He asked her to make up a small box of groceries for Mr Earle, things she knew he liked and that could be easily prepared. 'You can put it on my account,' he said.

She bobbed her head. 'Very good, Doctor.' He didn't have an account. Mrs Case didn't approve of them – they could lead to unpleasantness – but for the doctor she would make an exception. She saw men as largely unknowing, important men, educated ones, as the most unknowing.

She fetched a cardboard box from beneath the counter. 'And how's Mrs Parry?' she asked.

He nodded. He was studying the line of tins on the shelf at the back of the shop. Irene's father had called him yesterday evening when he was already on his third or fourth drink. Irene was safe. There had, of course, been trouble with the trains. He had not asked and had not been told what her plans were, and it was only afterwards it occurred to him that he still didn't really know where she was. She seemed not to be at her parents' house, unless he had missed something, which was possible. The call had ended with a series of hesitations, each man laying down his silence like a hand of cards. In all likelihood, none of this would ever be spoken of between them again, or referred to in any way.

'She's well,' he said. He took down a tin of mulligatawny soup. 'And stick this on the account too, will you?'

The first time she woke the room was a landscape, a lake at dawn with mist on the water. At the desk by the typewriter her father was sitting in the red cardigan she had made for him (it had taken months). He was smoking, looking towards the door rather than at her, or perhaps not really looking at anything. Thinking, remembering. He had come for what? For her? She knew it wasn't a dream because she could smell the smoke of his cigarette.

'Dad?'

He turned to her and smiled. 'Return of the invisible man,' he said.

The second time she woke the room was light, the uniform was gone from the back of the door, and the other side of the bed was cold. She lay with just her head above the covers and looked at the poster for *The Day the Earth Caught Fire*.

The INCREDIBLE becomes real. The IMPOSSIBLE becomes fact. The UNBELIEVABLE becomes true. The picture that gives you a front seat to the most jolting events of tomorrow!

There were stills from the film – men talking urgently, a crowd grasping at whatever pleasures it could find in the few hours remaining to it, the male lead (introducing Edward Judd) stooping to kiss Janet Munro.

She swung her legs from the bed. She was wearing her slip. The room was cold, though not as cold as the farm. She felt terrible but she felt all right, muddled but clear. She gazed down at the roses of her knees. One plan – she had brought it out of sleep with her – was to go back to the farm and take all the pills she could find, wash them down with whatever there was to drink (cider?). But in her sleep the lingerie drawer was crammed full of pills; awake, she knew she didn't have enough. She would need at least twenty of the Seconal to make sure of it, something like two thousand milligrams (who had told her the dose? Someone she danced with at the club?). If she took everything she had, added the half-bottle of aspirin in the bathroom and hid somewhere – the apple room, the barn – she might manage it, but the chances were they would find her, pump her stomach and send her home. Or send her to live with her father? How easy that was to imagine. Her first day on the ward.

She stood, swayed, steadied herself and went to the window. It was above the flat roof of the bathroom on the floor below. After a struggle she got it to slide up on its sashes. She leaned out, brushed away the crust where it was speckled with soot, scooped up a double handful of the cleaner snow and pressed it to her face until it stung.

'Do it or don't do it,' she said, addressing the print of her face in the palms of her hands. 'Don't *half* do it.'

She tossed the snow back onto the roof and shut the window. She put on the candlewick robe and went in search of her dress. It was hanging over the back of a chair in the kitchen. It was dry. The Guinness stain was a subtle cloud in the fabric. She carried it back to Gloria's room. When she was dressed she sat at the desk, the typewriter in front of her. There was a fresh sheet of paper wound into the platen. She stared at it, then lifted her hands and began to type. In her pomp at City and County she'd had sixty words per minute. She typed for a minute. She didn't read it back.

From her purse she took out the picture of the cow with its garland of flowers and slotted it into the mirror frame next to the postcard of the blue hills. It was, she thought, what she had come to do. Hello, goodbye, hello, goodbye.

She was starting to feel sick. She went to the kitchen to look for something to eat. She found a box of Ritz crackers, ate three, drank a mug of tap water and left the flat. She was in Brunswick Square before she realised she had left her rabbit-skin hat at Gloria's, though the more she thought about it, the more likely it was she had left it at the Pow-Wow. For some reason it made her laugh. 'Run, rabbit, run, rabbit, run run run!' An older woman, walking the other way, gave her a tight-lipped, quick-eyed glance, a bird's glance.

She crossed through strings of sullen traffic, walked up Union Street towards the bombed-out arches of St Peter's. She stopped in a café beside the market, ordered a sausage sandwich and a coffee with steamed milk. When it came, she drank the coffee but left the sandwich untouched under the folded serviette. She was sitting on a stool by the window. There was a wireless in the kitchen playing band music. The Dambusters? She lit a cigarette and unwrapped the last Nembutal from its nest of tissue, considered it, then wrapped it again. There were no voices this morning. She felt for them, but the place they had been was scraped and silent. Had they finished their work? Made way for something new? Was that what her father had come to tell her? She glanced around at the four or five others who shared the café with her. At what point do you stop a stranger to ask for help? And which one? The one who looks most like you? Least?

There was a phone box at the end of Corn Street. She walked through the market. The box was occupied by two teenagers, a boy and a girl. They seemed to be singing down the phone. When they came out they walked either side of her, a bit rudely, but she didn't mind. The box smelt of the perfume the girl had been wearing, something unusual, new, smoky, something she was already too old to wear. She found the number in her purse, written on a bus ticket. She lifted the handset, loaded her pennies into the holding slot and dialled. When Mrs Bolt answered, she asked if she might speak to Dr Miklos, but Mrs Bolt was still talking and it was as if she had been replaced by something that was just pretending to be Mrs Bolt. There were a few seconds of silence, and then it started again. 'On Saturday the twelfth of January Dr Parry is on call.' The voice recited his number. 'On Sunday the thirteenth of January, Dr Miklos is on call . . .'

She listened to it again, then dialled Dr Parry's number. She had some idea that she would ask for Irene, but when he picked up she couldn't speak at all.

'Hello? . . . Hello?'

His breath, hers. She hung up, left the box and walked down to the old bridge that crossed the floating harbour. Halfway over she stepped to the rail. Below her the water was frozen solid. The barges with their smoking stovepipes were locked in (not that they ever went anywhere). A pair of herring gulls strolled to the centre of the ice, then, with shrieks of anger, lifted abruptly into the air. There were skaters coming, three of them from the Redcliffe end, their hands clasped behind their backs, their bodies leaning into what they travelled through. It didn't look like a race but they came swiftly, shoulder to shoulder, swaying, pushing themselves into long glides, their faces shadowed, schematic, blurred by cold and motion. And suddenly she could hear the sound of the skates, how they chimed like spurs! They shot beneath the bridge, startling her with a thrill of falling so that she gasped, clutched at the rail and felt her belly cut with the shadow of their passing. For a minute she was stranded there, the strange white flower of her face, her gloved hands gripping the iron rail. Then, like one already wounded, already bleeding, she crossed the remainder of the bridge. Around her the city went on with its business, the day like a sheet on which it showed its wares. Even some of the small dark churches were for sale. Their bones were full of the river and they had seen too much.

The Scouts came. They had a sledge they had made into a sleigh. It had a seat and room for the legs. There were no wolf skins or bear skins, but there were blankets and a piece of oilcloth, a red cushion from the Scout hut. Their leader was a boy of seventeen. He had clear green eyes, the face of one who would later be a cardinal or the loved colonel of an elite regiment, or simply good. He introduced himself as Orlando. He blushed when he spoke. Irene and the housemother were in awe of him.

The children were hurried into their coats. The sleigh was drawn up outside the front steps. Five other boys waited there, holding the traces. The housemother (coatless) stood on the steps, the wind gusting the ash from her breasts. She held Irene tight. 'You won't forget us, will you, dear?'

Irene breathed her in. The other's body, with its lumps and strappings, its terrible softness, was an animal you meet in a dream and must placate with songs and silences; a wicked witch who turns out to be a middle-aged woman with poor circulation and some unsheddable grief you are free to look away from. Irene took her place in the sleigh. The blankets and the oilcloth were drawn up. She wrapped her scarf around her head. As Orlando assisted, he took care not to look at her, or he did so with quick little sweepings of his green eyes. Then he went to where another boy held out the line to him. Three boys on one side, three the other. There was a jolt as the lines tautened. The prow of the sleigh lifted slightly and they began to move.

'Goodbye, dear!' called the housemother. 'Goodbye!' The children cheered and waved, their gazes spread out in a fan as if a dozen sleighs were setting out, some in the air.

They crossed the lawn, passed under the wings of the cedar. The dog bounded after them and was called back. A bell sounded, very distant. It was the middle of the day. Fitful glassy sunlight, scudding snow-clouds. The boys leaned into their work, silent mostly, though now and then Orlando called the direction they would take, the presence of an obstacle. They went at a brisk march. In places they jogged, perhaps for the joy of it. They were, she thought, glad to be used. They cut across fresh snow. If one lost his footing, the others laughed, companionably. It was open country. Low chalk hills, the dark lines of woodland littered with snow. She wanted to call, is it far? But they would have had to stop and attend to her, then have the labour of setting off again. And what did it matter how far it was? She was in no hurry. Whatever she had said to her mother on the phone, she had no real doubt about what the letter had meant. What doubt could there be? She was going back to a type of failure and to whatever dull explanations it occasioned. She saw them, she and Eric, either side of the kitchen table, each staring into the dark of themselves to say what no longer really mattered. It was, she supposed, unavoidable. It was what people did, people in their situation. And there was something shaming in that too, their being caught up in what they would once have thought of with contempt, or a shudder, as if considering an illness (the sort one didn't discuss at table) others might suffer from, but you knew you never would . . .

The sleigh, one of its runners, bounced over something hidden under the snow and the whole thing rocked like a rowing boat, then righted and steadied, and went on. A chain is twenty-two yards. The shapes of snow are the shapes of water. They dragged her, her loyal boys, as if she was the empress of somewhere that still mattered. How *odd* this is, she thought, and leaned back in her seat, hands on the heat of her belly, gathering the moment in as a gift.

He spoke on the telephone to the district nurse. A couple of patients rang. Then there was a call, from a phone box, in which no one spoke, though there was obviously somebody there. He thought it had probably been Irene. It had unnerved him, filled him again with uncertainty.

He had his soup (was there much difference between mulligatawny and tomato? There didn't seem to be). The day thickened. He smoked. He had two fingers of whisky from a bottle he had bought at the grocer's in the little rank of shops next to the surgery (Tilly had waved to him through the window of the chemist's). Feelings came and went. At one point he was almost faint with desire, the need to press his mouth to the heat of another's body – he didn't really care whose – to be obliterated. Half a minute later he was thinking about his father, and then of Mr Earle, and then some residue of last night's dream in which Irene, enormously pregnant, stood in the nursery, laughing like a mad woman. There had been a lot of nasty dreams recently and he wondered if what he really wanted, wanted most of all, was just to be free of them and whatever it was they grew out of, to be not just untroubled but innocent.

*

In the garage the car started at the third time of asking. He let it idle a few minutes then shifted the lever by his knee to engage the suspension. The car rose. You had to smile when it did that, the cleverness of it. He got out to unbolt the garage doors then drove slowly into the light, watching the light ride up the bonnet as if peeling it. He went up the lane in second. Before the junction with the main road it climbed steeply and he was worried about the brakes holding, but the car was equal to it; the car was dependable. A single-decker bus went by, Bristol direction, mostly empty. He pulled out. The main road looked clear enough but he would, he decided, keep his speed to thirty or below. No point pushing his luck.

Ahead of him, a dark shape that resolved itself into a horseman – or, as he got closer, a horsewoman. He swung wide. Usually they acknowledged it with a lift of the riding crop but not this one. When he looked in his mirror he saw it was the girl from the party, the teenager who had come with the Strangs. Not beautiful, not even pretty, but a face you didn't forget. Cissy? Cassy? She sat with a fine straight back. You could see she'd been riding most of her life. God help the fox *she* went after.

He wondered if that was where Frank was. Apparently he spent a lot of time at Strang's house now, a loyal lieutenant, the heir apparent, flirting with the depressed wife, flattering the old man. Alison had said he always wore a cravat when he went over there because Edward Strang had a taste for them. She'd had to show him how to tie one because he'd had no idea.

He passed the surgery, passed the straggling houses (it was neither village nor town here), then out between fields again. So far so good. The snow was holding off. The land was settled, dream-locked under the white drifts. It was woods on either side of him now. He came down the hill to the turning. The side road was unscraped, but the moon-coloured snow was compacted and someone had scattered a reddish grit on it. He slowed to walking pace by the entrance to the first driveway, saw the boot of Alison's car, kept going and crawled into the second driveway, parking in his usual place opposite the white metal door of the garage.

The big house looked closed down for the winter, as if awaiting the arrival of some cheerful family on a warm morning in May. He switched off the engine, got out and stood there, listening. Riding on the gusts of wind was the sound of a klaxon from the quarry. What always struck him as curious was how, after the klaxon ended, you never heard the explosion or felt any disturbance of the air or ground. He couldn't explain that. He had often found himself waiting for it.

He walked around the side of the house. The snow had been partially cleared and there were boot prints going either way in what remained. The pool should probably have had a cover it on but didn't. The snow lay in it unevenly. The changing chalet was a toy, a souvenir of Switzerland. He went up the steps to the French windows and leaned towards the glass. The room was unlit, the expensive furniture floating in shadow. He tapped, waited, tapped again. In ten years, he thought, in five, none of this will matter a jot, we'll struggle to remember it. He tried the door; it was unlocked. He kicked the snow off his shoes and went in.

'Alison?'

He closed the door behind him and stepped deeper into the room. He wasn't a house-breaker, he was a doctor. And hadn't he done something similar at Mr Earle's bungalow this morning?

The room's warmth was, as always, excessive. As a medical man and a type of socialist, he didn't approve. It was, however, distinctly pleasant, a relief from the endless struggle with the cold, the way this bloody winter never let up. For a second or two he had the wild thought of stretching out on the sofa and taking a nap. She would find him there, asleep like Goldilocks, and wake him with a kiss (though that, of course, was a different story. The bears did not kiss Goldilocks. What did they do with her? A girl alone in a house of bears, bears she had offended).

There were no glasses on the table, no unwashed coffee cups. The magazines – *Country Life* – were neatly stacked; the ashtray was empty. He tried her name again but found himself speaking it softly, floating it in the heat-cushioned air as if, in some odd game, she was standing just the other side of the shut door to the hall. It seemed impossible she had forgotten their meeting. It was *she* who had called him – it had been her idea. She had wanted to have a proper talk – though possibly it was he who had said that part.

Go up to the bedroom? He knew his way well enough. But to go up he would have first to go past that shut door, and for some reason he didn't care to. He went back to the French windows (you could move completely silently on this carpet) and looked out at the changing chalet. He opened the door and re-entered the cold, closing the door behind him. He went down the brick steps to the lawn and peered up at the bedroom window. The curtains were drawn. He was surprised he hadn't noticed that when he first arrived. Or had they not been drawn then?

Above the bare trees at the end of the garden, the rooks were startling at something they could see but he could not. He began to feel foolish, caught in a play of glances he didn't understand. Inside the house he had unbuttoned his coat; now he buttoned it again. He decided to leave. He would do it without delay, swiftly and quietly. He would leave and go where he could think about it, this feeling he wasn't going to give a name to yet.

When he reached the corner of the house he saw his car, the *bleu nuage* a single shade brighter than the dusk. Another three strides and he stopped. The garage door was open. Inside, quite unmistakably, the black gleam and big silver grille of the Zodiac.

'Hello Parry.'

Somehow, Frank was behind him. Eric turned. 'Hello Frank.'

He had on a battledress blouse, camouflage trousers. From his left hand he dangled the longbow. In the other hand, an arrow.

'Come to see Alison?'

'That's right. She called the surgery. Yesterday, I think.'

'Perhaps she's unwell.'

'Is she?'

'You're the doctor.'

They looked at each other. Frank was smiling. In the garage, the narrow space between the car and the wall, something moved. It was the boy, John. He came out carrying his cricket bat. The men watched him.

'I'd been wondering for a while,' said Frank, 'what to do about you.' He fitted the arrow to the bow, notched it. 'Then John had a bright idea.'

'If Alison's not in,' said Eric, 'I have other patients to see.'

'Oh, she's in,' said Frank. 'My wife. She just doesn't want to see you. Not any more. Did you think you knew her? I can assure you you didn't. Perhaps you thought you knew me too, a clever chap like you. The fact is, Parry, you're a nasty piece of work and this little show is to help you remember to keep your trousers buttoned.' He raised the bow.

'Are you drunk?' asked Eric. He knew that he wasn't but it seemed one had to say something. His life had just entered a place called Chaos, but it was a place not without rules, a certain formality.

'This arrow,' said Frank, 'has a field tip on it. It will bring a stag down at sixty yards. How far would you say you are from me now? Five? So you stay nice and still and enjoy the show.'

The boy approached the Citroën. He walked to the driver's side, stood a couple of seconds looking at the car, admiring it even, then raised the bat and swung it. The windscreen exploded.

'Watch out for the glass,' said Frank. 'Though we do have a doctor here, of course.'

The boy circled the car. At each window he swung the bat. When he put in the rear window, Frank said, 'That was definitely a six.'

Once the windows were done he smashed the lights, front and back. He began on the body. Two, three, four swings at the bonnet. The steel creased like paper. He hit the roof of the car twice before his father called him off.

'I'm going to have to get him a new bat,' said Frank. To his son he said, 'Give the man some room or he'll think you're going to brain him.'

Eric walked to the car. He opened the driver's door and, with his hand, swept the broken glass from the seat into the well. He could not for a moment find the key; then he found it and got the car started. He twisted his body to peer through the hole where the rear windscreen had been. He reversed, very carefully, as if giving a demonstration, as if he was a man in a government training film about reversing. At every movement he felt and heard the glass beneath him. He knew they would be watching and that it was important he did not look back. When he reached the road he started speaking to himself. It was gibberish, it frightened him, and he stopped. At the junction he pulled out onto the main road. Instead of the inside car smells of tobacco smoke and seat leather, he had the sharpness of the outer world. As he picked up speed the air rushed across his face in a way that quickly became painful. His right hand was wet. When he glanced at it he saw it was cut and bleeding, the blood winding over his wrist and falling in dark drops to his lap. The passenger seat was covered with glass, a strange throne. A car came towards him. As it passed him, both driver and passenger turned to stare. A ghost car, driven by a ghost! Were they patients of his? He couldn't see them clearly enough.

At a farm gate he pulled over, got out and crouched beside the offside door. He pressed his hands to his face, then remembered the cut: he must have blood all over his cheek now. He thought of the girl on the horse coming by, looking down from an immense height and seeing him, this cowering man with his smeared face. She was of an age where she might still imagine she could choose the kind of world she lived in. She would not offer help.

He searched his pockets for his cigarettes. He found them and used the lighter in the car. It seemed surprising that so many things still worked after what the boy had done. He smoked half the cigarette and threw the butt into the shadowed ice at his feet. He started driving again. He needed to get off the main road before it was fully dark. He had no plan other than to return to the cottage and hide, but as he passed the unlit surgery he suddenly knew exactly what to do. He took the next right, then right again, and drove for a minute beside the yellow windows of early evening before pulling onto the forecourt of a large grey-stone house. It was a place with peaked gables and arched windows that must, once, have stood on its own in the midst of tended grounds, but possessed now only a single cherry tree, like a slapped girl, at the corner of a concrete parking area.

He stopped the car where there seemed least light, and sat for a while trying to master himself, to stop this unbearable sinking into the body. Then he got out and went to the entrance. The house had been divided into flats. He pressed the bell for the top floor. When the door opened his face was so numbed from the cold there was no possibility of a smile, of any expression at all. When he said hello he sounded as if he'd had a stroke.

'Come inside,' said Gabby. He stood back, then guided Eric up the stairs, one hand lightly between his shoulder blades. In the flat they went through to the kitchen-dining room. The house might be old but the interior was quite modern. Gabby pulled out a chair from the head of the dining table and sat Eric down on it. He fetched his medical bag. The cut – on the thenar of his left hand – was ragged and surprisingly deep. Gabby cleaned it and dressed it. It was interesting to see the way he worked, the little differences. From the corner cupboard he fetched two small glasses. Into each he poured an inch of colourless liquor from an unlabelled bottle.

'I have been promising you some of this for a long time.'

'The plums?'

'Yes.'

They drank. Eric still had his coat on. He picked a piece of the windscreen from it and placed it on the table. He told Gabby what had happened and why. Gabby did not interrupt. When he finished he began on a second version – longer, looser. He mentioned his father. He mentioned one or two practical matters (he was still on call). He did not mention Irene by name, though he seemed to be speaking about her. He asked if he could stay the night.

'Naturally,' said Gabby. He said he would go down and place something over Eric's car. He had a storage space in the basement and something in there, a tarpaulin, he thought was big enough. Then he would go to the surgery – there was a path behind the house, it was only a few minutes' walk – and change the message on the answer phone.

'You know how to do it?' asked Eric.

'In fact,' said Gabby, 'I showed Mrs Bolt how to do it.'

He topped up Eric's glass and left the flat. Eric continued collecting fragments from his coat, pieces of crystal, shards, splinters. He would, he thought, be shedding the stuff for weeks. Everywhere he sat down he would leave a little of it behind, enough to prick a finger.

At intervals of roughly seven or eight seconds he had the fantasy of killing Frank Riley and his son, battering them with a tyre iron, their bodies sprawled on the drive. Then, presumably, he'd go inside and do for Alison. She had betrayed him, for what? A warm house? He had a vivid picture of the blood coming through her hair. It made him shake again. He also imagined himself on Seven's table, the arrow in his chest still. My God, how interested Seven would have been in that! He created a touching graveyard scene, Irene and the child hand in hand next to a grassed mound. But the fantasies were all brief; they were hurried through and quickly corrected. For the moment, the truth was a more bearable version than its alternatives.

He drained the glass. The liquor was fiery, mineral, faintly medicinal, like something distilled from stones rather than fruit. He started to notice his surroundings. He had been in the flat before – he had helped Gabby to move in – but this was the first time he had seen it with everything laid out in its chosen place. There was no bachelor mess, no lingering whiff of fried food. Cream walls, blue curtains, a yellow lampshade. On the wooden floor a couple of good-quality Turkish rugs. There was a shelf with books in two languages, and beside it a painting of a house with eaves and shutters, not English. And then there was the dining table, big, possibly an antique, a tablecloth starched and thick as an altar cloth. Four chairs down one side, four down the other, a chair at the far end, plus the one he was sitting on. Ten chairs. For Gabby? Gabby who lived so quietly? Who were they for, all these chairs?

He came down from his room to say goodbye. He had the holdall, he had the briefcase. His mother was in the little room. He went to kiss her and she flinched.

'If you ever fancy some country air,' he said.

She nodded. 'Your father's got an appointment at the Brompton next week.'

'Has he?' He thought of the Brompton Oratory, Brompton Cemetery.

'With a surgeon.'

'You could let me know how it goes.'

'He's frightened,' she said, 'but he won't let you see it.'

And then, as in a play, he joined them. He was holding a pair of handcuffs. He took Bill's left hand, snapped one of the cuffs around his wrist and the other around the flayed leather handle of the briefcase. He held up a small key.

'You should swallow this,' he said. He slid the key into the breast pocket of Bill's jacket.

'Thanks,' said Bill. It was six o'clock. He had meant to leave at least two hours ago. The reason for the delay seemed to be his entire past life, his connection to these people, this house. It didn't matter. He had the briefcase. He had what he had come for. In truth he had vastly more than he had come for. If there was time he would call Rita from Paddington. He would drop hints, he would tease her. He wondered if the flower stall might still be open. He would walk into the farmhouse with more roses than she had ever seen.

'Where's Charlie?' he asked. Charlie was going to give him a lift to the station.

'He's brushing his hair,' said his father, slyly.

'He's going bald,' said Bill.

'He is *not*,' said his mother. 'What nonsense you both talk.'

Colin came in with the trolley. It was the second round of early-evening drinks. They raised their glasses to their lips like strangers at a bar.

Charlie arrived, strolled in. In his head, perhaps, he heard applause or laughter. He took his glass from Colin and drank it like water. 'You ready?' he said.

It was time. Bill turned to his father.

'Bye, Dad.'

'Bye, Bill.'

He could not, anyway, have embraced him, not with the briefcase. He smiled at his mother but was careful not to think about her. It was incredible to him that he had once lived inside her, had floated in her, the dark of her body. 'Look after yourselves,' he said.

'Don't wait up,' said Charlie.

The brothers went out to the not quite adequately lit square.

'Should I have given Colin something?' asked Bill.

'What – like a hand job?'

'I was thinking of some money.'

'Have you got any?'

They lowered themselves into the car and drove to Soho.

'A quick sharpener,' said Charlie. 'Drape your coat over the chain.' He helped Bill to do it and they went up the stairs.

In the club, a man with a ruined face kissed Charlie's hand, looked at Bill, the briefcase, the coat, grinned and tried to wink, but his face had passed beyond his control and he managed only a kind of tic, a malarial shudder. They stayed for two drinks. It was a different barman tonight and he put in the full optic. When they left, descending through the scuffed pink of the stairway, Charlie went ahead to check for muggers.

In the car they lit fresh cigarettes. 'I'll tell you what,' said Charlie, but he didn't, not until they were climbing the back of the Chiswick flyover and not even then, not until London started to bleed out in the glimpsed night-yards of warehouses, the widening gaps between the sodium lamps.

'If Paddington's out here,' said Bill, 'I'll be surprised,'

'I'm going to drive you,' said Charlie. 'On the train some klumnik will hack off your hand with a penknife.'

Bill nodded. It seemed possible. He was snug with gin, the heater was on high. On some stretches of road the window glass vibrated, on others, smoother, it was silent. They passed terraces of small brick houses. Light stood in pools at the junctions. The larger signs pointed west: mileage, B roads, the prospect of a cathedral.

In the glovebox there was a half-bottle of Beefeater. 'We'll just wet our lips,' said Charlie.

Off to the left somewhere, the airport. Bill looked for the lights of circling planes.

'Hurricane or Spitfire?' asked Charlie.

'Hurricane,' said Bill.

'Mark two?'

'Obviously.'

'Despite the dodgy fuel tanks?'

'Fixable.'

'You would have been an ace.'

'You too.'

They had found again, for the moment, a way of speaking they'd had as boys. At twelve and ten they had understood themselves to be hostages, child prisoners of a dangerous foreigner and the woman who shared his bed and his secrets. They had codes, had passed on warnings, had sometimes crept about the big house at night tethered to one end of a beam of torchlight. Looking for what? Food, evidence of sex, a gun. The truth about their father? About themselves?

After Maidenhead the road straightened. The car cut through darkness.

'You'll meet Rita,' said Bill. He laughed. The idea seemed absurd.

Charlie held out his hand for the gin. 'What's it for?' he asked.

'What's what for?'

'Marriage.'

'There are answers to that,' said Bill. He took back the bottle, rubbed the glass mouth with his hand and took his own sip.

'I'm not the marrying kind,' said Charlie.

They had not discussed what kind Charlie was. Charlie existed; he had interests; he had a purple car. The man in the bar, the one with the face like a crushed rose who had kissed his hand, had called him Carlotta.

'I sometimes think,' said Bill, picturing Rita with her back to the Rayburn reading a novel about Martians, the stillness of her face, like the serious sister of the one who danced to the radio, 'I know her less now than I did before. You know?'

'When she was just a shag.'

'Her father tried to burn down his own house.'

'Dad might have burned down a couple.'

'This wasn't an insurance job. It was some sort of protest.'

'Well, a man's entitled to burn his house down. This is England.'

'Apparently not. He's in the funny farm. Try not to mention it when you meet her.'

Slough town hall, abandoned; curve right at Taplow. Going through Reading required concentration. Even though he wasn't driving, Bill concentrated too. Midgham seemed to have been evacuated. They roared through Thatcham.

On a stretch of nowhere they stopped to urinate into the dark. The car throbbed discreetly at their backs. They went on. The bottle moved between them again. For five minutes or half an hour, Bill slept. When he woke he tried to lift his hand to scratch an ear. The chain snapped taut. He swore then laughed. 'You should open a club of your own,' he said.

'Has Dad got much left?'

'Ask him,' said Bill. 'A club makes more sense than anything I came out with.'

'But it was you who came out with it,' said Charlie. 'I thought I'd explained that.'

The road was lined with trees and then it wasn't. Occasionally, as they rounded a bend, the headlights probed a field. A thatched house blew past; it was painted pink; smoke twisted from its chimney. Bill wondered if he could unlock the handcuffs now. Out here, wherever they were – the Wessex Downs? – there were, surely, no klumniks to hack off his hand.

They talked about the future. It turned out neither of them believed in flying cars.

'What do you believe in?' asked Bill.

'Pleasure,' said Charlie.

'Because your life is so full of it?'

'And we'll be vegetarians. Every man Jack.'

'I hope not,' said Bill.

They could not remember if they had been through Marlborough. Nor were they really certain they were still on the A4. The carriageway was narrower, and here and there the snow lay in tongues across the road.

'We're not lost,' said Charlie. 'We're still going west. You can tell by the stars.'

'There are no stars,' said Bill. They had been in the car for hours. One more Gitanes in the packet. They crested the brow of a hill they had hardly been aware of climbing. There was a turning to the left and Charlie took it.

'That's better,' he said. 'End of detour.'

The road descended. It was narrower than the one they'd just been on.

'Next time we'll get you that suit from Mr Nencel,' said Charlie. 'A man without a suit . . .'

'Rita's doctor,' said Bill, 'I think he might have some numbers on his arm. He started telling me about it once. We were at a party.'

'They shaved off the women's hair,' said Charlie, 'afterwards. They used it to make socks for U-boat crews.'

'Is that true?'

'Stuffing for mattresses, rope for ships. Think how much hair you need to make a rope for a ship.'

'No,' said Bill. 'I'd rather not.'

The car's clock was set into the same dial as the rev counter. Bill leaned to try to see the time and as he did so the car started to travel sideways. It flipped onto its side, then onto its roof. There was a great deal of noise, some of which was the brothers shouting, then it was over. They lay together on what was now the floor of the car. Time passed. Bill opened his eyes. He could make no sense of this new world. There was a weight across his chest that turned out to be one of Charlie's arms. There was light from somewhere. There was a ticking sound he could not identify, a strong smell of petrol. Something amiss with his left cheekbone, something wrong with his right knee. He experimented with movement. One hand was free. It waved in front of him, like a puppet. The other was trapped, or not trapped but caught in something, snared, and it took him a few seconds to remember. He called Charlie's name but there was no answer. He started to struggle. It hurt but it was necessary. He found the door; he couldn't open it. He touched the roundel of the window crank. The window opened upwards. He crawled out into the snow. One of the headlights was still working. Very slowly, he stood up. The briefcase dangled from his wrist. He could not remember where his father had put the key. With his free hand he searched himself and found the key in his breast pocket. He limped into the beam of the headlight and tried to unlock the cuffs. The key did not fit the lock. It was the key to a different set of handcuffs, or it was the key to something else entirely. His father had made a mistake, or it was a sort of joke.

On his hands and knees he reached into the car. When he touched Charlie's foot, it twitched. He started to drag him towards the window. Charlie cried out but Bill kept dragging him. He didn't know what else to do; he thought the car might explode. He got his brother's feet out, his legs. This is like delivering a calf, he thought, I need some twine. Once he had him clear of the window, he hauled him over the snow into the light of the headlamp. The light was slowly dimming. Through its beam, Bill noticed the patient beginnings of a fresh fall. He sat down in the snow next to a sign lying on its back that presumably said something like 'Road closed'.

'We've had a smash,' croaked Charlie. The cold seemed to have revived him, though he made no attempt to sit up.

'Listen,' said Bill, 'we can't stay here.' He got to his feet. His knee throbbed, his face. He saw that one of his shoes was missing. He went back to the car, knelt by the open window and reached around until he found it. When he had put the shoe on (his fingers too cold to tie the laces) he saw that Charlie was upright, swaying slightly and talking to himself.

'We'll find a farmhouse,' said Bill. 'A village.'

Charlie held something out in the palm of his hand. It looked like teeth. They started back along the road they had driven down. Charlie leaned on Bill. He whimpered. Every ten steps they stopped to rest. They seemed to be making no progress at all. Something – perhaps just the nature of their injuries – veered them to the left. They moved through a line of trees. When they came clear, the drifts were deeper and it was obvious they were no longer on the road. The sensible thing was to turn around, but somehow this was unthinkable. Whatever was going to happen, it would happen ahead of them, in the grey wasteland they were walking into. It occurred to Bill that he could die here, chained to a briefcase full of money, his brother beside him. Some Wiltshire farmer would be alerted by the busyness of crows, would cut the chain with a hacksaw, bury the bodies in the field, hide the E-Type in a barn.

In places the snow was up to mid-thigh. They were walking out to sea. The effort was tremendous. Charlie folded, sank down, swooned perhaps. Bill bullied him up again. He shouted at him. He had no idea what he was saying. Despite the cold, he was sweating. He scoured his mind for something to keep himself from giving up. The money gave him ten yards, Rita ten more, the child another five. He thought of abandoning his brother. No one could blame him. No one would know? Then he fuelled himself with rage; it seemed he had it, that it was some sort of birthright, part of being a grown man, the slag heap of blunted desires. He pushed them on, the briefcase like a dead animal he had been tethered to in fulfilment of a curse, an archaic punishment, his free arm locked around his brother's waist. Suddenly the field stood up in front of them, a wall of snow, angled and three times their height. It glowed. Bill studied it awhile, panting. He thought he knew what it was. He shook his brother and they struggled upwards, as if under the weight of breaking waves. At the top they found the rails, an up-line and a down-line, and in the distance, flickering through the mass of tumbling snow, the green spark of a signal.

PART THREE

Live Your Life

1

It was the same Victorian cemetery his father was in. He climbed the hill in search of him, moving along paths lined with stones, crowded, almost toppling over each other. The snow confused him. He would, he thought, have known his way without it. These graves, pale stone, the ground around them tended, were war graves. So, left here? Left, and further up beyond the trees? Somewhere behind him they were burying the poor knocked-about body of Stephen Storey. He had stood at the back of the chapel. There were very few of them. Stephen's mother, and with her another woman of about the same age, who stood close and sometimes comforted her. Ian, the nurse from the asylum. And the policeman, Orton, out of uniform, who turned at the sound of Eric's arrival and gave a brief nod of acknowledgement. The chaplain had the singsong voice they must all be trained in. Grievous loss, the flowers of the field, the mystery of our lives. No attempt at a hymn. How long since a suicide would have been refused entrance here? Or was there always a corner of unconsecrated ground, somewhere for those Victorian lady poets who went to bed with a bottle of strychnine?

When the bearers came in to shoulder the coffin he slipped out ahead of them and walked away towards the cemetery gates, then uphill in search of his father.

He didn't know where Stephen's place would be, where the new plots were. They must have used a mechanical digger to break the ground. The graves he was passing now, with their mourning angels, their stone garlands and urns, stone ivy around which real ivy had wound itself, these were among the oldest. He paused to read a date: 30 March 1863. Almost exactly a hundred years! What was the news in 1863? Were we fighting a war? When was the Crimea? Earlier? Later? Then a sudden memory of a teacher at his junior school reading out the Tennyson poem and beating time with a ruler, the same one he used on the boys' hands, the backs of their knees.

He came to a bench. This, too, was a memorial. He cleared the snow with a gloved hand and sat down. The Labour leader Hugh Gaitskell was dead. He had died the night before, about nine o'clock. The cause of death seemed uncertain. Pleurisy, though they also mentioned his kidneys. He was fifty-six. A decent and principled man, probably the next prime minister. Not right on everything (wrong on Europe) but decent, courageous and decent. The *Herald* had a big spread on its front page: 'The World Mourns'. His wife was with him at the end. She had held his hand, or so the paper said.

He lit a cigarette, but before he could draw on it he found himself weeping. It seemed to be for Gaitskell, to be part of the world's mourning, but he knew there were other shades attending and that he had at last found somewhere he could show the little derangement they required. It didn't last long, a squall, ten ragged breaths. He was surprised by it, startled even, but pleased. When it was over the air was clearer. He was light-headed from lack of sleep (he was still in the spare room, had no notion of when that might end, *if* it would end) and for a few seconds he watched himself – his spirit or some part of him split off – disappearing around the bend in the path, chattering away, full of noise and narrowness. Farewell, old friend. Don't hurry back.

Then the mood was broken: someone was coming up the hill. He pictured the funeral party swaying into view with the coffin. He stood, and was ready to hurry off when he saw that it was just the nurse, Ian, on his own, also having a smoke.

'Is it over, then?' he called.

'Yes,' said Ian, trudging closer. 'Or most of it. I didn't think I needed to stay.'

'It was good of you to come.'

The nurse shrugged. 'We try to make sure someone's there.'

'Is that policy?'

'Not official, not as far as I know. But otherwise it might just be the chaplain and the undertaker.'

'No family.'

'None that will own them.'

'At least he had someone – Stephen.'

'Yes.'

'I was looking for my father,' said Eric.

'He's here?'

'Died in sixty. But the place is a maze.'

'Can't find him, then.'

'No.'

They looked, quizzically, at the old stones around them. It was too cold to stand there talking. They put out their cigarettes, tidying the butts to the edge of the path.

'How are you getting back?' asked Eric.

'There's a bus.'

'Fancy a lift?'

They walked down the hill, the city ahead of them like a field of burned stubble.

'New car?' asked Ian. He knew the Citroën.

'That's right,' said Eric. It was a Hillman Husky, the sort of car he thought a small grocer might drive. Engine like a lawn-mower, everything rattled. It was one of the hair shirts he had arranged for himself. He had bought it second hand and paid thirty quid for it. The Citroën was still under a tarpaulin at Gabby's. It could, surely, be repaired, though he would need to take it somewhere he was unknown. The damage did not look like a shunt or as if a tree had fallen on it. It looked like what it was. He would take it, perhaps, to a garage in some area of the city where cars were often beaten and nobody thought to ask awkward questions.

On the journey they spoke about Gaitskell. Ian, too, was a Labour man. He thought Wilson would take over the party but Eric thought it more likely to be George Brown. Brown had the unions with him. It was pleasant to talk politics, to rest in an impersonal passion.

At the hospital, the nurse got out, then ducked his head to lean back in and shake hands. Eric watched him go into the building. He liked Ian. He would have liked to tell him about his father, the ex-ganger, to explain or make clear that they were, if you stretched things a little, the same class, with the same class enemies. They could, conceivably, be friends. But imagine Ian at the cottage with the Duckworths and Irene's London crowd! Poor fellow would stand in the corner with his glass, wondering how soon he could leave without giving offence.

As usual, there were a few figures out of doors, hunched against the cold, walking aimlessly on the drive, the concrete paths around the edges of the hospital, killing time. What class were *they*?

He started a three-point turn and was at the end of the second short reverse (why not put a nice little dent in the Administrator's Wolseley?) when his rear-view mirror filled with a familiar face. He stopped and wound down the window. After a moment, the man appeared there.

'It's Martin, isn't it?'

The man nodded. With his yellow fingers he held out a small box. 'You'll give this to her?'

'To?'

'My daughter. You live by her, don't you?'

'That's right. What is it?'

'Spinning tops. We make them in the woodwork shop. With Mr Hitchcock.'

He passed the box through the window. A wooden box with a hinged lid, all neatly made.

'May I see?'

'If you want.'

Eric placed the box on his lap and opened it: three pretty wooden tops inside. One was unusual.

'That one,' said Martin, 'will jump onto his head when you spin him.'

'Yes?'

'It takes a bit of practice.'

'If these are for the child, you know there's plenty of time. You could give them to her yourself.'

'As you're here,' said Martin. The wind caught at him and he seemed to ripple like dry grass. He was, thought Eric, a man with as close to nothing as made no difference. The inmate of an asylum; someone who could not possibly look back at his life with any kind of pleasure. Yet there was, in the thin light of his winter eyes, a certain slaty grandeur, as if failure had raised him up, had scoured him in a way one might almost envy.

After his conversation with Rita at the party, Eric, on a routine visit to the hospital (and mindful too of the Administrator's wish that his medication should be adjusted, that the midnight 'peregrinations' be put an end to) had pulled out Martin Lee's medical record, a scuffed manila file he didn't think anyone had looked at in quite a while. He had read the short paragraph about the fire. His own house! Then, on the following page, read a note, added in ink in the margin, undated, unsigned, informing him that Martin Lee had been with the British army at the liberation of the camp at Bergen-Belsen, April 1945.

'Any message for her?'

Martin shook his head.

'Right-oh,' said Eric. He put the box on the passenger seat and wound up the window.

2

In the dream he was walking the railway line again. The briefcase had become a suitcase in which, he understood, he carried all he had been able to pack in the minutes before they fled. His brother was some manner of shape-shifter, a golem, hot under his arm, and best not examined. And in the dream they did not find the house where the man (he raised fancy fowl) met them with a shotgun thinking they were foxes. Had they started to sound like foxes? Inside the house, Charlie collapsed. The man did not possess a sofa so they laid him on the floor and covered him with a horse blanket (he possessed horses). He made them strong tea. He cut, at Bill's request, the chain of the handcuffs (his bolt cutter went through the links like snipping thread). In the morning he drove them both to the hospital in Devizes. At no point did he give his name or ask for theirs. He was the type of man who butchers his own meat, who wears in his hat a pheasant's feather and it is no affectation.

Waking, Bill reached across the bed for Rita but she wasn't there. He turned onto his back, wincing. He was still tattooed with bruises, some of them big. His knee was bandaged, the leg usable if he kept it straight – but set his foot down carelessly and he knew about it. He had a black eye that was, after a week, mostly green and yellow. His jaw didn't seem quite right, though he had, unlike Charlie, kept his teeth.

The money was under the bed. He couldn't drive yet – next week perhaps. Then, surely, even Harrison's composure would be tested. He would call in his senior clerk to do what Bill had already done in the farmhouse office (curtains closed, lights on). The clerk would do it more quickly, a stained rubber thimble on his finger, but he would come to the same conclusion. It was, to the pound, exactly what his father had said it was.

When he had shown the money to Rita, widening the case's mouth and lifting the money out, piling it on the kitchen table, she had, predictably, made a game of it. He was the bank robber and she was his moll; he was Clyde, she was Bonnie. Then, as if her concentration was that of a young child, the game was over. She made lunch (opened tins, toasted bread), leaving him to put the money back into the case, someone whose news had not astonished in the way he had hoped, who had told a joke that turned out to be not as funny as he'd thought.

He had dusted off and oiled Mr Earle's shotgun. There was a box of pink cartridges in the workshop, cobwebby, though probably still serviceable. He told Rita to stay schtum, not to speak of the money to anyone, certainly not while it was still in the house. Like who? she asked. He suggested Mrs Case in the shop. She nodded, seemed to understand, then added a long list of others, only some of whom he knew. He was annoyed with her. He also wondered why, since his return, she had not once looked him in the eye.

He lifted his head to see the green hands of the alarm clock. Nearly four. Teddy would do the morning milking, thank God. He wasn't ready for that yet. One shove from a cow and he'd be on his backside. The bull, said Teddy, needed to be with the herd again; he was getting mazy. Bill had agreed and asked him to take care of it. Could he? Oh, yes, said Teddy. The bull was just a big puppy, really. Bill thought a future in which he asked people (employees) to do things for him might be better than one in which he had to do them for himself.

If Rita was in the bathroom, she was taking her time. He listened, tensing himself against the silence. The curious sensation of the house listening back . . .

He had written again to the man at Poor Tree Farm, the farmer in Ireland with a similar sort of enterprise. Now that the way was clear, he felt less sure than he had when there was still the obstacle of the money. He needed more advice. He needed not to blunder. Every third or fourth time he thought of the money, of what you could get for ten thousand pounds, he saw himself walking away from all this, the farm, the madness of the animals, sometimes with Rita and sometimes without. Half the money would buy him five hundred acres in Argentina. It would buy him horses, servants . . .

He dozed, then sat up. The clock said twenty past. He pushed himself out of bed and hobbled to the door. He went down the black passageway to the bathroom. The door was open, the room unlit. He pulled the cord, narrowing his eyes against the light. One of the sink taps was dribbling and he went to shut it off. He looked at the window but it showed him only himself, a man swathed in night.

He went to the top of the stairs. 'Rita?'

The sound of his own voice unnerved him a little. The house was stupidly cold. He had, in the last week, ordered two new convector heaters, top of the range, a company in Bristol. With luck, the van would deliver on Monday or Tuesday. One for the bedroom, one in the bathroom. A start.

He flicked on the bedroom light, pulled on a jumper (smell of cows), some thick socks (flecked with straw), and went downstairs. He looked in the kitchen. He had expected to find her there, her usual place against the Rayburn, but the kitchen was empty. He touched the swell of the teapot. It was cold. He looked into the office, then went upstairs again. With his bandaged knee, going up and down the stairs was awkward; the other leg had to do all the work. He looked into the room where the apples were stored. He shouted her name. You wouldn't put it past her to be playing some ridiculous game in which she hid in the wardrobe. He opened the wardrobe in the bedroom. Her clothes, his. The smell of her clothes.

He went to the front door. Since the money came to live with them, he kept it bolted. Now he saw the bolts were drawn. He shoved his feet into boots, took a coat from the rack. There was a torch on the shelf above the hooks, but there was a more powerful one in the cupboard under the stairs and he took that. Outside, he shone a beam across the yard.

'Rita?'

It must be half-four by now, quarter to five. He did not want to run into Teddy. He did not want Teddy to find him searching in the dark of the yard for his wife. He went to the shippon, dot and carry. He shone the torch over the backs of the cows. Some turned towards him and their eyes shone like strange glass. He crossed to the barn, calling her name as he went. The car, the bath, the lamp, the pony, the dry cows. There were no sick cows. Now Teddy had taken over the milking the animals thrived.

Back to the yard. He stood by the midden, forcing himself to think. She had walked down the track? She had walked into the fields? Or she was lying up in their bed, wondering where he was? He limped to the cart shed. Imagine if he found her curled on the straw, her head pillowed on the flank of the drowsing bull. But the bull was not drowsing. It was balanced on its slender legs like a grand piano. It met him with a stillness more complete than the night's, its musk the last warm thing in the world.

He went around the side of the shed to the orchard. He was having a conversation in his head with Constable Hill. He would say 'abduction' rather than 'kidnapping', and when the policeman asked who might wish to abduct his wife he would say my father, her father, the Richardson gang, the man who drives the library van (it had called on Wednesday, but she had not wanted anything). And there was just time for the thought that he himself had murdered her, strangled her and buried her like a dead calf in the field and all this hunting was just a sham, a desperate ten minutes of self-deceit before he faced the unsurvivable guilt of it, when his beam snagged in the gold of her hair and he found her standing under a tree by the orchard gate. She was gazing towards the field.

'What are you doing?' he asked.

She turned, blinking at the light of the torch. 'I thought I heard someone come in,' she said.

She was wearing her duffel coat but had nothing on her feet but the socks she had been sleeping in. He picked her up and swayed back to the house with her. He was like Frankenstein's monster carrying away some poor girl from the village. He closed the door with his back and carried her into the kitchen. He sat her on one of the chairs and dragged it close to the Rayburn. He worked at her feet, pressing them, squeezing them. He touched her hands and face. 'You're bloody freezing,' he said.

He half filled the kettle and set it spitting on the hotplate. He stared at her. She was sitting very still, gazing vacantly ahead. Hard to say what, if anything, she saw. Call Gabby Miklos? (Sorry to wake you, Doctor. A strange thing just happened . . .) But what if it was the other one, if it was Parry on call tonight? Though Parry, of course, could be there much more quickly.

He bent to her and wrapped his arms around her. 'Come on, old girl,' he said. He held her as tightly as he dared. After a minute, a deep shiver went through her. She lifted her arms, her hands settled on his back, and she held him too.

3

The oil tank had been filled and the house was warm. Mrs Rudge had come in again to clean and Irene freed herself from the habit of cleaning the house beforehand. She spent more time in bed (the spare room), more time reading (*The Uses of Literacy*). She had long conversations with Veronica. These were not urgent. She was not, in any obvious way, discussing her marriage. They had resumed something of their old style, those afternoons they had sprawled on their beds in the room with the sloping ceiling, the window that looked over the garden (where in summer their father held up the skirts of the willow tree to mow the grass beneath). Were these calls expensive? Probably. At one time Eric would have suggested she send an airmail. Now, if he passed her, walking around her as she sat with a cup of tea at the bottom of the stairs, he went quietly, a tight little smile on his face.

He was being very polite, very attentive. He had an absurd new car, like a biscuit tin. They had talked. The story of the smashing of the Citroën was one she thought about a lot. If she were to see him – Frank Riley – what would pass between them? They were the injured parties but Frank, at least, had done something about it.

They did not touch. A couple of times he had reached for her hand, but if you choose to you can make your hand like a dead thing.

A dark line was spreading down her belly. She asked him about this; she didn't show him. He said it was called *linea nigra* and would disappear after the birth.

He had said she should be able to hear the heartbeat now through a stethoscope. He held out to her his own in its leather bag, and she had gone upstairs with it and moved the cool silver ear across her skin and finally she found it and had to bite her lip not to cry out.

He asked if she would like a trip into the city, see a film, supper at Marco's. It seemed childish or pointless to turn him down and, anyway, she liked the idea. She had spent too much time in the cottage.

It was the last week of January, the last Saturday of the month. The Air Ministry had hinted at a thaw but there was no sign of it yet. The thermometer outside Eric's study rarely rose above zero in the day and sank well below at night. They drove to Bristol in the new car and parked on Old Market. It was a street – a thoroughfare – the city had turned its face from. It would, soon, be on the wrong side of a new ring road. It dangled its feet in the eighteenth century, the seventeenth. It had shops you might go into to see what exactly it was they sold. The only brightness was the cinema. He had told her in the car the name of the film, *A Night on Bear Mountain*, and she hadn't questioned it. Now, under the cinema canopy, coats pulled tight, they regarded the poster. It showed monsters (a werewolf, Frankenstein's botched man) and women with improbable figures in improbable bikinis. No monster, announced the poster, had ever had it so good. You would (it promised) see Frankenstein do the twist with Miss Hollywood. It was a night on Bare Mountain rather than Bear Mountain. It had all been filmed in Sexicolor.

'I thought,' said Eric, 'it would be about Canada or something.'

A young man carrying a large wooden cross approached them. He had the cross sloped over one shoulder like a rifle. 'There's another cinema around the corner,' he said. 'You don't want this.'

They walked around the corner. The other cinema was darker. Above its door in tired neon: the Continental. Inside, it was like a bar or a club, smoky, softly lit, but apparently clean. If there was a large photo of Brigitte Bardot, there was also one of Ingmar Bergman. There was a scattering of people Eric might have described as beatniks. He bought tickets for a film called *Vivre sa vie*. The poster for the film was pink, possibly purple, and showed a woman with bobbed hair. She was not smiling. Her gaze was direct and hard to read. It was this or go out into the cold again.

'With luck,' said Eric, 'there'll be a power cut.' But there wasn't. Everything worked perfectly.

Afterwards, at Marco's, they both had the cannelloni. Marco came to their table as if they were favourites of his, though they had only been there two or three times. When he left them (to perform the same show at a neighbouring table, a whole life like this), they talked about the film. Something at the Continental, the plush seats, the shifting light, the film too, of course, had changed the mood between them. They spoke without struggle, almost companionably, people on a journey, weary, making the best of it. The film had made no sense to either of them. It was very French, slightly boring. The actress had a face like a beautiful clown. If the film was serious, it was a seriousness they didn't recognise. If it was a sort of comedy, it wasn't funny. A prank? What was amusing about people saying things that didn't really mean anything? Eric had taken a magazine from the cinema foyer. He read to her from an article about the film. She heard the Midlands in his voice, his old beginnings.

'"Only the surfaces,"' he read, '"are realistic."' He laughed. He had drunk almost a whole bottle of Chianti on his own.

'Is it existentialism?' she asked.

He scanned the article, shrugged. 'We should have stayed on Bare Mountain,' he said.

When the bottle was finished and Marco had treated them to little glasses of sambuca (Eric drank both), they set off for the cottage. In the car he smoked, flicking ash onto the floor in some gesture of contempt (car as ashtray). It was a clear night, a crescent moon sometimes visible, more so as they got free of the city. The heater was on full and eventually the air it blew was warm. They didn't speak. She thought the next occasion would probably be when they said goodnight to each other and went to their rooms at different ends of the house. She closed her eyes. The ribbed seats of the car had not been made for pregnant women, but the journey would not be a long one. In her head she watched the film again. It expanded in her like one of those dried-sponge 'magic' flowers children place in water, but this time, in its hollowness, in the round, frightened face of the actress (a face, she realised, that reminded her strongly of Rita's), in its slyness, its clumsiness, in those long, pointless conversations ('The more we talk, the less words mean'), the film addressed her with a directness she had not known since the fifteen minutes of *An End to Murder*, watched as a girl. It was like a word in a new language naming a mood she could not have experienced without the word, without learning it. It excited her, and she opened her eyes. The car, the moon, Eric's face (now the face of an actor) were all changed. She looked at him, his concentration (there was ice out there), his frowning into the onrush of night. She might just sit there, do nothing, say nothing, but it no longer felt inevitable. Her anger, at that precise moment, was absent. The anger, the fear, the shame, the wound that had to be tended like a wayside shrine. And what had replaced them? Only this: the rattling of the little car, the whirr of the heater, the shards of light beyond the edges of the road. A sadness she could live with. Some new interest in herself.

4

In February the snow came back. There was a blizzard on the night of the fifth that the weatherman on the wireless, his voice surging through gusts of static, said was the worst of the winter. The West Country took the brunt of it. What had been cleared, opened (much of it by men with shovels, grey-faced, bizarrely cheerful), was covered again, buried. Once more the sea stiffened. Lambs were born into the snow and died there. Fires were lit beneath the axles of coal wagons because the coal they carried was frozen into a single unbreakable block. In the village, you could not get down the lane but you could ring America. From his study, Eric could hear her on the phone again to Veronica. What was it with women and talking? This need to exhaust each subject they landed upon? Two men – himself and Gabby, for example: it was unimaginable. That night at Gabby's, later on, after three or four unavoidable questions had been asked and answered, they had sat in near silence reading medical journals and getting slightly pissed on Gabby's homemade brandy. And it was in one of those journals he had seen the advertisement he was now cutting out, carefully, with the very sharp scissors from his Gladstone bag. There was something called the British

Antarctic Survey. They were looking for a doctor to serve at their base on the Brunt Ice Shelf. There was a picture of the base. It looked like a row of Scout huts. There was an address in Cambridge you could write to for more information. He thought it significant he had seen the advertisement the very night after it happened, the event, the incident, that thing he still had no easy name for, because what do you call it, a schoolboy circling your car, taking out the windows with a cricket bat while his father watches you down the length of an arrow? Had Gabby known it was in there? Had he placed the journal at the top of the pile? You wouldn't put it past him.

They wanted someone in post by the end of March, someone who would do the southern winter. It would mean missing the birth, of course. Did that matter? It would mean missing the first several months of the child's life, but a father played no important part in the first year of life. He would see to it she had some money. She could move back in with her parents if she wanted. She could move in with her sister in America, and good old Morris, a man who seemed a fount of tedious good sense.

There was, he thought, something elegant about it as a solution. It struck the right note. Short of going into outer space, it would remove him from the scene in about as complete a way as possible. It would shift his identity from cheating husband to polar hero. It would give him the company of serious men, sober, intent. A community! Was that what he had been looking for? He thought that his father, if he had not disowned him entirely, would probably approve, see it as correct. And when Alison heard? It was almost worth it for that alone. Frank would announce it as a joke and she would say, 'Oh,' and turn away, busy herself with nothing, and in her head hear the sound of her life shutting like the bronze doors of a mausoleum. Another forty years with Frank. The descent into unloveliness. And in time, Frank would betray her, if he hadn't already. He would feel entitled to.

He put down the scissors and placed the advertisement in the desk drawer. His eyes settled on the box Martin Lee had given him for his daughter. He should have delivered it already, of course, but as she wasn't expecting it she wouldn't miss it. He raised the lid, reached in and took out the top he was interested in, the one like a little apple, a crab apple, red and green, with a half-inch of dowelling as a stem. This was the one that could jump, though as her father had warned him, it took some practice. Spin it too gently and it didn't have the energy, too hard and it became chaotic, went bouncing and tumbling off the desk and had to be retrieved from dusty corners of the study. He cleared a space on the desk, dangled the top from its stem, stilled himself, then flicked it into life. Almost at once he snatched it up again and sat back in his chair, head cocked. Irene was calling. About what? The back door? Then he heard it for himself and went out to the lobby and opened the door.

'Hello,' he said. 'You all right?'

Bill started to explain. He was in his overalls. He was breathing hard, flushed, big-eyed. He was frightened and not trying to hide it.

'Right-oh,' said Eric. 'You go straight back. I'll fetch my bag and follow.'

His bag was in the study. He snapped it shut, then opened it again and put in the scissors. He was pulling on his boots in the lobby when Irene appeared.

'What is it?' she asked.

He told her; it would have taken longer not to. He reached for his coat and she reached for hers.

'What are you doing?' he asked.

'I'm coming too.'

'Stay here,' he said.

'She's my friend.'

'It will be a mess,' he said.

'What does that matter?'

She held his gaze. This was, and was not quite, the woman who had walked into the shade of the trees that afternoon at the tennis party, feigning surprise at finding him there. He nodded and picked up his bag, wondering what he had lost, who.

He jogged across the garden; she strode after him, buttoning her sheepskin. Over the new snow they followed the path that Bill had made. The glassy air of a February afternoon, the sieved light, some exhaustion of stillness. The snowman, which appeared to be both melting and growing, had lost his eyes now, the little pieces of coal that must be under the snow somewhere. At the gate into the orchard, Eric stopped to look back. Irene called something that might have been 'Go on.'

The front door of the farmhouse was open. 'Hello?'

'Up here!' called Bill. 'The bathroom.'

He went up. The bedroom door was wide, the tousled bed, clothes on the floor. He walked down to the bathroom. Rita was sitting on the toilet. She had a blanket around her and was slumped against her husband. Her eyes were shut, her face colourless, waxy. Bill stared at Eric with that expression of silent pleading that had, the first time Eric saw it in a patient's house, been so impressive.

He crouched in front of her. He spoke her name. He looked under the blanket.

'I was outside,' said Bill. 'I don't know when it started.'

Eric removed his coat and draped it over the edge of the bath. He noticed he could see part of his own house through their bathroom window. He wasn't wearing a jacket: he had the Guernsey on. He pushed up the sleeves and washed his hands at the sink.

'Right,' he said. 'Can you fetch a couple of clean sheets and another blanket?' He wanted Bill out of the room. When he had gone, he took out the scissors (he should probably sterilise them, but they had only been used on a piece of paper) and cut the cord. There was, in the bowl, a great deal of blood. It looked as if the placenta was still to come. She spoke, a few words, like some stunned oracle, one who has served the god too long, who has been hollowed out by prophecy.

'I didn't take anything . . .'

He nodded. 'Are you in much pain?'

But she had withdrawn again, lain down behind the whiteness of her shut eyes. He wondered if she might like a sip of the mixture. It was in his bag. It seemed the solution to all sorts of things. In the last fortnight he'd had several sips of it himself. He thought he'd probably take the bottle with him to Antarctica.

Irene came in. He was glad to see her. He asked her to stay with Rita while he tried to get a helicopter. A helicopter was the only way she was going to reach a hospital.

He met Bill on the corridor, his arms loaded with linen and blankets. 'Where's your phone?'

Bill told him. Eric went down. This was the room he had seen her in that night, her face in the flaring of a match. He called the surgery. He didn't know who, if anyone, would have made it in, but Mrs Bolt answered at the third ring and for once he was pleased to hear her voice. Yes, Dr Miklos was there but he was presently with a patient. He asked her to put him through, and when she started to demur (she knew, of course, all about Alison Riley, about his car; it had changed things), he cut across her and instructed her to do as she was bid. For a few seconds there was silence and he wondered if she had put the phone down on him. He stared at the shotgun propped against the wall beneath the window. He had time for two or three thoughts, a flickering of images, hot as bile. Then Gabby picked up and everything was easier. Very little needed to be explained.

'Naturally,' said Gabby, 'I will make them come.'

In the bathroom there was a convector heater though it seemed the sort that warmed only a block of air directly above itself. Irene was crouched beside Rita, an arm around her shoulders. Bill was poised by the sink, still clutching the bedding.

'Let's get her down to the office,' said Eric. 'A bit snugger down there. We can make a stretcher out of one of the sheets.'

They laid a doubled sheet on the floor and lifted her. The sheet was more of a sling than a stretcher. Bill led the way, backing out of the bathroom. Though Rita had only been on the floor for half a minute there was blood, and both men had managed to tread in it. Irene stayed behind. When she heard them begin on the stairs (a pair of removal men calling instructions and encouragement to each other), she stripped off her coat, pushed up the black sleeve of her sweater, and lowered her hand into the toilet bowl. The water was slightly warm. She did not know if she was doing the right thing. She touched it and it bobbed away from her. She slid her hand beneath it and raised it. I will dream of this for ever, she thought, I will never not see this.

It was not quite the length of her hand and, despite its coat of blood, almost transparent. Feet no bigger than the nails of her little fingers, ten toes, the articulated knee. The way the spine was curled, like a fern or a fish, curled as she herself curled each night in the bed in the spare room above the garage. Was this what *her* baby looked like now? Of course. And this was what she had looked like. And Rita, and Eric, and the guards at Belsen.

At one end of the bath was a dry and passably clean-looking blue flannel. She took it, placed it on the tiled sill above the washbasin, and with her free hand spread out the flannel, smoothed it, and laid the baby on it (for it *was* a baby and she must call it so). Eric's scissors were on the floor and she used them to tidy away the cord. The stump wept and she sealed it with one of the grips from her hair. She wrapped the baby, swaddled it. Cover the face? She covered the face, the infinite softness of those sealed eyes. There was, surely, some better place to leave it, but she couldn't think of where, so it must stay where it was, a bottle of aspirins for a headstone, the light of the world resting on the crown of its head where the flannel did not quite hide it. She washed her hands. She tried to think how she would tell Bill what she had done. As she went down the stairs she heard the flat ringing of the phone, then heard Eric speaking to someone, from his tone probably Gabby.

In the office, Rita was on the sofa under a green rug. If someone insisted she was dead you wouldn't question it, or not until you were close enough to see the trembling of her finger-tips. Irene lowered herself to the floor beside the sofa. She knelt; she kissed Rita's brow and began to tidy the hair from her face.

'Is it coming?' asked Bill, when Eric had put the phone down.

'From the base at Yeovilton,' said Eric. 'Should be here in half an hour. Less with any luck. They'll call when it's airborne.'

'They can set it down in the field between us,' said Bill. 'She's got a red dress upstairs. I'm pretty sure she has. I could take it out and wave it.'

'All right.'

'Thank Christ it's light still.'

'Yes.'

'Can they come out at night?'

'I suppose so. If we lit a fire or something.'

'Douse a couple of bales in diesel,' said Bill. 'Though hay's like gold dust now. Diesel, too, for the matter.'

Eric nodded. He had heard, he hadn't heard. He reached into a pocket in search of his cigarettes but touched instead an object, solid, smooth, that he could not at first identify. Then he realised it was the spinning top and that he must have pushed it into his pocket when he went to answer the back door. Bill was staring at his stricken wife like a man coming slowly to understand something. Eric slid the toy from his pocket and placed it discreetly on the desk next to something he remembered noticing on the floor when he looked in that night, but which now, inside the room (in circumstances he might have predicted?), he could see was no alarm clock but a gauge of some sort, one he thought he recognised from RAF days, his training on bombers. He picked it up, handled it. A boost gauge? What the devil was it doing here? And he held it out, ahead and a little to the right, more or less where he would have seen it on the instrument panel along with the other three underneath the ignition switches. He had no difficulty remembering the ignition sequence. Starboard inner, starboard outer; port inner, port outer. Then bring them all up to around 1200 revs. Turn on the DR compass. Turn the ground-flight switch to flight . . .

Rita screamed. She writhed and tore away the rug.

Eric placed the gauge back on the desk and went over to her. He looked down at her.

'Atta girl,' he said. 'Nearly there.'

So out into the orchard, a sky veined with the boughs of apple trees. How easy it was to move now – effortless! The others, she decided, were ahead of her and she was the last. The house – that hopeless cold house – would be shut up. Someone, somehow, would take care of the animals.

As she came through the gate she saw that it was already in the field, waiting for her. Smooth, silver, a perfect disc, it sat silently in the bitter air like a boat on still water. Closer, she saw how its body – steel? Glass? – was streaked with small burns, a thread-like scarring, the marks of flight, of those undreamable distances it had travelled through the silken grain of empty space.

If she was nervous she was also excited. She had waited a long time for this and now she would know. One last glance back and she was inside. The hull sealed behind her. Though she could see her way it was not particularly bright, and she was glad of that. What light there was seemed to come from the small oval windows that were set at regular intervals into the smooth walls of the cabin. There were seats at the centre of the cabin. Bill and Eric were sitting together. They had at last found something to talk about. Something mechanical?

They glanced over to her, grinned, nodded, and went back to their conversation. They looked younger, and pleased to be at the beginning of an adventure, one she herself, perhaps, was responsible for.

The crew of the craft remained hidden; they would be shy of their difference. When the time was right they would reveal themselves. They would not wish to cause alarm. All this she understood.

She started to process around the rim of the cabin, pausing to look out of different windows. Though she had not felt the movement – no countdown! – they were already at some distance from the ground. Field, farm, cottage, village. There was the station, the snaking rails. There, the slated roof of the asylum, tiny figures in the grounds. Useless to wave from here of course, but she lifted her hand anyway. At her side, wordlessly, Irene appeared. She, too, was altered; she, too, looked younger, unburdened. For several seconds they gazed at each other. Then they turned to the window, faces close, their cheeks almost touching. The land was hidden now, lost to sight. They rose swiftly through the subtle banding of the light. All around them, meaningless and lovely, the endless dark flowing of the snow.

Acknowledgements

With warm thanks to the following: Sarah and David Arathoon; Carole Welch and Jane Borodale; my agent, Tracy Bohan (who said, wonderfully, 'Keep it weird'); to my ever-patient editor, Fede Andornino, and to the whole team at Sceptre, my publishers for so many years now. Also – once again – my gratitude to Beatrice Monti della Corte at the Santa Maddalena Foundation, where parts of this novel were written and revised. And finally, to my daughter, Frieda, who, without having read a word of this, somehow knew exactly what I was trying to do, let me bang on about it, and gave me courage.